Michelle,

Sandustee
The Search for the Nazarene's Code
The Legend of 13

Enjoy the Search for the Clues to the puzzle.

My best,

Bob Adamov

11/22/13

Other *Emerson Moore* Adventures by Bob Adamov

Rainbow's End	Released October 2002
Pierce the Veil	Released May 2004
When Rainbows Walk	Released June 2005
Promised Land	Released July 2006
The Other Side of Hell	Released June 2008
Tan Lines	Released June 2010

Next *Emerson Moore* Adventure

Zenobia

This book is a work of fiction. Names, characters, places and incidents are either products of the author's imagination or are used fictitiously. Any resemblance to actual events, locales or persons, living or dead, is entirely coincidental.

ISBN: 0-9786184-3-2
978-0-9786184-3-8

Library of Congress Number: 2013930447

Cover art by Lange Design
www.langedesign.org

Submit all requests for reprinting to:
BookMasters, Inc.
PO Box 388
Ashland, Ohio 78735

Published in the United States by:
Packard Island Publishing, Wooster, Ohio

www.bookmasters.com
www.packardislandpublishing.com
www.BobAdamov.com

First Edition – February 2013

Printed in the United States

Acknowledgements

For technical assistance, I'd like to express my appreciation to Chris Winslow, The Ohio State University's Stone Lab Co-Manager; underwater videographer Roger Roth, Barry Vermeeren, Scott Pansing, John Hildebrandt at Cedar Point Amusement Park, Steve Stapleton of the *Restless*, Denis Lange of Lange Design, Bruce Roberts and TJ Wright at Harbor North, and Lieutenant Mark Cherney from the Collier County Sheriff's Office.

I'd like to thank my team of editors: Andrea Goss Knaub, Hank Inman of Goldfinch Communications, David Noble, Jackie Buckwalter, Peggy Parker, Cathy Adamov and the one and only Joe Weinstein.

Dedication

This book is dedicated to my beautiful, loving and caring sweetheart of a wife, Cathy.

In Memoriam

Over the last 18 months, I've seen a few of my friends pass away and am dedicating this book in their memory – Ellen Meyers, Paul Izzo, Sam Hibbs, Hank Ruppel, Paul Wolfe, and Lou Knowlton. You all are missed!

They that wait upon the Lord shall renew their strength; they shall mount up with wings as eagles; they shall run, and not be weary; and they shall walk, and not faint. – Isaiah 40:31

Donations

The **Stone Lab** will receive a portion of the proceeds from the sale of this book.

If you would like to help with the restoration of **Cooke Castle**, please send your donation to:

Cooke Castle Restoration
The Ohio State University
1314 Kinnear Road
Columbus, Ohio 43212

If you'd like to support the **Stone Lab's Sustaining Fund,** which is used for equipment purchases to support courses and research at the Lab, please mail your donations to:

Stone Lab Sustaining Fund
The Ohio State University
1314 Kinnear Road
Columbus, Ohio 43212

Checks should be made payable to OSU. Donors can also donate to these funds on line at http://stonelab.osu.edu/fosl/give/

For more information, check these sites:

www.ohioseagrant.osu.edu
www.MillerFerry.com
www.cusslersociety.com
www.Put-in-Bay.com

Lake Erie Islands

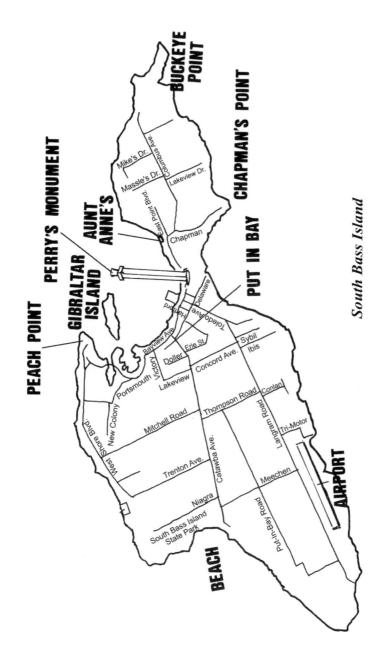

BUCKEYE POINT

CHAPMAN'S POINT

PERRY'S MONUMENT

AUNT ANNE'S

PEACH POINT

GIBRALTAR ISLAND

PUT IN BAY

Mike's Dr.

Massie's Dr.

Columbus Ave.

Lakeview Dr.

East Point Blvd.

Chapman

Delaware

Hartford

Toledo Ave.

Bayview Ave.

Victory Ave.

Doller

Erie St.

Sybil

Ibis

Lakeview

Concord Ave.

Portsmouth

New Colony

West Shore Blvd.

Mitchell Road

Thompson Road

Langram Road

Conlan

Tri-Motor

Trenton Ave.

Catawba Ave.

Meechen

AIRPORT

Niagra

South Bass Island State Park

Put-In-Bay Road

BEACH

South Bass Island

Gibraltar Island

LAKE ERIE

BARNEY COTTAGE

PERRY'S LOOKOUT

SWIMMING HOLE

LAKEVIEW

COOKE'S CASTLE

HARBORVIEW HOUSE

STONE COTTAGE

VOLLEYBALL COURT

GAZEBO

BAT HOUSE

GIBRALTOR HOUSE

DINING HALL

STONE LABORATORY

GLACIAL GROOVES

Basement Captivity
Bodrum, Turkey

A foreboding haze hung over the seaside resort city of Bodrum, much like a fog from hell. Warmed by the rising sun, a stench rose from the town's streets like an evil harbinger. It wasn't from the pungent odors from apartment kitchens, the exhaust fumes from passing cars or gasses from the small industrial complex. It was something hateful and vile. The smell of death emanated from one building's basement.

A rough burlap bag encased Emerson Moore's head. The stench of urine and excrement, which had previously saturated the bag, filled Moore's nostrils. The smell was stifling and caused Moore to choke on virtually every breath.

The sack was like a black cloud shrouding his face. The rough burlap irritated his skin. The bag was intended to diminish his senses so that he wouldn't be able to identify the location of the hell he was forced to endure. Moore tried to heighten his hearing to catalogue and memorize any sounds he heard. He was determined to survive his torturous ordeal and return to reap a hateful revenge on his captors.

For over forty-eight hours, Moore had suffered sleep deprivation as his tormentors prodded him as he sat naked in the chair. His legs and arms were tied securely to the chair legs and its arm rests. His feet were numbed by the bucket of ice water in which they had been thrust. He had tried repeatedly to lift them from the water, but he couldn't since his legs were so tightly bound. His buttocks ached from sitting on the worn, wooden chair. His body had been tormented from the beatings. It was black and blue and bruised with welts. His body shivered in the cold basement.

He could feel the electrodes affixed to his wrists. They were a constant reminder of his captors' brutality. They had shocked him when he tried to sleep or when they wanted to prod him for information. So far, he hadn't provided them with anything. He knew that they couldn't kill him, at least until they were able to wring out the information they needed to solve the puzzle.

A door opened and people entered the small basement room. When Moore heard the switch thrown, his body shifted in anticipation of a painful surge. Feeling nothing for a change, he relaxed.

He heard something being dragged on the floor. A faint, familiar smell penetrated the sack and greeted his nostrils. He stiffened as he recognized the scent and realized who might be wearing the perfume.

"Throw her into that chair," Yarian grumbled as he turned to look at Moore and snarled, "You feel like talking yet?"

Moore didn't respond. He couldn't see the 280-pound, six-foot, gray-haired Turk reach for the switch – and it wasn't the light switch.

Yarian threw the switch that zapped Moore with a short, strong burst of electricity. Moore's body began to spasm, and he clenched his teeth as his body twisted in pain. He never knew how much of a charge or the length of the charge they'd give him.

"You want to answer me now, Mr. Tough Guy?" Yarian asked as he switched off the charge.

Moore remained silent as his body relaxed. He was thankful that they couldn't see the tortured look on his face. He also knew he wasn't going anywhere with this madman.

"I thought so." Yarian turned to Gorenchenko. "Take the gag out of her mouth and remove the blindfold."

Gorenchenko, the powerfully built Chechen with the shaved

head, did as he was instructed.

When the blindfold and gag were removed, the captive's head looked to her left. Her eyes widened as she stared in shock at the beaten body in front of her.

Seeing her look of horror, Yarian smiled. "Your lover boy looks different now." Yarian looked from her to Moore. "When we're done with him, no one will recognize him – not even you."

Moore heard the woman's voice plead.

"Let him go."

Moore recognized the voice instantly, and cringed with the realization that she was about to be tortured. For the first time, he spoke. "Yarian, you need to let her go."

"Isn't this sweet? Bring the two lovebirds together and they began to sing a love song for each other."

"She doesn't know anything, Yarian."

"Emerson, don't tell them anything," she said.

"Oh, I think he will tell us exactly what we want to know now that you're here. Am I correct, Mr. Moore?" Yarian asked in his heavily accented English. "Is the little lovebird willing to sing to protect his mate?"

Filled with a mixture of growing anger and anguish, Moore struggled for a response. He wanted to protect her. He also knew that once he gave them the information, Yarian would kill both of them. He decided to stall while he tried to fabricate a plausible answer to the questions they had been asking him.

"I'm weak. I can't think straight," Moore feigned.

Yarian roared. "Do you think I'm a fool?" He walked over to Moore and struck Moore's head with his fist.

Moore's head snapped to the side in reaction to the unexpected blow.

"You're not the first person I've interrogated. I know pain threshold limits. It may differ amongst people, but you are nowhere close to it. Now, answer my question and don't play with me," Yarian stormed.

Moore's mind raced with ideas for his next parry with his swarthy foe. Before he could respond, he heard the sound of a struggle and clothing being torn.

"You're taking too long, Moore," Yarian said as he watched Gorenchenko rip the shirt off of her. "In less than a minute, she'll be as naked as you."

Hearing the shredding of her clothes and her screams, Moore lost his control and exploded uncharacteristically, cursing as he pleaded for them to stop. His body twisted as he attempted to escape his bonds.

A sinister laugh emitted from Yarian's grotesque mouth as he nodded to Gorenchenko, who was preparing to follow the next step in Yarian's plan. Gorenchenko smiled. He was going to enjoy the next step. He bent to his task.

Moore heard a struggle taking place. "What are you doing?"

The only response was a chuckle from Yarian and a grunt from Gorenchenko. A few seconds later, a gunshot echoed through the small basement room.

"No! No! Don't kill her! I'll tell you what you want to know!" Moore screamed as the sound from the gunshot filled the basement room. This made absolutely no sense to him. What were they thinking? What kind of torture was this? They didn't push him for an answer. They just killed her. His body began shaking in rage and grief.

"Too late, my dear Mr. Moore," Yarian said as he laughed evilly. "I really don't need her to get you to talk. This was just for fun."

Moore heard Yarian walk over to him and he tightened his stomach muscles in anticipation of a blow to the ribcage.

"Nervous, Mr. Moore?" Yarian snickered. "Why, there's nothing to be nervous about. Not quite yet."

Moore felt something being poured on top of the bag over his head. It began to seep through the burlap and slowly flow from the top of his head down his face.

"Wondering what that is?" Yarian asked.

Moore didn't respond as the warm fluid seeped across his eyes and nose, mixing with his silent tears.

"It's her blood," Yarian gloated. He could picture the emotional trauma he was causing his captive. "We'll leave you now so that you can wallow in misery. I want you to know that you are responsible for her death. You should have answered my questions. If you had, we wouldn't have had to kill her."

Moore's heart sank. His shoulders and head, which had been defiant throughout his torture sessions, sagged as the reality of her death crushed him like a bus being dropped on his shoulders. The blood seeping through the sack tortured him as nothing else could.

The emotional game was working according to Yarian's plan.

Moore heard her body being dragged from the room as the two

torturers exited. The door closed shut with a loud bang. The lock was secured. Moore was isolated in a tomb filled with silent anguish. His mind berated himself for allowing her death. This was far worse than any physical pain he had endured. All he could do now was weep – and wait.

Washington, D.C.
March 1791

Along the banks of the Potomac River and near the thriving port towns of Alexandria and Georgetown, President George Washington chose the site for the fledgling nation's Capitol. Congress authorized the establishment with an act in 1790 and named the new town Washington, D.C. President Washington delegated the design of the new city to a Frenchman, Pierre Charles L'Enfant.

L'Enfant had come to America to fight in the Revolutionary War and became a friend of Washington. He was an established architect and a trusted city planner. When L'Enfant arrived that rainy night, he was accompanied by John Williames, a young English-German mason. Williames would assist L'Enfant in surveying the area and platting the city.

The plan included a large public area, today's National Mall. The Capitol was located at the highest point and overlooked the National Mall for two miles to the Potomac. Wide diagonal avenues, named after the states, radiated from Capitol Hill. Pennsylvania Avenue stretched a mile northwest from the Capitol to the White House.

Williames worked tirelessly in assisting with the planning and building of the Capitol. But as the years progressed and he became more experienced, Williames hungered for an opportunity to design a city. In 1814, Williames received an offer and decided to accept it.

After informing his mentor of his plan to move on, Williames returned to the rooming house in which he was living. Early the next morning, he crept into the basement and went to the far wall. Pulling a knife from his belt, he began to work it around a brick in the wall. He worked at loosening the mortar, which to the trained eye was lighter in color than the mortar surrounding the other bricks. It was evident that the brick had been removed earlier and replaced several times.

Williames withdrew the loose brick and reached into the hollowed area. He withdrew an item wrapped in oilskin. This was his life's calling, according to his father. He was to guard this with his life as would any Freemason.

Williames placed the item in his rucksack and replaced the brick in the wall. He made his way up the stairs to the main floor, rummaged in the cupboard and found one loaf of bread left from the previous day. He took it and walked out of the house.

He headed west into the wilderness on his adventure. He was excited about designing the layout for a new town. It would be called Portland.

The White House
April 14, 1865

It had rained during the night. The windows were open, allowing an early morning breeze to invigorate the Oval Office. From his office windows, President Abraham Lincoln could see the partially constructed Washington Monument. The construction had been halted by the country's focus on the war, but now that the war had nearly ended, it was scheduled to resume.

Lincoln returned to his desk and, using his elongated fingers, picked up a sealed envelope. Holding the envelope, he began to tap the edge of the envelope on his desk top.

"Is that for me?"

Lincoln was so preoccupied that he hadn't noticed that his contentious Secretary of War, Edwin Stanton, had entered the office. "Is what for you?"

"The envelope?" Stanton had been curious about the private meeting held the day before between Lincoln and the German ambassador. Since the meeting, Lincoln had seemed distracted.

Lincoln stopped tapping the envelope as he looked at it, and then turned to Stanton. "No, it's something that I've put together since yesterday's meeting."

"The one with the German ambassador?" the rotund Stanton asked rhetorically.

"Yes."

"A treaty proposal?"

"No, it's much more than that."

Lincoln slipped the envelope into his interior coat pocket. He would find himself taking it out and holding it in his hand throughout the day and during the play that evening. Lincoln turned and looked again at the Washington Monument. "I've made several changes to the plans for the monument's construction. Let me show you."

Stanton walked across the room and joined Lincoln at a nearby table where the plans were displayed. After glancing at the plans, Stanton asked, "What's this coloring about?" Stanton was referring to the checkerboard-like coloring of the granite blocks.

Lincoln peered over the top of his spectacles as he looked down on his Secretary of War. "I thought it looked bland. By taking this approach, it will stand out for all visitors to our grand Capitol."

"Don't like it," Stanton huffed.

"Mr. Stanton," Lincoln began, "I appreciate your opinion, but this is my decision."

"I think you better dwell on it before we move forward," Stanton suggested.

"Thank you for your thought, but my decision on this is final. Take the plans with you and make the necessary changes. I need to redirect my energy to reconstructing the South." Lincoln turned from the desk and Stanton rolled up the plans to take with him.

"Mary and I plan to attend a play at Ford's Theater tonight. Would you like to accompany us?"

"Can't. I have plans," Stanton responded gruffly. He preferred not to socialize with Lincoln unless it was a state event. His disdain and scorn for the nation's president continued to grow.

"It's supposed to be wonderfully humorous. It's the play, *Our American Cousin*. And now that the war has ended, I feel it's time for a good laugh," Lincoln said, smiling. His face had been so strained and somber over the last four years.

"So, I've heard," Stanton muttered dismissively as he exited the office with the rolled plans in his hand.

The Boardwalk Restaurant and Bar
Put-in-Bay, South Bass Island

The late morning sun shimmered across the tranquil harbor on Put-in-Bay, the picturesque island resort town located on South Bass Island in western Lake Erie. Also known as the "Key West of the Midwest," Put-in-Bay was a short ferry ride on the Miller Ferry from the Ohio mainland at Catawba Point or the Jet Express in Port Clinton and Sandusky.

Put-in-Bay and the surrounding islands were known for being a tourist "hot spot" and a great getaway weekend. Visitors from Michigan, Indiana and Ohio flocked to the islands in droves to swim, sail, boat, fish, jet ski, dine, and party at the various attractions and venues. Visitors also toured the Ohio State University's Stone Lab on Gibraltar Island in Put-in-Bay's harbor to learn more about the marine environmental issues in the lake. Another venue was the Perry Monument, which towered over the island and offered bird's eye views of the surrounding islands and the site of Admiral Perry's victory over the British fleet during the War of 1812.

From his vantage point over the harbor on the upper deck of the Boardwalk Restaurant and Bar, a tanned, 6-foot-2 man with glossy black hair and dark brown eyes was engaged in conversation with two bikini-clad female tourists. His name was Emerson Moore, an investigative reporter for *The Washington Post,* who used his aunt's East Point home on the harbor as his base of operations.

"You live here?" the blonde asked in wide-eyed awe.

"I do. See Perry's Monument?" Moore pointed to the tall structure overlooking the harbor on the east. "Then look past the first two houses, you'll see a two story taupe-colored house on the waterfront."

"That's where you live?" the blonde asked.

"Yes."

"All by your lonesome?" the brunette asked demurely.

"Not quite," Moore grinned as he recognized where she wanted to go with the conversation. "It's my aunt's house. I help her take care of it when I'm home."

"Is she home now?" the brunette asked with a flirtatious wink.

"Yep. She has an OWL meeting at the house today. That's why I'm here munching on a perch sandwich. You should try one."

"I'm a vegan. I don't eat fish," the brunette replied. "But I could have a salad if you don't mind the company," she teased.

"What's an OWL meeting? Do you raise owls on the island?" the blonde asked.

"Not really. It's the Old Women's Literary Society."

"Oh, I get it," the blonde replied.

"Hey, there're the two guys we met last night at the Beer Barrel," the brunette said as she spotted the two men on a boat, which was docked in the harbor. "Hey Rick," she yelled.

The guys returned her call and beckoned the two girls to join them on their Sea Ray.

"Nice talking with you," the blonde said as her friend began to pull her away from Moore. "Looks like we have to go."

Moore grinned. "Have fun."

The brunette looked back over her shoulder and said as she continued walking, "You can count on that."

With that the two girls disappeared down the steps to the main floor and shortly afterwards, appeared on the Sea Ray where drinks were already flowing.

"What the matter for you? You let those two get away?"

Moore turned around with a smile as he recognized the deep, rough voice. "They weren't keepers. Those are the ones you hook and throw back into the lake," Moore grinned as he saw his rascally friend, Mike "Mad Dog" Adams. The burly Adams had been an island fixture for over 33 years as he entertained tourists with his singing prowess and sharp humor from the stage at the island's Round House Bar.

"I don't know about that. The blonde was cute." Adams grinned as he sat on a high bar stool next to Moore. "What've you been up to other than trying to assassinate the president? You sure caused a commotion around here."

Thinking back to his involvement with President Benson's disappearance and the drama surrounding the nomination convention in Cleveland, Moore commented, "It sure made for a good story."

"Yes, it did. I bet your editors loved you for breaking the story on that one. The only thing I get to break around here is wind from time to time," Adams joked as he gazed across the harbor at Gibraltar Island. "And I want you to know, I didn't once believe any of that crap about you trying to assassinate the president. I figured it was a palace coup and I was right."

"What people do for power and greed never fails to amaze me," Moore replied stoically.

"You working a story now?"

"Yes, I am. Heading to Steinbach, Germany tomorrow."

"Steinbach, Germany! What ever for?"

"My curiosity is up. I got a note from a guy who used to be in German intelligence. The note was intriguing enough that I pitched it to my editors and they've given me the go-ahead to follow up. Not sure if there's anything there, but I'll check it out."

Adams slid off of his chair and stood. "You be careful, my friend. You've been lucky with your near death experiences. Cats only have nine lives. You better count up how many of your lives you've used up."

"I'm always careful."

"But you sure do some stupid things. Quit pushing the edge of the envelope so much," Adams warned.

"With the business I'm in, I have to," Moore said as he stood and began to walk away.

"Just remember what I always say. Every day above ground is a good day," Adams said, repeating the tag line from his show.

"Will do," Moore responded as he walked toward his parked golf cart.

JFK Airport
New York City

Moore watched as the blue-haired woman made her way down the plane's aisle. She walked slowly and carried a large bag. She seemed determined to hit every passenger with the bag as she made her way down the aisle. She was muttering to herself as she progressed.

Moore steeled himself in anticipation of being hit by her bag, but she stopped within inches. "Sir, you are sitting in my seat."

Moore looked up to see that she was addressing him. "Let me see," he said as he reached into his jacket pocket for his boarding pass. Pulling it out, he glanced at it. "It says 9D."

"That's the same as mine. See!" she responded as she thrust her boarding pass in Moore's face.

Moore looked at the pass and said, "It says 8D. That's the seat in front of me."

"It does?" She squinted her eyes and took a closer look at her boarding pass. "Oh my, it certainly does. I am so sorry," she said as she turned, swinging the bag. The bag narrowly missed Moore's head as he ducked.

The lady tried to lift the bag into the overhead storage unit, but couldn't lift it high enough. She struggled with it several times.

Seeing that no one else was assisting her, Moore unbuckled his seat belt and stood. "Could I do that for you?"

She turned and looked at Moore. "Why thank you, young man," she said appreciatively.

Moore quickly deposited the bag in the overhead storage compartment. "There you go," he said as he returned to his seat and rebuckled. He watched as she took her seat and was pleased that he had avoided the bag's impact.

He kicked off his shoes and stuck his sockless feet under the seat in front of him. As the flight attendants began their safety pitch, he felt the impact of his Tylenol PM. He began to drift into a deep slumber.

About four hours later, Moore woke suddenly as a warm liquid dripped onto his feet. He saw the lady in front of him reach for the call button as the smell of urine began to permeate the cabin.

He grimaced at the realization of what was making his feet wet.

"Yes?" the attendant asked the lady in front of Moore.

"I'm afraid I had a little accident," she whispered. The whisper was loud enough for Moore and passengers around her to hear.

Sniffing the air, the attendant said, "Let me help you." She assisted the passenger from her seat and down the aisle to the lavatory. A few minutes later, she returned and grabbed the lady's bag from the overhead compartment. She looked at Moore and whispered, "I'll be back in a second and freshen up this area."

"My feet need more than freshening up. Looks like they were in the drip zone," he said.

"Oh, I am so sorry."

"No problem. Those things happen at that age. I just hope folks are as understanding when I get to that point in my life." Moore unbuckled his seatbelt and stood. "I will go wash off my feet, though," he said as he eased himself into the aisle and began to walk to one of the open lavatories.

"When you return, I'll have this cleaned up." She smiled at the handsome reporter.

"Thank you."

When Moore returned to his seat, he found the area free from odor and that the lady had returned to her seat. She was apparently oblivious as to what had happened to him. Moore settled into his seat and the balance of his flight to Frankfort was uneventful.

Steinbach
Germany

With the rain beating harder against his windshield, Moore slowed as he guided the rented Audi through a tight curve. He had made it nearly to Steinbach when the storm broke. The dark clouds overhead unleashed a torrential downpour. The constant beating of the windshield wipers drummed in his ears as Moore peered through the windshield in the diminishing light.

Following his GPS instructions, Moore arrived at the address he had programmed. He parked his car in front of the house and walked to the home's entrance where he knocked on the door. As he waited under his umbrella, he looked around the neighborhood.

Across the street and down a few houses was a parked car. He thought he saw the shadows of two people sitting in the car. Moore wondered if they were guarding the house or if the house was under surveillance. He expected the former since Kalker had retired from the intelligence field.

His knock was answered with a voice responding in German, "I'm coming."

Within seconds the door swung open to reveal a stout gentleman with curly gray hair. Perched on his nose was a pair of rimless glasses. "May I help you?" he asked in German.

Moore shook his head. "I apologize but I don't speak German. I was looking for Andreas Kalker. Could you tell me if he lives here?"

Switching to near perfect English, the man replied. "I am Andreas. And you must be Emerson Moore."

Moore nodded, but before he could comment further, Kalker spoke. "Come in. Come in. It is nice to meet you in person since our e-mails and phone chats."

"Thank you, Andreas," Moore responded as he followed Kalker into the house and into the front room. He sat down when Kalker gestured to a chair. Moore noticed that the man seemed to be sweating profusely and his skin tone had a pasty pallor.

"Good flight?" Kalker asked as he coughed twice.

"Yes."

"Good. Good. And your drive here was fine?"

"Easy drive thanks to the GPS. I do love technology."

"Good, Good. How about a beer or schnapps?" Kalker asked. "And I have some fresh pastry from the baker. Would you like some?"

"Yes, I would. A small schnapps, please."

Kalker scurried out of the room to get the refreshments. While he was gone, Emerson allowed his eyes to roam the modestly appointed living room. Nothing here that would seem out of the ordinary, Moore thought to himself.

Kalker returned and, after setting the refreshments on a small table next to Moore's chair, sat in the chair on the other side of the table.

Moore reached for his glass of schnapps and turned to Kalker, who had his glass in hand. "To our good luck in meeting each other," Moore toasted.

"Probst." Kalker toasted in turn as the two drank the schnapps.

Moore then reached for a pastry and tried one. "Tasty," he remarked.

"Yes. Yes. They are quite good, aren't they? The baker is a little too close to my home as you can see by my girth," Kalker grinned. "Where shall we start?"

"Let's start with the note you mailed me. I must admit I found it very intriguing. What made you decide to contact me when there are hundreds of people who would love to learn more about this?"

"True. True."

Moore noticed that Kalker had a propensity to repeat himself.

"It was through our mutual friend, Steve Nicholas. He thought that you had a strong investigative background and a fresh perspective outside the intelligence world."

Interesting, Moore thought to himself, that Kalker knew cyber code breaker Nicholas, who had been in a top level position at the National Intelligence Agency and had also worked at the National Security Agency, or NSA. "How do you know Nicholas?"

Kalker took another swallow of schnapps before responding. Quietly he replied, "Many years ago, Nicholas and I were assigned by our governments to work together on a project. That's how we got to know each other. He spent a lot of time in Germany."

"You worked in the same domain as Steve?" Moore asked.

"Yes. Yes. For the Bundesnachrichtendienst. The BND." He coughed again.

Moore was aware of Germany's Federal Intelligence Service

from his discussions with Nicholas over the years. The BND heavily used wiretapping and electronic surveillance internationally to collect and evaluate information on international terrorism, organized crime, illegal weapons sales, human and drug trafficking, and information warfare.

"Is that how you came across the Legend of 13?"

"Yes, and from what I've been able to piece together over the years. Some of which I've shared with Nicholas."

"Why do you bring it up now?" Moore asked.

"I'm dying. I have inoperable cancer. I should have quit smoking years ago. Nothing can be done," the 68-year-old replied and smiled weakly as he wiped his sweating brow and coughed again.

"I'm sorry to hear that."

"As you Americans say, 'I'm playing the cards I've been dealt.' I just didn't expect this card of death to be in my hands so quickly."

"There is nothing the docs can do? No treatments? How about in the U.S.?" Moore asked sympathetically.

"No, nothing. I've checked all of the avenues."

"Again, I am so sorry," Moore repeated. After a pause, he continued, "So, tell me about this Legend of 13."

"It goes back. It started with Jesus and the twelve disciples."

Moore arched his brow. "How's that?"

"How many were there?"

"Thirteen when you count Jesus."

"Exactly. The number thirteen has had a significant impact in world events and for some strange reason that number holds the key to this puzzle. Look at the groups or individuals who had thirteen affiliated with them. There were the European Union, United Kingdom and, most recently, Osama Bin Laden. All have thirteen letters in their names. Play with it and you'll be amazed with key historical links to the number thirteen." Kalker sat back in his chair.

"I don't get it. Why are you and Nicholas so excited about this number thirteen stuff?" Moore asked with a wrinkled brow.

"I have a theory that this Legend of 13 leads us to solving a major puzzle which the world has been seeking to solve."

"Which is?"

"The location of the Nazarene's Code."

Moore looked directly at Kalker. "The Nazarene's Code? What's that?"

"The existence of this document has been rumored for centuries. Myself, I took it as nothing more than rumors. Jesus allegedly authored the Nazarene's Code a short time before his arrest and crucifixion. It reportedly contains the key to using the powerful forces of heaven and earth to change lives - and it reveals hidden secrets to controlling nations."

Moore sighed in undisguised disappointment. "Sounds like wishful thinking to me. It's probably nothing of substance." Had he come all the way here for a religious hoax? He thought he had heard them all.

"That's how I felt until earlier this year when my doctor, who is Jewish, asked me if I had heard about the missing scroll. I told him that I had heard rumors of it over the years and asked why he was inquiring. He said that he thought I'd know more because he knew that I worked in intelligence. I told him working in intelligence doesn't make me more intelligent." Kalker stopped as a giggle slipped from between his lips.

Moore nodded.

"I prodded and asked him again why he was inquiring. He answered that his brother in Israel was an antiquities professor and researcher. His brother confided in him that he found evidence of the code's existence and believes the whereabouts of the scroll is tied to the Legend of 13."

Moore was growing restless, and it showed.

Kalker grew very serious. "Mr. Moore, I have been involved in intelligence all of my life. I am no conspiracy theorist or follower of fairy tales. Believe me when I say I would not have reached out to you if I didn't think there was something to this."

Moore took out his cell phone. "All right. Could I have your doctor's name and phone number? I'd like to talk to him about this."

"Sure. It's Doctor Levy." Kalker provided the contact information.

"This is helpful. I'll get in touch with Levy and see if I can talk my way into visiting his brother. I'd like to talk to him, too."

"Levy's brother won't have anything to say."

"Why's that?" Moore asked.

"He's dead."

"What?"

"Yes, two weeks ago, Levy said that his brother became suspicious that he was being followed. He thought someone searched his apartment and downloaded data from his computer. Then, a few days later, he was found murdered."

"How do you know all of this?"

"Levy told me. He knew that I had worked for the BND and wanted to see if there was anything I could do to help. There wasn't."

Moore's interest jumped a quantum leap. Shaking his head side to side in disbelief, Moore reached for his cell phone and dialed the doctor's number. "Excuse me, Andreas. I'd like to get this meeting set with your doctor right away."

"I'll get more schnapps," Kalker said as he wiped his brow, then stood and walked into the kitchen, coughing as he walked.

Moore worked quickly in setting up an appointment and then, continued to talk with Kalker. After further discussion over the next hour, Moore thanked Kalker for the information and excused himself to go to the meeting with Kalker's doctor.

As Kalker walked Moore to the door, he said, "One more thing."

"What's that?" Moore asked.

"Nazarene's Code."

"Yes?"

"It has thirteen letters."

Moore looked at Kalker, "Interesting." He turned and began to walk to his car.

"Emerson?" Kalker called.

Moore stopped and turned. "Yes?"

"I have thirteen letters in my name."

Moore quickly counted the letters in his own name. "I'm in the clear. I only have twelve in my name unless I count my middle initial."

He entered his car and drove to Levy's office.

Dr. Levy's Office
Steinbach, Germany

Entering Dr. Levy's second floor office, Moore checked in with the receptionist and took a chair in the sparsely decorated lobby. He picked up a worn, dog-eared magazine and leafed through the pages, primarily looking at the pictures since he didn't read or speak German. He was just returning the copy to the end table and picking up another magazine when the door to the examination rooms opened.

A voice called. "Herr Moore?"

"Yes," Moore said as he stood.

"The doctor will see you now. Please come this way," she responded in broken English.

Moore followed the nurse past three examination rooms and into a small office.

"Please have a seat. He'll be right with you."

Moore squeezed into a chair in front of the small desk. As he waited, he looked around the small office and noticed how tidy it was. Moore took a mental note to try to do better with his rather messy office. His thoughts were interrupted by a deep voice from over his left shoulder.

"So, my friend Andreas has sent you to see me?" the bespectacled doctor asked as he firmly shook hands with Moore and sat in the swivel chair behind his desk. The chair seemed to groan as the slightly overweight doctor sat down.

"Yes, he did. I was sorry to hear about Andreas' health condition."

"Yes, I'm sure he told you his prognosis?"

Moore nodded. "He doesn't have much time left."

"Unfortunately, that is true. Now, what is it that I can do for you?" Levy asked, even though Moore had mentioned the topic when he set up the appointment.

"Andreas told me about your brother's work."

"One moment please," the doctor interrupted Moore. He stood, walked across the office and closed his door. He then returned to his chair. "I need to be careful when talking about my brother, especially if I think you are going to talk with me about the information I shared with Andreas."

"That's why I'm here."

"So, Andreas told you about my brother's research? He must have told you because you work in the same field as he, is that correct?"

"Yes, he did tell me and no, I don't work in intel if that's what you're getting at. We have a mutual friend, who suggested to Andreas that he get in touch with me about the Nazarene's Code."

Levy nodded as he listened.

"Andreas told me that your brother had been murdered. Was the murderer caught?"

"No."

"Do you know what the motive was?"

"I don't," Levy said as he took off his glasses and looked at a smudge on them. He opened his desk drawer and withdrew a cleansing cloth that he used to clean the smudge. Returning the cloth to his drawer and resettling the glasses on his face, Levy added, "I believe he was following the trail of the Nazarene's Code."

"I'd like to see his apartment in Israel and look through his office to see if I can find any clues. Could I have your permission and a key to his place?"

"I'm not sure that you'll find anything there."

"Why is that?"

"I've been to his apartment and his office. I didn't find anything. Besides, the police had already gone through his apartment twice according to the landlord."

"Are you sure it was the police both times?"

"How would I know?" he asked with a raised eyebrow.

"I'd still like to take a look if you'd give me the keys and addresses."

For a moment, Levy looked at the stranger in front of him. "It's because Andreas thinks so highly of you that I will give you my permission." He began to write down the addresses.

"And while you're at it, could you note where he was killed? I'd like to assess the murder location while I'm there."

"I can write it down, but the murder didn't take place there."

"It didn't?"

"No, it took place in Turkey in a small town near Bodrum."

"Turkey? Why Turkey?"

"I don't know. Other than he may have been on the trail of the Code."

"Did your brother send you any files, notes or e-mails which could help us in our investigation? Did he say anything to you on the phone?"

"The day before he was killed, he called me. Otherwise, no."

"And what did he say?"

"It's not so much what he said as it was the tone in which he said it."

"How's that?"

"My brother was always a confident person. When we talked last, he was rushed and I detected fear in his tone. He seemed nervous. When I asked if he was okay, he replied that he thought he was being watched."

"Did he say by whom?"

"No. Then he said he had to go. He was leaving for Turkey

within the hour."

"Could you note the location of his murder for me?"

"I can do better than that. I can give you the name of the police officer, who called me, and a newspaper clipping, which I have here." Levy pulled open his desk drawer and pulled out a copy of the story that had appeared in the local Turkish newspaper. "You'll need to have the story translated," he said as he took the clipping to the copy machine where he made a copy. Returning to his desk, Levy replaced the original in his desk drawer and handed the copy to Moore.

"Thank you," Moore said as he arose from his chair. "Anything else I should know?" he asked as he handed Levy his business card.

"If I think of anything else, I will give you a call."

Shaking hands, Moore again thanked the doctor and exited the office. He made his way back to his car and drove to Kalker's house where he began to make plans to visit Levy's brother's apartment in Haifa.

Kalker's House
Steinbach, Germany

Welcoming his overnight guest, Kalker beckoned Moore to follow him to the second floor guest bedroom. "How did your visit with Levy go?"

Carrying his small suitcase and his briefcase that contained his notebook computer, Moore responded. "Interesting. Very interesting."

"How so?" Kalker asked as he led Moore into his bedroom.

"Levy said his brother thought that he was being watched. He was suspicious that his apartment and computer were searched," Moore responded as he looked around the bedroom.

Wrinkling his brow, Kalker asked, "And what's your take on this?"

"Obviously, something's not quite right. He must have found something and someone was on to him. Not sure what he found, but I'm intrigued enough to fly to Haifa to see what I can learn."

"When are you flying there?"

"Tomorrow." Moore set his notebook on a small desk near the bed. "Do you have Wi-Fi here?"

"Yes. You should be able to access my network. It's a secured network."

"Good. And what password do I use?"

"Meine Liebe."

"Meine Liebe?" Moore asked.

With a smile, Kalker responded, "Yes. Translated it means 'my dear'. I may be dying, but I'm not there yet. I still chase the pretty girls. The only difference is that they are older and I'm much slower."

Moore chuckled softly.

"Are you married, Emerson?"

"I was." Moore paused before commenting. "My wife and son were killed a couple of years ago in a car accident in D.C."

"I am sorry to hear that," Kalker said.

"And you?"

"Four times. I've been married and divorced four times. In my business, it's difficult to have a normal home life. It seemed like I was always out of the country on missions. Not many women tolerate long absences."

Moore nodded.

Changing the topic, Kalker said, "It's near dinner time. Would you like to go to one of Steinbach's fine restaurants?"

"Sounds like a plan," Moore said as he plugged in his notebook and turned it on. "I'd like to make my flight and hotel arrangements first, if you don't mind."

"Go ahead. You come downstairs when you are ready to go." Kalker exited the bedroom as Moore sat on a chair in front of a small desk and began to log on.

Within fifteen minutes, Moore had booked his flight and hotel and returned to the home's main floor to his waiting host. The two went to Zum Goldenen Stern, the Golden Star, at nearby Born Hollow for dinner. The restaurant was one of the oldest in the town and was situated in a traditional half-timbered house. The two enjoyed a meal of large portions, several glasses of wine from their excellent wine list and additional dialogue about Levy's murdered brother.

Afterwards, they returned to Kalker's house and Moore returned to his room to research Haifa on-line before his trip.

From the Airport
Haifa, Israel

After the Frankfurt-to-Haifa flight landed, Moore quickly cleared customs and caught a cab. He gave the cab driver the address of the hotel and settled in the seat to enjoy the ride through Israel's third largest city, which was built on the slopes of Mount Carmel.

On the cab ride, Moore recounted his quick research of Haifa. It was a city besieged and ruled by invaders over the years including Saladin, Richard the Lionhearted and his Crusaders, Napoleon, the Egyptians, the German Templars, and the Ottoman Turks. In 1918, Indian horsemen serving in the British Army captured the city from the Turks.

The Brits ruled Haifa and developed the city into a major industrial port with a strong railway service. After Israel declared its independence in 1948, Haifa became the gateway for Jewish immigration into Israel.

The cab worked its way up the slope of Mt. Carmel. It pulled to a stop at 51 Palmach Street on top of Mount Carmel and in front of the Marom Haifa Hotel. Moore paid the driver and exited the cab with his luggage. He entered the hotel and walked across the stone-tiled floor to guest registration.

Once he completed his registration, he deposited his luggage in his room and returned to the lobby where he caught another cab for the University of Haifa.

The university was located on top of Mount Carmel amidst the green forests of Carmel Mountain Park, commanding a panoramic view of the city below and the eastern Mediterranean Sea along the shores of Haifa.

The cab dropped off Moore at the university's Zinman Institute of Archaeology, where Moore entered the building and located the director's office. He was greeted by a friendly administrative assistant.

"May I help you, sir?"

"Yes. I have an appointment with Professor Josef Steinmetz. My name is Emerson Moore."

Before she could respond, a gregarious man with thick white hair appeared in his office doorway. "Welcome to the Zinman Institute of Archeology. I'm Josef Steinmetz," he said as he greeted Moore. "I am sorry that we meet under such circumstances." He ushered Moore into his office where the two sat around a small round table.

"Yes, I agree. This has been very difficult for Dr. Levy's brother."

"Do you have the letter from his brother? I'll need it for our files."

Moore reached into his sport coat's inside pocket and withdrew the letter that he had secured from Levy before leaving Steinbach. The letter authorized the Institute to release Levy's personal items in his office to Moore. He slid the letter across the desk to Steinmetz, who quickly read through it.

"It looks to be in order." Steinmetz placed the letter on the table and asked, "If I could see your passport, please?"

Moore produced his passport and Steinmetz stood. "If you don't mind, I'll make a copy of your passport to attach to the letter as proof that we verified who you are."

Moore nodded, "No problem. I understand."

Steinmetz returned within two minutes and returned the passport. He then called to his administrative assistant, "Eva, would you escort Mr. Moore to Professor Levy's office so that he can pick up his personal belongings?"

Within minutes, Moore had left the director's office and followed Eva.

As they walked, Moore engaged Eva in conversation. "Eva, what area did Professor Levy specialize in?"

"Biblical research. That's where he spent most of his time."

"Any particular area of the country?"

"He split his on-site research time between Jerusalem and Nazareth."

Moore's eyebrows lifted. "He did?"

"Yes, until recently."

"What happened recently to change that?"

"He received several special grants from the Israel Antiquities Authority that allowed him to focus on the Crusader period."

"And is that the reason he was in Turkey?"

Eva looked down the hall toward the director's office before she answered. "I believe so." She hesitated before commenting further to the affable stranger. "I filed the approved travel authorization form."

"Did it state the purpose of the trip?"

"Yes. He was following a lead on a missing scroll which may have been stolen by the Knights Templar during the Crusades."

"Do you know where he was going in Turkey or who he was going to see?"

Eva's voice dropped to a whisper. "I don't know who he was going to see, but his destination was Gumusluk. He flew into Bodrum, but he was murdered in Gumusluk." She paused in front of an office door and produced a key to unlock it. Swinging the door open, she said, "This is - was his office."

Moore entered the small office and looked around at the shelves filled with books. He quickly scanned the titles. "Did the police go through his office?"

"Yes, why do you ask?"

"Since his death was a murder. But then again, it took place in Turkey."

"The Turkish authorities said he was murdered during a robbery."

Moore spotted a box on the desk filled with Dr. Levy's personal belongings. Moore sat on Levy's chair and saw a Dell laptop computer. "Is this his personal computer?"

"I believe it belongs to the Institute."

"Could you check to be sure? If it's his, I'd like to take it with me."

"I'll go check." Eva left the office and Moore powered up the laptop. As he waited for it to come up, he pulled open the desk drawers to see if there was anything of interest. He noticed one drawer would not close completely. He pulled the drawer out and peered inside where he spotted a small notebook taped to the back of the drawer. He detached it and put it in his sport coat pocket. He then replaced the drawer into the desk.

At the same time, the laptop powered up. Moore pulled out a flash drive and was about to insert it when approaching footsteps signaled the return of Eva. He quickly returned the flash drive to his pocket.

"I'm sorry, Mr. Moore, but the laptop is university property. It must stay."

Moore was frustrated in not being able to dump the "C" drive onto his flash drive, but he also realized that he didn't have the password to sign on to Levy's laptop.

"I understand," Moore said as he rose from the chair and picked up the box. He took one last look around the office and said, "I think that does it here. Could you show me the way out?"

"Certainly," she responded as the two exited the office and she relocked the office door. When they reached the entrance, she asked, "Would you like me to call you a cab?"

"Yes, I would. I'll just wait here. Thank you for your help today, Eva."

"You are quite welcome. And please express my deepest sympathy to Professor Levy's brother."

"I will," Moore said as he sat on a chair in the lobby to await his cab.

Within five minutes, he was in a cab and had provided the driver with the address for Levy's apartment. Moore pulled out the notebook from his sport coat. He opened it to the first page and breathed a sigh of relief when he saw it was written in English. The title page read: My Search for the Nazarene's Code. Moore's eyes widened as he began to read. He was so intent on the notebook that he didn't see a car pull out from its parking space and begin to follow the cab.

When they arrived at the apartment building, Moore had the driver wait while he checked out Levy's apartment. Twenty minutes later, Moore returned to the cab. His search of the apartment had not been fruitful.

Arriving at the hotel, Moore paid the driver and walked inside, through the lobby and to his room where he sat in a chair and began to devour Levy's notebook.

The car, which had been following Moore's cab, pulled into one of the hotel's parking slots. Its driver reached for a cell phone and made a call. Receiving instructions to tail Moore wherever he went, the driver rang off and settled into the front seat.

In his hotel room, Moore continued reading through Levy's comments. The notebook chronicled Levy's discovery of the Nazarene's Code. He had found several scrolls that mentioned it and its power to control the world. Further investigations and logical assumptions pointed Levy to Turkey to follow the trail.

Moore turned to his notebook and sent an e-mail to Kalker to tell him that he'd return to Steinbach the next day. Moore then began rummaging through the box of Levy's personal effects. Not finding anything of interest, he turned to his laptop and began Googling Gumusluk and Bodrum in Turkey to gather information on the Knights Templar activities there.

Kalker's House
The Next Day

Moore had begun to update Kalker on the results of his trip when they were interrupted by a knock at the front door.

"Excuse me, that must be my niece," Kalker said as he stood

from the chair. "I asked her to join us tonight. You'll like her. She's an antiquities researcher, specializing in Israel and Turkey."

Moore sat back, nodding his head. "That could be helpful."

Kalker returned a few minutes later with his niece in tow. "Emerson, this is my niece, Katrina Bieber."

Moore stood to greet the tall, svelte, buxom blonde, who was wearing a white linen shirt and black jeans. The jeans looked like they had been painted on. She had sparkling blue eyes and her lips were colored with a bright pink lipstick. Moore was awestruck by her Germanic beauty. He made a mental note that he'd buy Kalker a case of wine for introducing her to him.

Moore beamed as he arose from his chair and shook her extended hand, "This is indeed a pleasant surprise. Nice to meet you, Katrina."

Bieber eyed the handsome American. "My friends call me Kat," she purred in English with a heavy German accent.

"Then, Kat it is," Moore grinned.

Kalker had been watching the exchange between the two, and smiled. "Now, let's get down to business," he said as he produced another glass, filled it, and sat in his chair.

Bieber took a seat at the table and reached for her glass. She quickly downed her schnapps and sat back. "So, what do we have here that I can help with? My uncle gave me a quick briefing over the phone when he called."

Moore, trying not to let her blue eyes distract him, recounted the events of the last week including Levy's murder in Gumusluk and the ensuing investigation by a Turkish police officer named Ekrem Tabak.

"Interesting," Bieber said as Moore finished and she turned to her uncle. "Sounds like something I'd like to help with."

"Kat, why don't you fly with Emerson to Bodrum and help him with the next step?" her uncle asked.

Kat raised her eyebrows and looked at Moore.

"Sounds like a plan to me. Would you like to go?" Moore asked. "I can always use an extra set of eyes and ears, especially from someone with a background in this stuff." Moore also looked at this as an opportunity to become better acquainted with the beautiful woman seated across from him.

"I'd love to," Bieber responded. "I've spent time on the Bodrum Peninsula and in Gumusluk. When do we leave?"

"I have a commitment to keep in the Red Sea," Moore began.

"Parting the waters?" Bieber teased.

Grinning, Moore nodded. "Maybe on my next trip. Actually, I have to meet a friend of mine for a dive trip. It's been planned for some time and I don't want to break my commitment. We can meet in Bodrum three days from now."

"*Das ist gut.* That works for me," Bieber said.

They went over their travel details and continued their conversation. An hour later, Moore excused himself and returned to his hotel. He had decided not to stay at Kalker's on this visit to be more in control of his time. As he drove to the hotel, he found himself looking forward to spending time with Kalker's attractive niece, and reminded himself not to let her become a distraction.

Suddenly, Moore realized that there were thirteen letters in Katrina Bieber's name. This is beginning to become maddening,

Moore thought to himself. Then, he realized that his next destination, the Strait of Gobal, also had thirteen letters.

Strait of Gobal
The Red Sea

The *Aeolus* rocked gently at her anchor as the warm wind blew across her bow. She was appropriately named *MY Aeolus,* which means *God of the Wind.* She was a new 85-foot dive boat with four double cabins, a spacious salon, dive deck, and a sun deck on top behind the captain's wheel.

Karim, the boat's captain, had picked up Moore at the resort city of Sharm el Sheikh after Moore had taken the one-hour flight there from Cairo. They drove for fifty minutes to Dahab where nine boats were docked at the jetty. Karim's *Aeolus* and Roger Rothman, an old friend of Moore's, were awaiting their arrival so they could be moored on a special shipwreck by sundown, ready for an early morning dive.

Rothman was internationally renowned for his underwater videography and filmmaking. The wiry Rothman had filmed for National Geographic and Discovery Channel and had helped Moore recently in his adventures in the Cayman Islands.

"It's been awhile, my friend," Rothman greeted Moore as he exited the parked vehicle.

"It has," Moore agreed. "And I hope that our dives here are more relaxing than the ones in the Cayman Islands." Moore started to grab his gear, but Karim waved him off.

"You visit with your friend. I'll grab your gear," Karim said.

"Thanks," More said as he and Rothman began walking to the

ship. Moore looked over his shoulder at Karim and then back to Rothman. "That Karim bears an uncanny resemblance to an author we have in Put-in-Bay. They could be twins," Moore observed as the balding, deeply tanned, brown-eyed captain effortlessly hoisted Moore's gear onto his shoulders.

"They say we all have twins somewhere," Rothman said as they boarded the ship.

"I'll have to take a picture to take back to Put-in-Bay," Moore said as he walked aboard.

Karim assisted Moore in getting him settled in his stateroom. Then, he and Rothman gave Moore a quick tour of the ship before Karim excused himself to get underway.

The next morning, Moore and Rothman prepared for their dive. Moore couldn't pass up diving with his friend, especially when it came to diving in new seas. Moore was especially excited about diving on the *Thistlegorm,* rated as one of the top ten dives in the world. Strong currents at the surface and at the wreck site made it a challenging dive.

The *Thistlegorm,* Gaelic for "Blue Thistle," was a British vessel that was bombed and sunk in 1941 after an air attack by the German Luftwaffe. She was carrying a cargo of war supplies: ammunition, rifles, generators, motorbikes, and Bedford trucks. On her deck, she carried two Stanier locomotives with their respective tenders and water bowsers. A nose-diving German Henkel He 111's bombs struck the hold aft of the bridge where the ammunition had been stored. The ensuing explosion peeled back that section of the *Thistlegorm*'s deck like a sardine can.

Karim fired up the zodiac and helped Moore and Rothman into it from the dive platform. He took them to just above the stern of the wreck and a little off to starboard. It would make it easier to descend in the current and hopefully end up at one of the locomotives that had been blown off the deck. They were sitting at a depth of ninety-five feet next to the *Thistlegorm.*

The two divers seemed to fly through the water as they descended. Their dive plan worked perfectly as the locomotives loomed ahead. Rothman chose the locomotive that offered more sunlight since it would be better for his videographing.

A large green moray eel appeared magically in front of Moore from underneath the locomotive. The suddenness of its appearance caused Moore to jerk backward in surprise and move away from this eel of sea serpent proportions. Its head was larger than a human's. The eel ignored Moore and continued swimming under the locomotive looking for prey.

Hearing a knife tapping on a tank, Moore turned to look at his dive partner. Rothman's eyes were filled with mirth in reaction to Moore's encounter with the humongous eel. If Rothman didn't have his mouthpiece in, Moore would have seen Rothman's huge smile.

Rothman pointed to the wreck and then began to swim toward it. As they swam directly at the wreck, the current carried them towards the bow where the huge anchor chain still hung from the hawse pipe to the sand where it had been dropped while supposedly in safe anchorage on that October day in 1941. The pair slipped to the port side out of the current and Rothman filmed an upshot of the bow with the port anchor still mounted and the sunlight coming over the railing.

Rothman ascended over the bow railing and continued filming as he swam toward the huge anchor winches still tightly holding their chains. He was the first of the pair to leave the protection of the ship and realized that the current had subsided. This made the swim aft ward much easier than anticipated.

Moore quickly followed as he enjoyed observing the fish life as he swam. There were schools of brightly colored anthias dancing above the winches with striated fusiliers schooling higher in the water column. As a school of batfish swam by, a masked puffer fish kept a wary eye on the pair while Moore studied a small pipe-fish at the base of a capstan.

The two divers dropped over the end of the foc'sle and swam to the main deck, then down into the first hold. There were large rubber tires strewn about the tween decks level along with the damaged Bedford trucks and a number of Norton motorcycles awaiting riders. Descending deeper to the lower deck, they spied a single Wellington thigh boot on the floor and Moore wondered if it might have belonged to one of the crew.

Finished with shooting in the first hold, Rothman motioned to Moore to follow him through a small doorway, which led to the number two hold. BSA motorcycles were lined up next to each other almost exactly like the day they were loaded. Each Bedford truck in this hold also had three motorcycles loaded on their beds to save cargo room. Rothman rubbed off some silt and growth from one of the batteries and Moore could clearly see the im-printed logo of the Lucas Company of Birmingham, England and a production date of 1941.

Knowing that their time underwater was waning, Moore mo-tioned to Rothman that it was time to ascend to the main deck. He then swam past the port side of the wheelhouse where a green sea turtle was heading to the surface for a breath of air. They passed over the peeled-back steel deck to the area that had been blown apart by the explosion.

It was strewn with two tank-like Bren gun carriers, boxes of rifles, and unexploded munitions. Then, Moore noticed one shell in a box of four. Its end had been rubbed clean displaying a date of 1929. Moore showed it to Rothman to film.

They swam along the starboard rail slowly ascending as they

went, until they spotted the mooring line that had been fastened amidships near a davit. This davit and the metal stairways leading from the main deck to the foc'sle were grim reminders that sailors once used these in their everyday lives. Now, they had become part of an unofficial war grave from WWII.

The pair slowly ascended up the mooring line to fifteen feet below the surface. There they spent five minutes doing their safety stop to off gas, releasing the nitrogen that had built up in their bodies during the dive. Both divers hung onto the mooring line and watched other divers explore the wreck. Near the end of their safety stop, they watched a huge eight-foot Napoleon wrasse swim over the wreck as if it were the official sentinel.

Once their safety stop time was up, they swam from the mooring line to the ladder of the *Aeolus*, took off their fins, and broke the surface.

"Awesome dive wasn't it?" Rothman asked as he bobbed on the surface.

"Frozen in time," Moore responded. "I appreciate you inviting me, Roger. It exceeded my expectations!"

"I thought you'd get a kick out of this one," the bearded Rothman replied.

The two divers climbed onto the dive platform where a member of the crew started to help them remove their tanks. As he did, the crew member slipped and fell into the water.

"You okay?" Rothman called when the man's head surfaced.

"Yes. Yes, I'm fine," the man replied as he swam to the dive platform and pulled himself aboard. "Just lost my balance."

"Hakan!" Karim's voice bellowed.

"Yes, Karim," Hakan replied as he quickly stood to his feet.

"Go help in the galley."

"Yes, yes," Hakan replied as the young man disappeared toward the kitchen.

"And don't loose your balance!" Karim's voice trailed after the young man. Karim looked at his two divers. "I apologize. He's not a regular member of my crew. He's my cousin's friend and is replacing one of my regular crew members, who is in the hospital."

"Hope it's not something serious," Moore said.

"Just minor surgery." Karim looked in the direction in which Hakan had disappeared. "Hakan means well, but he's clumsy."

Grinning, Moore replied, "I'll say. You should have seen how big his eyes were as he fell."

"Emerson, tell me. Did you see any mermaids when you were diving today?"

"No, I didn't," Moore smiled.

"Back you go until you find one." The powerfully built Karim tossed Moore overboard as if he weighed ten pounds. Moore hit the water with a splash and surfaced.

Karim turned to Rothman. "Roger, did you see any mermaids on your dive?"

Rothman nodded his head as he spoke, "Saw three this trip."

"Good. Let's help your friend on board."

As Karim and Rothman helped Moore onto the dive platform,

Karim asked again, "Did you see any mermaids this time?"

"Yes, I did - and the redhead was the most beautiful," Moore said now that he knew the drill.

Karim helped them with the rest of their gear and then escorted them to the salon to snack on fresh fruit before preparing for dinner.

The ship's guests had completed another day of diving and would be treated to a sumptuous buffet meal of fish and squid.

After dinner, two couples from Illinois remained in the salon playing cards as they savored glasses of red wine. Two Armenian guests were standing near the dive deck, smoking cigars and talking in hushed tones.

Upstairs at the wheel, Captain Karim was studying his GPS, but quite aware of Moore and Rothman as they approached either side of his driver's bench. Rothman, with a Jim Beam in hand, sat down next to Karim.

"Did you enjoy the diving today?" Karim beamed as he asked, confident in receiving a positive response.

"Excellent," Rothman responded.

"Exceeded my expectations," Moore added.

"So Emerson, you mentioned that you are going to meet a woman in Turkey?" Karim asked.

"Yes. We're meeting in Bodrum."

"A very nice area in southwest Turkey. It's a resort on a bay with good diving," Karim beamed. "I've been there several times. I've also coordinated flights for my divers who wanted to try diving there."

"Could you help me with a flight?" Moore asked.

"Better than that. I'll drive you tomorrow to the airport and introduce you to an American expat, Ray Grissett. He runs a small charter service there. You'll pay less flying with Ray than one of the other charters or a regular flight," Karim offered.

"Sounds good to me," Moore responded.

"Sure you don't want to take another dive tomorrow?" Rothman asked as he sipped his drink.

"I promised to meet her tomorrow. As much as I'd like to do another dive, I'd better pass," Moore replied. Moore turned to Karim. "You ever hear anything about a Nazarene's Code?"

Karim thought a moment before responding. "In this part of the world, we hear about all sorts of legends, codes and lost cities. What is this Nazarene's Code?"

"I'm still putting this all together," Moore began. "It has something to do with a code which gives the holder the power to control the world. Again, I'm still chasing this down."

"Sounds like something my ex-wife thought she had," Rothman grinned as he peered over the top of his glass.

"Sometimes truth is stranger than fiction," Karim said quietly. "Tell me more," he encouraged Moore.

Recalling Karim's Turkish ethnicity and Rothman's knowledge of antiquities, Moore shared his involvement with the Nazarene's Code and the Legend of 13 including the letter count in Kalker's and Bieber's names.

After Moore concluded sharing his adventure to date, Rothman sighed, "Guess I'm not special. Missed it by one. Only twelve letters in my name. Wait, there're thirteen if I include my middle initial." Rothman grinned at the two in front of him, and then continued, "Actually, I have heard about the Legend of 13 and the Nazarene's Code."

"Do you really think there is anything to them?" Moore asked Rothman.

Rothman took a sip of his drink. Then, he looked directly at Moore. "The Legend of 13 may be nothing more than coincidence. It seems strange that so many names and places can be linked based on thirteen letters. I'm sure you could do the same with other numbers of letters."

"I hadn't tried that. I suppose you could," Moore agreed.

"Now the Nazarene's Code is another issue. If it exists and if its powers are real, then you wouldn't want it to end up in the hands of the wrong people, if you know what I mean," Rothman said.

From the stairs leading up to the upper deck, Hakan had been eavesdropping on the conversation. He hunkered down to hear more and then decided to make a call. He stepped away to his quarters and found his cell phone. He quickly keyed in the numbers and his call was answered on the second ring.

"Yes," the voice answered.

"Mr. Yarian?"

"Yes. Who is calling?"

"It is Hakan."

"Hakan? I'm surprised that you're calling me. I heard that you left the country so that you could hide from me. You still have not repaid the loan."

"I know. That is why I'm calling."

"Are you here?"

"No. I'm out of the country, but I miss being home."

"I would understand that."

"Mr. Yarian, I may have some valuable information for you. I was hoping it would help repay my loan. Could it?"

"Depends on the information. What do you have?"

"I have overheard some men talking about a mystery."

Yarian sat straight up in his chair. "What did you hear?"

Hakan quickly related what he had overheard, including Moore's comment about having discovered a notebook.

"Are they still talking?"

"Yes."

"I want you to go back immediately and see what else you can hear. Then, I want you to call me."

"Yes, yes. I can do that. Will this repay my loan?"

"We will see. It depends on how factual this information is. You go back and listen. Be sure to call me back, and I will consider your request."

"Yes, yes. I will do that." Hakan disconnected the call and raced back to his listening post. He was hoping that he hadn't missed any critical information while he was gone.

Ahmet Yarian stared in disbelief at his cell phone. Could this boy have stumbled upon the key to controlling the world? If he did, Yarian may be on the verge of becoming one of the world's most influential power brokers. He would be able to turn his back on his white slave trade, drug running and other nefarious activities.

The muscular Yarian extracted a Turkish cigarette from its package. He inserted it in his mouth and struck a match to light it. He inhaled and then expelled a cloud of smoke, which dissipated through his small office in Istanbul. His dark face with piercing black eyes was reflected in the window as he glanced over the city.

Back at the boat, Hakan returned in time to hear Karim as he hung up his satellite phone.

"We're set to visit Ray tomorrow. He'll be at the hangar."

"Good. I can meet Kat and we can interview the Gumusluk police officer," Moore said eagerly.

Karim smiled. "Gumusluk? What is the officer's name? I may know him."

"Because he's looking for you?" Rothman asked with a sly grin.

"No. Because I think half of Turkey is related to each other. He may be a cousin."

Moore obliged. "His name is Ekrem Tabak."

"Not related," Karim said with a twinkle in his eyes. Karim relayed then what he knew about the history of Bodrum and Gumusluk.

After twenty minutes lapsed, they changed topics and began to walk onto the bow for fresh sea air.

Sensing that they were done, Hakan slipped back to his quarters and called Yarian. He updated him on the balance of what he had overheard.

"You have done well tonight, Hakan."

"And my loan, can we consider it repaid?"

"Not yet. I will call you and let you know. It depends on the actual value of this transaction. Patience young man. Patience."

"I will be patient. I just want to return to Turkey." Hakan looked at the cell and realized that Yarian had already disconnected the call. Hakan hoped that his information would be valuable enough for his loan to be forgiven. He would be patient as difficult as it would be. He had no choice.

Yarian ended the call and speed-dialed another number. He couldn't wait to share the news. Karapashev and others would pay handsomely to have the Nazarene's Code in their possession.

Miracle Airlines
Dahab, Egypt

The Land Rover pulled to a stop in front of a rusty metal hangar. It seemed to be on the verge of collapsing from lack of repair and upkeep. There was a sign askew over the doors. Its faded blue lettering read "Miracle Airlines".

"Not a very good first impression." Moore looked from the sign to Karim.

"Not to worry. This guy has walked away from more plane crashes than he deserves."

"Oh, that sounds very encouraging," Moore commented.

"With all of the plastic and metal parts he has in himself, I'd say he's almost bionic." Karim added. "I should clarify that most of his plane crashes were due to being shot down."

Moore's head whipped around. "And who is shooting him down and why?"

Karim grinned. "Relax my friend. Those were in his younger days when he ran with a wild crowd in the Mideast. He worked both sides - CIA and drug smuggling. All that's behind him now. He just runs this very ordinary charter service now."

"I hope so," Moore said as he looked toward the hangar.

As the two men exited the vehicle, they could hear an engine sputtering as it tried to run, and then failed. The men approached the hangar where they saw a tired-looking airplane that had definitely seen better days. A figure jumped out of the plane and ran to the port engine where he began to work on it, grumbling as he did. The slim man wore a soiled New York Yankees baseball cap, greasy tee shirt and worn khaki shorts. He was oblivious to his visitors.

He talked to himself as he coaxed his engine, "Come on baby, you still have another 1,000 air hours in you. I know what you're thinking. I said that 2,500 air hours ago. Just 1,000 more, baby. Come on."

Moore's eyebrows arched as he looked at Karim. "You want me to fly in that?"

"It's no problem. He's quite a good mechanic."

"Airplane engines need a major overhaul at 2,000 hours," Moore stated proudly as he recalled conversations with his Put-in-Bay island friend, who owned Dairy Air, the only island-based air service.

"Like I said, he's a good mechanic." Karim looked at the man and called, "Ray, you've got company."

"What's that?" the man said as he whirled around in surprise. His long gray hair was sticking straight out from underneath the ball cap.

"I've brought you a paying customer, Ray," Karim grinned.

"That's always the best kind, Karim," the man responded as he wiped his hands on an oily rag and walked toward the two men. "Ray Grissett," he said as he extended his hand to Moore.

Shaking hands, Moore responded uncomfortably, "Emerson Moore. This is your airline?"

"Yep, it is. Miracle Airlines. Our motto is 'If we land in one piece, it's a miracle'," he chuckled as he sensed Moore's uneasiness. "Had a close one last week. The starboard engine fell off midflight."

Seeing Moore's eyes widen, Grissett guffawed. "Kidding! Just kidding!"

Trying to reassure Moore, Karim offered, "I've brought several of my diving guests here so that they could take a short hop to Turkey. They've all raved about the flight."

"Yeah, I haven't lost any yet," Grissett grinned as the three ambled toward an equally decrepit office. "Come on in for a drink."

The office contained a worn desk. Underneath it were three thick telephone books stacked upon each other, replacing a missing desk leg. The desk was littered with paperwork, including a number of bills stamped "past due" in red. An upside down desk chair revealed a missing caster. Behind the desk was a rusty metal folding chair. Two more were folded in a corner. Another corner contained a dented metal filing cabinet. An ancient refrigerator sat next to a small table that held an old two-way radio and a 1970s radio playing Turkish music.

Reaching into the dented fridge, Grissett said, "Hope you don't mind a warm drink. Fridge is busted. Warm beer or warm water?"

"Water," the two visitors responded in unison.

He handed Karim and Moore bottles of warm water as he grabbed a beer for himself and popped the tab. Sitting in the chair behind the desk, he motioned for the two to use the other two chairs. "Now what can I do for you?"

Karim spoke first. "Emerson needs to be in Bodrum this afternoon or tomorrow. Could you fly him there?"

Grissett sat back in his metal chair and rubbed his unshaven jaw. "Probably." He looked at Moore. "Nothing illegal going on here, right?"

Moore looked at Grissett. "No, just a simple flight. I have a meeting to attend in Bodrum."

Grissett grabbed a fly swatter and used it to kill a fly that had landed on his desk phone. "Killed six flies so far today. Three male and three female."

Moore's face had a bewildered look. "How did you know they were male and female?"

"The three on the beer can were male. The three on the telephone were female." Grissett laughed at his joke. The lanky Grissett stood and wandered over to a table covered with maps. He shuffled through several to find a particular map. "I've flown into Bodrum before and it shouldn't be a problem."

After negotiating the fare and paying Grissett, Moore asked, "Would you like me to come back in the morning?"

"What for? Got your gear with you?"

"Yes, but it sounded like you were repairing one of the engines."

"Aw, it's fine. It should get us there okay."

Moore arched his eyebrows again, to Karim's amusement. "It's really not a problem, Emerson. I've heard his engines sound worse and he has made it through every time."

"You get your passport stamped over yonder, grab your gear and I'll meet you at the plane."

Moore walked over to an overflowing trash can and discarded his empty water bottle.

"Hey, don't throw that away!" yelled Grissett.

"Sorry, I didn't think you'd recycle," Moore said as he retrieved the bottle and set it on Grissett's desk.

"I don't. I just refill them from the cistern out back."

"After you wash them, right?" Moore asked as he looked at Grissett.

"No need to. Nobody knows." Grissett thought a moment, and then continued. "I only know of two people who came down with a case of the runs after drinking my water. Doesn't bother me a bit."

Moore shook his head from side to side in disbelief. He was

hoping that he wouldn't be one of the chosen few to become ill, especially during the upcoming flight.

The three men exited the office. Grissett walked to his plane as Karim and Moore headed to the parked Land Rover.

"You're sure about this?" Moore asked.

"I wouldn't let you get on board if I didn't trust him. Grissett's a bit eccentric, but he's a genius as a mechanic."

"I hope so," Moore commented.

The two entered the Land Rover and drove to the main terminal where Moore had his passport stamped. Within minutes, the Land Rover returned to the Miracle Airlines hangar.

Pulling his gear out of the vehicle, Moore said, "Thanks for the diving experience. It was incredible. And that mermaid was spectacular."

Karim winked and shook hands with Moore. "Come any time. I'm glad that Roger had you join us and I got to meet you. Have a good flight."

Moore cautiously approached the four-seater, a Piper PA-30 twin Comanche.

"Ray, I was just curious," Moore said as he stowed his gear behind the front seat.

"About?"

"How old is this plane?"

"Built in 1965 in Pennsylvania. They used to call me the Ancient Wonder, but I call this plane that," Grissett beamed as he tapped the fuel gauge. "Sometimes, this doesn't read right." He tapped it several more times, then stopped. "We're probably all right." Grissett grinned to himself as he teased the wary passenger climbing into the plane.

Grissett fired up the plane and began taxing onto the runway. The engine on the port side had trouble starting. Once it did start, it didn't seem to be running at full horsepower. "It'll be fine," Grissett told his nervous passenger as the plane began to pick up speed. "Sorry I don't have the flight attendant on board today. I gave Rose the day off." He paused and then continued, "You'd like Rose. She has more curves than a road through the Appalachian Mountains."

Moore shook his head from side to side and didn't comment.

Halfway down the runway, Grissett turned to Moore, "Emerson?"

"Yes?"

"You got any religious background?"

"Yes, why?"

"Cause I'd suggest you start praying we clear them trees at the end of the runway!" Grissett chortled as he pushed the throttle forward.

With widening eyes, Moore said a quick prayer as the end of the runway quickly approached. Just before getting there, the port engine caught and roared as it unleashed its full horsepower. The small plane narrowly cleared the trees and began a bank to the left as it headed toward its destination.

"We made it," Moore sighed with relief.

"So far. Thanks to your prayer. I'd keep that prayer handy if I was you."

Moore hated to ask, but did. "Why?"

"Might need it again if that port engine quits or when we land. Been having some problems with the front landing gear releasing properly. It's a bigger miracle if we land in one piece."

Moore stared at Grissett for a moment. He wasn't quite sure how much of this tale he was going to buy. He settled back in his seat and listened quietly to the ravings of his erratic pilot. From time to time, the plane dropped suddenly as the port engine quit running, but Grissett was able to coax it back to life each time. After three hours, they entered Turkish airspace and Grissett was cleared for landing at Bodrum International Airport.

Grissett brought the small plane down smoothly and taxied to the main terminal. "Looks like the landing gear worked. You praying again?"

"I don't think I ever stopped," Moore responded seriously.

"Sometimes I think the world would be a better place if more people flew with me. They get religion real quick," he grinned. "Now, you're going to have to be quick about yourself here."

"How's that?" Moore asked as he prepared to exit the plane as soon as she rolled to a stop.

"See those three Turkish soldiers heading towards us?"

Moore looked to where Grissett was pointing and saw a military vehicle racing toward the plane. "Yes?"

"The guy in the back is waving a piece of paper. I'd venture a guess that it's an unpaid bill I have here for fuel and I have no plans on paying him today. So you better skedaddle," Grissett said as the plane stopped rolling forward.

Moore barely had time to grab his gear and exit the plane before its engines roared with horsepower and the plane moved swiftly away from the approaching soldiers. Seeing they didn't have a chance at catching Grissett, they instead pulled to a halt in front of Moore. Moore found himself facing two loaded weapons.

Moore produced his passport and was ushered into the terminal where he underwent questioning. Finally satisfied with his responses, the soldiers allowed him to leave and make his way to the baggage claim area and ground transportation where Moore said another prayer of thanks and caught a cab for Bodrum, thirty-two kilometers away.

From the Airport
Bodrum, Turkey

Bodrum lies on the southwest coast of Turkey on a peninsula, which reaches into the Aegean Sea. Settled around 1000 B.C. by Greeks, Bodrum has been conquered over the centuries by the Persians, Alexander the Great, and the Ottoman Turks. The town was also the home of the Greek historian Herodotus. The Knights of Rhodes constructed the Castle of St. Peter with its English, French and German style towers.

This seaport resort town is fronted by a protected harbor on the Aegean Sea and, during the summer months, teems with visitors, much like Moore's Put-in-Bay. The heart of the tourist area is a street named Cumhuriyet Caddesi. It's better known as Bar Street. It's their version of Key West's Duvall Street and New Orleans' Bourbon Street. The street is filled with boutiques, bars, discos and restaurants, serving a wide variety of international fare.

Nearby are sandy beaches with water sports and boats to take visitors fishing or diving.

The cab from the airport deposited Moore at the Hotel Karia Princess, a white-washed, stone building with a European flair and sixty guest rooms. He marveled at its elegant beauty as he walked into the large, marbled lobby and checked in.

When Moore gave his name to the front desk clerk, a thick, muscular man seated in the lobby, lowered the newspaper he'd been reading to stare at Moore. Once he had identified his target, Yarian smiled and looked across the room where Gorenchenko was standing. He nodded to his henchman and then pointed his head toward Moore. Gorenchenko nodded his head to acknowledge he also saw Moore.

Once he had his room key, Moore stepped into the elevator and took it to his floor. He walked down the luxurious hallway to his room and threw his gear on the double bed. Walking to the minibar, he inserted a key and opened the door. He was pleased when he spotted three cans of Pepsi and withdrew one. Closing the door with one hand, he held the ice cold can to his face and allowed it to cool him as he rolled it down across his skin.

Next, Moore slid open the patio door and stepped onto the balcony that was framed by an arch. He enjoyed the view of the lush gardens and sat on one of the small patio chairs. He popped open the can and allowed the caramel colored beverage to stream down his throat, cooling him further.

Within a few minutes, he returned to his room and reached for the phone. Dialing the lobby, he had them connect him to Kat's room.

"Hello," her sensual, feminine voice answered.

"Kat, it's Emerson. I just checked in."

"Great. Would you like to freshen up and meet on the rooftop patio for a drink?"

"Sure." Moore glanced at his watch. "How about in thirty minutes? That'll give me time to get out of this tee shirt and shorts."

"*Das ist gut.* See you there in thirty minutes," she purred.

Her tone was not lost on Moore. This could be a very interesting evening he thought to himself as he quickly stripped down and stepped into the shower of the marbled bathroom. Turning on the hot water, Moore allowed it to cascade on his taut, muscular body – washing away the tension from his flight with Grissett.

Reaching for the bar of sweet smelling soap, Moore lathered up and rinsed off. Stepping out of the shower, he grabbed a thick Turkish towel, which was folded neatly on a nearby shelf and dried himself. He reached into his kit bag and grabbed his shaving gear.

As he began to shave, Moore surprised himself. He caught himself humming a song. It was a tune from Mad Dog Adams, his Put-in-Bay island singer friend. The tune had a lively Caribbean beat and was from *The Other Side of Hell* CD. He just hoped that he had crossed over and was headed for paradise.

He smiled at himself in the mirror. This was the first time in a long time that he was truly excited about spending time with a woman. Ever since his wife died, he had met many attractive, willing partners who should've made his heart race – but didn't. He didn't know if the timing was suddenly now right, or the chemistry was inexplicably just right – but he didn't care to overanalyze it. Either way, he liked it.

Moore extracted a soft yellow polo shirt and a pair of khaki slacks from his duffel bag and quickly touched up the wrinkles with the iron he found in the room. Slipping into a pair of tan

Clark boat shoes, he dabbed on Calvin Klein's *Obsession for Men*. He knew he was back in the game when he cared about how he smelled.

Smiling, Moore exited his room and walked toward the elevator. Preoccupied with his thoughts, he didn't notice the man watching him from the other end of the hall. After Moore stepped into the elevator, the man raced to the closing doors so that he could see which floor the elevator was going to stop. It stopped on the top floor.

Gorenchenko pulled a cell phone from his pocket and called Yarian. When Yarian answered, Gorenchenko said, "He's on the roof. Probably the bar."

"I'll be right up," the voice responded, ominously.

Rooftop Bar
Hotel Karia Princess

The rooftop patio bar overlooked the hotel's lush tropical gardens filled with towering palms, red hibiscus and sky blue plumbago. The gardens also contained purple, orange, pink and white bougainvillea as well as red, pink, white and yellow oleander. Fragrant orange, tangerine and lemon trees were mixed in with other tropical plants.

Moore exited the elevator and stepped into this oasis-like retreat. The late afternoon sun cast growing shadows across the garden as Moore took a seat at the bar. He was staring at the patio below when he heard her voice, adding magic to the air.

"That's illegal in this country."

Moore swiveled around on his bar stool to see Bieber a couple of steps away. "What is?" He tried to sound nonchalant, but his heart was racing.

"For a good-looking man like you to be sitting alone at a bar," Bieber teased with a warm smile.

"I think I'm beginning to like the Turkish legal system," Moore beamed as he eyed the woman in front of him. She was wearing fitted black slacks and a light blue, silk blouse with the top three buttons undone, revealing the swell of her ample breasts. She had on black sandals and an alluring perfume. Her blonde hair was pulled back in a ponytail, with soft tendrils framing her oval face.

"Have a seat." The words seemed to erupt from Moore's mouth.

Shaking her head, Bieber pointed to an unoccupied table near the wall overlooking the garden. "Let's sit over there."

"Anywhere you like."

Moore stood and accompanied Bieber to the table where they both sat.

A waiter appeared instantly. "Welcome to the Rooftop Bar. Could I take your order?"

Before Moore could respond, Bieber answered. "We'll both have raki."

The waiter nodded and disappeared to get the drink.

"Have you ever tasted raki, Emerson?"

"Never had anything Turkish before," Moore responded. "This is my first trip to Turkey."

"Then, we'll need to make this trip memorable for you."

"I was counting on that," Moore smiled.

"I'm sorry. What did you say?" Bieber had read between the lines and knew exactly what Moore was hinting, but she wanted to hear him say it again.

"Oh, nothing," Moore said, thinking that he might have appeared too eager.

The waiter returned with two glasses of raki and set them on the table. He then presented two bottles of water and meze, a small dish of roasted eggplant and cheese. The waiter returned to the bar where Yarian and Gorenchenko were seated, watching Bieber and Moore.

"So, what is this raki that I'm about to drink?" Moore asked.

"It's the national drink of Turkey. Very light. Tastes like Greek ouzo or Italy's sambucca," Bieber said as she opened her bottled water and began to pour water into the glass of raki.

"What are you doing?" Moore asked.

"You drink raki by adding about two thirds of a cup of water," Bieber explained as she finished adding her water and sat back to watch Moore add water to his drink.

"I suppose you could tell me just about anything and I'd believe you," he said.

Bieber raised her glass to Moore.

Likewise, Moore raised his glass and toasted. "To our adventure."

Bieber smiled as she looked over the rim of her glass. "To our adventure," she echoed seductively.

Drinking half of the raki, Moore set his glass on the table. "Tastes like licorice."

"Some people think so," she agreed as she began to eat the meze. "Try some."

Moore sampled the meze, "Quite good," he said as he enjoyed the cheese.

They finished their raki and the waiter was quick to reappear and refill their glasses.

Looking over the edge of the wall at the garden, Moore commented. "Beautiful garden."

"Yes, it is."

"I'd expect paradise to look like this," Moore said. "Sort of like the Garden of Eden."

"And you're Adam and I'm Eve. Oh," she said in feigned surprise as she looked at Moore. "Adam, you're clothed. How disappointing!"

Smiling, Moore responded as he finished his second raki, "I could take care of that right now, but I don't think the patrons in this bar would appreciate it."

"Some of us would," she said flirtatiously as she finished her raki and motioned for the waiter to return.

Moore found himself being seductively pulled into a dangerous position. He decided the conversation was being influenced a little too much by the raki and their mutual attraction for each other. He spoke to the waiter who stood next to him with refills. "We're done. Bill this to my room."

"Already?" Bieber asked in mock disbelief.

"Let's go for a walk and find a place for dinner. You can show me around a bit," Moore suggested as he provided his room number to the waiter. The waiter left and reappeared within minutes with the bill for Moore to sign.

After signing the bill, Moore and Bieber stood and headed to the elevator.

"I'll take you down Bar Street," Bieber suggested.

"Sounds like trouble to me," Moore said as the two stepped into the elevator.

"Oh, I'm quite sure that you know how to handle trouble, Emerson," Bieber commented as the doors closed.

"Sounds like trouble to me!" Yarian mocked Moore's comment. "Your trouble is just getting ready to start, Mr. Emerson Moore."

Yarian watched the waiter key in Moore's room number. "Let's go," he said to Gorenchenko.

The two paid their bill and took the elevator to Moore's floor. They walked to the door of Moore's room and Yarian extracted a passkey, obtained earlier in the afternoon by bribing one of the housekeepers. He quickly inserted and withdrew the card, unlocking the door to Moore's room.

Entering the room, Gorenchenko checked Moore's shaving kit while Yarian carefully went through Moore's belongings.

"Nothing here," Gorenchenko said as he walked toward Yarian.

"Find the notebook!" Yarian bristled as he continued searching the room.

Bar Street
Bodrum, Turkey

Stretching from the back of the castle and along the waterfront, Bar Street is an assortment of shops, tourist traps, bars and restaurants. As the late afternoon turned to dusk, Moore and Bieber made their way through several shops as they looked at the local merchandise.

"I'm famished," Bieber said as they exited one of the shops.

"Let's find somewhere to eat, then." Moore looked down the street and spotted the Berk Balik restaurant. "How about that one?" Moore asked as he pointed.

"Let's do it," Bieber said firmly.

The two entered the restaurant that specialized in fresh fish and other Turkish cuisine. They took seats near the open front of the restaurant so that they could enjoy the harbor view.

"And what can I start you off with?" asked the plump owner with a large smile and an equally large clump of graying hair on his chin and head. He was a retired Turkish army cook and ran the restaurant with his German wife.

"Raki," Bieber responded without hesitation.

"Raki it is." The owner disappeared to get their drink order.

"That raki is dangerous stuff," Moore said as he looked into Bieber's eyes.

"But not as dangerous as me," Bieber cooed.

I bet you can be dangerous, Moore quietly thought to himself.

Before Moore could comment aloud, the owner returned with the raki and water. Setting them in front of the two, he asked, "Is this your first visit to my restaurant?"

"Yes," they responded, almost in unison.

"This is my first trip to Turkey," Moore added.

"Welcome to my country, sir." The owner turned his attention to Bieber. "And you? From Germany, yes? Your accent is like my wife's."

"Yes. I've visited Bodrum several times. I've done archeological research at various sites in Turkey, including Bodrum," Bieber answered.

"Then, you are aware that Bodrum was the site of one of the Seven Wonders of the Ancient World?"

"Yes, the Mausoleum. I've been to the site remains," Bieber said.

"And you've been to the castle here built by the knights from the Greek island of Rhodes?"

"Yes, several times," Bieber said.

Moore interjected, "I've been to Rhodes and saw where another of the Seven Wonders of the Ancient World stood, the Colossus of Rhodes."

"Did you tour the castle in Rhodes?"

"Yes, it's more like a fort overlooking the port," Moore said.

The owner nodded his head. "I've been there, too. It is only a short ferry ride from here." Changing the topic, the owner pointed to a food-filled table next to the wall. "Please help yourselves to our starters. We have pepper and grape leaves stuffed with rice currants and pine seeds. There are fried slices of eggplant with garlic yogurt and humus."

"Sounds delicious," Bieber said as she eyed the table. "What's the featured course tonight?"

"We specialize in fresh fish. We have dark-fried calamari, flat-head in batter, and slabs of blue grenadier. Our special tonight is lamb fillets marinated in onion juice."

"Do you have a seafood platter?" Bieber asked.

"Yes, I do."

"I'll take that. Emerson?"

"Same for me."

"I'll start you off with a salad of calamari cubes, feta cheese and tomato on lettuce," the owner said as he quickly turned and went to the kitchen.

Finishing a sip of her anise-flavored raki, Bieber began to stand. "Shall we try the starters?"

Moore quickly stood and followed her to the table where they selected their starters and returned to their table with full plates.

"Delicious," Moore said as he munched on a grape leaf filled with rice pilaf.

"Always," she responded as she finished a bite of pepper filled with humus. "The fun thing about Turkish cuisine is that it has been so influenced by being at the crossroads of Europe, the Mid East and Africa. It seems like every nationality has left its mark here."

"Including the Crusaders."

"Yes, they did."

Thinking of the next day's meeting, Moore asked, "Kat, was your uncle able to set up a meeting for us tomorrow?"

"Yes, he did. He used some of his old intelligence contacts to set up our meeting with the investigating officer, Ekrem Tabak."

"That's great."

Their discussion was interrupted by the arrival of the owner with the seafood platters. The plates were filled to overflowing with an array of seafood, fruit and vegetables. "Enjoy," he said as he turned to greet four couples who had entered his restaurant.

Between bites of the sumptuous meal, the two continued their conversation.

"Let me tell you a bit about this area and why I think Levy may have been here."

"Please do," Moore urged.

"Gumusluk is about a thirty minute drive from here. It's a small sleepy, fishing port surrounded by a number of hills. It's built on the ruins of the ancient city of Myndos that was partially destroyed during an earthquake. The seafront sections of Myndos slid into the bay and you can dive the bay to explore the sites."

"Really? Diving is a hobby of mine."

"They only permit snorkeling there. They don't want anyone staying down too long and tampering with the underwater site."

"Why do you think Levy was in Gumusluk?" Moore asked.

"Don't know. If he was on the trail of the Knights Templar, I think he would have focused on Bodrum."

"Interesting. Do I need to get a rental car?"

"Already handled. I rented one at the airport. I'll drive us over in the morning."

"Finished? Can I take you plates?" the owner asked as he returned to their table and eyed the half-empty plates.

"I'm full," Moore said as he pushed away his plate.

"Me, too," Bieber said. "Have to save room for dessert. I'd like baklava."

"I'll have a slice also," Moore said as the owner picked up the plates.

"We have a large selection of desserts."

Before the owner could continue, Bieber interrupted him. "Baklava is all I want."

The owner nodded and smiled. "A woman who knows exactly what she wants."

"I do," Bieber said as she gazed at Moore.

The owner looked at Moore.

"That's all for me, too." For some reason, he blushed.

The owner chuckled. "Then, you shall have it. It's the best baklava in Turkey," he boasted as he headed for the kitchen.

"They all say that," Bieber grinned.

"Tea or coffee to go with your baklava?" the owner asked as he reappeared with the baklava.

"You pick," Moore said as he looked at his dinner guest.

"Coffee."

"And which do you prefer – sade, orta or sekerli?"

Moore looked from the owner to Bieber. "Help me here."

Bieber smiled. "Sade is no sugar. Orta is with a touch of sugar and sekerli is with a lot of sugar." Looking back at the owner, she responded, "Sekerli for me."

"I'll take the orta," Moore replied.

Within minutes, the owner returned with two small mocha cups of their respective coffees. The two slowly drank their beverages.

"Emerson, I noticed that you don't wear a wedding ring. Are you single, or married and pretending not to be?"

"I was," he replied as he looked down as his plate. Memories began to flood his mind at the thought of his marriage's tragic ending. "I don't really like to talk about it. My wife and son were killed in an accident a couple of years ago."

Bieber practically choked on her drink. "Me and my big mouth. I am so sorry."

"You didn't know," he said as he shuddered.

"I can tell that you really loved her," Bieber said softly.

"I did and still do," Moore said as he lifted his head to look at her. "She was one of the kindest and most caring people who ever walked this planet."

The depth of the emotional attachment to his departed wife was not lost on Bieber. "I can tell from the way you just described her that she was a very special person."

"An understatement," Moore said. Changing the direction of the conversation, Moore asked, "But life moves on, and I must, too. What's next?"

"Next, I need to freshen my lipstick." Reaching into her pocket, Bieber withdrew a tube of lipstick. She opened it and applied the lipstick to her full lips, leaving a pink sheen.

"Pink. One of my favorite lipstick colors," Moore grinned.

"My uncle's too. He surprised me with this," she smiled.

"Your uncle is buying you lipstick? That's a bit strange."

"His wife used to wear this color because it was her favorite, too. He always said that a woman wasn't properly armed unless she had her lipstick on."

"I guess I could agree with that," Moore said as he looked at her pink covered full lips one more time. He felt desire stir within him for the first time in a long time.

Moore paid the bill and the two stepped onto the sidewalk.

The moon cast a bluish glow across the harbor in front of them and outlined the masts of the boats at dock. To their left and at the end of the harbor, the castle was bathed in a soft yellow light. The lights from the houses on the hills surrounding Bodrum seemed to be like twinkling stars.

"Would you like to enjoy the evening's magic?" Moore asked.

"There is indeed something magical in the air tonight," Bieber said as she suddenly twirled around in a circle. "I want to go dancing. Do you dance, Emerson?"

"I do."

"Then, let's go to Halikarnas over there." She pointed to a nearby building. "It's the third largest open-air nightclub in Europe and tonight is foam night!"

"Foam night?"

"Oh, you'll love it. Come on."

The two walked to the disco, paid their cover charge and entered the facility where the techno beat was bouncing off the walls.

"Welcome back, Kat," one of the handsome Turkish bouncers said as he greeted Bieber with a kiss on the cheek.

"Amal, it has been too long," Bieber responded.

"How long are you in town?" he asked eagerly as he looked past her to Moore.

"Just overnight."

"That's too bad. Save a dance for me later after the foam starts," he grinned.

"Maybe next time I'm here." She winked at him as she talked. "Amal, this is my good friend, Emerson Moore."

"Mr. Moore, the pleasure is all mine." Amal reacted coolly as he shook hands.

Moore's radar was on full alert. "Nice to meet you."

Bieber hooked arms with Moore and began to walk away. "Talk to you later, Amal."

Amal winked at her and allowed his eyes to roam her figure as she began to disappear in the crowded club.

"You come here often?" Moore asked, peeved by the familiarity displayed between the two.

"When I'm in Bodrum on extended archeological research, I sometimes wander down here to take a break." She sensed the jealousy in Moore and was pleased by his interest in her. "This is a fun place!"

Looking at the walls as they entered the open-air nightclub, Moore exclaimed, "This is like being in a Greek amphitheater." He was amazed at the Greek-inspired architecture and the size of the club that could hold 4,000 partygoers and attracted them as far away as Ankara and Istanbul. On the hill outside of the club, he could see St. Peter's Castle, bathed in muted light.

"Come on, Emerson. Let's dance," Bieber said as she grabbed his hand and led him to the dance area in front of the stage. Bieber began to shimmy her shoulders and hips as she began dancing on the crowded dance floor. Laser lights danced over the gyrating bodies.

Moore wasn't particularly fond of techno music, but he was fond of his dancing partner. He quickly began to match her moves.

After ten minutes of dancing, they took a break at one of the nearby bars where they could watch the crowd dancing. Bieber downed three rakis within thirty minutes while Moore nursed one raki.

Bieber stood and almost fell. The raki was having its effect on her.

"Time to dance, Emerson," she said as she grabbed his hands and pulled him along to the dance floor.

No sooner had they returned than the dancers began to be covered by a sea of foam shot from several hoses on the stage. Foam was everywhere. Moore found the foam to have a cooling effect and, to his surprise, more enjoyable than he expected.

With her arms draped liquidly around Moore's shoulders, Bieber whispered in his ear. "I've had too many drinks. You need to take me back to my room. Could you do that for me, Emerson?" She pursed her full lips and planted a wet kiss on Moore's cheek.

"You've had quite a few drinks, tonight," he agreed as they left the dance floor and began to weave through the crowd and away from the pulsing music.

"It wasn't the drinks that intoxicated me tonight," she said as she seductively bit his ear. "It was the company."

Moore smiled to himself at the compliment and especially as Amal saw the two of them leave. "See you next time, buddy," Moore smiled victoriously at the bouncer as they walked back.

Amal wasn't smiling. He just stared sinisterly.

Moore hailed a cab and the two cuddled together in the back seat as the cab went up the hill to the hotel. Moore paid the driver and, half carrying Bieber, walked through the lobby to the elevator, which they rode to her floor.

When they reached her room, Bieber produced her room key and handed it to Moore. Moore unlocked the door as she stood unsteadily.

"My bed," she murmured as she stumbled toward it with Moore's help. She plopped face down onto the plush mattress.

Moore sat on the bed and stroked her hair. "Kat, you are so beautiful."

Much to Moore's surprise, Bieber responded with a snore.

"Kat? Kat?" Moore asked.

In return, Bieber rolled over and groaned. "I'm so tired. Emerson, be a sweetie and say good night."

Moore looked at the semi-comatose figure in the bed and shook his head. He should have slowed her drinking. She had certainly had more drinks than he had that evening. He was disappointed the night had to end like this, but preferred her sober company, anyway. "Good night, Kat."

Moore stood, walked to the door, turned off the lights and let himself out of the room. He took the elevator to his floor and returned to his room.

As soon as the lock clicked on her door, Bieber rolled over and stretched. She stood and walked over to the mini-fridge where she helped herself to a cold bottle of water. Walking onto the balcony, she looked over the city. She thought about the handsome man who had just left her bedroom. He's very attractive, she thought to herself. I need to be careful about becoming emotionally involved when we have work to do. He is so damn cute she thought to herself as she returned to the darkened room and lay on the bed. Within minutes, she was asleep.

Rooftop Bar
Hotel Karia Princess

"Good morning, sleepyhead," Moore said as Bieber walked over to his table. He drank in her fresh, natural beauty. She had minimal makeup on, and her hair flowed softly over her shoulders. Even in a loose blouse and shorts, she looked stunning.

"My head is throbbing," she feigned as she sat and picked up the waiting cup of coffee.

"Too much to drink last night?"

"Probably," she responded as she looked over the rim of the cup at Moore and smiled, "I told you last night that you were intoxicating." She reached out and patted Moore's arm.

"I'll be more careful next time," Moore smiled. "Fruit?" he asked as he passed the plate filled with assorted fruit to her.

"Yes," she answered as she forked several pieces onto her plate. "Did you enjoy last night, Emerson?" she asked as she took a bite of fruit.

"It was a wonderful evening, especially the foam dancing. I must admit that I've never done anything like that before," Moore grinned.

"All the young do this when they visit Bodrum," she smiled.

"I like the use of the word 'young'," Moore grinned.

"And you enjoyed the food and raki?"

"Delicious. Absolutely delicious." Moore gazed onto the tropical garden below, then commented, "There was only one thing disappointing about last night."

Bieber placed her fork on the table. With a look of concern, she sighed. "I'm so sorry that I ruined your evening. I had too much to drink and passed out," she explained.

"I wasn't referring to that," Moore said seriously. And besides, he wasn't one to take advantage of an intoxicated female.

Bieber ran through the events of the evening together. "Emerson, I'm at a loss. What was so disappointing?"

"Someone broke into my room last night."

"Did they get Levy's notebook?" she asked anxiously.

"No, I had his notebook in my pocket last night and fortunately the foam didn't ruin it. I had placed it in a plastic bag when I was on Karim's boat."

"That's good," she said with a sigh of relief. "Did they get anything else?"

"They ransacked the room, but the only thing they stole was my laptop," Moore said as he sipped his coffee.

"You've lost all of your data!"

"Not quite. That's my travel laptop, so I don't keep a lot on it." Moore held up a flash drive. "I also back up to a flash drive after using it each time. A reporter can't afford to lose his data, you know," Moore grinned.

"They didn't find your flash drive in the room?"

"Nope. It was in my pocket with the notebook."

Bieber pushed her empty plate to the side and took a long drink from her coffee cup. "Did you report the break in?"

"Yes. I called the hotel manager this morning. He and a police officer visited with me this morning, but they don't expect that I'll see my laptop again."

Bieber shook her head in disbelief. "I'm sorry to hear that." She looked at her watch and back to Moore. "We should get started on our drive to Gumusluk. I have a rental car downstairs."

"I'm ready," Moore said as he motioned to the waiter to bring them their bill.

"Let me pay for this," Bieber said as the bill was placed in front of Moore.

"No can do, Kat. You're helping me research. Besides, my newspaper is picking up the tab," Moore said as he paid the bill.

They stood from the table and began to walk toward the elevator.

"It's a beautiful drive. We'll pass the Peksimet Strait and you'll see the windmills on the hill."

They chatted amicably as they boarded the elevator.

Police Outpost
Gumusluk, Turkey

Gumusluk is a seaside village and fishing port situated on a cove west of Bodrum. The remains of the foundations of buildings of the ancient city of Myndos can be clearly seen in the bay.

The police outpost overlooked the bay. Inside the two-story concrete building, the whirling black blades of an old fan did little to relieve the heat in the small office. The office's occupant had aimed a small fan directly on himself as he sought relief from the heat.

His shirt was too small for the overweight man. Its buttons strained to contain the volumes of flesh hidden by the blue shirt.

It seemed like they were on the verge of popping. The area under the man's armpits was covered with a growing wet sweat stain.

The man grunted as he wiped the sweat from his face with a dirty handkerchief. He looked up from the report his fat fingers were typing. His eyes centered on the air conditioning unit in the window. It had been broken since last year with no funds available for repair or replacement. But the man smiled to himself. He had found a way to finance its replacement with a much stronger unit. It would be delivered within two days and provide him with a cool working environment.

He had wrestled with the idea of selling information, but he had seen other policemen taking bribes for looking the other way on certain transactions. He decided that he would do it just once, but not again. He wanted to be above the other officers.

He turned back to typing the report. His focus was so intense that he did not hear the door to his office open. Nor did he hear the approaching footsteps.

Beads of hot sweat dripped on his keyboard as he typed. Within moments, they were replaced by red beads of blood. The red beads were replaced by a torrent of red as the blood flowed from his lethal wound onto the keyboard. His body slumped in its chair and then slid onto the floor where it lay.

The assassin wiped his knife blade on the officer's uniform shirt and replaced it in its sheath. Then the assassin returned the way he came in.

Moments later, a car pulled in front of the police outpost. Moore jumped out of the car and asked an approaching police officer, "Are you Ekrem Tabak?"

"No," he said as he watched the blonde woman step out of the car and join Moore. "He's inside."

"Good. We have a meeting with him this morning," Bieber announced.

The officer looked again at the tall blonde. "And could I have your names?"

"Yes, I'm Emerson Moore," Moore responded.

"And I'm Katrina Bieber."

"Yes, we were told to expect your visit. Headquarters called and said to extend you every courtesy. It was in regards to the Levy murder," he said as he responded and continued to stare at Bieber.

"Yes," Bieber nodded.

"Your uncle must still have a lot of influence," Moore said to her.

Smiling, Bieber said, "He sure made this connection easy."

"Excuse me," the officer said as he continued staring at Bieber.

"Yes?" she asked.

"Have you been here before?"

"Yes. I've done research on Myndos."

"Ah. That is why you look so familiar. I have seen you here in town," he said.

Bieber responded before he could comment further. "And today, we are researching a murder. Mr. Tabak was investigating the murder of my uncle's friend, Dr Levy."

"Yes, I'm somewhat familiar with the murder. Let me take you to Sergeant Tabak. It's his case." The young officer beckoned for the two to follow him into the small outpost.

They walked down a short hallway and the officer knocked on Tabak's office door. "Sergeant Tabak? Your visitors are here. May we interrupt?"

There was no response.

The officer asked again, "Sergeant Tabak? May we interrupt?"

When there was no answer, the officer pushed open the door and they saw Tabak on the floor. The officer rushed to Tabak's side and felt for a pulse.

"Gone," the officer said as he stood. "If you could please have a seat out here, I need to call this in."

Moore allowed his eyes to quickly scan the room before the two were escorted into the outer office area. They sat on two chairs while the officer returned to Tabak's office and called in the murder. Within five minutes, he returned to join the two.

"I hope you understand, but under the circumstances, I really do not have time to talk with you," he said.

"But we are only here this morning. We have flights out of Bodrum this afternoon," Moore said.

"Could you help us with a few answers?" Bieber asked. "What we're investigating may be related to this tragedy. I'm sure that my uncle will alert your headquarters to how cooperative you were, especially under the circumstances."

The officer looked at the pretty blonde in front of him and then acquiesced. "Only a few questions, please."

Moore led the questioning. "What can you tell us about Levy's death? Where was he murdered?"

"Not here."

"What?" Moore asked in bewilderment. "The newspapers said he was murdered here."

"We don't tell the papers everything. And they got it wrong."

"Where was he murdered?" Bieber interjected.

"We don't know, although we suspect in Bodrum and then his body was dumped here."

"What makes you think that?" Moore asked.

"Levy didn't have a rental car. Working with the Bodrum police, we were able to confirm that he didn't hire a driver to bring him out here. His luggage was packed in his hotel room and his watch and wallet were on his nightstand. We shipped everything to his brother in Germany, except the ticket which must have fallen out of his wallet."

"The ticket? Ticket to where?"

"That's why we think his body was dumped here. His body was found at eleven o'clock in the morning. His ticket was for the nine o'clock ferry."

"Ferry to where?"

"Rhodos," the officer replied, using the local name for the Greek island of Rhodes.

Moore's eyebrows arched in response to the comment. "I bet Levy found a link between the Knights from St. Peter's Castle to the Knights at Rhodes."

"That could be," Bieber nodded.

"Now, please I must excuse myself," the officer said as he stood. Moore and Bieber also rose and thanked him for his assistance and expressed their condolences on the death of Sergeant Tabak.

Walking out the doorway, Moore said, "That was an interesting twist."

"Yes, it was." Seeing a small bar two doors away, Bieber suggested, "How about something cool to drink? It was so warm in there."

"Sure."

The two walked in and took a seat in the open front restaurant and bar that overlooked the cove.

"Let me order," she said to Moore as the waiter approached them. "Two Ayrans."

The waiter nodded affirmatively and went to get the drinks.

"Now, what am I drinking?"

"It's a drink for hot days and I need something cold. It's yogurt diluted with water and with a touch of salt. It'll cool us right down," she grinned.

Moore wasn't that keen on a yogurt style drink, but decided to go ahead and try it. After a few seconds he suggested, "I think we need to change our travel plans."

"To Rhodes?"

"Yes," Moore replied. "I have a hunch that Levy believed the Nazarene's Code was transported to Bodrum. We know that the apostle Paul preached in Turkey. What if he or another of the Christ followers carried the Code to Bodrum and it was hidden there for centuries until the Knights found it?"

"That's quite a bit of supposition," she said with a concerned look on her face. "You don't have the facts."

"No, I don't, but a reporter follows his instincts and my instincts tell me to go to Rhodes."

The waiter delivered the icy drinks to their table and left them.

Taking a sip, Moore groaned with delight. "Hmmm. Nice and cold."

"I told you you'd enjoy it," she smiled as she took a second drink from her glass. "So, where do we start in Rhodes?"

"The castle and its archives."

"And how much time do you have to spend there?" she asked.

"I know, I know. Not a lot. But it's a starting point for me. You have to trust me on this."

"I think you're running off half-cocked."

"Guess you'll have to just trust me," he repeated.

The two finished their drinks and Moore watched as Bieber refreshed her pink lipstick.

"Enjoying this?" she asked as she smacked her lips together.

"You know, there's just something about a woman applying lipstick to her lips that is…" He didn't get to finish his comment.

"Tantalizing?" Bieber asked demurely.

"That would be a good description." Moore sighed as he stood from his chair.

They left money on the table to pay for their bill and walked out of the restaurant. They returned to their car and drove to Bodrum.

Two men seated at a table at the other end of the restaurant watched when Moore and Bieber left. The one reached for his knife and the other placed his hand on the first one's arm to restrain it.

"Let them go. There will be plenty of time to take care of him. You've spilled enough blood today," Yarian said to Gorenchenko as he stood. "We need to follow them and see where they go next. It was good that Hakan heard Moore talking about Tabak."

"Yes. It was good for us and bad for Tabak," Gorenchenko said as his thin lips broke into a deadly smile.

The two walked to their car and quickly drove out of town. They spotted Bieber and Moore and tailed them from a discreet distance back to Bodrum.

On the Ferry Boat
Island of Rhodes

The hydrofoil ferry entered the harbor at the island of Rhodes. It had made the journey from Bodrum to the spearhead-shaped island in two hours and ten minutes. The city of Rhodes was located at the northern part of the island, which was about fifty miles long and twenty-four miles wide. Its hills and valleys are surrounded by some of the best beaches in the Mediterranean.

Rhodes was an important cultural and financial center during Greek times. Its strategic location in the eastern Mediterranean Sea placed it at a cultural crossroads. It was occupied over the centuries by the Romans, Knights Templar, Ottoman Turks and Italians.

Moore pointed to the stone-lined channel as they passed through it. "See those stone columns?"

"Yes."

"That's where the Colossus of Rhodes stood with one leg on each side of the channel. It was one of the Seven Wonders of the Ancient World."

Bieber nodded her head as Moore talked about his previous visit to Rhodes.

The two had checked out of their Bodrum hotel and made arrangements to stay on Rhodes while they followed up on Levy's ferry ticket purchase. Traveling together and discussing mutual points of interest made business quite a pleasure, Moore thought.

They caught a cab from the ferry landing to the Hotel Mediterranean. The six-story hotel was located on the island's most popular beach and had balconies overlooking the beach. The hotel was next to the casino. Behind the casino and on a lofty perch on the hill, the Castle of the Knights of St. John loomed over the city and the harbor.

The two walked through the marble-floored lobby to the front desk where a cheerful blonde with a magnetic smile greeted them. Sandy Rana was inscribed on her name badge.

"Hello, Sandy," Moore said as he set his luggage on the floor.

"Welcome to the Hotel Mediterranean," she smiled. "Do you have reservations?"

"Yes, for Moore and Bieber," Moore said as he smiled in return.

Rana's fingers flew across the keyboard as she searched for their reservation. "Yes, here they are. I can't give you adjoining rooms, but I do have two rooms on the same floor. Would that be acceptable?"

"Fine with me," Moore said as he looked at Bieber, who nodded her head in agreement.

After checking in and dropping their luggage in their rooms, they caught a cab for the old city. The cab dropped them off at one of the entrances to the old walled-city, which was filled with a labyrinth of narrow streets and cobbled alleys. As they walked, Moore looked through a brochure that he had picked up in the hotel lobby.

Reading from the brochure, Moore commented, "Looks like the Knights Hospitaller began their occupation of Rhodes in 1309 and modeled the city on the style typical during European medieval times. That's when they built the Palace of the Grand Master, the castle."

"Do you know the origin of the name Knights Hospitaller?" Bieber asked.

"No, I don't recall. I know bits and pieces about the Knights Templar, but hardly anything on this order."

"It came from the fact that they originally worked in the hospitals," Bieber responded.

"Interesting." Moore continued reading from his brochure. "They held Rhodes until 1522 when they were ousted by Suleiman and the Ottoman Empire. Then, the Knights fled to Sicily and later Malta."

"Our next stops on this journey?" Bieber asked.

Grinning, Moore shrugged, "Don't know. Let's see what we find. I think our first stop should be the Archaeological Museum. I bet they have archives there."

They stopped in front of a two story building on the cobblestone road that led to the castle. It was formerly the Knights' hospital.

"Here we are," Moore said as he opened the door and the two stepped into the air-conditioned main floor, which served as the museum's gallery. Looking through the building, they could see an internal courtyard lined with porticos. They spotted a Hellenistic statue of a lion in the courtyard.

"May I help you?" a young lady asked from behind the counter.

"Yes, we are interested in visiting the archives," Moore replied. "Is the museum director available?"

"I'll see if he's available." She disappeared around the corner.

Within minutes, a stout, balding man walked into the main entranceway and greeted them.

"I'm Marcos Nassos. I understand that you're interested in visiting our archives?" he asked.

The two introduced themselves and Moore said, "Yes, we'd like to see information on the Knights."

"Is this in regards to a newspaper story you're working on, Emerson, or research you're working on, Katrina?" he asked as they walked to an elevator and took it to the basement level.

"Both," Bieber responded.

"I see. Then, is there anything in particular so I know where to direct your attention?" he asked as he unlocked the door to the archives and swung it open.

"Are you familiar with the Nazarene's Code?" Moore asked.

A smile crossed Nassos' face. "Yes, many of us have heard about this Code, but no one has been able to confirm its existence. It's either a well guarded truth or an intriguing story."

"We are trying to determine which one," Moore explained. "We have a feeling that the Code was carried to Turkey by either one of the apostles or a trusted Christian and then possibly to Rhodes."

"And on what are you basing your conclusions?"

"The research of a University of Haifa professor and archeologist who, we believe, followed the trail to Bodrum. He was murdered and we think it was by somebody who is also looking for the Code."

Nassos' head had been cocked as he listened carefully to the explanation. "And why do you come to Rhodos?"

Bieber responded to this question. "We believe that the professor made a link to the Knights. He was carrying a ticket to Rhodos in his wallet when he was murdered. The connection to the Knights makes sense if you connect the castle in Bodrum to the castle here, both having been built by the Knights."

"So, where do you think this document is now?"

"My gut tells me that it's here," Moore offered.

"Do you have any hard facts?" Nassos asked.

"No. It's a journalistic hunch."

"And you know the Knights were dispersed from here?"

"Yes, they ended up in Malta," Moore said.

"There's more to it. Have a seat." He gestured to a conference table with several chairs. "Let me give you some insight. Some of it you may be aware of, but bear with me.

"The Knights were founded in 1022 in Jerusalem by monks as a religious order to take care of the sick and poor. Over time, it changed and became a military organization under the Catholic Church's control. This occurred in 1099 with the First Crusade's conquest of Jerusalem. The Knights became known as the Knights Hospitaller.

"When Islam regained control of Jerusalem, the Knights withdrew to Rhodos where they ruled for almost 200 years. The Knights Templar was dissolved in 1312 and all of their assets were given to the Knights Hospitallers."

"I didn't realize that," Moore commented.

"They evacuated Rhodos when the Ottoman Empire conquered it and went to Sicily and then to Malta. You are already aware that they built the castle here. In 1494, they built St. Peter's Castle in Bodrum as a stronghold to begin an attack on the growing threat from the Ottoman Empire.

"However, I doubt that the Knights would leave something as sacred as the Nazarene's Code here, if they had it. They would have probably taken it with them to safety so it wouldn't fall in the hands of the Ottoman Turks."

"So, are you suggesting that they took it to Malta?" Moore asked.

"I am suggesting that, and please note my use of the word 'suggesting.' I believe that the Knights most likely would have taken it with them during the diaspora."

"Malta?" Bieber asked Moore as she looked at him.

"I guess so," Moore said.

They finished their discussion and the two left the building. After touring the castle, they returned to their hotel.

"I'll check on flights and then why don't we meet on the beach?" Moore asked as they entered the hotel lobby.

"Good. I'll see you over there," Bieber responded.

Moore made their travel arrangements and returned to his room where he slipped into his swimming trunks. He returned to the lobby where he saw Bieber getting off the elevator next to his.

"Perfect timing," he grinned as he looked at the stunning blonde in her bright blue swimsuit cover up.

"It is," she commented. "How did you make out with the flight to Malta?"

"The best deal I could get has us returning on the ferry tomorrow to Bodrum and flying out in the afternoon to Malta. Does that work for you?"

"*Das ist gut*," she said as the two crossed the road and walked onto the beach packed with sun worshippers.

They found two lounge chairs and paid the attendant for their rental fee. Moore spread his towel and sat down. He retrieved a tube of suntan lotion and turned to Bieber. "Kat, would you like…?" He didn't finish his question as his eyes bulged at the view in front of him.

Bieber had tossed aside her cover up, revealing that she was only wearing a pink thong bottom. Her firm, bare breasts were staring at Moore's surprised face.

Chuckling at Moore's reaction, she asked, "Did I surprise you?"

"That would be an understatement," Moore stammered as he looked away and sought to compose himself. "I just, um, didn't expect it."

"Life is full of surprises, Emerson. Europeans enjoy being topless at the beach. It's part of our culture. Don't you have topless beaches in the United States?" she asked as she noticed him blushing.

"We do," he stammered, unsure as to where to look.

"Look at the beach – it's full of topless women!"

"That's not the issue. You just surprised me, Kat." Then he added, "Completely surprised me."

"Get over it and put some of that sun tan lotion on my back and legs," she smiled as she laid face down on her beach chair. Moore dutifully complied as he squeezed a large amount of lotion on his hands. He then began to rub the lotion into her upper back, massaging her muscles.

"Hmmm. Feels good," she murmured as he firmly applied the lotion.

"These hands have been trained to provide the finest in muscle relaxation techniques," Moore teased as his hands worked their way down to her lower back.

"Keep on doing what you are doing. At least for another four hours," she teased back at Moore.

Moore paused to squeeze more lotion on his hands and resumed working on her back. He then passed over her exposed buttocks and began applying lotion to her firm thighs and toned calves, working the lotion in with deep penetrating motions. He also rubbed the lotion into her feet and onto her toes. When he finished, he stared at her buttocks and tried to decide what to do.

He didn't have to decide. Bieber decided for him.

"Emerson, you missed my butt. I certainly don't want it to burn."

"Yeah, okay, I can do that," Moore said as he reached for more lotion. After squeezing more onto his hands he reached for her left cheek and awkwardly began to lightly rub lotion on it.

"Emerson, don't be shy. Rub it in like you did the rest of me," she ordered. "It's not like you're making love to me in public!"

Red-faced, Emerson responded, "Just trying to be a gentleman." He began to knead her cheeks as he applied the lotion.

"I don't need a gentleman right now. I need sun protection, so get over it and get on task," she said as she rolled her eyes.

Moore worked diligently in applying the lotion.

"That's more like it," she cooed as Moore completed his task and returned to his chair where he applied lotion to his face, chest and legs. He sat back, adjusted his sunglasses on his face and allowed his eyes to take in the scenery on the beach. Before he realized what was happening, he began to doze.

After thirty minutes, he was awakened by Bieber stirring in her lounger. He looked over and saw that she was applying lotion to her chest. Sensing that he was watching her, Bieber commented. "I can do these myself. Wouldn't want to make you feel any more uncomfortable than you already are."

"Kat," he smiled weakly, "this isn't something that I'm used to doing."

"Apparently!"

Changing the topic, Moore asked, "Ready to get wet?"

Bieber looked at the inviting, sky blue water and looked back at Moore. "Oh, why not? I need to cool off."

Me too, Moore thought to himself as the two began to walk to the water's edge and into the sea. They playfully splashed each other and swam a short distance. After twenty minutes, they returned to their beach loungers.

Moore dropped face down onto his lounger. "Your turn to do me."

"I'd love to do you," Bieber smiled as she squirted lotion on her hand and began to apply it to Moore's muscular back. She worked the lotion deeply into his muscles.

"Hey, you're pretty strong," Moore said as she worked her magic.

"Like I said, I'm full of surprises, Emerson," she said as she finished and squirted more on her hands. She then went to work on his left calf. Slowly her hands began massaging upward on his thigh. She really has strong hands, Moore thought to himself as she moved to his other calf and repeated the procedure.

When she finished, she reapplied lotion to her front side and sat back on her own lounge chair to relax.

After three hours on the beach and two more applications of

sun tan lotion, the two decided to return to their hotel rooms to clean up and meet for dinner.

Thirty minutes later, the two met in the lobby. Moore, who was wearing a light blue polo shirt and khaki slacks with sandals, arrived first. He watched the doors to the elevators and was finally rewarded with Bieber emerging from one of the elevators. She looked devastatingly gorgeous in a black dress and black open-toed heels. Her blonde hair was pulled back in a ponytail.

Moore took a deep breath and exhaled. With all of the sophisticated and technologically advanced weaponry known to man, there was but one ultimate weapon in a woman's arsenal – and one that could be a fatal WMD, weapon of mass destruction, to men. It was the little back dress. The dress that Bieber was wearing violated every dress code possible. It was semi-sheer and low-cut as well as body hugging.

"You like?" Bieber said as she pirouetted in front of Moore.

"That would be an understatement."

"You say that a lot. I wanted you to be surprised," she smiled demurely.

"That you did, Kat," Moore smiled at the beautiful woman in front of him. "That you did," he repeated again.

"I told you that I was full of surprises."

"Yes, you did! That is such a unique dress."

"Thank you. I bought it at the hotel's shop a little while ago. Lucky that they had it in my size."

"Yeah. Lucky for me," Moore said.

"Hungry?"

"Very." His eyes told her exactly what he was hungry for.

Bieber grinned. "Let's go to the casino. We can grab something to eat there and gamble." She looked at him and asked seductively, "You do gamble, don't you?"

"I'd say that life's a gamble. You play the cards you're dealt."

"I know what you mean," she agreed. "So, what do you play? The slots? Roulette? Blackjack?"

"A little of each. I'm not a real player."

Bieber winked at Moore. "I gathered that."

"Thanks, but I was referring to gambling."

"I know exactly what you were referring to," she said as a smile crossed her face. "Let's go."

Bieber linked her arm into Moore's arm and the two walked the short distance from their hotel to the casino. They had a light dinner and several drinks while they played roulette, blackjack and a few slots.

Four hours later, they stood outside of her hotel room door.

"Emerson, you are such a gentleman," Bieber said as she placed her arms around him and he reciprocated.

"I don't always want to be," he said sincerely as her blue eyes melted him.

"I'd love to invite you in," she said, "but I don't think it's a good idea to mix business with pleasure."

Moore bent down and kissed her lightly on her lips. "I usually agree, but under the circumstances, I'm reconsidering." He kissed her again, but with passion.

A moan escaped from between Bieber's lips. "Boy, can you ever kiss!"

Moore didn't reply other than pulling her body closer to his. He continued to kiss her until she suddenly pulled away.

"This is going to be very difficult, Emerson," she said as she held up an outstretched hand to Moore's chest. "I know I've flirted with you – I can't help it – but it can't go further. We must keep this on a professional basis."

She gave him a quick kiss on the lips and turned her back to open her door. Opening it, she stepped in, saying, "I had a fun evening, Emerson. Let's not ruin what we have going. Good night."

The door closed in Moore's face.

Women, Moore thought, they can look so good and tease you, and then when the game gets to the ninth inning, I strike out. Confused, he turned and walked back to his room.

The Next Morning
Hotel Mediterranean

The elevator doors opened and Moore stepped into the lobby. He walked to the registration desk and set his duffel bag on the floor as he handed the desk clerk his key.

"Checking out?" Sandy Rana asked.

"Yes," Moore responded.

"I already checked out," a familiar feminine voice whispered into his right ear after she had quietly approached Moore.

Moore swung around and faced Bieber. "Good morning, Kat," Moore greeted her coolly.

"Hmmm. Not sure that I like the tone I hear in your voice."

"Give me a second to finish checking out." Moore reviewed the bill itemizing his stay. "Looks fine," he said to the desk clerk as he signed it and placed a copy in his duffel bag.

"Kat, we need to catch our cab if we're going to make our ferry ride," he said as he pointed to the lobby exit.

"Sure," she said as she grabbed her luggage and walked to the exit where they seated themselves in one of the cabs. As the cab pulled away from the hotel, Bieber asked, "So, what's bothering you this morning? As if I don't know."

"I'm confused."

"Confused?"

"Yes."

"Why?"

"The last few nights, you went beyond flirting with me – you were very warm and suggestive. But when we returned to our hotel, you abruptly doused the flames."

Bieber turned her head away from Moore and looked out her window at the passing scenery.

Hearing no response from Bieber, Moore continued. "You're sending me mixed signals, Kat. If you want me to be just business, I can do that. Is that what you really want?"

When Bieber turned her face back toward Moore, her eyes were brimming with tears. She reached over and gently caressed Moore's left cheek. "There's something I didn't tell you last night."

"And that would be?"

"I'm dying, Emerson. I – it wouldn't be fair to get too close to you."

Moore's eyes widened. "What?" he asked as he placed his hand on hers and began to stroke her soft skin.

"Yes, I have an inoperable brain tumor. Radiation treatments haven't been effective in reducing the tumor. There's nothing that can be done. It's only a matter of weeks, maybe months."

Moore's arm encircled her and he pulled her close to comfort her. He leaned his face into hers. "I'll take you back to the states. We've the best hospitals there and the latest technology."

"Our German medical doctors are just as good as yours," she retorted. "My uncle has worked his contacts and so have our doctors in Germany. Nothing can be done."

Moore looked into her eyes. "There must be somewhere else you can go."

"No, there isn't. I'm dealing with the reality of my situation. That's why you sense me cooling things down at the end of the evening. I just don't want to become emotionally involved with anyone. I don't have much time left."

Moore was stunned. "Why didn't you tell me sooner?"

"No need to. I didn't know how fast we were becoming attracted to each other. It's – distracting. We both need to be professional and focus on our task at hand," she said as she pulled away from Moore's embrace. "Please – I don't want your pity."

Before either could comment further, the cab pulled to a stop at the ferry dock. Moore paid the cab driver and the two walked quietly to the ticket booth where they purchased the tickets to Bodrum.

Other than briefly chatting, they rode the ferry in silence, each filled with a range of emotions. When they arrived in Bodrum, they returned to Bieber's parked rental car.

Moore looked at his watch as he tossed their baggage into the back seat. "Looks like we should make our flight on time."

"Yes, and time to spare," Bieber said as cheerfully as she could. Bieber started the rental car and drove it out of the ferry parking lot.

Nearby, Gorenchenko started his car. "There they go."

"Don't follow them too closely," Yarian smiled evilly as the car pulled out of its parking space and followed Bieber's car from a discreet distance.

Halfway to the airport, Yarian directed Gorenchenko. "It's time."

Gorenchenko's foot placed more pressure on the black Mercedes' gas pedal and the car shot forward to close the distance with Bieber's rental car.

Seeing the speeding car in her rear view mirror, Bieber commented, "The joker behind us sure is in a hurry."

Moore looked at his outside mirror. "Looks that way."

Bieber moved her vehicle closer to the edge of the road to give the Mercedes extra room to pass.

As the Mercedes pulled around and abreast of Bieber's car, Yarian produced a Sig Sauer P6 pistol, which he pointed at Bieber.

"He's got a gun!" she screamed.

Moore leaned forward so that he could see around Bieber. When he saw the gun, he advised, "Better pull over. They look like they mean business. Probably a carjacking."

"They want this car?" Bieber asked.

"For parts? Who knows? Let them have it. It's a rental."

Bieber was shaking as she pulled the car onto the berm and slowed the car to a stop. The Mercedes pulled in front of it and parked. Its two occupants, with guns drawn, walked back to the parked rental car.

Bieber and Moore remained in the car, but had lowered the windows so they could speak to the carjackers.

As Yarian approached Moore's side of the car, Moore asked, "What's the meaning of this?"

Gorenchenko had arrived at Bieber's window and shoved the barrel of his pistol against Bieber's temple. "You don't ask questions," he growled as Moore's head turned to face him. "All I have to do is pull this trigger and you can say bye bye to your girlfriend."

With Moore's attention distracted, he didn't see Yarian pull out a hypodermic needle that Yarian plunged into Moore's neck. Before he lost consciousness, Moore thought to himself, this was going to be one of those days. He slipped into oblivion.

Basement Captivity
Bodrum, Turkey

When he regained consciousness, Moore found himself on a bare metal bed with a thin mattress in a basement cell. He rose slowly and swung his legs over the edge of the bed. He looked around his relatively bare surroundings. There was a wooden table and two chairs at the table. Nothing else was in the room.

Hearing a latch being thrown on the metal door, Moore stood and faced the door as it swung open to reveal his two captors. They entered the room, closing the door behind them. The captor with the shaved head stood next to the door.

The other captor spoke as he sat on one of the chairs at the table. "Mr. Moore?"

"Yes?"

"Please join me here at the table. You can call me, Mr. Yarian."

Moore stood wobbly and carefully walked the short distance to the table. He sat. As he did, he asked, "Where's my friend?"

"Katrina?" Yarian grinned.

"Yes."

"Not to worry. She's being taken care of. Gorenchenko is making sure of that."

From the doorway, the ape-sized Gorenchenko chuckled.

"I don't want anything to happen to her."

"And nothing will, provided you cooperate." Yarian produced a pack of cigarettes and a lighter. "Would you like one?"

"No, I chose to quit years ago."

"Your choice then." Yarian extracted a cigarette and lit it. He inhaled deeply and exhaled a blue plume of smoke. He watched as it dissipated in the air. He then turned his head toward Moore. "And speaking of choices, you have a choice to make."

"How's that?"

"You can choose to make this little session easy or difficult."

"I really don't know what this is all about. We thought you were carjackers."

"You thought wrong."

"Then, what's this about?"

"Mr. Moore, we are interested in the notebook."

"Notebook?"

"Don't play coy with me."

"I don't know what you're talking about," Moore bluffed.

"I'm talking about the notebook which you stole from Dr. Levy's office in Haifa. Does that help jog your memory?"

Moore's heart sank. He guessed that his captors had tortured Bieber to get the information about the notebook's existence. "I don't know anything about a notebook."

"That's not what your girlfriend told us!" Gorenchenko called from the door.

"She's not my girlfriend."

"Whatever!"

"Who are you guys?" Moore asked as he glared from one to the other.

"It's of no significance to you. Just call us contractors. We work for different people at different times and sometimes for ourselves. But we digress. I want to know where the notebook is."

"Did you break into my room and steal my laptop?" Moore pushed.

"Was it a Dell Inspiron?"

Moore nodded his head as he realized that they were responsible for the theft.

"I don't know anything about it," Yarian lied. "Mr. Moore," Yarian said as he leaned toward Moore, "I'm going to ask you nicely one last time to cooperate with us or we'll accelerate our interrogation techniques, just as we did with your girlfriend. Where's the notebook?"

"I don't know what you're talking about."

"So be it." Yarian nodded to Gorenchenko, who walked quickly over to Moore.

Before Moore could react, Gorenchenko delivered a blow to his body that sent him sprawling from the chair onto the floor. Gorenchenko picked up the chair and set it at the table as he looked at Moore, who was beginning to sit up.

"Do you want to answer his question now?" Gorenchenko growled.

"Like I said, I don't know what you're talking about," Moore responded stubbornly.

Gorenchenko picked up the chair. He raised it over his head and brought it crashing down onto Moore's head, knocking him unconscious.

Yarian tamped out his cigarette on the table and stood. "Strip him and bind him to the chair. Then, get your water and electrodes."

Gorenchenko nodded as he picked up Moore as if he were nothing more than a limp rag doll.

Two Days Later
Bodrum, Turkey

A rough burlap bag encased Emerson Moore's head. The stench of urine and excrement, which had previously saturated the bag, filled Moore's nostrils. The smell was stifling and caused Moore to choke on virtually every breath.

The sack was like a black cloud shrouding his face. The rough burlap irritated his skin. The bag was intended to diminish his senses so that he wouldn't be able to identify the location of the hell he was forced to endure. Moore tried to heighten his hearing to catalogue and memorize any sounds he heard. He was determined to survive his torturous ordeal and return to reap a hateful revenge on his captors.

For over forty-eight hours, Moore had suffered sleep deprivation as his tormentors prodded him as he sat naked in the chair. His legs and arms were tied securely to the chair legs and its arm rests. His feet were numbed by the bucket of ice water in which they had been thrust. He had tried repeatedly to lift them from the water, but he couldn't since his legs were so tightly bound. His buttocks ached from sitting on the worn, wooden chair. His body had been tormented from the beatings. It was black and blue and bruised with welts. Moore shivered in the cold basement.

He could feel the electrodes affixed to his wrists. They were a constant reminder of his captors' brutality. They had shocked him when he tried to sleep or when they wanted to prod him for information. So far, he hadn't provided them with anything. He knew that they couldn't kill him, at least until they were able to wring out the information they needed to solve the puzzle.

A door opened and people entered the small basement room. When Moore heard the switch thrown, his body shifted in anticipation of a painful surge. Feeling nothing for a change, he relaxed.

He heard something being dragged on the floor. A faint, familiar smell penetrated the sack and greeted his nostrils. He stiffened as he recognized the scent and realized who might be wearing the perfume.

"Throw her into that chair," Yarian grumbled as he turned to look at Moore and snarled, "You feel like talking yet?"

Moore didn't respond. He couldn't see the 280-pound, six-foot, gray-haired Turk reach for the switch – and it wasn't the light switch.

Yarian threw the switch that zapped Moore with a short, strong burst of electricity. Moore's body began to spasm, and he clenched his teeth as his body twisted in pain. He never knew how much of a charge or the length of the charge they'd give him.

"You want to answer me now, Mr. Tough Guy?" Yarian asked

as he switched off the charge.

Moore remained silent as his body relaxed. He was thankful that they couldn't see the tortured look on his face. He also knew he wasn't going anywhere with this madman.

"I thought so." Yarian turned to Gorenchenko. "Take the gag out of her mouth and remove the blindfold."

Gorenchenko, the powerfully built Chechen with the shaved head, did as he was instructed.

When the blindfold and gag were removed, the captive's head looked to her left. Her eyes widened as she stared in shock at the beaten body in front of her.

Seeing her look of horror, Yarian smiled. "Your lover boy looks different now." Yarian looked from her to Moore. "When we're done with him, no one will recognize him – not even you."

Moore heard the woman's voice plead.

"Let him go."

Moore recognized the voice instantly, and cringed with the realization that she was about to be tortured. For the first time, he spoke. "Yarian, you need to let her go."

"Isn't this sweet? Bring the two lovebirds together and they begin to sing a love song for each other."

"She doesn't know anything, Yarian."

"Emerson, don't tell them anything," she said.

"Oh, I think he will tell us what we want to know now that you're here. Am I correct, Mr. Moore?" Yarian asked in his heavily accented English. "Is the little lovebird willing to sing to protect his mate?"

Filled with a mixture of growing anger and anguish, Moore struggled for a response. He wanted to protect her. He also knew that once he gave them the information, Yarian would kill both of them. He decided to stall while he tried to fabricate a plausible answer to the questions they had been asking him.

"I'm weak. I can't think straight," Moore feigned.

Yarian roared. "Do you think I'm a fool?" He walked over to Moore and struck Moore's head with his fist.

Moore's head snapped to the side in reaction to the unexpected blow.

"You're not the first person I've interrogated. I know pain threshold limits. It may differ amongst people, but you are no-where close to it. Now, answer my question and don't play with me," Yarian stormed.

Moore's mind raced with ideas for his next parry with his swar-thy foe. Before he could respond, he heard the sound of a struggle and clothing being torn.

"You're taking too long, Moore," Yarian said as he watched Gorenchenko rip the shirt off of her. "In less than a minute, she'll be as naked as you."

Hearing the shredding of her clothes and her screams, Moore lost his control and exploded uncharacteristically, cursing as he pleaded for them to stop. His body twisted as he attempted to es-cape his bonds.

A sinister laugh emitted from Yarian's grotesque mouth as he nodded to Gorenchenko, who was preparing to follow the next step in Yarian's plan. Gorenchenko smiled. He was going to enjoy the next step. He bent to his task.

Moore heard a struggle taking place. "What are you doing?"

The only response was a chuckle from Yarian and a grunt from Gorenchenko. A few seconds later, a gunshot echoed through the small basement room.

"No! No! Don't kill her! I'll tell you what you want to know!" Moore screamed as the sound from the gunshot filled the basement room. This made absolutely no sense to him. What were they thinking? What kind of torture was this? They didn't push him for an answer. They just killed her. His body began shaking in rage and grief.

"Too late, my dear Mr. Moore," Yarian said as he laughed evilly. "I really don't need her to get you to talk. This was just for fun."

Moore heard Yarian walk over to him and he tightened his stomach muscles in anticipation of a blow to the ribcage.

"Nervous, Mr. Moore?" Yarian snickered. "Why there's nothing to be nervous about. Not quite yet."

Moore felt something being poured on top of the bag over his head. It began to seep through the burlap and slowly flow from the top of his head down his face.

"Wondering what that is?" Yarian asked.

Moore didn't respond as the warm fluid seeped across his eyes and nose, mixing with his silent tears.

"It's her blood," Yarian gloated. He could picture the emotional trauma he was causing his captive. "We'll leave you now so that you can wallow in misery. I want you to know that you are responsible for her death. You should have answered my questions. If you had, we wouldn't have had to kill her."

Moore's heart sank. His shoulders and head, which had been defiant throughout his torture sessions, sagged as the reality of her death crushed him like a bus being dropped on his shoulders. The blood seeping through the sack tortured him as nothing else could.

The emotional game was working according to Yarian's plan.

Moore heard her body being dragged from the room as the two torturers exited. The door closed shut with a loud bang. The lock was secured. Moore was isolated in a tomb filled with silent anguish. His mind berated himself for allowing her death. This was far worse than any physical pain he had endured. All he could do now was weep – and wait.

24 Hours Later
Bodrum, Turkey

The unlatching of the cell door awoke Moore from a restless sleep. His head lifted off of his chest as he heard the door swing open and two people enter his cell.

Yarian walked in front of Moore. He was the first to speak. "Pleasant dreams or tormenting nightmares, Mr. Moore?" Yarian snickered.

Moore didn't respond.

"Not talking today?"

Moore remained quiet. His mind turned as he tried to determine how he could escape, but they had been too careful when they bound him.

"Don't want to talk?" Yarian queried as he turned and picked up a sharp knife. "Then, I guess you don't need a tongue."

Moore's head jerked back in revulsion.

Yarian moved in closer to Moore and motioned Gorenchenko to move behind Moore. As he did, he roughly removed the blood soaked sack from Moore's head. Moore's eyes closed in reaction to the light in the room. He winced several times before opening them again. When he did, he quickly looked to his right where Bieber had been. On the floor he saw a pool of dried blood.

The head movement was not lost on Yarian. "Yes, that's your girlfriend's blood. And you will carry that responsibility for the rest of your life although I don't anticipate that your life expectancy is that great."

Yarian touched the side of Moore's face with the side of the knife's sharp blade.

As Moore began to pull his head away, Yarian warned, "Be careful how you move. This blade is very sharp, Mr. Moore. I could shave you with it if I wanted." Yarian nodded to Gorenchenko.

Gorenchenko stepped up and pulled Moore's head against his bulging belly. At the same time, the fingers on Gorenchenko's right hand applied a metal clamp to Moore's nose, forcing Moore to open his mouth to breathe. Gorenchenko's fingers moved to Moore's mouth and fought to keep it open as Yarian moved in with the blade.

"If you can't answer my questions, you don't have any need for your tongue. Would you agree?" Yarian asked as he moved the knife's blade closer to Moore's mouth.

Moore's eyes widened and he squirmed in his chair, but he couldn't move. Gorenchenko had a strong grip on Moore's head and mouth. For one second, Gorenchenko eased his grip and Moore made his move – even though it wasn't a wise move.

Moore's teeth chomped down on two of Gorenchenko's fingers, causing Gorenchenko to scream and release his grip on Moore's mouth. Yarian backed away in surprise as a raged-filled Gorenchenko took aim and launched a powerful shot to Moore's right jaw. The blow was so strong that Moore tipped over in his chair and his head slammed into the cold concrete floor. His ankles scrapped hard against the side of the water-filled tub as they came out of their icy prison.

"So foolish, Mr. Moore," Yarian said as he and the furious Gorenchenko righted the chair containing Moore and placed Moore's feet back into the tub of water.

Moore's jaw ached from the blow and the left side of his head throbbed from hitting the concrete floor.

"Secure him," Yarian ordered Gorenchenko. Gorenchenko tightly gripped Moore's shoulders as Yarian again approached Moore with the deadly knife. "I'm not going to cut out your tongue. At least not today. Tomorrow, maybe. Or maybe, the next day. You just dwell on when I'm going to cut it off. Or, maybe you'll decide to talk."

Yarian ran the sharp blade down Moore's hairy chest. He wielded it expertly like a surgeon as he shaved off parts of Moore's chest hair. He then moved the blade down Moore's naked torso and shaved hairs off Moore's abdomen.

Moore tensed. Then, a smile cracked his strained face as he decided to give Yarian a surprise of his own. Moore allowed a stream of urine to spurt onto Yarian. Yarian jumped back in disgust and began swearing at Moore.

Moore laughed. That was the last sound he heard as Gorenchenko's powerful blow to the side of his head returned Moore to the now-familiar world of darkness.

"Emerson? Emerson, can you hear me?"

Moore fought his way back to consciousness. He'd been dreaming. He thought he'd heard Bieber's voice.

The familiar voice repeated itself. "Emerson?"

Moore opened his eyes. In front of him was Bieber. Moore shook his head from side to side. He flinched at the pain in his right jaw. It was throbbing. He hoped it wasn't fractured.

"Kat?"

"Yes, it's me."

Eyes widening in disbelief, Moore stammered, "I thought they killed you."

"They were playing mind games with you," Bieber replied as she cut the plastic ties which bound Moore's arms to the chair.

"But the blood he poured on my head and the pool of blood on the floor? Where did that come from?" Moore groaned as he flexed his arms and circulation was restored.

"When they took the blindfold off me, I saw that they had dragged two of us into the room. I don't know who the other guy was. It looked like he was either dead or unconscious." She snipped the plastic ties from around his legs and carefully lifted his feet from the tub of cold water.

"So, they shot the other guy," Moored deducted. He looked at Bieber and asked, "Why didn't you say something after they shot the guy?"

Bieber was kneeling on the floor in front of Moore. She was rubbing his cold feet, trying to warm them and restore circulation. "I vaguely recall hearing a gunshot. That bastard Gorenchenko plunged a hypodermic needle in my neck and I was off to la la land."

"These guys are good. But I still don't get why they didn't torture you or me more while you were in here. I'm not sure I would have been able to withhold information if they tortured you."

Bieber allowed a smile to cross her face as she looked up at Moore. "You would have given them the information they wanted?"

It was Moore's turn to smile. "Let's just say I would have given them information to stall them and send them on a false trail. They wouldn't have killed either of us until they were able to confirm that the information was correct. But, again, these two animals aren't normal."

"Who is?" Bieber questioned.

Moore nodded his head in agreement. "Did they harm you?" Moore asked as he looked at Bieber, who was wearing a man's worn shirt and slacks, which were too big for her.

"No, other than stripping me. I found these clothes and put them on." Looking at Moore's chest, she asked, "So, who groomed you?"

"Yarian. With his knife blade."

Bieber allowed her eyes to drop to Moore's abdomen. "Looks like he left your happy trail," she grinned. "And everything else," she added in a teasing tone.

"I'm lucky that he didn't castrate me after what I did to him."

"What did you do? I'd say you were pretty helpless."

"I pissed on him!"

"Oh, no! Aren't you the risk taker!"

"Or stupid! I'm just fortunate that they just took it out on my head." He winced again as his jaw throbbed. "I just hope he didn't fracture my jaw."

"Oh, I'm sorry about that," she said.

Moore looked down at the beautiful woman in front of him. He wrinkled his brow and asked, "How did you get free?"

"Apparently, I regained consciousness quicker than they expected. I was on my cell floor and the cell door wasn't latched. It was partially open. I tried to stand, but was too dizzy from whatever they had in that injection. I sat up and waited for my head to clear, and when I was able to stand, I eased the door open. When I looked down the hall, I didn't see anyone, so I figured I'd better find you. This was the third cell I looked into."

"We have to be quick. Did you see anyone in any of the other cells?"

"No, they were empty." Bieber looked at Moore's feet. "How do your feet feel now?"

"Much better, but you better help me stand. We can't waste much time here. They'll be back to check on you. When they find you missing, it will be a matter of minutes before they show up here."

Bieber stood and walked to Moore's side. She placed one of his arms around her shoulder, causing him to groan. "Did that hurt?"

"Everything hurts," he said as he tried to move.

"Let's walk around the room and loosen your muscles," she suggested as she allowed him to lean against her.

"Good idea, but we don't have a lot of time." They moved slowly around the cell as Moore took in everything. "And I'll need clothes to wear if we're going to escape."

"I can look down the hallway," Bieber offered.

"Just let me lean against this table while you go and look."

Bieber slowly walked Moore to the table. "You'll be okay?"

"Sure," he said as he slowly bent over to rub his aching legs.

"I'll be right back." Bieber disappeared for a few minutes. When she returned, she produced a guard's uniform and a pair of over-sized shoes. "How's this for starters?"

"Not quite Jos. A Bank Clothiers, but looks good to me. Did you find socks? My feet are begging for a pair of socks."

"Here you go," she said as she bent down and slipped them on his cold feet.

In a matter of minutes, Moore was dressed in the baggy uniform. "Must be Gorenchenko's," Moore commented.

"Now what?"

"I need your help with these wires," Moore said as he grasped the wires that had been used to electrically shock him.

"What are you going to do?" she asked as she pulled out excess cord and Moore approached the cell door.

"I'm wiring the door handle. When they grab it from the other side, they'll get a little payback for what I've been going through." Moore finished attaching the wires and stood back. "Could you throw that switch?" He pointed to the switch and she threw it, allowing the electricity to surge through the line.

Moore beckoned her to follow him into the hall. "It goes without saying, but don't touch the doorknob."

Bieber smiled at the obvious.

In the hallway, Moore took only a few steps. "I'm still weak. Can I lean on you?"

With her big blue eyes, Bieber looked at Moore and asked, "Is that the only reason?"

Moore grinned. "Right now, yes. Later on, maybe not. Now, let's get out of here before someone comes looking for us."

The two made their way down the hallway and quietly up a flight of stairs to ground level. They looked through the small window on the door and saw an old van parked ten feet away. Slowly, they opened the door and peered outside. They saw no one in the small courtyard.

"We'll take the van," Moore said as they stepped through the doorway and began walking toward the van.

"What about keys?"

"I'll hot-wire it if it's necessary," Moore said. "I had to do it a couple of times on my uncle's old truck."

"Oh, not always the good boy?" Bieber asked demurely.

"Not always."

As they neared the van, Bieber asked, "Are you able to drive or should I?"

"I can." Moore's eyes widened when he saw a key in the ignition. "We're in luck. The key is here." He slid into the driver's side as she ran around the van and jumped into the passenger side.

Moore pumped the accelerator four times and turned the key. The van started and Moore threw it in gear. He slammed his foot on the gas pedal and the van roared out of the courtyard and turned right onto the street.

Bieber leaned toward Moore and gave him a kiss on the cheek. "We did it!" she smiled.

"Yes, we did," Moore responded, "but it all seemed too easy." He had a growing feeling that something was amiss.

"Some times people forget and leave the key in the ignition," Bieber said. "We can just be thankful."

Moore nodded, but worry continued to gnaw at him as he drove.

Back at the building where Moore was tormented, Yarian and Gorenchenko huddled together in a small office filled with monitors. They had watched every move of Bieber and Moore's escape.

Leaning back in his chair, Yarian smiled confidently. "Just like we planned."

"Moore is a fool," Gorenchenko observed.

"Yes, he is. So is his stupid girlfriend."

"I hope this works. We need them to lead us to Levy's notebook."

"It'll work. Go down to the cell and disconnect his booby trap. Careful you don't get shocked." Yarian reached for a phone. "I'm going to alert our government friends to watch the airports, ferries, trains and border crossings. Let's see how creative this Moore can be in leaving the country."

Gorenchenko's bulky frame stood and he walked to fulfill his task.

In the van, Moore constantly checked his rear view mirror to see if they were being followed.

Bieber tried to calm his fears. "Anyone behind us?"

"No," Moore responded as he turned a corner.

"See? All is well. Now, where are you taking us?"

"Our hotel."

"But we checked out," Bieber said, confused. "Neither of us has any money and we don't have our passports."

Moore's eyes sought the fuel gauge and he saw that he had a quarter tank of fuel left. "Trust me," he said as he eased the van into a parking spot in front of the hotel. Fifteen minutes later, Moore returned with a sack, which he set between the seats.

"How did it go? What did you do?"

Moore seemed to relax as he spoke. "Great! I talked to the front desk people who remembered me. I explained that I had been robbed and was able to talk them into pulling my credit card number from their file. I charged some food and was able to get a $100 cash advance from my credit card number which they had on file."

"That won't get us far."

"No, but it's a start. I made arrangements for a flight to Steinbach."

"But there's no way we'll clear passport control without our passports," she said as the van left the outskirts of Bodrum and headed toward the airport.

"I've got that covered. You'll have to trust me."

Bieber was silent as she stared out the window.

Moore continued. "We'll be okay. But we need to stop along the way and have you call your uncle."

"My uncle?"

"Yes. He'll need to call his local buddies and influence them to allow a small charter plane to land in Steinbach with no questions asked. The plane will touch down and drop us. After refueling, the plane will take off."

"You chartered a plane?"

"In a matter of speaking. I hired transportation. I'm not sure that it's really a plane. It'll be a miracle if we get there in one piece," Moore joked. "Ask your uncle to meet us at the Steinbach airport tonight around seven o'clock. He'll also need to call you back after he makes his arrangements and provide an identifying flight number for my friend so that he can get landing clearance and no one hassles us when we land."

"I can do that."

Spotting a small boutique hotel off the road, Moore turned into its parking lot. He found a parking spot near the rear of the building where the van would be partially hidden from the road.

"Why don't you go inside and make your call?" Moore asked as he handed her some of his cash. "And be sure to let him know that we're expecting a return call."

Taking the money, Bieber exited the car and walked to the inn's lobby. Within ten minutes, she returned to the van.

"Over here," Moore called from beneath a shady tree, where he was seated at a patio table. "Did you connect with your uncle?"

"Yes. He had so many questions and I told him that I couldn't talk; there were too many people around. I told him that I'd explain when we saw him."

"He's going to make the arrangements at his end?"

"Yes. He said it might take some time."

"We have some time before we meet our flight. It will take him about four and a half hours to fly to our rendezvous point."

"We're not going to Bodrum's airport?"

"No. Be patient. You'll see." Moore pointed to the food and beverages that he had purchased at the hotel. "Have some cheese and bread. I was famished," he said as he took a drink from the bottle.

"Raki?"

"Yes. Thought it might help me relax a bit," Moore said as he set the bottle on the table. He slouched in his chair. "I might grab a nap. You'll need to wake me if I sleep too long. There's a clock on the van's dash you can use."

"What time do we need to leave here?"

"In four hours," Moore said as he allowed his head to tilt to the side and he slipped into a deep sleep. His adrenaline level had dropped and he was exhausted from his captivity.

"Emerson? Emerson?"

Someone was calling his name. Emerson fought his way out of dreamland and back to reality. He slowly opened his eyes and focused them on the attractive blonde who was calling his name.

"Emerson. Wake up," Bieber said as she stared.

Shaking his head and pulling himself up in his chair, Moore asked, "How long did I sleep?"

"Four hours."

"Four hours? But it seems like I just fell asleep." He looked around the parking lot to assess their safety. Seeing nothing of concern, he looked back at Bieber. "Hear anything back from your uncle?"

"Yes. He called about two hours ago. All is taken care of. The identifying code is ND346. That will give our pilot priority landing."

"Good. Sure is nice having an uncle as well placed as yours."

Bieber smiled. "He's just amazing."

"Any raki left?"

"Probably a couple of swallows."

"Good." Moore reached for the bottle and took the final two swigs of the alcoholic liquid.

"Feeling rested?"

"Somewhat, but my jaw is still throbbing from the hit I took in my cell. You didn't sleep?"

"No. I wanted to be sure to take my uncle's call and I kept an eye on the road in case those two guys appeared."

Standing, Moore looked at the van. "We should go. Don't want to be late for our pick up." He picked up the leftover cheese and bread and replaced them in the sack while Bieber threw the empty raki bottle in a nearby trash can. They walked to the van.

"How far of a drive is it to our pick-up point?"

"It's about five miles southwest of the airport. I have written directions," Moore said as he pulled them from his shirt pocket and reviewed them. He started the van and they drove to the point without further incident.

After making several turns and driving down three side roads, they arrived at their meeting point. Moore pulled the van off the road and parked. "Nothing to do now but wait," Moore said as he scanned the sky to the southwest.

Thirty minutes elapsed before Moore thought he heard the faint rumblings of an airplane engine. He squinted his eyes and spotted the familiar Piper Comanche four-seater belonging to Miracle

Airlines.

The plane bobbed in the wind as it descended to the gravel road. As it neared, they could hear that one of the plane's engines seemed to be running irregularly.

"Sounds like that plane is in trouble," Bieber said worriedly.

"Nah. That's the way he likes them to run," Moore grinned as he thought back to his experience a few days earlier.

As the plane's altitude dropped to within twenty feet of the road, the port engine died. The pilot skillfully guided the plane to a safe landing and he taxied to where his passengers were waiting. Cutting his remaining engine, the pilot jumped out of the plane. He was carrying a toolbox.

"Hi, Ray. How was the flight?"

The lanky pilot looked from Moore to the tall blonde. Ignoring Moore's question, Grissett nodded to the blonde. "Well, good afternoon, sweet thing."

"Ray, this is Kat Bieber. She'll be flying with us today."

"Iffen I knowed that I'd be flying Miss Universe today, I'd have shaven and cleaned up," Grissett said. "I'd give you a big hug sweet thing, but I've got some grease on my shirt."

Bieber looked past Grissett to the plane. "Is that plane going to be safe for us to fly in?"

"Once I make a couple of adjustments here, we should be good to go. And if she has trouble, we'll just put her down and I'll fix whatever needs to be fixed," Grissett said. "You guys go ahead and put your luggage on board and I'll just be a couple of minutes."

"We don't have any luggage," Moore said.

Grissett stopped in midstride. "You sure are traveling light. No passport you said on the phone and no luggage. Tells me that you both are in deep do do."

"I would say that we don't have a lot of time to waste," Moore replied.

"Climb in then." Grissett went to the port engine and adjusted the fuel injectors. He then returned to the plane.

"Fixed?" Bieber asked nervously.

"Your guess is as good as mine," Grissett announced. He fired up both engines and listened for a few minutes. Both were running although the port engine was still running rough. Grissett turned to Bieber. "You have any religion in your upbringing?"

Moore, who was seated in the co-pilot's seat, leaned toward Bieber in the rear. "I think Ray asks everyone that question, isn't that true, Ray?"

Turning to his right, Grissett grinned at Moore. "It don't hurt to have someone praying for your plane while you're flying it, especially if that someone is a passenger."

"You guys are not giving me a warm and fuzzy feeling," Bieber said as she looked at the two rascals in front of her.

"My flying's not that bad," Grissett said as the plane began picking up speed on its takeoff run. "One time, I dumped a cup of coffee in my lap. I accidently reacted by putting the plane into a dive. When I pulled out of it, I told my passengers that the front of my pants was all wet. Guy sitting where you're sitting, Kat, said 'that was nothing. You should see the back of my pants.'"

Moore and Grissett laughed while Bieber allowed a tentative smile to cross her face as the port engine began to run smoothly and the plane became airborne.

"We gotta fly low until we clear Turkish airspace," Grissett said as the plane went into a sweeping turn and began to head west. "Don't want to get picked up on their radar and have a couple of fighters appear off our wings."

"You've had encounters with them before?" Moore asked.

"Just a couple of times, but we're not going to discuss that."

Within minutes they were flying over the Aegean Sea and Grissett turned to Bieber. "There's a parachute under your seat. Think you could reach under there and pull it out for me?"

With a quizzical look on her face, Bieber tugged the parachute out and handed it to Moore, who passed it to Grissett.

"Where's my parachute?" Bieber asked as she looked under the seat next to her and couldn't find one.

"I only carry one in the plane. Iffen we get in trouble, I'll put it on and jump to go find help," he grinned.

"Ray, you're incorrigible," Bieber smiled from the rear.

"Iffen that means I'm smart, I guess I'd agree with you, Kat."

Their flight path included refueling stops at two small airports. Grissett knew no questions would be asked as long as he paid an expensive surcharge for his fuel.

As they approached Steinbach's airport, Grissett turned and looked at Bieber. "Now, you're sure that your uncle has all the right connections so that I'm not finding my plane impounded and me locked up when we land?"

"I can assure you that my uncle's contacts are at the highest levels in the German government. Everything will work out fine."

"Okay, here goes." Grissett radioed the tower and provided the ND346 identifying code.

The tower cleared them for landing and Grissett sighed in relief as he lowered his airspeed and aligned the small aircraft on his approach.

Once they landed and began to taxi, Bieber pointed to a car parked near the edge of the tarmac. "That's my uncle's car."

Grissett nodded and taxied the plane toward the car. When they reached the car, Grissett shut down the plane's engines and exited the craft, and then helped Moore and Bieber exit.

"Sounds like you two had a very bad experience," Kalker said as he shook Moore's hand and hugged his niece.

"Yes, we did," Bieber responded. Looking at Grissett, she said, "But we don't want to go into detail now."

"I don't want to hear anything that doesn't impact me. The less I know the better it is for me," Grissett commented. He knew from past experiences that being in the dark on certain things played to his favor. "And who is going to pay me for my charter services?"

Moore looked to Kalker. "Andreas, did you bring the cash?"

"Yes," he said as he reached inside his jacket pocket and extracted an envelope, which he handed to Moore. "It's all there."

"Thank you. I'll make sure that we reimburse you." Moore handed the envelope to Grissett. "Thanks, Ray. You really bailed us out on this."

Bieber chimed in, "Thanks, Ray. And the flight wasn't as bad as I anticipated."

"Oh, sometimes I stretch how bad things are so I can rattle my passenger. That's just part of me being me," Grissett said. "Now, I need to fuel up and take a pee, but not necessarily in that order."

Kalker pointed toward the fueling area. "If you taxi over there, they should be able to accommodate your needs without any hassle."

"Good." Grissett shook Moore's hand. "Maybe I'll see you around again sometime. You've got my number."

"Maybe. The world is getting smaller," Moore said as he watched Grissett climb into his plane and taxi away.

"What? No lipstick?" Kalker exclaimed as he looked more closely at his niece.

"They took everything," she explained.

"I'll replace it. I have one more at the house. Can't have a woman walking around without her lipstick on," Kalker said as he coughed twice. He turned to Moore and began, "A woman isn't properly armed unless…"

"She's wearing her lipstick," Moore finished the sentence for Kalker.

"You are learning, Mr. Moore."

The three entered Kalker's car and returned to his home. As they drove, Bieber and Moore caught him up on their adventure from the time they left Steinbach to their return to Steinbach.

"Interesting. I have a number of questions for you. Let's start with Levy's murder," Kalker said as they parked the car and entered his home. Kalker motioned for them to sit at his kitchen table and he produced three glasses that he filled with schnapps. After they downed their schnapps, he refilled the glasses and sat back.

Bieber opened the discussion. "The police suspect that Levy was killed elsewhere and his body dumped in Gumusluk."

"Yes," Moore concurred. "It appears that someone, and I'm suspecting our friends, Yarian and Gorenchenko, are also on the hunt for the Nazarene's Code. They were probably involved with Levy's murder. Dumping Levy's body in Gumusluk was a false trail to steer us away from Bodrum. The real link appears to be from Bodrum to Rhodes to Malta with the Knights Hospitallers."

"Let me see if I understand your supposition. Based on what you read in Levy's notebook, you suspect that Paul or one of the apostles carried the Nazarene Code to Turkey, maybe to Ephesus where Paul preached or Bodrum where it remained until the Knights discovered it. Is that correct?"

"Yes. Levy's notes provide the link from the apostles to the Knights," Moore nodded as he spoke.

"And then you believe that the Knights took the Nazarene's Code to Malta?"

"We do, Uncle Andreas," Bieber replied.

"But you don't have any proof, Katrina?"

"Correct. But we need to follow up and see what we can discover," Bieber said.

"I agree. We shouldn't stop our research on this," Moore added.

"I'd like to see the notebook. Do you have it, Emerson?" Kalker asked.

"I have it," he responded, "in a safe place."

"You left it in Bodrum?" Kalker asked.

"A friend of mine has it for safekeeping. I can show it to you when I have it again."

Kalker nodded as he thought.

After a few minutes of silence, Moore asked, "What about these two guys, Yarian and Gorenchenko? Can you find out anything about them?"

"That I can do. I'll talk to my connections in Turkey and see what we can learn. Then, we can decide how to deal with them. I may need my Turkish friends to locate them and interview them." He chuckled when he used the word interview. "Interview them as they did you," he added.

"They're bad characters," Moore said.

"Very dangerous," Bieber added.

"What about Malta?" Kalker asked. "Do you want to make arrangements to visit there?"

"Yes!" Bieber responded.

"I think we should divide and conquer," Moore suggested.

Bieber seemed stunned at the strategy. "What do you mean?"

"Why don't you go to Malta and see what you can learn?" Moore looked at Kalker. "I need to pay a visit to our mutual friend, Steve Nicholas in Washington. I want to run the results of our research past him to get his take on the Nazarene's Code and where we are in the process."

"I think that would be a wise move," Kalker agreed.

"Only one thing," Moore said.

"Yes?"

"You need to provide some sort of security for Kat when she goes to Malta. We can't be too careful with Yarian and Gorenchenko running about."

Bieber smiled. "Emerson, you're very thoughtful."

"I'll have a couple of my former BND friends accompany Kat to Malta. That should not be a problem. And I'll also be more comfortable knowing that she has protection."

"Thanks, Andreas," Moore responded.

"Thank you, Uncle," Bieber echoed.

"Not necessary to thank me. Now, let's get you two cleaned up and go out for dinner. Emerson, you can shower here and I'll provide you with a change of clothes." Kalker stood, coughed twice and walked out of the room.

"Glad we have him on our side," Emerson observed.

"Yes, me too," Bieber concurred.

"You sure that you're okay with going to Malta without me?"

"I don't see any problems, especially with a couple of security guys along."

"Good. I need to see Steve and I also need to check in at my office. They've got to be wondering where I've disappeared. I need to keep them in the loop. This has the makings of a good story for the *Post*."

Before Bieber could comment further, Kalker returned to the room. "Kat, here's another tube of lipstick. You need to freshen up."

Taking the tube that he handed to her, she removed the cap and began to apply the pink coating to her lips. Completing the task as the two men watched, she smacked her lips together.

"Much better. Thank you, Uncle Andreas." She stood and slipped the tube in her pant pocket, then hugged her uncle. "I'll borrow your car and run back to my place to shower and change. Then, I'll be back."

"Good," Kalker said.

Bieber grabbed the keys off the table and began walking to the door. "See you in a bit, Emerson."

"Looking forward to it," Moore grinned.

The growing attraction between the two was not lost on Kalker. As the door closed, he asked, "So, what do you think of my niece?"

"Smart, ambitious and attractive." Moore summed it up in three words.

Kalker smiled to himself. "Yes she is. I appreciate you taking care of her these last few days. I wouldn't want anything to happen to her."

"Andreas, I wouldn't want anything to happen to her either." Moore looked at Kalker. "She told me."

"She told you what?"

"She's dying."

Kalker looked down. He didn't speak for a moment. After coughing twice, he looked back up at Moore. Tears welled in his eyes.

"I didn't expect her to tell you." Kalker looked toward the wall. "She's my only living relative. The others are gone."

"And there's no medical solution for her situation?"

"No. We've checked with the best. It's inoperable. Nothing can be done."

"I am so sorry to hear that," Moore said with heaviness in his voice.

Kalker coughed twice. "This is a bit macabre, but we have a bet on who is going to die first."

Moore's faced showed disbelief at the comment.

"When I introduced you two, I didn't expect that you two would become emotionally involved."

"Neither did I," Moore responded. "She's a very special lady."

"That she is. That she is," Kalker repeated. Kalker changed the topic. "Now, we need to make a few phone calls to replace your missing passport and fly you back to the U.S."

After placing the calls and starting the process, Kalker excused Moore to clean up. While Moore was showering, Kalker placed a call to Turkey to follow up on Yarian and Gorenchenko.

Within the hour, the three were reunited and driving to dinner in Steinbach.

Washington Sailing Marina
Alexandria, Virginia

Making his way through Reagan National Airport, Moore caught a taxi and headed to his home away from home, a houseboat docked at the Washington Sailing Marina, on the Virginia side of the Potomac River.

Moore had sold his Alexandria townhouse after the death of his wife and son - it held too many memories. One of Moore's friends had decided to sell his houseboat and offered to sell it to Moore at a fair price. Since Moore moved his permanent residence to his aunt's house in Put-in-Bay, he decided to purchase the houseboat. It was named *Serenity* and served as his new Alexandria residence.

The taxi turned left off of George Washington Parkway and drove down the peninsula's tree-lined Marina Drive, which ended at one of Moore's favorite restaurants, Indigo Landing. As the taxi followed the lane on Daingerfield Island, Moore gazed at the rows of watercraft at dock. They rocked gently in the light breeze. The marina held a number of sailboats, powerboats and houseboats.

The taxi made the turn in front of the restaurant.

"Where do you want me to drop you?" the driver queried.

"Here is fine," Moore responded. He paid his fare and exited the cab. Moore turned and walked to A dock.

As he walked, he glanced at the Potomac and smiled as he saw a number of sailboats taking advantage of the late afternoon breeze. He silently wished that Kat could be here to enjoy it with him.

"Haven't seen you in awhile, Emerson."

Moore's head turned toward the gated entranceway to A dock and he saw the dockmaster. Dino Dorman's face had a large smile as he looked at Moore. The slim sixty-year-old dockmaster had retired from working at the nearby Pentagon three years ago to pursue his dream of working at the marina.

Dorman wiped his hands on a rag. "Careful there, just finished painting the gate. Don't have my 'Fresh Paint' sign up yet."

"I'll be careful," Moore responded.

"Staying long?"

"I should be here for a few days. Everything shipshape on the *Serenity*?"

Dorman nodded. "She's just fine. She awaits your command."

Moore had hired Dorman to keep an eye on the houseboat and maintain her. Dorman would bill him for any maintenance work that was needed.

"Thanks, Dino," Moore said as he walked down to the *Serenity* and stepped aboard the 1987 Adam cruising houseboat with twin 170 hp Detroit diesels. She was sixty feet long with a breadth of twenty feet. Her flying bridge was huge and, according to the previous owner, could hold up to fifty people for a party.

The accommodations included the stateroom with a queen-sized bed, a crew's quarters with two side-by-side single beds, and a sofa bed in the lounge. The boat also had a head with full bathroom facilities. The modern galley was located aft of the living room. The interior was trimmed in a highly glossed teak wood and contained hunter green carpet.

After stowing his gear and going over the houseboat to check it, Moore walked the short distance to Indigo Landing. The low green structure on the banks of the Potomac provided an island-like atmosphere with its overhead paddle fans and teak wood decor. From its large windows, Moore could view the Washington Monument and the Capitol. He also could view the party deck where a local singer was providing island music to the crowd of young Washingtonian office and government workers.

Moore was seated on the first tier and ordered his drink, Pyrat rum and coke. When the waitress returned with his drink, Moore declined her suggestion of a fresh salmon dinner since he wasn't a big salmon fan. Instead, he ordered the day boat scallops with goat cheese polenta and an herb emulsion.

Sipping his drink, Moore's thoughts once again drifted to Kat. She was right – their personal relationship was distracting, and shouldn't go further. For now, he forced himself to think about the task at hand, and planned for his meeting with Nicholas in the morning.

Nicholas' Office
Washington, D.C.

Behind the Supreme Court building was a residential area. It was made up of a collection of homes of varying styles. One townhouse, in particular, on East Capitol Street NE and within a block of the Supreme Court, did its best to blend in with the others. The owner didn't want to attract any undue attention from the outside.

From the inside, though, it was unique amongst the other homes in the area. It had an underground tunnel that connected to the Supreme Court building. It also connected to a tunnel from the Supreme Court building to the Capitol. The tunnels were there so that the home's occupant could easily make his way unnoticed from his residence to testify or consult at closed-door congressional intelligence committee hearings. At times, the intelligence community members would make their way through the tunnels to the owner's home for consultations. The tunnels also provided him access to the service garages beneath the Supreme Court building and the Senate where waiting government vehicles could whisk him away to meetings at The White House.

Steve Nicholas owned this unusual home. He had taken early retirement as Assistant Director of the top secret National Intelligence Agency. Nicholas' career had skyrocketed as he moved from intelligence agency to intelligence agency to strengthen their covert activities. His expertise, at which he was unusually adept, was code-breaking and cyber warfare, but he also had covert field experience early in his career.

In the cluttered office, sunlight was trying to penetrate the partially closed wooden shutters that faced East Capitol Street NE. The office was filled with fine leather chairs, a large mahogany desk and several bookcases. Its walls were filled with pictures of Nicholas with presidents and senior members of Congress.

Moore was pacing as he began to air his frustrations to Nicholas, who was seated behind the large desk. Nicholas split his attention between Moore and the two 22-inch monitors in front of him as his fingers flew across the keyboard.

"Since you got me into this mess, you need to help me out of it," Moore said to his sixty-eight-year-old friend, who looked like he was in his early fifties. His full head of hair and bearded face, which was just starting to show a hint of wrinkles, complimented his trim physique.

"Every now and then rumors swirl anew about the Nazarene's Code. When Kalker asked for help, I thought of you. Never know what you might run into. I just thought it could be an interesting story for your readers," Nicholas noted.

"I certainly hope that my encounter with Yarian and Gorenchenko was not part of your plan," Moore said in a serious tone.

"Of course not. That was unfortunate and brutal. I'm sorry that you had to go through that, but glad that you escaped relatively unfazed."

Rubbing his jaw, Moore said, "They gave me a lingering reminder. I took a pretty hard shot to my jaw while I was being interrogated. It might be cracked."

Nicholas looked up from his monitors. "If you think you have a cracked jaw, you should have it looked at."

"I guess so. Let's just see if the pain continues."

"As far as Yarian and Gorenchenko, I'm sure Andreas will run them down and eliminate any future encounters with them."

"Eliminate?" Moore asked with concern.

"Not that kind of eliminate. I'm sure that he'll have the authorities hold them. I wouldn't expect them to bother you further."

"Did you get a chance to review the notebook?"

"Yes. Good thing you mailed it to me from your hotel in Bodrum."

"After my hotel room break in, I didn't want to chance it disappearing on me. What did you think?" Moore pressed.

"I went through it and it sounds like you're on the right track. It'll be interesting to see what this Bieber woman discovers in Malta."

"I hope that the trail doesn't go cold. Maybe I should join her."

"Up to you, though it certainly sounds like she can handle it herself."

Moore nodded and looked at Nicholas. "Do you trust Kalker?"

Nicholas raised his eyebrows. "What makes you ask?"

"Nothing, really. I actually feel sorry for the guy. You know that he's dying?"

"Yes, I knew. He and I had a very good relationship over the years. There are things which we did together that helped each of our countries."

"Like?"

"I'd have been disappointed if you didn't ask, but some things must stay buried."

Moore nodded and smiled. "I had to try."

"Yes, you did."

"The bad thing too is that his niece is also dying. Inoperable brain tumor."

"An unfortunate coincidence," Nicholas said. "He hadn't told me."

Nicholas stood up. "Emerson, I appreciate the update on your misadventures. Let me give it some additional thought now that we've talked. I'll see if I can come up with any other connections. A lot of it will depend on what Bieber discovers in Malta."

"Yes. It's really our only other lead at this point."

"Oh, there's one other thing I should mention to you. It may be connected to the Nazarene's Code," Nicholas said.

"What's that?"

"The Legend of 13," Nicholas said.

"Kalker mentioned it to me."

"It's something that dates back to the rumors swirling around the Nazarene's Code. Count the letters."

Moore responded, "I know. There are thirteen letters."

"Exactly. If you spent some time in antiquities, you'd learn that for centuries, people have felt there was a link between the Nazarene's Code and the number thirteen. Think about it. Jesus and the twelve disciples. Thirteen present at The Last Supper, which also has thirteen letters. God and the twelve tribes of Israel.

"There's always been a strange aura about the number thirteen. Thirteen colonies formed the United States and our flag has thirteen stripes. The Cuban Missile Crisis lasted thirteen days and there are thirteen letters in the names Osama Bin Laden, Saddam Hussein, Jack the Ripper, Charles Manson, Jeffrey Dahmer and Theodore Bundy." Nichols paused, then added with a mischievous smile, "And don't forget Marilyn Monroe."

Moore chuckled. "You've got too much time on your hands."

"Well, you never know what is a lead and what is coincidence. Just thought you should be aware and consider it as you research this."

"Thanks, Steve. I will. But for now, I'm going to head over to the *Post* and report in, and then I'll head back to Put-in-Bay to wait."

Moore shook hands with his friend and started to walk out of the office.

Nicholas called to Moore. "You realize that I have thirteen letters in my name, don't you?"

Moore quickly counted. "I guess you're right. So, that means that you're part of the solution?"

"Hopefully."

As he walked, Moore said, "There are thirteen letters in Andreas Kalker and Katrina Bieber."

"Interesting."

"And if I include my middle initial, I have thirteen letters in my name," Moore said as he walked to the door.

"That's a bit of a stretch," Nicholas laughed as his friend left.

The Washington Post
Washington, D.C.

After parking his car, Moore walked up 15th Street. He neared the tan brick building, which held the offices of *The Washington Post*. He was carrying a cup of coffee, which he had purchased at Starbucks, located half a block away at the intersection with K Street.

He walked up the four steps and turned left into the lobby.

"Well, aren't you a sight for sore eyes!" exclaimed the slightly overweight, black female security guard, seated in the security booth that guarded the entrance to the elevators.

"Hi Emily," Moore greeted her. "You're going to have to give me a visitor's badge today since mine is missing."

"No problem, we'll have your old one deactivated and replace it today with a new one. You know the drill. Step over here so that I can take a photo of you."

Moore obliged and stepped into the area where a camera had been set up.

Emily adjusted the focus and then looked at Moore. "Say 'Emily, please go on a date with me'."

Moore's face immediately broke into a large smile and Emily depressed the shutter. "Got it," she smiled. "That line works every time."

"But, I'm the only one who would be interested," Moore teased.

"Now, you just go ahead and get yourself out of here," she said as she shooed him toward the elevator door with his visitor badge in hand. "I'll have your replacement badge ready when you leave."

"But, I mean it," Moore yelled as the elevator's doors closed and took him to his floor.

Sure, sure you do, she thought to herself as she smiled. That man is a real heartbreaker, she thought.

When the elevator reached his floor, Moore walked briskly to the entrance to John Sedler's office. Moore's hard-nosed, but soft-hearted editor had his back to the entranceway as he reviewed a story on his monitor.

"John?"

"What is it now?" Sedler grumbled, not realizing it was Moore's voice. Sedler whirled around in his chair. "Emerson! I thought you'd been abducted by aliens!" he teased. "Where have you been? Other than an e-mail from you in Germany, which I might mention was very cryptic, you've been incommunicado."

"I've been…"

"Working on an interesting story. I know. I know," Sedler interrupted as he finished the line he'd heard so many times from his Pulitzer Prize-winning reporter. "What are you chasing now? Some scroll?"

"The Nazarene's Code."

"That's right. Oh, this should be interesting. Go on." Sedler said in a mocking tone. He sat back in his chair and prepared to listen to Moore's story.

Moore told Sedler about his meeting with Kalker, his trip to Haifa and finding the notebook, the research in Bodrum, Gumusluk and Rhodes, and the torture in Bodrum.

"Nasty bit of business," Sedler reacted upon hearing of the torture. "We need to make a few phone calls about that."

"Already handled. Kalker is in touch with his contacts in Turkey. They're tracking down Yarian and Gorenchenko," Moore explained.

Sedler nodded his head. "Then, how did you escape from Bodrum? You didn't have your passport or any money."

Moore smiled. "You're going to get an invoice from Kalker for the cost of our charter flight. He paid for the flight when we landed in Steinbach since I didn't have any cash and the flight operator prefers to do business in cash."

Sedler growled, "I'm sure it wasn't cheap!"

"It was well worth the cost. We didn't know who the good guys were, but I knew I could count on this pilot."

"And your return to the U.S.?"

"Kalker expedited my replacement documents and covered my flight cost here as well as giving me an advance in cash. He'll include all of this on his invoice."

"I'm sure he will." Sedler leaned forward in his chair. "Tell me more about this Nazarene's Code that is costing me so much money."

"Apparently there have been rumors about it for centuries, but no one has been able to track it down. I think we're in the hunt and have a good chance to take it to conclusion. Would be an interesting story."

"It better be," Sedler growled. "Tell me again what this code is about."

"It has the power to change lives."

"That's what people say about the Bible and Zumba, so I'm not sure that there's anything new there," Sedler said dismissedly.

"We don't know until we read it. You know what they say about rumors – there's usually some truth there. Whether or not it's legit, this could be more valuable than the Dead Sea Scrolls, even if for the sheer global curiosity of it."

Sedler shrugged his shoulders.

"Kalker said that it combines the power of heaven and earth to control nations. I'm not sure how that works realistically or logistically, but enough people think there's something to it that murder and torture are involved in the search for it."

"May be nothing more than pabulum!" Sedler said with an air of skepticism. "But it does sound like an interesting story that people would read. I'd like you to stay on top of it and let me know what Bieber learns from her Malta visit."

"Thanks, John. I appreciate the support," Moore said as he stood from the chair in which he had been seated and began to walk towards the doorway.

"And be sure to minimize your costs," Sedler cautioned as he turned back to his monitor.

"I'll do my best."

"I'm counting on it."

Moore walked down the hallway and into his office where he spent the rest of the day pounding out his story on his computer. By seven o'clock, he returned to his houseboat. The next morning, he planned to catch a flight to Cleveland and drive to Put-in-Bay.

Put-in-Bay's Harbor
South Bass Island, Ohio

The 38-foot restored vintage tugboat, *Restless*, motored out of the harbor and began to round Gibraltar Island on one of its chartered sunset cruises. The tug, which had been built in 1938 in Wisconsin, had been redesigned with the addition of an aft cabin, head and sleeping quarters. When one of the owners put her up for sale, Scott Market bought her and brought her to her new homeport at Put-in-Bay's Miller Marina. Market, who jointly owned the Miller Ferry with his siblings, made the craft available for cruises around the Lake Erie Islands.

Onboard, a party was underway. Moore had invited his aunt and Mr. Cassidy, his aunt's boyfriend. Cassidy was two years older than her and was an island farmer, fishing guide and a retired Miller Ferry captain. At the helm of the tug was Scott Market.

"You picked a wonderful evening for a cruise," Market said to Moore, who was standing next to him at the wheel.

"It certainly is turning out that way," Moore agreed. Moore had spent most of the day Googling the Nazarene's Code and potential links to it. His brain was filled to capacity, especially after the call with Kalker and Bieber earlier in the afternoon and subsequent call with Nicholas.

Moore looked down into the aft salon where he could see his aunt and boyfriend enjoying the cheese and bottles of wine, which Market had provided.

"They look like two teenagers," Market observed.

"That's for sure," Moore agreed. "I better join them," he said as he left the pilothouse and walked below. "You two kids having fun?"

"We're off to a good start," his aunt replied with a shy smile.

"We'll be having more fun once we down a couple more glasses of wine," Cassidy chimed in.

Moore took a seat across from them. "I'm glad you're enjoying yourselves."

"Thank you, Emerson," Aunt Anne responded. "It's about time you got back to the island. It seems lately that all you do is travel."

"That goes with my job. But, there's nothing like relaxing here at home in the islands." Moore didn't plan on telling his aunt that he was returning to Washington in the morning. He'd wait until early the next day to tell her.

The little tug plowed through the relatively calm waters to the western side of the island, which offered the best sunset views. Market spun the wheel to position the stern toward the sunset. The boat's three passengers scrambled up the stern ladder to sit on the waiting chairs to enjoy the orange yellow sun's disappearance below a bright blue, cloudless sky. The beautiful sunset signaled the end of another day on the islands.

As they sat, Cassidy asked, "Anne, you think this nephew of yours might also be spending some time with a woman?"

Aunt Anne's head turned and looked at Moore. "Take those sunglasses off. I want to see your eyes when I ask you a question."

Moore reluctantly removed his sunglasses.

"Is he right? Are you off seeing some woman?" his aunt probed.

Moore looked from his aunt to the sunset and back to his aunt before answering. "As a matter of fact..."

Before he could finish, his aunt pronounced, "You don't need to say anything else. That explains why you've been gone so much."

"No, it's not like that at all. I'm working with a woman researcher on a project. She's really smart, and the fact that she's beautiful isn't a problem for me. Are we romantically involved? No, we are not." At least not yet, Moore thought quietly to himself.

"Sure. Sure. I can read those eyes of yours, Emerson. I always could. Ever since you were a boy, your eyes gave you away every time," she retorted with a smile.

"There she goes," Cassidy said as the sun slipped below the

horizon.

They continued their cruise around South Bass Island before returning to port in Put-in-Bay and then returning to Aunt Anne's house.

Moore reflected on his day. Earlier, he had been pacing in his aunt's house, waiting for a response to his latest e-mail to Bieber.

The phone rang and his aunt answered it.

"Emerson, it's for you. Someone named Kat," she said with raised eyebrows and a grin on her face as she handed the receiver to Moore.

"Hello Kat," Moore said as he placed the phone to his ear. He walked out of the house and sat on the dock overlooking the harbor.

"Emerson, great news!"

"Yes, great news," Kalker's voice echoed in the background. "We've got you on the speakerphone."

"What is it?" Moore asked, anxious for more information.

"My research went well and I flew back to Steinbach today."

"Yes?"

"I'll give you the highlights of my research. I met with two archivists and it was probably good that you didn't come with me."

"Why's that?" Moore asked, puzzled.

"They were partial to blondes. So, I probably got more attention and cooperation than if you had accompanied me," she teased.

"I bet," Moore grinned.

"What I learned was that the German knights in the Hospitaller Order fell out of favor with the Grand Master of the Knights Hospitaller in the 1400's. They were banished from the Order. They returned to Germany and enlisted in the Teutonic Knights in Prussia."

"And how does that link into the Nazarene's Code?"

"That's the exciting part, Emerson," she exclaimed. "They were the designated guardians of the Code!"

"But I'm sure the Grand Master would have been aware of it. He wouldn't let them leave with it," Moore pronounced confidently.

"That's where this gets intriguing. The Grand Master was murdered the night that the German Knights slipped away. When the murder was discovered the next morning, a number of Knights were sent after the German Knights, but they never caught up with them because of the head start they had. It appears that they took the Code with them because nothing but rumors swelled around after that time."

"And you got all of this from the two archivists?"

"Yes," Bieber responded.

"Good work."

"That's what I thought," Kalker chimed in.

"So does this take us to Prussia?" Moore asked.

"I've already scheduled a flight there for tomorrow," Bieber announced.

Moore was surprised. It didn't seem as if she was including him. He decided to ask. "Would you like me to meet you there?"

"I think I can do this part myself. It may work better for us if I just go. Look how Malta worked."

Moore knew she was right, but he found himself missing the company of the blonde beauty. He decided to set his emotions aside and support her. "You're right. Besides, I don't speak German."

"Thank you for understanding."

"What about your escorts? Will they accompany you?"

"Of course," she said. "And we didn't run into any trouble from our two characters from Bodrum," she added.

"Good. Andreas, did you hear back from your friends in Turkey?"

"That was another reason for our joint call. I did. Those two are independent contractors. They work for the highest bidder. Most often, they work for the Russians."

"You think the Russians are involved with this?" Moore asked.

"It wouldn't surprise me. My friends in Turkey tell me Yarian and Gorenchenko have vanished. No one can find a trace of them."

"That's not good. Think they went to Moscow?"

"Could be. We're running more checks on them. My friends at Interpol are also helping."

"Kat, I'd suggest you keep looking over your shoulder," Moore commented. "If they're off the radar screen, they could pop up anywhere."

"We'll be careful," she said. "I'll plan on being back here in a few days. If anything earth-shattering comes up, I'll get in touch with both of you right away."

"Happy hunting," Moore said.

"Thanks, Emerson."

They ended their call. Moore set the phone on the dock and looked across the harbor. His mind replayed the conversation that had just ended.

Emerson reached for the phone and called Steve Nicholas to update him.

Nicholas' Office
The Next Day

The door buzzed open and Moore entered Nicholas' townhouse. He walked past the closed office door of Nicholas' assistant, Jody Walker, to Nicholas' office.

"How was the flight?"

"Good. I dropped my gear at my place and came right over," Moore responded. "Is Jody in today? I seem to keep missing her," Moore said as he thought about the attractive, 40-ish assistant. Moore had always been impressed by her positive demeanor and can-do attitude. "She always energizes me when I visit."

"She's out having her nails done," Nicholas replied. He was very liberal in giving his top assistant time off to accomplish personal business.

Moore sat down. "So, what did you learn?"

"Let me start with your two captors. They're bad news."

"That doesn't surprise me at all. Kalker said they were independent contractors."

"Andreas was right and they are working for the Russians."

"So, the Russians are in the chase?"

"Yes, they are. I'm going to call Andreas and discuss it with him. I'm also going to discuss it in more detail with some of my friends here."

"In the intelligence agencies? Think they'll help us?" Moore's questions spewed out of his mouth.

"Officially, they can't help. They can't get involved in something like the Nazarene's Code. But unofficially, they may be able to give me some information." Nicholas looked at his monitor and back at Moore. "And, you know, you can't…"

"Publish their involvement," Moore finished. He had heard it so many times from Nicholas over the years.

"I also did some research on the Order of Teutonic Knights as I promised."

"And?"

"I won't bore you with the little details. But they originated with the Teutons, a Germanic tribe with links to the Danes. In fact, their flag and the flag of the Knights Templar have the same colors as the Danish flag."

Moore nodded as he listened.

"There were numerous territorial battles as they expanded

their area of influence. Playing off the Legend of 13, I saw that, on 9/13/1309, they acquired the castles of Danzig, Schwitz and Dirschau. Don't think that has any impact on my analysis, but I thought I'd just mention it. By the way, there are thirteen when you count King Arthur and his twelve Knights of the Round Table."

"There's the thirteen stuff again," Moore grinned.

"I also noticed that the Knights Templar in France were arrested on Friday, October 13, 1307. That started the superstition of Friday the 13th as being bad luck."

"Once again."

Nicholas looked closely at Moore before offering the next tidbit of information. "You might be interested to know that Andreas Kalker is also a Teutonic Knight."

"Interesting. Is that a bad thing?" Moore asked.

"I don't think so. Andreas has a vested interest as a member of the order to understand where the Nazarene's Code went. It will help underscore his commitment to finding it. It seems to be a good thing."

Nicholas paused for a moment before continuing. "There's a guy you should meet."

"Oh? Who?"

"His name is Reggie Lawsons. Lives in London. His cover is a communications worker, but he's really employed by British Secret Intelligence, MI6, in Vauxhall. He has an apartment across the Thames in Pimlico. It's in central London."

"And he can help me?"

"I believe so. But you need to meet him in person. Here's his e-mail address." Nicholas scribbled down the address and handed it to Moore. "Get in contact with him and see if you can meet. I know Reggie. I'll call him and update him on your search for the Nazarene's Code. I'll suggest he help you as much as he can without getting himself in trouble."

"How is he going to help me?"

"He works in Section 13 and has thirteen letters in his name."

Moore rolled his eyes and smiled. "And how does that help me?"

"Section 13 works on cyber coding and cyber warfare. It is one of MI6's most elite groups; it's staffed with nothing less than the brightest minds in the service. Reggie has access to all kinds of data. On top of that, he's an antiquities hobbyist."

"Why can't I just talk to him on the phone?" Moore asked.

"Phones can be tapped. He'll be more relaxed talking to you in person. He may have documents to show that he wouldn't mention over the phone," Nicholas replied.

"Well, London it is, then. I'll grab my umbrella."

"Emerson, ever have your future read with Tarot cards?"

"No, why?"

"Thought you'd be interested to know that the thirteenth card represents death."

Moore shrugged as he stood. "I'm not much into superstition, though I'll keep that in mind during my research."

"Good luck," Nicholas said. "Keep me posted."

"Will do," Moore said as he left the townhouse and returned to his houseboat in Alexandria. He e-mailed Lawsons and made arrangements to meet. He also called Bieber and Kalker to let them know where he was going and why.

St. George's Hotel
Central London

The taxi pulled to a stop in front of the hotel's entrance at 25 Belgrave Road and the passenger paid the fare.

"Thank you very much," he said as he exited the cab with his suitcase and walked into the ornate hotel, which occupied two restored 19th-century buildings. The hotel was near the Vauxhall Bridge, which spanned the Thames, and was a block away from Victoria Station.

"Welcome to St. George's Hotel. May I help you?" the front desk clerk asked.

"Yes. I believe you have a reservation in my name. It's for Emerson Moore," he said as he set his suitcase on the counter top.

The clerk looked through his system and said, "Yes, we have it. If I could see your passport, please, and a credit card?"

As the man reached for them, the suitcase slipped and fell onto the clerk's side of the counter and then onto the floor. The man's wallet slipped from his hand and the contents fell on the floor next to him.

"I am so sorry, Mr. Moore," the clerk said as he bent to pick up the suitcase.

Flustered with the amount of cards in his hand that he needed to refile in his wallet, the man asked, "Could you send the suitcase up to my room right away? I'll get my wallet in order and then be back with it."

"Certainly, Mr. Moore," he said to the distraught gentleman across from him. "Front!" he called to the bellman. "Take this suitcase to Room 637."

"Here you go," the man said as he slipped a pound note in the bellman's hand.

"Thank you, sir."

"Was there a package delivered for me?" the man asked as he held tightly to his credit cards and wallet.

The front desk clerk looked in the cabinet behind the counter and said, "Yes. Here it is. Would you sign here, please?" He handed the man a clipboard and showed him where to sign.

The man signed, picked up the package and said, "Let me get organized for a moment. I'll be right back." He picked up the package and walked to a nearby chair where he began to sort through his credit cards.

Two more taxis arrived and deposited guests, who walked to the hotel desk. After checking in the first arrivals, the clerk turned to a tall, tanned man, who had just arrived. "Welcome to St. George's Hotel. May I help you?"

Setting his duffel bag on the floor, the man introduced himself. "I'm Emerson Moore. You should have my reservation."

Moore found himself faced with a clerk with a bewildered look on his face. "Is there a problem?" Moore asked.

"It looks like we have two Emerson Moores staying with us

tonight," the clerk stated. "The other one is seated over there."

Moore turned to where the clerk was looking and smiled as he saw nothing more than two empty chairs. "My twin must be invisible because I don't see anyone."

"He was right there." The clerk, closely followed by Moore, walked to the chairs and looked down the hallway. It ended with an exit onto St. George's Drive. "He's gone."

Moore smiled. "No problem. Now, let's get me checked in."

"But you don't understand, Mr. Moore. I gave him the package which was delivered today for us to hold until you arrived."

"Now, that is a problem," Moore fretted. "Didn't you check his identification?"

"In the confusion of dropping his suitcase and wallet, I didn't. It's not how we do things here, Mr. Moore."

Moore could barely contain his irritation. "I know it isn't. I've stayed here before. I'd like to report this to the police and your general manager."

"I understand." The clerk nervously called the hotel's general manager and then turned to Moore. "He'll be here within five minutes. He's ringing up the police first. Let me get you checked in." The clerk worked quickly and processed Moore.

Moore looked at his watch. "Your manager seems to be running late. Let me take my bag to the room and I'll be right back. We need to clear this up."

"Certainly, Mr. Moore," the clerk said as he handed the keys to room 637 to Moore. "I'll call him again and make sure he's here when you come back down."

"Good." Moore walked over to the elevator and pushed the button for the sixth floor.

Moments later, the clerk rang Moore's room to tell him about the suitcase which had been delivered there earlier. There was no answer as Moore was still on the elevator.

Five minutes later, an explosion destroyed room 637.

"Oh no!" the general manager said from where he stood at the front desk with the clerk, awaiting Moore's return. The explosion had reverberated throughout the two buildings.

The two policemen, who had been dispatched to take the theft report, rushed into the lobby. When he saw them, the general manager beckoned them to follow him up the stairs. At each landing, they opened the door to each floor and checked the hallways. When they reached the sixth floor, they encountered thick smoke from the fire that had originated in room 637. They cautiously eased themselves onto the sixth floor, checking each room for occupants and directing them to the stairwell.

When they reached room 637, they couldn't enter the room as the fire raged. They did hear the sirens from approaching fire trucks, responding to the explosion. The two police officers and the general manager continued their way down the hallway and assisted guests in walking to a fire exit at the other end of the hall.

Within thirty minutes, the fire had been brought under control and the firemen were continuing their room-to-room evacuation of the building. The desk clerk was fervishly assigning guests to rooms in the adjoining building when a familiar voice said, "I guess I'll need another room, too."

The clerk looked up and saw Moore. His face paled upon recognizing him. "Mr. Moore, you're okay!" he exclaimed.

"Yes. But, I can't say the same for my room."

The general manager appeared at Moore's side in response to the clerk's beckoning. "Your visit today has been very extraordinary. I'm so sorry."

"I agree," Moore grinned.

"May I ask how you escaped the blast?"

"Sometimes, it pays to be a gentleman. This kind lady next to me," Moore pointed to an elderly lady in a wheelchair, "needed assistance in getting to her room on the fourth floor. I offered to roll her to her room. Good thing for me."

The lady looked up to the manager and firmly said, "I want you to know that I do not make a habit of asking younger men to my room." She looked at the handsome American and continued as she winked at Moore, "But today, I made an exception."

"And am I ever glad you did," Moore responded as he returned the wink. "She's going to need a room, too."

"Make it adjoining," she teased.

"But, of course," the general manager said as he motioned for the clerk to accommodate both of his guests. "Mr. Moore, could you meet with me in an hour? Things will have settled down and I'll have the police here to take your report."

"Yes, I need to get that package," Moore said as he took the keys for his new room and for the lady's room. He turned to the lady. "Would you like me to take you to your room?"

The lady's face was filled with a big grin and she gave him a coy look. "Most certainly, young man."

Looks like I have a real cougar on my hands, Moore thought good-naturedly to himself. "Then, it's off we go."

After helping the lady to her room, Moore went to his new room, set his duffel bag on the bed, and sat in a chair. It was near the window and overlooked the array of fire trucks, police cars and ambulances below. It was the first time that he had sat down in some time. As he relaxed, he thought about how close he had come to being blown to pieces. This assignment had turned from dangerous to deadly. A shudder ran through his body as he reached for his cell phone and called Bieber.

She answered on the second ring. "Hi, Emerson. You're in London?"

"Yes."

"Good. Get my package?"

"Not so good," he replied. He then recounted the events of the last hour.

"Oh, great! I bet it was our two buddies."

"I don't think so. It sounded like it was someone more sophisticated."

"Then, it may have been the Russians," she deduced.

"That's what I thought."

"I can duplicate the file, but I'll personally deliver it."

"You don't need to do that," Moore protested. "I'd love to see you, but I don't want to put you in danger."

"I don't mind a little danger. Besides, it'll give me a chance to see you." She paused before continuing. "I've missed being with you."

"Oh?"

There was another pause. "Well, you're kind of fun to hang out with."

Moore smiled at the provocative tone she used. "I'm glad that you feel that way."

"I bet you are," she teased. "I'll text you and let you know when my flight arrives. It may not be until later tonight or tomorrow morning."

"I'll be watching for your text. And trying to track down who-ever took that package."

Moore set his cell phone on the table and looked at his watch. It was time for him to go to his meeting with Lawsons.

Lawsons' Apartment
Pimlico in Central London

There was no response to Moore's knock on the dark brown door on the top floor flat. "Lawsons, are you home?" Moore called as he checked his watch to make sure that the time was right.

Out of the corner of his eye, he saw something amiss with the doorknob. The wood surrounding the latch was splintered. More splinters lay on the floor of the hallway. It was as if someone had tried to force his or her way into the modest flat. Moore pushed gently on the door and it swung open.

"Lawsons?" Moore called. "Are you home?"

A movement on his left caught Moore's attention, He swung around quickly and then relaxed. A small breeze blowing through the open window had caused the drapes to move.

"Lawsons," Moore called. "Are you here?"

Moore looked around the flat and saw that several chairs were overturned as if a scuffle had taken place. Emerson moved cautiously from the living area to the rear bedroom. It was empty. He then began to push open the door to the small bathroom.

When the door opened, his eyes focused on his grim discovery. It was a gruesome sight. Lawsons' body, or what was left of it, was in the bathtub. The body's appendages had been removed and could be seen sticking out of the top of a sports bag next to the tub. Blood was everywhere.

Moore peered at the lifeless eyes. They were rolled back in the victim's head. The head had a large lump on the temple. The chest was peppered with stab wounds. Moore surmised that the assailant had forced his way into the flat, struck Lawsons with a blunt object and was dismembering the body when his knock interrupted him.

Backing out of the bathroom, Moore walked around the flat, looking for any clues that might help him. On a small desk, he saw a docking station for a laptop, but the laptop was missing. Taken by the assailant, Moore guessed.

He made a cursory inspection of the rest of the flat, but didn't find anything of interest. He walked over to the landline phone and dialed the operator.

"May I help you?"

"Yes, you can. Could you call the police and let them know that someone has been murdered in this flat?" Moore provided the address.

"Yes, I'll call them straight away."

Moore replaced the receiver and walked over to the open window. It opened onto a fire escape, which Moore surmised served as the assailant's escape route. He leaned through the window and filled his lungs with fresh air. This was becoming a day full of surprises.

Moore had been standing there no more than ten minutes when he heard noise at the front door, announcing the arrival of the police. He turned and began to walk toward the doorway.

Three police officers entered the flat.

Moore spoke first. "You'll find the body in there," Moore said as he pointed to the bathroom door that was slightly ajar.

One officer approached Moore. "And who might you be?" he asked firmly.

"I had an appointment with Lawsons. When I arrived, I saw that the door had been forced open."

"And you entered the crime scene?"

"Officer, I didn't realize it was a crime scene. Yes, I entered the flat."

Before he could continue with his questions, a man in a suit entered the room. The officer quickly updated the man, who occasionally looked around him and at Moore. When the officer finished, the man thanked him and motioned to Moore to take a seat. The man took one of the overturned chairs and righted it, then sat on it.

"I'm Inspector John Richardson. And you are?"

"Emerson Moore."

"Could I see your identification, please?"

Moore handed his passport to Richardson, who quickly reviewed it and returned it to Moore.

"Tell me what brings you to a meeting with our departed Mr. Lawsons."

"He was going to answer a few questions for me about an old legend that I've been tracking down."

"So, you are an antiquities researcher?"

"In a way. I research all sorts of topics," Moore responded.

"What exactly do you do, Mr. Moore?"

"I'm an investigative reporter for *The Washington Post*," Moore explained.

"I see," Richardson said as he scribbled notes on a pad that he produced from his inside suit pocket.

"Excuse me, inspector. There're two men here from MI6," an officer, who had approached Richardson, whispered in the inspector's ear.

Richardson nodded his head. "I'll be right there." He turned to Moore and said, "If you could excuse me for a moment."

"Sure. No problem," Moore said.

The inspector walked into the hallway outside of the apartment's entrance door where he talked briefly with the two officials from MI6, who had been notified of Lawsons' death.

"I understand," Richardson said. He turned and called to his officers. "Let's go, boys. This one is out of our jurisdiction."

The police officers cleared the apartment and were replaced by investigators and a clean up team from MI6. As Richardson was leaving, he updated the two senior MI6 officers about Emerson Moore.

They thanked him as he left and one used his cell phone to make a call to MI6 about Moore. The other walked into the room where Moore was sitting and said, "If you could be a bit patient with us, we'll get back to you shortly."

Over the next sixty minutes Moore sat in the chair and observed what he could as the investigators scoured the apartment for clues. The MI6 officer, who had talked with him earlier, returned to stand in front of Moore.

"Mr. Moore."

"Yes."

"Other than the e-mails which you had sent to Mr. Lawsons, did you have any other contact with him?"

"No." These guys were good. They had apparently scanned Lawsons' e-mail records, Moore thought.

"You had no other contact with him?"

"None."

"And who helped you in setting up this meeting with Mr. Lawsons?"

"Steve Nicholas. He's a friend…"

"We know of Mr. Nicholas," the officer said as he interrupted Moore.

– 165 –

"Any idea of who would do such a thing to Mr. Lawsons?"

"No. A package of information that was meant for me was stolen. It may have contained information that included Lawsons' name. I don't know."

"And you reported this theft to the police?"

"Yes."

"Why don't you give me a high level overview of what you've been working on and how you expected Lawsons to help you?"

Before Moore could start, the other senior M16 officer walked into the room. He motioned for the other one to join him near the window where they talked in hushed tones. Moore overheard them mention Nicholas' name and guessed that someone in M16 had been in touch with Nicholas.

The two officers returned to stand in front of Moore. The one, who had been asking the questions, said, "You may leave now, Mr. Moore. If anything comes to mind which you believe we should know, please give me a call." He handed Moore his business card.

"Be glad to help in any way that I can," Moore said as he rose from his chair and headed toward the apartment's door. He was grateful that Nicholas was able to extricate him from this mess. He made a mental note to call him to thank him.

St. George's Hotel
Central London

Nicholas had been quiet throughout Moore's recap of the day's events. He had asked a few questions and was ready with an overall comment. "Today's events certainly turn this up several notches. I'm sure the Russians are behind this, but I don't know what drives them to this level. What has driven them to make an attempt on your life and kill Reggie? This baffles me."

"Me, too," Moore agreed. "We must be getting too close to something big."

"I'm going to conference Andreas onto our call. Hold on." Nicholas was able to connect with Kalker and brought him into the call.

"Hello, Emerson."

"Andreas," Moore responded.

"Steve tells me that you have some interesting developments to share with me. Katrina did call me and tell me about the attempt on your life at your hotel, but please tell me. I'd like to hear it in your own words."

After Moore quickly recapped the day's events, Nicholas asked, "What do you make of this, Andreas?"

"It makes me curious on several fronts. First, how did the Russians know that you were staying at the St. Georges Hotel and why would they try to kill you – or was it meant as a warning? Second, how did they know that a package was being delivered to you? Third, why did they kill Lawsons and was there anything on his stolen computer? I would be surprised if there was. The Brits are so careful about securing data. Most of all, why are the Russians killing people over this?"

"My exact thoughts," said Nicholas. "Do you think Karapashev is behind this?"

Kalker paused as he thought. "He might be. I heard his name surface when I made my initial inquiries. Let me check with my contacts and probe further. I wouldn't be surprised to hear if he is involved."

Moore was agitated. "This really is going too far. Why are they murdering people? I want Katrina out of this mess now."

"There must be more to this Nazarene's Code than we realize. Andreas, your thoughts?" Nicholas asked.

"I've been trying to figure that out myself since we started this conversation. Let me think more about this and get back to you. As for Katrina – she makes her own decisions."

"Have you heard from her?" Moore asked. He was worried.

"Not recently. When she called me, she was on her way to the airport. She's flying in early tonight."

"Let's wrap this up. Andreas, you're going to follow up to see if Karapashev is pulling any of the strings on this search for the Nazarene's Code and, more importantly, his potential involvement in today's events."

"Yes. I'll get back in touch with you within twenty-four hours."

"Good, we can get back together on a call then."

The three ended the call and Moore saw a text message on his cell. He opened it and read that Bieber would be arriving at the hotel by seven o'clock. He texted back and offered dinner. When he didn't receive a reply, he assumed she was in midflight. He decided to take a shower and try to relax.

The events of the day had taken an emotional toll on him. He selected his attire for the evening and touched them up with an iron that he found in his room. He then stripped and headed to the bathroom where he turned on the water in the shower stall.

When it was hot, he entered the stall and allowed the hot stream to run over his muscular body. The water was invigorating, helping to release the day's tension. He lathered up and washed his body and hair. When he was done, he shut off the shower and stepped on to the ceramic floor. Briskly drying himself, he plopped on his bed and quickly fell into a deep sleep.

Two hours later, his cell phone began to ring. Moore rolled over in the bed and reached for his cell phone. "Hello?"

"Emerson, it's Kat. I'm in my room."

Moore sat up and turned so that his legs hung over the bed's edge. "Great."

"Give me five minutes and I'll meet you in the lobby."

"Sounds like a plan," Moore said. "See you in a few." Moore slipped into his khakis and a soft yellow, casual dress shirt. From his shaving kit, he withdrew a small bottle of Calvin Klein's *Obsession for Men* and splashed some on his face. He looked in the mirror and quickly ran his comb through his thick, dark hair. Looking good, he thought to himself as he left the room and hurried to the elevator.

The doors to the elevator opened in the lobby and Bieber stepped out. From across the lobby, Moore, who was seated in a chair, stood and allowed his breath to escape at the sight of the woman walking toward him. Her blonde hair flowed in soft curls over her shoulders and her trademark pink lipstick accented her heart-melting smile. Her low cut, blue knit sweater accentuated her blue eyes. Her khaki miniskirt and tan heels highlighted her tanned legs.

"Emerson," she smiled as she floated across the lobby toward him.

Moore beamed as he closed the distance between them. They

exchanged hugs and she gave him a small peck on the cheek. He was breathless, speechless.

"Hmmm. Somebody smells good," Bieber purred as she nuzzled Moore's neck and smelled his cologne.

"Thanks." He didn't want to release her from his arms. "It seems like it's been forever since I've seen you."

"It does," she agreed. "Miss me?"

Looking into those deep blues of hers, Moore could only nod.

"I missed you, too," Bieber said. She locked her arm with his arm. "Let's go get something to eat. I'm famished."

Moore nodded and the two walked through the lobby's exit doors. "How does fish sound to you?"

"Das ist gut" she replied.

"So far, that's the only German I know. I'm guessing it means 'that is good.' Right?"

She nodded. "I will teach you more later."

"You can teach me anything you want. For now, let's go to a place called Seafresh. It's about two blocks from here."

They walked down Warwick Way and turned left at Wilton Street. "This is it," Moore pronounced as he steered her inside the pub with a wooden façade.

The maitre'd escorted them through the crowded restaurant to a table at the rear and handed them menus. Within a minute a waiter appeared at their table to take their drink orders.

"This sounds interesting," she said. "What is this unoaked chardonnay Corvinus?"

The waiter replied, "It's one of our specialty wines. It's from Hungary. It has the flavor of ripe peaches from the hills above the Danube. Very good. Very creamy."

"I'll try it."

"And you, sir?"

"Bacardi and Coke."

The waiter nodded and disappeared.

"Rum and Coke? You're not too adventurous tonight," she teased.

"Oh, I'm adventurous tonight," he retorted good-naturedly. "Just not for wine."

She smiled back at the handsome Moore as she read between the lines. "We better look at the menu so we can get down to business," she said as she shifted gears.

Within minutes the waiter returned with their drinks and asked for their meal selections.

Bieber ordered first. "I'll start with the fresh Scotch salmon salad and then I'll have the deep fried calamari."

"Thank you. And you, sir?" the waiter asked.

"I'll try the roast chicken salad and the haddock fillet."

"Thank you. It shouldn't be long." The waiter scurried away to place their orders.

Bieber raised her glass to Moore. "To our adventures," she said as she looked over the rim.

Moore raised his rum and toasted, "May they be safe adventures."

Taking a drink from the beverages, they set them on the table as Bieber leaned toward Moore. "So, tell me. You haven't said anything about your meeting with Lawsons."

Moore paused before answering and gazed at the pretty face staring across the table at him. "Your uncle didn't tell you? This could ruin your meal."

"No. Now, what? Tell me. I can stomach it."

Moore recounted the circumstances surrounding Lawsons' death.

When he finished, Bieber said, "How awful! That's absolutely horrible."

Nodding his head, Moore agreed, "It was. He wasn't even officially a part of this investigation, and look what happened to him."

Bieber nodded. "And now we don't have the data he was going to provide us."

Moore nodded as the waiter arrived with their salads and main dishes.

"Did you get any leads on your visit to Prussia?"

She shook her head. "It was very frustrating. I couldn't find anything," she responded in an irritated tone.

"Great. Our trail just went cold," Moore lamented.

They continued to chat and finished their meal. After paying the bill, Moore watched as Bieber withdrew her lipstick from her pocket and took off the cap. She then applied it to her full lips.

Noticing that Moore seemed captivated by her application, she remarked, "Never leave home without it."

"I'd second that," Moore said appreciatively.

The two walked out of the Seafresh restaurant and walked toward Warwick Way. They didn't notice that a taxi pulled away from the curb and began to follow them. As they began to walk onto Warwick Way, a man stopped them on the sidewalk.

"Excuse me, folks. Might I bother you for a light?" he asked.

The taxi had also stopped and the driver and passenger exited the taxi. They rushed up and behind Moore and Bieber, plunging their syringes into their necks. Moore and Bieber crumbled to the ground.

"Here, give me a hand," Yarian ordered the man who had stopped the couple.

Gorenchenko had already picked up Bieber and was carrying her to the taxi, which he had stolen earlier and was driving.

Working together, the two carried Moore to the cab and they dumped him onto the floor next to Bieber. Yarian and the man sat in the back of the taxi so that they could keep an eye on their two captives.

Gorenchenko turned left onto Warwick Way and the taxi headed to a warehouse across the Thames River in the Pennington Park light industrial complex.

"Wake up!" Gorenchenko's gruff voice ordered as he threw a bucket of cold water in Moore's face.

The shock of the cold water on Moore's nude body brought Moore to a conscious state. Moore looked down and saw that he was once again restrained Gorenchenko-style in a chair.

"Not again," he mumbled, angry at himself for not being more aware and careful.

He moved his feet and realized that they weren't submersed in a bucket of water.

Moore scanned his surroundings and noted that he was in a fairly clean warehouse. There was a closed office door and a wooden garage door. Inside and in front of the garage door was parked the stolen taxi. There were pallets filled with boxes throughout the dark warehouse. Only the lights over them were turned on.

Moore heard a groan and looked to his right where he saw Bieber, lying on the floor. Her feet were bound and her hands were tied in front of her.

"Where's your partner in crime?" Moore asked when he saw the giant step in front of him.

"You'll find out soon enough," Gorenchenko chortled as he stared at the beautiful woman on the floor. Gorenchenko walked over to the woman. "You and I have some unfinished business," he said as he looked at her ravenously.

Bieber returned his look with an icy stare.

Gorenchenko pointed his head toward Moore and said, "If you don't cooperate with me, I'll be glad to perform surgery on your friend." Gorenchenko produced a knife and opened it. "This time he won't get away."

"Don't touch him," she warned from her prostrate position on the floor.

"You think you're going to cut me up the way you did Lawsons?" Moore asked unexpectedly.

Anger flashed in Gorenchenko's eyes. "So you figured that out?" He looked from Moore to Bieber and back. "I'm going to cut you up into smaller pieces. Take my time."

Moore smiled inwardly that he was able to bait Gorenchenko so easily. "Too bad you ran off like a scared rabbit when I got there," Moore prodded.

A deep laugh emitted from Gorenchenko. "Look who's talking? You are the little rabbit. You run from us, but we track you down. You can never get away from us, little rabbit." Gorenchenko laughed as he turned and approached Moore with the blade pointed at Moore's neck. "Let's see if I can make this rabbit scream."

Moore tensed his body as he prepared to launch himself at Gorenchenko. But Gorenchenko saw Moore lean forward and anticipated the launch. He deftly stepped aside as Moore launched his body and missed Gorenchenko.

Gorenchenko laughed so hard his belly fat was shaking. "Oh! The rabbit tries to take down the lion! You are so amusing and pathetic," Gorenchenko said.

Moore tried to roll over, but he felt excruciating pain in his left arm. He hoped he hadn't broken it when he landed.

Gorenchenko knelt over Moore, pinning him to the ground with one hand as he placed the tip of the knife under Moore's chin. "Please. Try that move again."

"Let him go. I'll do whatever you want," Bieber called from across the room.

Gorenchenko paused and pulled the knife blade back from Moore's neck. "Anything?" he asked ominously.

"Anything," she said softly in a submissive tone.

Gorenchenko stood and walked toward Bieber.

"There's only one thing I need," she said as she rolled onto her side so that her back was facing Gorenchenko. Her skirt had slid up, exposing more of her firm thighs.

"What's that?"

"My lipstick. It's in my back pocket if you could get it for me."

"Don't Kat. You don't need to do anything for me," Moore groaned.

"This is for us," she said.

Gorenchenko chuckled and raised an eyebrow. "Well," he said gruffly, "I'm glad you want to pretty yourself up for me, but you don't need to."

"Yes, I do," Kat replied as Gorenchenko kneeled next to her. Before reaching into her pocket, he ran his hand over her firm buttocks.

"Nice," he said as his hand reached into one of the pockets and extracted her lipstick. "Pink," he said as she rolled to a sitting position.

Bieber didn't respond. With an icy look that could have frozen hell, she took the lipstick tube from Gorenchenko. "With my hands tied, it's rather difficult for me to take off the top. Could you?"

Gorenchenko moved in closer and removed the top of the lipstick tube. As he did, she quickly pointed the tube at his forehead and depressed the hidden trigger in its base.

There was a popping noise as the lipstick gun fired the bullet squarely into Gorenchenko's forehead. His face filled with surprise as he dropped the knife and fell over. He was dead.

A smile crossed Bieber's face as she looked from the fallen Gorenchenko to Moore. "Like I told you, lipstick is a woman's best friend."

She reached for Gorenchenko's knife and scooted across the floor to Moore.

"Where did you get that?" Moore asked in disbelief.

"My uncle," she replied. "He gave these to his female agents when he was working. And had a few at the house. He wanted me to have extra protection."

"Glad it didn't go off when we dined together," Moore said as she held the knife in her two bound hands and sawed away at Moore's restraints. He was surprised that she showed no remorse or emotional response for killing Gorenchenko. "Are you okay?"

Bieber didn't respond right away. "I guess I am. I surprised myself," she said. "I never thought I'd actually have to use it. Look at me. I just killed someone and I seem to be fine. Must be the adrenaline."

"Must be," Moore agreed. "Nice shot by the way."

"Thanks. My uncle coached me on that. He said if I ever had to use it that I should get as close as possible and aim for the forehead. I just did what he told me to do."

"This has been a day full of strange happenings."

"I'll say. Look at you now. Naked again," she giggled.

"Yeah, and for all the wrong reasons," Moore commented as his hands were freed. He took the knife and cut the restraints on her hands and feet. She then finished freeing Moore.

Moore rolled over and seeing his clothes, began to dress himself. "Check the office and see what's in there. Yarian and his other friend could be returning at any moment."

Leaving the office door open, Bieber began to rummage through the office. "Found a couple of laptops," she said.

Moore joined her in the office. "That one is mine, the one stolen in Turkey." He looked at the other laptop. "I wonder if this one is Lawsons' laptop." He picked up both laptops. "See anything else of interest?"

"No."

"We need to get out of here." Moore walked over to the taxi and looked inside. "The keys are in the ignition."

"I'll get the door." She ran over to the door and depressed the button to raise the doors. She quickly returned to the taxi and they roared out of the building. Moore quickly oriented himself and drove back to the hotel.

When they returned to the hotel, he parked the taxi in front and pulled out his wallet. He extracted the card from Inspector Richardson and called him from the front desk. He quickly related what had transpired and provided the address to the Pennington Park warehouse.

"We'll send investigators to the warehouse. I'd like to come over right now to talk with the two of you and pick up Lawsons' laptop," Richardson said.

"Sure. We'll be right here or in the bar."

"Good. I'll be there within ten minutes."

Moore turned to Bieber. "Richardson is coming over. He wants to interview both of us and pick up Lawsons' laptop."

Bieber cast a glance at the clock in the lobby. It showed a few minutes after midnight. "This has been a long day."

"I'll say. It's been one of the longest days in my life," Moore concurred. "How about a drink?"

"Long overdue," she responded as they headed toward the bar off of the lobby.

They had been barely served their drinks when Richardson and another inspector walked into the bar. After introductions, Richardson started his interview.

"Quite an evening for you two, it sounds," Richardson commented.

"Yes, it has been," Moore said as Bieber nodded her head.

"Okay, let's take it from the top," Richardson said.

The two took turns explaining what had happened from the time they left the hotel until they had returned. From time to time, Richardson or the other inspector would interrupt and ask questions.

When they had completed relaying the evening's events, Richardson looked at Bieber. "Could I see your lipstick?"

"Sure. I haven't had a chance to reload it," she said as she handed it to him.

"And I doubt you will since we have to keep it temporarily as evidence," Richardson said as he looked at the weapon. "Very clever. Very clever, indeed." He dropped it in a plastic bag that he produced from his pocket.

Richardson then turned to Moore. "And which laptop is Lawsons?"

Handing the laptop to Richardson, Moore said, "Here you go. The other one is mine."

Richardson passed it to the other inspector and looked at the two people in front of him. "Tell me now. What are you plans for tomorrow?"

"I have a noon flight from Gatwick back to D.C.," Moore responded. "Here's my card with my cell number if you have any additional questions for me."

Richardson looked at Bieber. "That shouldn't be a problem. Miss?"

"I fly back to Germany tomorrow morning from Heathrow. I have an early flight. It's at eight o'clock."

"That is a problem. I'll need you to postpone your flight at least until the afternoon. We'll want to take additional statements from you since you killed Mr. Gorenchenko. Nothing more than routine paperwork. Can you change your flight?"

"I can do that."

"Good. Be at my office at ten o'clock sharp." Richardson handed her his business card as he and the other inspector stood. "I hope the rest of the evening goes better for both of you." He said as the two officers left the bar.

"Me, too," Moore said as they walked away and he finished his drink. "Ready for bed?"

"Long overdue."

Moore picked up his laptop and carried it with him as they walked to the elevator.

"You'll need to stop by my room so I can give you the replacement package," Bieber said as the elevator doors opened.

"Sure. I'd like to have it."

The elevator reached her floor and they walked to her room. Bieber inserted her keycard and unlocked the door. For a moment, Moore thought he saw a movement to his right. He swiveled his head to look, but didn't see anything. He put if off to being tired.

Bieber, closely followed by Moore, walked into her room, which was dominated by a king-size bed. Moore glanced at the bed and Bieber noticed.

"Oh, Emerson, what am I ever going to do with you?" she asked provocatively with a raised eyebrow.

"I can think of several things. What did you have in mind?" he asked with an expectant grin as he looked from the bed to the seductive blonde.

"Emerson, Emerson, Emerson," she repeated.

"Yes?" he asked with eager anticipation.

"We do need to call this a night. We both have had a tremendous strain today and flights tomorrow. As difficult as it is for me to say, I must say goodnight."

Moore couldn't hide the disappointment from his face. "Kat, hear me out. I know we can't get too distracted until our research is over, and that you don't have much time. But whatever time you have left, I'd like to share it with you. I'm – falling for you. You're strong and smart and beautiful and – you tan well all over. Not to mention you saved my life." He laughed, trying to lighten the mood.

Bieber said nothing as she handed the package to Moore. He took it and looked at her expectantly.

"I pour my heart out to you and this is all I get in return?" he pleaded.

She gave him a quick peck on the cheek and said, "I just – can't. Not right now. I'm sorry. It wasn't my plan for this evening to end this way." She looked down.

"Nor mine," Moore said gruffly as he forced himself to leave. "Thanks for the package. I'll be in touch."

"I'm counting on it," she said as she closed the door.

Moore returned to his room where he washed cold water over his face and tried to clear his mind. He checked his laptop. None of his files had been deleted. He once again was glad that he had kept all critical information on his flash drive. He opened the package from Bieber and saw the file on the results of her research of the Teutonic Knights. He decided he'd review it on the flight home.

He called the front desk and scheduled a wake up call for the morning. He then disrobed and dropped onto his bed, exhausted. Within minutes, he was in a deep sleep.

"All is not lost," Nicholas said to Moore, who had been pacing the office in frustration.

"What do you mean? I didn't get a chance to talk with Lawsons."

"There's one thing about Reggie that you don't know."

"What's that?"

"He always planned for the unexpected. He always had a back up in place. Taking what you learned from the Bieber woman and her plans to visit Prussia to follow up on the Teutonic Knights, he conducted a data base search of his country's records and then Germany's records. The Brits are almost as anal as the Germans in recordkeeping. He e-mailed me his search results."

"Great! Did you see anything interesting?"

"Yes, I did. He was able to trace a young Mason of German and English descent, who may have transported the Nazarene's Code to the United States."

"Now that's progress. Give me his contact information and I'll interview him."

"That's going to be difficult to do."

"What do you mean?"

"He's dead."

"What? How do you know?"

"Because he came to the United States during the Revolutionary War."

"Oh," Moore said with a discouraged tone.

"His name was John Williames."

"Can't get much more of a common name than that. That's going to be a difficult one to trace," Moore moaned.

"Don't be discouraged. He worked with Pierre L'Enfant and helped lay out this city. There's only one John Williames who did that."

"Too bad I can't interview the one and only," Moore said sarcastically.

"Let me have Jody help me run this down. We'll see what we come up with." Nicholas stood from his desk and walked to the window at the rear of the room. He pulled back the drape and peered at the roses in his garden. They were his pride and joy. He found a quiet energy from planting, pruning and fertilizing them.

"There's one more thing which turned up in Lawsons' research."

"What's that?"

"The German ambassador visited with Lincoln the day he was assassinated."

"And how does that tie in?"

"Don't know if it does. But I wonder if the two mysteries are tied together. It was rumored that the German ambassador left a letter with Lincoln. The letter was mentioned in Secretary of War Stanton's memoirs. The letter was never found."

"You think the letter is connected to the Nazarene's Code?"

"I'm not sure. Maybe, maybe not. But there's more to Lincoln's assassination than people know."

"Oh?"

"When Booth fired the .50 caliber bullet into the base of Lincoln's head, Lincoln dropped an envelope which he was holding."

"An envelope?"

"Yes. If you read the transcripts of the interview with Major Rathbone, you'd see that he mentioned the envelope and that Booth picked it up. He stuffed it in his coat before he leapt from the Presidential Box to the stage floor."

"What was in it? The letter from the German ambassador?"

"Who knows? But no one has seen the envelope since that night."

"What about the Garrett farm where Booth was captured and killed?"

"Nope. Booth's body was searched and nothing was found. The barn where they found Booth was destroyed by fire. If the envelope was hidden there, it would have been destroyed also." Nicholas paused for a moment, and then continued. "Booth was killed by a single shot."

"I knew that."

"When his co-conspirator Herold was surrendering, one of the sergeants thought Booth was raising his carbine to fire. The sergeant fired, intending only to wound Booth in the arm. But a sudden movement by Booth brought his head in range and he took the bullet in the head. You know what's strange about the kill shot?"

"What's that?"

"The round entered Booth's head exactly one inch below where his bullet entered Lincoln's head. Strange coincidence, isn't it?"

"I'll say," Moore responded. "Any chance that Booth hid the envelope on his escape route from Washington?"

"Oh, sure he could have. Most likely it would have been at the home of Dr. Samuel Mudd. That's where he was treated for his broken leg."

"And Mudd went to trial for being a conspirator."

"Yes, he did. They were all hanged in Washington in July 1865, except for Mudd and two others. Mudd escaped a hanging conviction by one vote and was shipped out to Fort Jefferson in the Dry Tortugas, off of Key West."

"I visited Fort Jefferson several years ago," Moore said.

"I do recall that there were rumors amongst the archivists at the National Archives that Mudd was observed spending an inordinate amount of attention to his right boot."

"Think he may have hidden a letter there? In a hollow heel or inside the boot itself?"

"Don't know."

Calculating quickly, Moore grinned. "Thirteen letters."

"What's that?"

"Fort Jefferson."

"You think the envelope is there?" Nicholas asked.

"Maybe. It's worth checking out his cell. Whether it's related to the Nazarene's Code or not, it's an interesting story. Besides, I look for any excuse I can get to visit Key West." Moore counted letters again. "There are also thirteen letters in The White House and Dr. Samuel A. Mudd.

"Hmmm. There are also thirteen letters in John Williames and Pierre L'Enfant," Nicholas added. "I wish you luck. Hope I was helpful."

"You were." Moore rose from his chair as did Nicholas.

"I'll walk you to the door," Nicholas said.

When they reached the door, Nicholas opened the door for Moore. "One other thing. I'll take a look through the file you gave me from Bieber. I'll see if anything grabs my attention."

"Thanks. I looked at it on the flight back, but didn't see anything earth-shattering."

Moore flagged a taxi and took a seat in the rear. He called on his cell phone to make ticket reservations for a flight to Key West. He was able to schedule a flight to Miami where he would make a connection to Key West. Completing his reservations, Moore called his ex-Navy SEAL buddy, Sam Duncan, in Key West and made arrangements to crash at his doublewide.

Washington Sailing Marina
Alexandria, Virginia

After dining at Indigo Landing, Moore listened to the band playing on the outside deck. In the distance he could see the setting sun, the Washington Monument and the Capitol Building.

As he sat drinking a rum and coke, he replayed the events of the last ten days. It had been a whirlwind. He was still stunned by the lack of emotion shown by Bieber when she killed Gorenchenko. Then again, she may have been in shock, he thought to himself as he sipped his drink. It was all probably just hitting her.

As dusk turned into night, Moore paid his bill and walked the short distance to his houseboat, *Serenity*. He had decided to make it an early night and, since he'd be up at sunrise, to pack his duffel bag for the flight the next morning.

He boarded the houseboat as it rocked gently and entered her main salon where his laptop was set up. He accessed the Internet and printed his boarding passes for the flight to Miami and the connecting flight to Key West. He then walked to his stateroom in the stern. Within minutes, he had disrobed and was asleep.

Two hours later, a scuba diver aimed his Torpedo DPV (Diver Propulsion Unit) into the marina's harbor. He had been traveling up the Potomac River at a speed of two mph, surfacing a few times as he neared the harbor entrance to check his bearings. The underwater personal propulsion device saved the diver valuable energy for the next steps in his mission.

As he entered the harbor, he rose again to take a bearing on the *Serenity*. He then pointed the Torpedo's nose toward the dock where the *Serenity* was tied. Once he reached the dock, he secured the Torpedo to one of the pilings. He pulled off his fins and attached them to the Torpedo. Then he took off his BCS and tank, securing them to the Torpedo as well.

Slowly, he surfaced under the dock and tilted his mask off his face. Listening carefully, he heard the band playing at Indigo Landing. He continued to listen for five minutes before he made his move. He swung up and onto the dock where he crouched in the shadows. Again, he looked around and listened.

Seeing and hearing nothing of concern, he padded down the dock to the *Serenity* and cautiously stepped aboard, withdrawing his knife from a scabbard strapped to his leg. He opened the door and quietly stepped inside. He paused and listened for two minutes before pulling a small penlight from his waist belt. He flicked it on and flashed it around the bow compartment. Seeing nothing, he made his way midship and again paused. When he flicked on the flashlight he saw Moore's boarding pass on the counter. His inspection revealed Moore's plan to fly to Key West. That would be important to know, even if Moore wouldn't make the flight.

The assassin waited a few more minutes as he listened. Not hearing anything, he slowly eased open the door to the stateroom. He again paused. The only noise he heard was the breeze blowing through the two large portals, which Moore had opened earlier for cross ventilation.

The assassin saw the bed with the covers drawn over Moore. He sprang to the bed and began to stab Moore. But something was amiss.

The lights suddenly came on and a voice thundered, "Looking for me?"

The assassin's head whipped around in the direction of the voice. He was speechless for a few moments as his eyes adjusted to the light. "Sir," he began with a heavy Russian accent. "I believe this is a mistake."

"It sure is on your part, friend. I wouldn't do anything stupid if I were you," Moore said as he pointed his Glock 26, the Baby Glock, at the intruder. "Baby has a sensitive trigger on it." The subcompact weapon held ten rounds and it was fully loaded.

The Russian abruptly threw his knife at Moore, hitting Moore's arm and causing Moore to drop the Glock. The Russian launched his body like a missile at Moore, knocking Moore midships and onto the floor where the two grappled. The Glock and knife were on the floor close to the stateroom's doorway.

As they fought, Moore realized that the Russian was stronger than him and in a fight based on endurance, Moore would probably lose. He was able to rotate his body so that his legs were around the Russian's waist. Moore pulled hard on the dive mask, which had now slipped around the Russian's neck.

The Russian struggled for air as Moore tightened the tension on the mask. Suddenly, the Russian threw his head back and snapped it onto Moore's forehead, causing Moore to lose his grip and allowing the Russian to roll free.

The Russian made a beeline for the knife and Glock. Reaching the Glock, he grabbed it and turned to fire at Moore. In the meantime, Moore had reached under the counter where he had hidden another Glock. He gripped the Glock and aimed at the Russian.

As the Russian fired, Moore reacted by diving out of the open doorway onto the dock. When the Russian appeared in the doorway, Moore fired twice from his prone position and the Russian dropped to the deck.

Sirens from approaching police cars could be heard from the Parkway. Dorman came running down the dock toward the *Serenity*.

"Emerson, are you okay? I heard a shot and called the police."

"I'm okay. But we better check on my visitor." Moore approached the Russian, who was lying inside the houseboat and on the deck. Moore saw blood on the carpet as he kicked the fallen Glock away from the Russian, who was writhing in pain. "Looks like we're going to need an ambulance," Moore said to Dorman.

"Yeah, and a cleaning crew," he said as he looked at the bloody carpet. He grabbed a couple of towels and held them over the Russian's wound, trying to stem the blood flow.

At the same time, Moore held his weapon on the Russian until the police arrived, followed shortly by an ambulance. The ambulance whisked away the bleeding Russian and a police officer, who was assigned to watch over the gunman.

"What happened here?" another police officer asked. "You know this guy?"

"Never saw him before. I couldn't sleep and went topside to watch the stars. Shortly afterwards I heard a noise and I watched this guy crawl onto the deck like some sea creature and try to kill my pillows."

"You think he was after you or was this a burglary?"

"Since he went straight to my berth, I doubt it was simple burglary," Moore responded. "It looks like he came to kill me."

The police officer and his team conducted a brief interview of Moore and looked through his houseboat for any additional clues. As they were concluding their investigation, the officer approached Moore. "We're leaving one of our officers on the dock overnight as a precautionary measure. We'll be back in the morning to search the dock for clues. We'll have a police boat and divers check under the docks to see if we can find his gear."

"Fine with me. I'll only be here for a short while in the morning. I've got a flight to Key West."

"Shouldn't be a problem."

The police officers, except for one, left and Moore returned to the houseboat. His adrenaline was so high that he knew he wouldn't be able to sleep. He decided to pack his duffel bag for the morning flight.

Reagan National Airport
Washington, D.C.

~~~~

Awaiting his flight to Miami to take a connection to Key West, Moore had just finished a call with Nicholas to relate the previous evening's incident. He looked up Kalker's number in his cell phone's contacts directory and depressed the call key.

Kalker answered on the third ring. "Hello, Emerson."

"Good morning, or I should say good afternoon," Moore said into his cell.

"No matter. How are things going?" Kalker asked.

"Good. I wondered if you could get Kat on the line with us."

"Certainly."

"Wait a second, Andreas. How is she doing as far as recovering from killing Gorenchenko?"

"Better now. I met her at the airport when she landed and it appeared that she had been crying. I think it was a delayed reaction. She spent the night at my place and seems to be doing better."

"I'm glad to hear that. Thank you," Moore said.

"She's my niece. Of course, I'd take care of her. Hold one moment and I'll get her on the line." Less than a minute passed and Kalker said, "She's on the line with us now."

"Hello, Emerson," the feminine voice cooed.

"Hi, Kat. I hear you're doing better."

"I am. I'm still having nightmares, but I'm sure it'll pass. Uncle Andreas is keeping a close eye on me."

"Great." Moore's tone changed. "You'll never believe what happened to me last night."

"Oh, no," Bieber said with concern as she sensed the seriousness in his voice.

Moore related the prior evening's incident to Kalker and Bieber.

"Russians again." Kalker stated matter-of-factly. "I'd bet anything that Karapashev is behind this. I should send you a security detail."

"That's not necessary."

"I could send you one of my lipsticks," Bieber offered.

"I'll pass. Not my color," Moore joked weakly. "It sounds like the Russians are behind this. I'll let you know what I hear from the officers investigating last night's incident," Moore said.

"They took the Russian to the hospital?" Kalker asked.

"Yes."

"But, you weren't hurt, were you?" Bieber asked.

"No." Then, Moore added, "I sure could have used your help last night. By the way, Andreas, that lipstick you gave Kat was deadly. Nice gadget."

Kalker chuckled. "A woman, who knows how to wear her lipstick, is deadly no matter what the circumstances are. In this case, she was dead on." He chuckled again.

"No woman should leave home without one," Moore retorted.

"It was something we had developed during my working days. I had a few around the house and thought my niece should have one," Kalker explained.

"I hope, and excuse my pun, I wasn't the trigger for you giving her one. She is quite attractive," Moore teased.

"No, she's had one for some time. I'm especially glad that she had it when you were in London."

"I'll bet." Turning the conversation to Bieber, Moore said, "Kat, I was surprised how accurate of a shot you were. Even more surprised that you were able to kill him. Not what I'd expect from a researcher." This was a question that had been gnawing at Moore since the incident.

"Surprised you, didn't I?" Not letting Moore respond, she continued, "What you didn't know was that I was a crack shot when I did my military time."

Kalker interjected, "It goes back before that. Katrina's father had always wanted a son. When their only child turned out to be female, he passed on his hunting skills to her. My brother and I were good hunters."

"That's right, Uncle Andreas. I loved to go into the forests on hunting excursions. It was mostly small game, but we did hunt deer on several occasions." Bieber paused for a moment, and then continued. "But Emerson, it's not the same as killing a person. When I returned to my hotel room, I threw up but didn't want to tell you. Don't want you to think I'm a softie."

"I see," Moore said as he closed his curiosity on the shooting. "But the next time I'm with you, I'd appreciate if you turned your head and looked to the side when you applied your lipstick. I don't want any accidents."

Both Kalker and Bieber laughed.

"I'll be careful. How astute of you to know that I have a replacement lipstick!"

"I didn't have any doubt," Moore grinned.

"You're off to Key West, then?" Kalker asked.

"Yes, Nicholas had a theory tied into this thirteen stuff. I'm running it down in case it's fruitful. Could be a wild goose chase, but I never pass up an opportunity to visit Key West."

Moore then remembered one other question he had for Kalker. "Have you heard anything more about Yarian or his friends from your London contacts? Are they still in London or do you think they're in the U.S.?"

"Nothing other than they seemed to have disappeared. My friends are still searching for them," Kalker responded.

"Let me know if you hear anything. I better go. I need to board my flight shortly," Moore said as he stood.

"Be safe," Bieber said as she hung up.

Moore speed-dialed Sam Duncan in Key West and Duncan answered on the second ring.

"E! Are you here, already?" Duncan's voice seemed puzzled.

"No. I'm still at Reagan."

"You had me wondering. What's up?"

Moore related the prior evening's incident.

"Russian?"

"That's my sense," Moore responded.

"I'm glad that you took my advice and had a couple of weapons hidden aboard. How about your aunt's house? Do you have any hidden there?"

"One, but I don't think I'll need it in Put-in-Bay." Moore paused, then continued, "It seems like these guys are on my tail wherever I go."

"Let's see if we can throw them off a bit. Stay where you are. I've got to make a few phone calls and I'll get right back to you."

"Okay. I have about twenty minutes before I board my flight."

"More than enough time," Duncan said as he ended the call.

While he waited for Duncan's return call, Moore walked over to the coffee bar and ordered a medium-sized breakfast blend to which he added six containers of hazelnut cream. He loved his cream. He paid for the coffee and returned to his seat near the jetway.

Sipping his hot coffee, Moore began to replay the events of the last few days. His vibrating cell phone interrupted his thoughts. He looked at it and saw Duncan's name appear.

"Sam?"

"Got you covered, E. Good thing I know the right people."

"As only you would," Moore smiled.

"Ever fly in a Grumman HU-16B?"

"Don't believe I have."

"You will when you arrive in Miami. It's a big amphibious cargo plane. My friends in Black Ops are running a shipment to a certain country that you don't need to know about. They're going to let you ride with them as a favor to me. They'll drop you in Key West. This way, we can put some distance between the Russians and you."

"Sam, I appreciate it," Moore said.

"No problem, E. You just get your butt safely down here and I'll see what I can do to help you more." Duncan provided Moore with the address to a small airport outside of Miami where Moore would catch his Key West flight.

The boarding announcement for Moore's flight echoed through the waiting area.

"They're calling my flight, Sam."

"Okay. See you later today."

Moore ended the call and walked to the jetway. There, he produced his boarding pass and walked down the jetway to catch his flight.

Two rows from where Moore sat, a well-built traveler pulled the ear buds from his ears and looked at his iPod. The iPod to the normal person wouldn't raise any suspicions, but it was a directional eavesdropping device. The man was able to hear both sides of Moore's conversation.

The man reached into his jacket and extracted his cell phone. He speed-dialed a number, which was answered on the first ring.

"Is there a problem?"

"Yes. Moore is catching a Black Ops flight from Miami to Key West. We could lose him," the man said with a Russian accent.

The man on the other end responded. "Give me the details and we will see what we can do."

The first man provided the address and then was told to board the flight to keep an eye on Moore.

Miami International Airport
Miami, Florida

Walking through the concourse, Moore made his way through baggage claim and outside to the hot, humid Miami air. He caught a cab and gave the driver the address of the small airfield outside of Miami.

As the cab pulled away, the man who was following Moore, emerged from the luggage claim doorway. His seat at the rear of the aircraft made it impossible for him to disembark from the plane as fast as Moore, who was seated near the front. Not realizing that Moore had stopped in the restroom, the man raced by the restroom's doorway to check baggage claim. Not finding Moore there, he walked briskly to the cab stand. Not seeing Moore there, he returned to baggage claim to find Moore. When he couldn't locate Moore, he reluctantly made a call on his cell phone.

"Yes?" the voice answered.

"I lost him," the man said.

"That shouldn't be a problem for us. We know where he's headed and I've arranged a surprise." The second man ended the call.

It was a thirty-five minute drive to the airport, which was west of Miami. The cab pulled in and deposited Moore at the hangar as instructed.

Inside the hangar was a 1955 Grumman HU-16B amphibious flying boat. It was painted an ominous-looking black. Ten of its twelve passenger seats had been removed so that the plane could carry a wide variety of lethal cargo. Today's cargo was a large container. It contained weapons and ammunition for a mercenary force involved in drug interdiction in a certain Latin American country. The plane would land in a small lake and unload the freight onto a nearby dock before returning to Miami.

"You lost?" a surly voice greeted Moore as he walked into the hangar.

"No. I'm looking for Jeremiah," Moore responded as he turned to face the source of the voice. He wasn't surprised when he saw the business end of a semi-automatic trained on him.

"And, why would you be looking for him?"

"My name's Emerson Moore. I'm flying with him today."

"I'm Jeremiah," a voice spoke from the shadows. A tall man, wearing a black tee shirt and camouflage-colored slacks, stepped out of the shadows behind the armed guard. "We were expecting you."

Jeremiah was smoking a cigarette. "We'll be boarding in a few minutes. Waiting for our new co-pilot to get here." He took a draw on his cigarette and exhaled. "Regular guy took sick," he added even though Moore hadn't asked.

The words were barely out of his mouth when a dark blue Jeep Laredo pulled up next to the hangar and parked. The driver locked his vehicle and rushed to the hangar.

"Sorry about the delay. I just got the call a while ago. I'm Joshua," the muscular man said. He was wearing a black tee shirt and khakis.

"No sweat off my back. Our human cargo just arrived so we should be good to go."

Moore nodded his head. "Appreciate the ride. Looks like I'm flying with J&J," Moore said weakly.

The surly guard interjected, "I'd say it's more like dumb and dumber." It was the first time Moore saw "Mr. Personality" crack a smile.

"Knock it off," Jeremiah snarled at the guard. Turning to Moore, Jeremiah spoke good-naturedly. "Let's mount up. That your gear?" he asked when he saw the duffel bag on the floor.

"Yes."

"Well, grab your gear and come along."

The two walked across the hangar to where the co-pilot had entered the aircraft that had been modified with a large doorway aft of the propeller on the port side and forward of the retractable landing wheels. They walked under the mounted wings, which held the aircraft's two engines, one on each wing.

"Reminds me of the PBY Catalinas used during World War II!" Moore commented.

"They were good planes. These planes are dependable sons of bitches," Jeremiah replied.

As they entered the plane, Jeremiah worked his way to his seat and Moore stored his gear. He then took one of the two empty seats behind the bulkhead separating the pilots from the passenger and freight area. Behind Moore was a large cargo container on wheels with the arms and ammunition. Straps secured it, with one end affixed to the plane's interior wall and deck. It had been rolled on board through a specially constructed large doorway.

Moore heard the starboard engine fire up and then the port engine fire up. He looked out his window and could see the blades spinning.

"Better fasten your seat belt," Joshua the co-pilot said as he walked by and closed the plane's large door.

"Right. Forgot," Moore said as he quickly fastened it.

"And don't expect any food service on this flight," Joshua said as he returned to the cockpit.

It was then that Moore realized that he hadn't eaten since breakfast. The thought triggered a gnawing in his stomach. "Don't suppose we could cruise through a McDonald's?"

Joshua turned his head toward Moore and glared at him. It was Jeremiah who came to the rescue. "Here. It's a submarine sandwich. I'll share it. I've got a thermos of coffee up here. You can have a cup of it if you want."

"Thanks." Moore caught the wrapped sub, which Jeremiah had tossed to him. "Would you have a knife I can use to cut it?"

"Just don't ask me to cut it for you," Jeremiah said as he tossed a sheathed Army knife to Moore.

"Thanks," Moore said as the plane taxied slowly from the hangar and onto the apron. The plane moved to the end of the runway where it revved its engines and then began its take off.

Moore unwrapped the submarine sandwich and cut off a third of it with the knife, which he had pulled from its scabbard. He then rewrapped the sandwich and resheathed the knife. Sitting back in his seat, he looked out the window and took a bite of his sandwich as the plane cleared the runway. The first bite was so good that Moore took larger bites and devoured the sandwich in a matter of minutes.

As the plane cleared the Everglades and headed over the open water toward Key West, Moore heard a small pop from the cockpit. He leaned to his left and into the aisle so that he could see into the cockpit area. What he saw made him almost throw up the food he just ate. Jeremiah was slumped back in his seat and blood was dripping onto the cockpit floor. Joshua was now swinging his weapon around to point at Moore.

Moore ducked back toward the window side of his seat, unfastening his seatbelt as he did. He heard a second pop, followed by a soft noise to the right of his head where the bullet lodged in his seatback.

Setting the plane on autopilot, Joshua called back, "Mr. Moore, I bring you greetings from your Russian friends."

Moore jumped from his seat and raced to the freight area of the plane. Two more pops followed, sending bullets into the crate he had hidden behind. Moore felt something poke his thigh and remembered that he had the sheathed knife in his pocket.

He withdrew the knife and quickly sawed at the strap restraining the wheeled cargo container, which had been secured at the plane's center of gravity. He then pushed the wheeled container between gunshots toward the cockpit. This action affected the distribution of weight in the plane. As the weight moved forward, the plane's nose began to inch down, bringing it into a dive.

Joshua was distracted and after sending another gunshot at Moore, pulled back on the yoke to level off the aircraft. At the same time, Moore pushed the wheeled container to the tail, causing the plane's nose to move up vertically, taking it dangerously close to a stall.

Joshua pushed the yoke forward, overcompensating as the wheeled pallets rolled forward and crashed into the bulkhead. Joshua pulled out of the dive and fought to level off the plane.

Meanwhile, Moore had opened the plane's door and saw that the plane's altitude had dropped dangerously low. He heard a noise and turned to see Joshua had left the cockpit. Moore began pushing the container toward mid-plane.

In his hand, Joshua held his gun. Once again, he began to train it on Moore. Moore reacted, ducking quickly as the bullets hit the planes interior wall. Out of ammo, Joshua advanced on Moore.

Moore saw the exposed fuel line and decided to puncture it. When he began to approach the fuel line with the knife, Joshua launched himself at Moore, knocking Moore to the floor and sending the knife spinning aftward.

The two men grappled on the floor as Joshua tried to break Moore's wrist. Moore slipped from his grasp and rolled toward the plane's doorway where he pulled himself to his knees. Joshua, filled with rage, launched himself from a crouch like a missile at Moore. Moore quickly sidestepped and the thrust of Joshua's action carried him through the open doorway. He screamed as he plummeted to the water below.

Moore peered out the open doorway, but couldn't spot Joshua. He closed the door and made his way through the cargo to the cockpit. With one danger out of the way, he needed to address the critical issue of landing the plane.

He walked past the slumped pilot and sat in the co-pilot's seat, fastening the shoulder harness as he sat. Looking at Jeremiah, he could tell he was long gone. There was no chance of rescuing the pilot, whose eyes stared lifelessly toward the horizon. It was at this point that Moore thought to himself how he wished he had completed those flight lessons he had started as a teenager. He was also devastated that his search for a story had resulted in the deaths of innocent people he had peripherally involved.

He couldn't dwell on that now. He familiarized himself with the controls and thought back to his flights on Lake Erie with the owner of Dairy Air. He remembered the basics, but there was a huge difference in the controls of a small two seater and this huge amphibious plane. Moore knew what he needed to do. He reached for the radio.

Moore located the altitude indicator, which displayed a miniature set of wings. It showed the plane was level. There was no need for him to be concerned about correcting the pitch upward or downward or banking the plane at this point.

He checked on the center of the glare-shield panel and saw that the autopilot was engaged. Moore placed the co-pilot's headset on his head and pushed the push-to-talk button on the yoke. "Mayday!" Moore called. He repeated it two more times.

"This is Key West air traffic control."

"I'm in trouble. I've got a dead pilot and a missing co-pilot. And I've never flown a plane like this." The words spewed out of Moore's mouth.

The controller looked at his radar and saw the blip representing Moore's plane. He also recognized the discreet transponder code as probably one of the covert flights out of the Miami area.

"Is your autopilot set?"

Moore rechecked the indicator. "Yes."

"Good. Look at the airspeed indicator. It's located toward the upper left of the instrument panel. What's you airspeed?"

Moore located the airspeed indicator. "Looks like 150 mph," he responded.

"If the airspeed starts to drop, then I'll need you to gently push forward on the throttles. But, be sure to do it gently," the controller warned.

"Got it."

The controller went through controlling the craft and its indicators with Moore acknowledging each control or indicator as he identified it. After taking the plane off autopilot and banking the plane over Key West as directed, Moore found himself lining the plane for a landing at Key West's airport.

Beginning the descent, Moore pulled back on the throttles, reducing power to the engines. This caused the nose of the plane to lower. Beads of sweat formed on Moore's brow as he listened to the controller's instructions. He appreciated the dangers of a neophyte landing a large plane like this Grumman.

"Lower your landing gear. It should be to the right of the center console. The end of the gear handle is shaped like a tire."

Moore glanced at the center console and located the gear handle. "Got it," he said as he lowered the gear. The plane continued to descend onto the approaching runway.

"Just before you touch down, you'll need to pull back on the yoke to raise the nose so that you land on the main wheels first."

"Right. I'll pull back on the yoke," Moore responded. He wiped the sweat from his eyes.

"Your approach looks good. Reduce your power."

Moore followed the instructions. His eyes were glued to the

single, 4,800-foot-by-100-foot asphalt, grooved runway. "How's my airspeed? Am I coming in too fast?" he asked nervously as his eyes darted to the airspeed indicator and back to the runway.

"You're doing fine, sport. Steady. Steady."

The plane's main wheels touched the runway and bounced several times before settling down.

"Reduce your power to idle and slowly apply the brakes. If you hit the brakes too hard, you'll put the plane into a skid." The controller snapped out instructions quickly as the plane moved across the runway.

Moore grabbed the throttle and pulled back to the idle position while his feet applied pressure to the top of the rudder pedals. When the plane came to a stop at the end of the runway, Moore slumped in his seat, mentally exhausted with the unexpected perils of the flight.

"You did a nice job for a first-timer," the controller grinned as he looked toward the plane from his lofty vantage point in the control tower.

"Thanks for all of your help. I'm glad I'm still in one piece," Moore said with a sigh of relief.

"Just sit tight. Our ground crew will be there in a few seconds and will taxi the plane."

"Will do." Moore looked out the window and saw the airport's fire and rescue vehicles beginning to return to their garage. He was glad that there had been no need to call upon their services.

Within minutes, a ground crew member had replaced Moore at the controls and taxied the plane off the runway and to an isolated area.

Leaning out of the co-pilot's seat and looking back to Moore, who had taken his original seat, the ground crew member said, "I'd bet those guys in the black suburban will want to talk with you."

Moore looked out the window and saw two men exit the vehicle that had parked next to the plane. "Police?"

"Nope. Government types, if you know what I mean."

"Thanks," Moore said as he grabbed his gear and stepped out of the plane. He approached the waiting men. They looked like two people you wouldn't want to meet in a dark alley.

"Guess you guys are going to want to talk to me?"

"Sounds like you had a real adventure up there," one said.

"That'd be an understatement," Moore replied.

The other man spoke. "They found the body of the original co-pilot in his apartment. He was murdered."

Moore nodded. "I guess I'd expect something like that."

For the next hour, the black ops guys grilled Moore as to what happened in the plane. One stepped away to make a cell call after Moore mentioned his involvement with Steve Nicholas. After completing his call, he returned and pulled his partner aside to have a private conversation. Then, they returned to where Moore was waiting patiently.

"We're done. I've been asked to tell you that all of this is confidential. You cannot report on anything that has happened here. In fact, nothing happened. Understand?" The man glared at Moore with a look that meant he was deadly serious.

"I do," Moore acknowledged, although he still planned on talking with Duncan and Nicholas about the event.

"You can go now," the first man said. "Terminal is over there."

Moore nodded as he bent to pick up his gear and began walking toward the terminal. His flight had been so tense that he didn't have a chance to enjoy his high level view of the clear, blue-green waters surrounding the mystical island, the anchor for the long emerald chain of fossilized coral and limestone islands which stretched southerly from the Florida mainland. They were like a jeweled necklace with Key West as the crown jewel.

On this flight, he had missed the alluring enchantment of the island paradise bounded by the Atlantic Ocean and the Gulf of Mexico with a wide array of boats at rest in the harbor, the church spires, and the Key West lighthouse. The plane had flown low over the luxuriant green island and parallel with Smathers Beach and Roosevelt Boulevard.

Moore walked up to the white airport terminal, which was trimmed in aquamarine. A sign on the terminal building with "Welcome to Key West" in bright red letters greeted arriving travelers.

Walking through the baggage claim area, Moore didn't spot Duncan. He decided to step outside where the honk from a waiting Jeep greeted him.

"E!"

"Hey, Sam," Moore said as he tossed his gear in the back of the Jeep and took a seat on the passenger side.

"You okay? I heard you had a rough flight," Duncan said as he pulled out of the airport and headed down Roosevelt Boulevard, passing Smathers Beach on his left.

Moore turned his head and looked at Duncan. "News travels

fast. Sorry about Jeremiah."

"In my circles, it does. Jeremiah was a good guy, but he knew the risks of his job. Tell me what happened."

Moore related the details of his flight.

"You were lucky. Still running on your nine lives," Duncan commented.

"I think I passed nine a long time ago. It seems that I have a habit of running into bottom feeders."

Duncan glanced at his friend as he turned on United Street. "You and me. That's what makes our jobs so interesting."

Duncan pulled the Jeep into a small mobile home park off of United Street. He carefully maneuvered the Jeep down a narrow lane, and parked next to a small mobile home that had a covered patio in front.

The patio was screened from the lane by white latticework desperately in need of a fresh coat of paint. The patio area itself was littered with three chairs in disrepair, which surrounded a worn and stained rattan table. A few potted plants dotted the patio. They were in need of water and nourishment. Hanging from the ceiling were a number of colored lights and two wooden parrots.

"Not much has changed since I was here last," Moore observed. "That lattice still needs a coat of paint."

"Yeah. Yeah. I'll get to it," Duncan said as he approached the door, unlocked it and stepped inside. "Not much changed inside either."

"Dishes still piled up in the sink?" Moore teased.

"Yeah. But they're different ones from what you saw last time," Duncan teased back.

Emerson entered the trailer. To the right was a small living room complete with an easy chair and small sofa. A beat-up coffee table was covered with magazines and files. Moore's eyes were drawn to one side of the room that housed the latest in Duncan's entertainment technology. There was a big screen plasma TV with sound-surround for the TV and the CD player.

"Still using the second bedroom as your spy center?" Moore asked as he remembered that it was filled with the latest in technology, including satellite uplinks to a number of covert agencies.

"Yep, and it's still off limits to snooping reporters," Duncan grinned. "And it's always locked," he added. "You can drop your gear here and use the sofa bed while you're in town."

"Good." Moore's eyes roved the kitchen countertop that was littered with crumbs, pizza crust and pieces of lettuce. There was a blackened banana in a fruit bowl and an empty milk carton. "You really do need to find a wife. She could help you keep this place tidy."

"Emerson Moore. I'm just shocked to hear you use four-letter words like that. I should wash your mouth out with soap!"

"But, you should settle down."

"Look who's talking! You need to put your loss behind you and find a woman," Duncan said as he referred to the death of Moore's wife and son.

"I'm working my way through it."

"And E, you need to get over that Martine woman. You still holding a torch for her?"

Memories of the redhead flooded Moore's mind as he recalled their flirtation a couple of years ago. "I think I'll always have a part of her in my heart."

"Maybe you'll get lucky and her husband will die, the little wuss." Duncan didn't lose any sleep over the twerp.

"Any other love interests? Come on, you can tell Uncle Sam," Duncan asked.

"Maybe. There's this attractive German lady I'm working with."

Duncan gave Moore a lecherous look. "And how is the chemistry?"

"Incredible, but still in the early stages," Moore mused as his thoughts drifted to her blue eyes.

"Well, well, first time I've seen that look in your eyes in a long time."

"Whatever. Hey, this doesn't have anything to do with you finding a woman."

Duncan shook his head. "Listen, when you live here in Key West, the Land of Oz, you find that it's filled with liars, tireds and bares. The women here are like a bus line. Another one will be along in five minutes. I'm not settling down with anyone," Duncan said as he espoused his philosophy on relationships with females.

Moore chuckled. "You will when you find the right one. Trust me."

"Enough of this talk. I'm famished. Want to head over to Jack Flats?" Duncan knew how much Moore enjoyed the fresh grouper sandwiches at the sports bar across from Jimmy Buffet's Margaritaville on Duvall Street.

"What time is it?" Moore looked at his watch. "I've got a dinner meeting with Kim Fisher and his wife at Kelly's in about an hour. Why don't you join us?"

"Sure. I love being with the Fishers. They're always finding more treasure on the Atocha." Duncan said as he thought about the recovery operations. "Why don't you freshen up and then we can drive over there?"

Thirty minutes later, Moore emerged from the bathroom after a long, hot shower and change of clothes. He was wearing a flowered shirt and khaki shorts. He had tried calling Nicholas on his cell, but Nicholas didn't answer. He'd plan on calling him later that evening.

Moore and Duncan quickly exited the mobile home and drove to Kelly's Caribbean Bar, Grill and Brewery. Parking the Jeep on Whitehead Street across from the restaurant, the two crossed the street and walked up the stairs to the wide entranceway.

Kelly's had been the site of Pan Am's first office and was currently owned by award-winning actress, Kelly McGillis. To the right of the entranceway was a small museum that housed Pan Am memorabilia and history. To the left was the bar, which was sided with a ribbed, galvanized aluminum. Upstairs, customers could be seated on a deck with several Banyan trees ringing it and overlooking the patio dining area below.

As Moore and Duncan approached the hostess, a lean, tall man with blonde hair and a deep tan walked up the stairs from the bricked dining patio, which was surrounded by lush green foliage.

"Emerson," the man greeted him. It was Kim Fisher. "And you've brought your buddy, Sam! We have a table over there."

The three shook hands and followed Fisher to his table where his wife, Lee, was seated.

"I've brought along my son, Sean, and his wife, Star."

Moore and Duncan greeted the lean, muscular son and his stunning, six-foot tall, long-haired brunette wife.

"You sure are tall," Duncan said appreciatively as he looked at Star.

"She is," Sean grinned with a twinkle in his eye. "She's so tall that she can wrap her long legs around me twice!" he teased Duncan as Star blushed.

Duncan moaned while Moore changed the topic. "Lee, the last time I saw you was right here. You had me stand up in the middle of the restaurant while you gave me a chiropractic adjustment."

"I remember. You had strained your wrist in a jet ski accident on the Atlantic side."

A waiter appeared and took their drink orders which included a Pan Am Panic of Bacardi light rum, strawberry puree and pina colada; Blue Lagoon Margarita of gold tequila and triple sec; a Jamaican Me Crazy of Appleton Reserve, pineapple and orange juice topped with Coruba dark rum; and a couple of beers.

As the waiter scurried away, Kim asked, "So, what's your latest adventure, Emerson? You seem to always be getting into something exciting."

Moore proceeded to update the group about his search for the Nazarene's Code and the Legend of 13, but didn't tell them about his flight from Miami to Key West.

About a third of the way through his explanation, the waiter returned with their drinks and took their meal orders. Moore ordered red Bahamian conch chowder and yellowtail snapper.

After Moore finished updating the group, Kim commented,

"You've had a tough road."

"Yes, it's been trying. I'm getting too old for this."

"Aw, that won't stop ya," Duncan teased.

"That's just amazing how the Legend of 13 is tied into this. Interesting how Dr. Samuel A. Mudd and Fort Jefferson have thirteen letters," Kim said.

"Hey, my favorite actor, Channing Tatum, has thirteen letters, too," said Star with a wink. "But somehow I doubt he is tied to all of this."

They all laughed, including Moore.

"Well, it does seem like a silly connection – it could be nothing."

"But then again, it may be something," Kim added. "You hoping to find a clue at Fort Jefferson?" Kim asked.

"I'm counting on it," Moore answered. "I'd like to go there tomorrow – just have to find a way to get there."

Sean Fisher spoke. "I can take you. I can borrow a go fast boat from my friends at the Taboo Racing team. They've got one that goes about 125 mph. It'd take us about forty-five minutes to get out there."

"Great. Where do you want me to meet you?"

"The docks outside of Schooner Wharf at ten o'clock."

The congenial group continued their discussions as their meals were served.

Two hours later, Moore and Duncan entered Duncan's mobile

home.

"I need to make a call to Nicholas," Moore said as he sat at the kitchen table.

"Go ahead. Make yourself at home," Duncan responded as he headed to his office in the second bedroom.

Moore speed dialed Nicholas and his call was answered on the second ring.

"Hi, Steve, It's Emerson."

"You had a good flight?" Nicholas asked.

"That's why I'm calling." Moore paused, and then continued, "I know it's late, but could you get Andreas on the phone?"

"Must be serious."

"It is and I don't want to explain it twice."

Within a minute, Kalker was connected into the call.

Moore began by apologizing. "Andreas, I'm sorry to wake you up in the middle of the night."

"You're not the first to disturb my beauty sleep. What is it?" He coughed several times as he responded.

Moore explained what happened on the flight. Then, he closed. "Innocent people are dying here. The Russians are turning up the heat and I need you to find them and stop it. Haven't your connections found anything concrete yet?"

Nicholas spoke next. "Andreas, I'm sure Karapashev is behind this."

"It sounds like it," Kalker agreed. "I've had our best people trying to track him, but we haven't been successful in finding him. We think we are close."

"Emerson," Nicholas asked, "what are your plans for tomorrow?"

"I'm meeting Sean Fisher at Schooner Wharf at ten o'clock and he's going to run me out to Fort Jefferson. We'll search Mudd's cell to see if we can find anything."

"Okay, but be careful."

"I will," Moore reassured him.

"And I'll turn up the heat on my people to get some answers and some action," Kalker, added before they ended the call.

De Novo Hospital
Alexandria, Virginia

The new red Volkswagen pulled off Seminary Road into the employee parking lot and parked in the last row near the hedges. Shutting off its engine, nurse William Somers smiled to himself with pride as he had parked his two-week-old vehicle where there was less chance of it being scratched and dented. He reached for his ID badge and its lanyard, which he'd left on the passenger seat the previous evening.

He threw the lanyard around his neck, opened the car door and stepped out. Before he could close the door, a figure clothed in medical garb emerged from the hedge where he had been evaluating potential targets before settling on Somers. The man rushed at Somers. All that Somers realized was the feel of a hard metal object behind his ear. The man pulled the trigger on his silenced weapon and then pushed Somers back into the new car.

The man grabbed the lanyard from around Somers' neck, and, seeing that it was already wet from Somers' blood, disconnected the ID badge from the lanyard. He threw the lanyard into the vehicle and closed its door. He then held the badge in one hand as he slipped the weapon under his top and into the waistband of his trousers.

He walked toward the employee entrance where he waited until a group of five nurses walked up to the entrance. He quickly fell in line behind them, swiping his badge as he walked in front of a distracted security guard.

Back in the employee parking lot, the new Volkswagen was no longer spotless. Blood from its dead owner, sprawled across the front seats, had streamed down the passenger's seat and puddled on the white-carpeted floor.

Inside the hospital, the man walked up to the emergency receptionist. He was carrying two cups of coffee, which he had poured from the waiting room's courtesy area. "I've got an extra cup. Would you like it?" he asked in a voice that hinted his Russian accent.

"Black?" the receptionist asked.

"Your lucky day, Annette," the Russian said as he read her nametag and handed one of the cups to her.

"Thanks. Saves me a trip," the receptionist said as she took the cup and sipped it. "Looks like it's going to be a busy morning."

Looking over the brim of his cup, the Russian asked, "Why's that?"

"Houston called off sick." The receptionist looked at the attractive man in front of her and caught herself. "Houston works with me here," she explained. "They're going to have someone come down and help me today."

"Yeah, but I bet you can handle it." The Russian smiled at her and took a sip of his coffee. "I heard that there was a shooting victim in here last night."

"That's nothing new," the receptionist retorted.

The Russian took another sip of his coffee before commenting again. "This one took place over by Indigo Landing. I have friends who work there, and I was concerned. Do you know who it was?"

"Gosh, I hope it wasn't one of your friends," she said. "Here, let me see if I can look at last night's records." The receptionist scrolled through a number of names and then found one linked to Indigo Landing. "Don't know if this is your friend. The name is unknown and he's in the secured area. He had surgery last night and is recovering."

"He hasn't been identified?"

"No."

The Russian smiled inwardly. "Maybe I'll go up and see if it's one of my friends. Annette, could you give me his room number? I'm so worried."

"Sure." She provided the room number. "I'd be surprised if he's one of your friends, though."

"Why's that?"

"He's in the area where criminals are kept."

"You're probably right. I don't know anybody in that category. Now that I think more about it, I'm going to pass." The Russian started to walk away.

"Stop back any time," the receptionist smiled. "Next time, I'll buy," she teased. He was kind of cute, she thought to herself. She didn't recall seeing him around the hospital in the past, but then again, they were hiring people every day.

"I'll do that," he said as he walked to the elevator and entered it. The receptionist turned back to her work and forgot about the exchange.

The elevator doors opened on the fourth floor and the Russian walked out. He acclimated himself to the room numbering scheme and began to walk toward the secured area. When he walked by the nurses' station, he saw one of the mobile carts with a laptop computer. It didn't look like it was in use, so the Russian powered it up and began pushing the cart in front of him as he walked to the secured area. He nodded at the police officer at its entrance and wheeled the cart down the hallway until he found the right room.

Pushing the cart into the room, he found his friend. He was heavily sedated as he recovered from his surgery. The Russian reached into his pocket and withdrew a syringe. He inserted the syringe's needle into the IV and depressed it, releasing a deadly dose of potassium into the line. In a matter of minutes, his accomplice would be dead and unable to recover for police questioning.

Finished with his task, the Russian pushed the cart out of the room and down the hallway. He walked past the police officer without being challenged and returned the cart to where he had found it. He then walked to the elevator, and took it to the first floor where he exited the building. He was smiling at having accomplished his mission and was looking forward to reporting to his boss.

Schooner Wharf Bar
Key West

The island music was playing overhead in the speakers. Moore had just finished another grouper sandwich and was watching the harbor for his ride to the Dry Tortugas. It had been feeding time for the hungry monsters, who dwelled in his stomach. Their growls had demanded attention and Moore succumbed to another grouper sandwich.

Schooner Wharf Bar and Turtle Kraals next door were two of Moore's favorite restaurants in Key West. He enjoyed their waterfront setting, overlooking an array of watercraft in the harbor. There were Zodiacs, small runabouts, fishing boats, sailboats and large cruisers.

Duncan had driven Moore to the waterfront restaurant for his meal and upcoming ride to the Dry Tortugas, and then left for the airport to catch a flight for Columbia. When asked, Duncan had been evasive as to what he would be doing. Moore guessed it was another of his covert adventures and didn't push further.

He watched and saw his ride making its way into the harbor. Moore stood and paid his bill. Then, he walked out on the docks to the end dock as he had been instructed the previous night.

As the boat neared the dock, Moore waved to Sean Fisher, who was standing stiffly at the wheel. Sean didn't smile or wave at all. Strange, Moore thought, he looks more like a mannequin than a person.

As the boat pulled up to the dock, two figures rose from the deck of the go-fast craft. Both were holding guns, which were quickly aimed at Moore.

"Mr. Moore, how nice of you to join us for a cruise," Yarian tittered as he looked at Moore and waved his weapon as an indication for Moore to board.

Moore froze. "How did you know I was here?"

"I can always track you down and hook you in, Moore. You aren't the smartest fish in the sea. Now, get on board. We're going for a ride."

Moore stalled. "Where to?" he asked without moving.

Yarian's cohort was scanning the docks to make sure that they weren't attracting any attention, and then returned to look at Moore. "Get in the boat," he said gruffly with a Russian accent.

"The Dry Tortugas, where else? We're going treasure hunting," he said as the boat nudged against the dock pilings.

Moore didn't respond nor did he move. He knew going with them would be the end for both Sean and him, but so would staying still.

"Come, come Moore. Don't make my chartered flight here a waste of my time. Get on board the boat," Yarian said in a gruff tone.

Moore's mind had been searching for an escape idea. He began to step onto the stern. "I'm not sure that I'm going to like this."

Yarian and the other gunman relaxed as Moore stepped onto the stern. As he did, Fisher winked at him. Fisher's next action upset Yarian's plans. He launched his body at the two ruffians, knocking one to the ground while spinning Yarian around.

Moore accelerated his steps across the stern and dove into the harbor. Fisher stood and prepared to follow Moore, but was stopped by an angry voice.

"Freeze!" Yarian exploded.

Fisher saw that Yarian was pointing his weapon at Fisher and decided it would be wise to follow Yarian's instructions. He may have an opportunity to escape later.

Holding his weapon on Fisher, Yarian snarled, "I'll shoot him when he surfaces. You can get me where I want to go."

"He's a master diver. He won't surface within firing range," Fisher said confidently.

Yarian cursed in Russian, and then snarled at Fisher. "Get us out of here!"

Smiling, Fisher threw the throttle forward and the boat leapt out of the water as they began to rapidly move forward. Fisher was intent on accomplishing two things. First, he wanted to put some distance between the boat and Moore to give Moore a safety zone in case his two captors changed their minds and wanted to shoot at the swimmer. Second, he hoped his violation of the "no wake" rule would attract attention from the Coast Guard or harbor police. It didn't. And the boat headed due west for the Dry Tortugas with Yarian raging about Moore's escape.

Within minutes, Moore's head emerged from the warm depths of the harbor. He had heard the go-fast boat's acceleration and was fairly certain that he could safely surface. He was greeted by the wake of the speeding boat as it left the harbor.

Moore spotted a ladder affixed to one of the pilings and swam to it. He quickly climbed it and walked back to the Schooner Wharf Bar.

"Shouldn't go swimming on a full stomach or fully clothed," his waitress greeted him upon his return.

"Yeah, I know," Moore said as he pulled his cell phone from his wet pocket. "Would I be able to borrow your phone to make a quick, local call?"

Remembering the size of the tip he had left her, she didn't hesitate in pulling her cell phone out of her pocket and handing it to Moore. "Yes. And take your time."

"Thanks."

"And I'll get you a sweet tea, too. It's on me."

"I appreciate that," Moore said to the waitress who had already started to walk away. Moore punched in Kim Fisher's number and the call was immediately answered.

"Hello?"

"Kim?"

"Yes," Fisher answered.

"It's Emerson. You still have that seaplane?"

"Yes. Why?"

"I need to get to the Dry Tortugas right away. Can you take me?"

"I thought Sean was taking you there in a go fast boat," Kim said, slightly perplexed.

"I'll explain when I see you. This is urgent. Time is of the essence."

Kim's voice became serious. "Sure. I'll fly you there. Where are you?"

"Schooner Wharf."

"Be out front in eight minutes."

"Will do. And thank you, Kim."

"You know that I'll do whatever I can to help you. I look forward to hearing what happened with your go-fast boat plans." Kim hung up.

The waitress appeared with the sweet tea and Moore returned her phone to her. "Thanks. Could I have this in a roadster?"

"A roadster?"

"Plastic cup for the road," Moore grinned. "That's what they call them in the Cayman Islands."

"You can start on this one and I'll get you a fresh one."

Moore took a gulp of the tea, allowing its cool sweetness to flow down his throat. When the waitress returned, he thanked her and took the cup. He then walked around to the other side of the bar where he waited for Kim to arrive.

While he waited, he replayed Yarian's comment. "I can always track you down." As he thought about it, Moore counted the number of times which Yarian had surfaced. He didn't believe his phone was tapped and he didn't believe that he was being tailed. Yarian's comment was beginning to haunt Moore. His thoughts shifted to the prior evening's phone calls after dinner. He had called Nicholas and Kalker. Maybe, he thought, one of their lines was tapped. He decided he wouldn't alert them until he had returned to D.C. and completed the next critical leg in his adventure.

A truck pulled to a stop in front of Moore and the window slid down. "Let's go, Emerson," Kim yelled.

Moore jumped into Kim's truck for the short drive to Key West's airport where they boarded Kim's Cessna 172 amphibious seaplane and began their flight to the Dry Tortugas.

The Dry Tortugas lie seventy miles west of Key West. They are comprised of seven islands made up of coral reefs and sand. When Spanish explorer Ponce de Leon, discoverer of the islands, saw the large sea turtle population and the lack of fresh water on the islands, he named them the Dry Tortugas. Tortuga is Spanish for turtle.

Garden Key is the home to Fort Jefferson, the largest all-masonry fort in the United States. Bricks for the fort were hauled by barge from Pensacola, Florida, until the Civil War broke out. Then, the bricks were hauled from New England. When the weight of the bricks caused the fort to begin sinking, construction was halted. The three-tiered, six-sided fort was then turned into a military prison.

Kim's plane flew at a low altitude of 500 feet for the thirty minute flight to the islands. Along the way Moore explained what had happened with Sean, Yarian, and the other goon. Kim was distressed that his son was in danger, and soon, Kim pointed to a speeding go-fast boat. "That's Sean's boat."

"Looks like they're heading for Fort Jefferson," Moore guessed.

Kim reached for the radio. "I'd better get some help out here. I'll put a call in to the Coast Guard." After finishing the call, they continued their flight in silence as their joint concern for Sean's safety troubled them.

Kim circled the Cessna over the fort and then descended for his water landing. He adjusted the plane's speed so that the floats would contact the water at a point aft of the step. As the floats touched the water and sent water billowing in the air, Kim closed the throttle and gradually applied back elevator pressure so that the plane wouldn't nose down.

He pointed the plane toward the shallow water and then shut down its engine. "You can get out now. I'll secure the plane and join you in a few minutes," Kim said. "We can't do much for Sean until the boat gets here, so let's see what we can find."

Moore stepped out of the plane and onto the float. He stepped into the shallow water and raced up the beach toward the main entrance to the fort. He crossed the wooden bridge across the moat and into the fort. He found stairs nearby, which he took to the second floor. Moore walked to the open air gunroom, which was over the main entrance to the fort.

Moore stopped at the wide entrance to the brick-lined gunroom, which had been occupied by Mudd and three others. Other than a brief three-month period when the four spent time in the fort's dungeon, this was their home. The room was barren. The far wall had three narrow windows through which Moore could see the seaplane.

Moore walked into the room and allowed his eyes to wander. He knew he didn't have much time. To his right and left were anterooms. They had large open gun ports through which the cannons would have been positioned for firing. Moore leaned against one of the cool brick walls and allowed himself to slide down to the concrete floor. He sat and continued to gaze around the room.

A few minutes passed and Kim appeared at the entrance to the room. "Find anything?"

Shaking his head in consternation, Moore replied, "I just don't know where to start. If Mudd were to hide a note here, it would be a perfect place to do it. All he would have to do is to loosen one of the bricks, insert the note in the opening and return the brick to its original position."

"Sounds simple enough, but which brick?" Kim wondered aloud as he looked at the brick walls.

"Yeah, that's the million dollar question," Moore responded.

"You don't think Mudd took the note with him when he was pardoned and returned to Maryland? The note could be right in your D.C. backyard," Kim suggested.

"I thought about that, but my gut tells me no for whatever reason. I've a hunch that the note is still here. I'm basing that on this linkage to the number thirteen and with there being thirteen letters in Fort Jefferson. I could be wrong, but I don't think so."

Looking at his watch, Kim said, "I'd accelerate your thinking process. We've got about fifteen minutes before Sean and your friends arrive. We have to be there to get Sean away from these guys – distract them or something."

Moore glanced at his watch as he stood. "I guess we'd better get started." He gazed out onto the grounds in the center of the fort. There were shrubs and tropical trees. The blue sky mixed well with the red-brick walls. "It's kind of peaceful here."

"Sure is if you don't mind not having a fresh water supply and cell phone access. This is a dead zone for cell phones."

"I didn't realize that," Moore said as he turned back to face the room. "Now, where would you loosen a brick? High or low in the wall? Near the window?"

"I think you're right in eliminating anything at normal eye level. Mudd would have wanted something less conspicuous."

"Yeah, that's what I was thinking," Moore said as he dropped to his knees and began inspecting the lower bricks with his hands. "And I'd rule out high, because that would be suspicious to anyone walking by as to what he would be doing standing on a chair or table. If he worked on it while he lay on the floor, it would be less obvious. And he had cellmates. So he'd probably would have tried to do it while they were out."

"That sounds reasonable," Kim agreed as he began to run his hands over the bricks on the opposite wall.

For the next ten minutes, the two men closely inspected and ran their hands over the first two feet of bricks, trying to find one which was loose or would seem not as tightly fitting as the others. It was near the far corner that Kim made a discovery.

"Emerson?"

"Yes?"

"I may have something here," he said as he produced a knife from his pocket. He opened the blade and began to dig around the brick as Moore joined him and watched closely.

"Think that's it?"

"Maybe. It looks like the dried mortar was just packed in around this one. See how easy it's flaking as I dig it out?"

Watching the dust from Kim's excavation fall to the floor, Moore said, "Sure looks that way."

Within a minute, Kim had loosened the packed mortar dust and began to slide the brick from its position in the wall. Holding it in his hand, Kim pronounced, "I'll let you have the honors." He stepped to his left and Moore peered into the opening.

"I think there's something in there." Moore reached in and his hand felt the oilskin wrapping. He pulled it out and showed Kim. "This may be it," Moore smiled.

He carefully unwrapped the oilskin to reveal a faded and yellowed envelope.

"Hate to ruin your discovery, but I'd suggest stopping," Kim warned.

With a look of consternation, Moore asked, "Why?"

"Two reasons. First, I'd suggest opening that envelope under a more controlled environment. You don't want to damage whatever is written there. We've had some similar experiences when we've brought up our discoveries from the *Atocha*. Granted it's a different environment. This isn't in sea water, but I'd be careful."

"Okay. What's the second reason?"

"Look out the window. We've got company."

Moore stood and looked at the center window. He saw the go-fast boat had docked and Yarian and another man were racing across the dock toward the sally port entrance.

"Now what do we do?" Moore asked. "I'd guess there's just the main entrance."

"Let them come in and we'll drop out the window, then head to the plane."

"Sounds good to me," Moore agreed as he rewrapped the envelope in the oilskin.

The two men moved to the adjoining cell, which had a large opening through which they could easily pass through and drop to the ground below. They watched as Yarian and his accomplice ran into the entrance and then dropped to the ground. They ran to the seaplane and entered the craft.

"Did you see Sean anywhere?" Moore asked.

"No. I looked for him, but I bet he ran off once he delivered his cargo," Kim said as he started the plane's engines.

Suddenly, a stern voice spoke from the storage area behind the two rear seats. "Today's the day!"

Moore and Kim swung their heads around and found themselves looking at the business end of a Smith & Wesson.

"Do we need this, Dad?" Kim's son asked.

"Stow it," Kim said. "How did you end up here?"

"Those clowns tied me up, but I was able to get loose. I ran to the plane to get your gun. When I heard someone starting to board, I ducked back here."

"I'm glad you're safe," the older Fisher responded.

"Me, too," Moore added. "And thanks for your help back at the docks."

"No problem. But how did they know to come after me and my boat?"

"That's what I'm trying to figure out," Moore said angrily.

"Yeah. It's like they knew."

A few minutes earlier, Yarian had stopped to talk to a park ranger who was standing inside the main entrance. "Excuse me, could you tell me where Dr. Mudd's cell is?"

"Certainly." The ranger gave him directions to the cell on the second level.

Thanking him, Yarian and the other man ran up the stairs to the cell where Yarian spotted the brick on the floor. Swearing, he walked over to the open cavity in the wall and reached in. He withdrew his empty hand as they heard the seaplane's engine spark to life.

Yarian rushed to the window and looked at the seaplane as it gathered speed. He swore again when he saw Moore seated in the plane, waving in Yarian's direction. The water flew over the plane's pontoons as it gathered speed and planed on top of the water. Within a minute the plane was airborne and headed back to Key West.

"Back to the boat," Yarian snarled as he pulled the boat's keys from his pocket. "I'm sure they got whatever they were looking for."

Nicholas' Office
Washington, D.C.

After being buzzed through the front door, Moore walked down the hallway to Nicholas' office. It had been two days since he had returned from Key West and delivered the oilskin-wrapped letter to Nicholas, who then gave it to a friend of his. The friend had formerly worked at the National Archives and was experienced in old documents and their preservation.

"Good morning, Emerson." Nicholas greeted Moore as he walked into his office. "I've already poured your coffee. Heavy on the cream, right?" he asked as he handed Moore the coffee in a brown mug and motioned for him to sit.

"Yes, good memory," Moore said as he raised the cup to his lips and sipped the hot, flavory brew. "What did you hear from your friend?" Moore asked eagerly.

Nicholas held up his hand with the palm outward to Moore. "Patience, my boy. Patience." Nicholas took a drink from his cup and set it back in its saucer. "Tell me. What have you been doing the last couple of days?"

Moore squirmed impatiently. "Been hanging around the houseboat. Caught up on the local happenings. Saw that my intruder was killed."

"Yes, I saw that, too," Nicholas commented, in the same manner as if he had been asked about the weather.

"The police visited with me, but didn't have any further news about the investigation. They're still running it down."

Nicholas nodded his head.

"Had dinner at Mango Mike's one night. Ever been there?" Moore asked.

"I believe so. It's in Alexandria. Tropical décor. Reminds you of being in the islands. Band on the outside deck. Great island food like jerk chicken."

Moore had a large smile on his face. "You certainly know the place."

"I've actually been there several times," Nicholas said.

"Yeah, the owner brings in two semi-truck loads of tropical plants each spring to enhance the island feel. I just love the place when I'm in town."

"Have you talked with Andreas or Katrina?"

"Yes. When I called you from Miami as I was changing planes on the way back to D.C., I also called them. I talked with them again yesterday on a conference call."

Nicholas nodded his head again. "Any e-mails to them?"

"No, why?"

"I'm just curious. So, tell me about your conversations. Did either one say anything about making a visit here?"

"They're thinking about it. They're as anxious as I am to see what the letter in the oilskin reveals."

"I'm sure they are," Nicholas said as he again sipped his drink.

"Okay, you're killing me with this melodrama! Tell me what you know," Moore demanded of his friend.

"It's the letter we were looking for. It's from the German ambassador to Lincoln. I researched the German ambassador's background. He was a member of the Teutonic Knights."

"He was!" Moore said, startled by the revelation. "And that provides linkage back through Bodrum."

"That's what I was thinking," Nicholas agreed. "The letter requested Lincoln's assistance in retrieving a document that was stolen from the Teutonic Knights."

"What was the document?" Moore pressed eagerly.

"Interesting enough it didn't say. It makes me think that the Germans didn't want to reveal the contents of the document because of its significance."

"Think it was the Nazarene's Code?"

"Perhaps. If it's as powerful as it was alleged to be, then no nation would want another nation to be aware that they were searching for it." Nicholas paused and glanced toward the morning sun's rays penetrating his sheer curtains. "The letter did point to a Mason, who immigrated to the United States during the Revolutionary War. It was suspected that his parent or grandparent was involved in stealing the document from the Teutonic Knights."

"Think it was John Williames?"

"It seems to point to him. He was a Mason of German and British heritage," Nicholas answered. "I already have some of my people conducting a search for more data on Williames."

"That's helpful."

"There's more."

"Oh?" Moore asked.

"Lincoln had a second meeting scheduled with the German ambassador."

"Were you able to get the details of the meeting?"

"No. The meeting didn't take place."

"Are you sure? Maybe they need to go back and check the records," Moore urged.

"I'm sure. The reason the meeting didn't take place was that Lincoln was assassinated the night before the meeting."

"Oh," Moore said dejectedly.

"There's one other thing."

"What's that?"

"There was a second document wrapped in the oilskin."

"There was?"

"Yes. My experts say the handwriting appears to be Lincoln's."

"And, what does it say?"

"It's only a sentence."

"Which is?"

"The Indian points the way, E Pluribus Unum."

"Thirteen letters. Out of many, one," Moore translated. "The words on the Great Seal of the United States. I don't think the Great Seal has anything to do with an Indian," Moore said.

"Your thinking parallels mine. I did some research on the Great Seal. The shield, which was designed in 1782, has thirteen stripes for the original thirteen states. In the eagle's talons are thirteen arrows, symbolizing our power to go to war. That's offset by the olive branch for peace held in its other talon. Over the eagle is a constellation of thirteen stars."

"There's that thirteen stuff again. And how does this link in to this mysterious Indian?" Moore asked.

"I don't think it does."

Moore looked around the office. "Do you have an extra laptop I can use?"

Nicholas smiled. "I always have a few spares around. Why?"

"Let's do additional searches on this. You can use your souped-up system and I'll Google away."

Nodding his head, Nicholas rose from his chair. "This should be fun."

Within a few minutes, Moore was set up with the laptop and had signed onto the Internet. He was quickly researching while Nicholas returned to his dual monitors and began to search.

No more than fifteen minutes had passed when Moore looked over at Nicholas. "I think I've found something."

"Yes?"

"The Freedom Statue."

Nicholas calculated. "Thirteen letters again. Go ahead."

"It's the statute of the top of the Capitol. Four blocks from here."

"Better check your date to see when she was installed. Was she there when Lincoln was president?"

Moore read the information in front of him and exclaimed, "Yes. She was installed in 1863."

Continuing reading his display, Moore said, "It says that she's more of a classical figure, but many think she's based on Pocahontas. She's holding the shield of the United States with its thirteen stripes. Her helmet has thirteen stars and has a crest composed of an eagle's head, feathers and talons similar to what American Indians would wear."

"Anything about a link to E Pluribus Unum?"

Moore read further and then stopped. "Here it is! It says that she stands on a cast-iron globe. Those words are inscripted on it. Looks like we found our Indian."

"It's funny how things are. As many times as I've been to the Capitol, I've been aware, but not truly aware of her on top of it. Can you display a picture of her?"

Moore scrolled down as Nicholas stood from his seat and walked over to Moore and his laptop.

"Here we go."

"Doesn't look like she's pointing to anything," Nicholas said as he stared at the screen.

"No, it doesn't." Moore studied the photo. "I'll bet that the clue is based on the direction she's facing."

"Could be." Nicholas looked at her again.

"Looks like she's facing the Mall."

"I think we should check this out in person."

"You mean go up there?"

"Exactly. There's a small balcony up there. You can visit it if you have a Congressman with you. And, do I know Congressmen or what!" Nicholas smiled as he picked up the phone.

"Who are you calling?"

"Your buddy from Ohio."

"Who?"

"The Speaker of the House, John Bettner. I thought you'd get an extra kick out of Bettner acting as our escort." Nicholas turned his attention back to his phone as his call was answered.

Within minutes, he made his arrangements and hung up. "All set," he smiled.

"That easy?"

"For as much as I help Congressional oversight committees and considering the work I do for the intelligence committees, they are more than willing to assist me in return." Nicholas looked at his watch. "We better get moving. Bettner is going to meet us in forty-five minutes."

"I'm impressed."

"Don't be," Nicholas responded. "This will give you a chance to experience my tunnel access to the Capitol. I don't think you've seen it."

"No. You had mentioned that you had this tunnel, but I haven't gone through it."

"Follow me." Nicholas walked over to his built-in bookcases and reached underneath one of the shelves, depressing a hidden button. The bookcase opened into the room and revealed an elevator door, which opened. "Step inside, Emerson."

Moore walked into the elevator as Nicholas depressed another button that returned the bookcase to its original position. He joined Moore in the elevator for the short trip two stories below. When the elevator doors opened, they saw a dark tunnel in front of them.

"Follow me," Nicholas repeated as he emerged from the elevator. His motion activated the motion detector system and lights turned on as they walked toward the Supreme Court building.

"Did I tell you that there were thirteen signers to the Declaration of Independence?" Nicholas asked as they made their way through the tunnel.

"No, but that would make sense since there were thirteen colonies," Moore responded.

Upon reaching it and a locked steel door, Nicholas placed his head into a bracket, which allowed for a retina scan of his eye. Once the scan was completed, the door unlocked and the two entered another underground corridor, which led them to the Capitol Building.

As they neared the end of the long corridor, Nicholas warned Moore, "We have a security check with the Capitol Police coming up. It should go fine."

The check went flawlessly, thanks to the officers recognizing Nicholas. They made their way to another elevator, which they took to the main level of the Capitol. They walked through the rotunda and to a small office door. It was the on-site office for the Speaker of the House.

Nicholas looked at his watch. "We're right on time."

At that moment, the office door opened and John Bettner stepped out. The tan, suave Speaker was impeccably attired in a dark blue suit, white shirt and bright green tie. "Steve," he greeted Nicholas with a handshake.

"Mr. Speaker."

Nicholas introduced Moore and then they headed for the elevator for a short ride to a stairwell that would take them to the balcony area. When they walked onto the balcony, they were greeted by a breath-taking view of the Mall and the city below.

From their perch atop the Capitol and below the statue, Moore, said, "What a view!"

"Where's she looking, Emerson?"

Moore glanced up and then in the direction the Freedom Statue was facing. "I'd think it's either the Lincoln Memorial or the Washington Monument."

"We know it couldn't be the Lincoln Memorial. It wasn't planned to be built in 1863. But each day, Lincoln could look from his office window and see the Washington Monument. I bet that's your next clue."

"Doesn't have thirteen letters," Moore offered as he scanned the Mall below.

"I know. I may be wrong, but I'd still start there. We can do more research when we return to my office."

They thanked their guide, who accompanied them down the elevator. They then returned through the underground tunnels to Nicholas' office.

Closing the bookcase door behind them, the two men returned to their respective chairs and started researching the Washington Monument.

Moore was the first to speak about his research.

"It says here that it's made of marble, granite and bluestone gneiss and it's the world's tallest stone structure and tallest obelisk at 555 feet 5 1/8 inches." Moore continued. "Work on it was halted during the Civil War which means Lincoln would have looked out of his window at a monument a third of the way completed."

"That's what I'm seeing here, too," Nicholas added.

"That partially explains why there's a discoloration between the stones laid earlier," Moore read. "Here's something else interesting. Each side at the base also measures 666 inches."

"Not sure that ties into anything we're working on."

"No, but interesting since it's a number strongly tied to religion."

"Back to the shading, I did hear a rumor over the years that Lincoln had given the Secretary of War instructions on laying the block in a certain manner based on shading. What if the shading translated into a code?" Nicholas wondered aloud.

Moore chuckled. "Wouldn't that be ironic? A code visible to all onlookers, but only the true message known to a few."

"Yes, it would be."

Moore zoomed in on a few on-line photos of the Monument and looked over at Nicholas. "It doesn't appear that the shading was implemented."

"No, it seems that after Lincoln's assassination, Stanton ignored the instructions Lincoln had given him."

Moore looked at several photos of the monument. "What if the monument was pointing to a message just like we think the Freedom Statue was pointing to a clue?"

"You know that there's a message at the top of the monument?"

"Yes, on the top piece, facing the Capitol. It says Laus Deo. That translates to Praise Be to God," Moore said as he read from his display screen.

"That's correct and that's thirteen letters." Nicholas offered.

"You think that the Freedom Statue was pointing to that message? I don't see how that helps with finding the Nazarene's Code."

"What if there's another message there? What if it involved the Masons when they built the monument? You know the laying of the foundation for the monument included a huge celebration by the Masons. And they were very supportive of the Monument's construction, especially when the site of the Monument had to be relocated."

"Relocated? I thought that it was always meant to be built in D.C."

"It was. But it had to be moved several feet because of integrity issues with the foundation. The original site couldn't support the Monument's weight."

"That's no big deal," Moore said as he wrinkled his brow, trying to understand the point that Nicholas was trying to make.

Nicholas added a dark line on his screen and partially turned the monitor so that Moore could see it. "Exactly thirteen blocks away from the Monument and now directly in line with it is the Masonic Temple."

Moore looked at the monitor and nodded, saying, "Eerie." Moore looked up at Nicholas. "How do we determine if there's anything else written on the top of the Monument?"

"There's someone we could check with."

"Who?" Moore asked.

"In August 2011, an earthquake really shook up D.C. It also damaged the Monument and cracks appeared in it."

"Yes, I remember watching a story on cable news about it. An engineering firm was hired to inspect the structural integrity of the monument."

"Your memory serves you correctly. There's a small access window near the top and the engineers had to hook their gear over the top of the Monument and rappel down the sides to inspect every part of it. I'd venture that they could confirm whether there's anything else written there."

"Wasn't the firm headquartered in Chicago?"

"Yes, but I don't recall that the engineers were domiciled there."

Moore's fingers flew across his keyboard as he researched the incident. "Here we go. They're in Northbrook, Illinois. I've got a phone number. Let's see what I can find."

Moore picked up his newly acquired cell phone as he stood. "I'm going to call from your front porch. I could use some fresh air."

"Go ahead. Do as you wish," Nicholas said as he continued to review his screen for additional information.

Moore's steps echoed down the hallway as he left to place his call. Twenty minutes later, he returned.

"I've got good news," Moore beamed.

"Oh?"

"The folks in the Chicago office were very accommodating. They gave me the number for one of the engineers and he lives nearby in Arlington. I called him and explained a bit about our interest in the Monument. He agreed to meet me in Alexandria at Mango Mike's for dinner tonight."

"That is good news."

"No, it gets better."

Nicholas, with a puzzled expression, glanced at Moore.

"He saw something etched below the inscription Laus Deo. He wouldn't tell me what it was until he has a chance to check me out on line. Assuming the check goes okay, he'll show up for the dinner meeting tonight."

"We should update Andreas and Kat," Nicholas said. "But, let's hold off until tomorrow. I'll send them an e-mail and set up a conference call for tomorrow morning. They have a new private number in case the other line was tapped."

"Sounds fine to me." Moore looked at his watch. "I think I'll head back to my place and freshen up before dinner. You have plans for tonight?"

Moore watched as a grin crossed Nicholas' face and he remained silent.

"I think I know what that look means. You're going to the White House again for dinner, aren't you?" Moore asked.

"There are some visiting dignitaries in town and they've brought some of their intel people. I'm joining some of my associates to mingle. Usual black tie affair."

Moore shook his head. "That's one thing I don't miss about D.C. - the pomp and circumstance. When I'm back in Put-in-Bay, it's island style - just a tee shirt, shorts and sandals."

"And a girl on each arm," Nicholas teased.

"Not quite. Thanks for all of your help today. It was productive," Moore said as he began to walk toward the hallway.

"And I hope your dinner is as productive," Nicholas said. "Call me if it is. I should be back by ten-thirty or so."

"I can do that," Moore said as he walked down the hall and out the front door.

Mango Mike's
Alexandria, Virginia

Parking his car in the restaurant's parking lot on Duke Street in Alexandria's West End, Moore entered one of his favorite restaurants. Mango Mike's was a tropical oasis in the middle of the Washington Beltway's hustle and bustle. The outside was flanked by full-grown palm trees and waterfalls. Inside, the Caribbean island-themed grille offered an escape to paradise. Its tropical plants and vibrant red, blue, yellow, and orange colored walls combined with island paintings to offer its customers a brief respite from the hectic Washington political scene.

Moore entered and turned to his right. He walked past the white shuttered doors to the restrooms and into the tiki hut themed bar. He saw a couple leaving a high top table and quickly secured it. As he sat on one of the high chairs, his cell rang.

"This is Emerson."

"Emerson, it's Nick Sheldon. I just walked in. Where do I find you?"

Moore saw the blond-haired engineer in the entryway with his phone to his ear. "I'm in the bar," he answered. "Tall, dark, and wearing Khaki's." When Sheldon turned his head, Moore waved and Sheldon headed for Moore.

"So, I checked out okay?" Moore asked as they shook hands.

"Yeah. It's not every day that you get a Pulitzer Prize-winning reporter wanting to meet up with you." He took the vacant chair across from Moore.

Moore smiled as he recalled the story from a few years ago where he solved a mystery from the Civil War amidst a nuclear terror threat in the Lake Erie islands. The story had won the award. "Been here before?"

"No, but I've wanted to try it. Just didn't get around to it. Nice place," he said as he looked around.

"You'll want to check out the outside deck when we're done. They usually have island music and, sometimes, steel drums."

"Cool," Sheldon responded.

A svelte blonde waitress appeared to welcome her two customers. "Welcome to Mango Mike's. Can I get you gentlemen drinks? Like to try a Margarita?"

"Sure, I'll give it a try. How about you, Emerson?"

"Make mine a Captain Morgan and Coke."

"I'll be right back," she said as she spun on her heels and walked away.

"Guess we better look at the menus," Moore suggested.

By the time the waitress returned with their drinks, the two men had made their dinner selections.

Sheldon ordered the Caribbean Platter. It was a seafood selection of fried rockfish, coconut shrimp, fried sea scallops, and a mini crab cake. It was accompanied by fried sweet plantains, mango cole slaw, and spicy cocktail and tartar sauce.

Having a fondness for jerk chicken, Moore ordered the Jerk Chicken Paillard. It was a grilled and sliced, jerk-marinated chicken breast dusted with jerk rub. It was served over rice with corn pudding, and seasonal grilled vegetables.

The waitress left them to place their dinner orders.

Moore raised his glass to Sheldon in a toast. "Nick, here's to your continued safety as you climb tall buildings."

Sheldon toasted back, "And to yours."

Thinking back to the events of the last few weeks, Moore wanted to say, if you only knew. Instead Moore commented, "You've got

– 246 –

a dangerous job, rappelling down monuments and all."

"It's not really that bad. You follow all of the safety rules and check your gear."

"I can't imagine climbing out of the little window near the top of the Monument, and then having to set up your rigging over the top of the Monument."

"It's not that bad. You do what you have to do. We're very careful. Can't make any mistakes in that environment." Sheldon sipped his drink. "This is good. Glad I chose this."

Moore nodded.

Sheldon looked at Moore intently. "I'm curious as to how you knew that there was more etched into the Monument than the general public knows. How did you know that?" Sheldon asked.

"I didn't. It was just a guess. As a reporter, sometimes my gut leads me down the right track. Sometimes, the wrong track." Moore pressed. "So, are you comfortable enough to tell me what was written there?"

"Sure. I don't think it's really that big of a deal. I believe it's the stone carver's name. It's Sandustee. It's cut in the stone, below the words Laus Deo."

"Sandustee?" Moore asked.

"Yes. Would you like to see it?"

Moore laughed. "There's no way I'm going up there."

"No, no. I have a photo on my cell phone."

"You took a cell phone photo while you were hanging there?"

Moore asked astonished.

Chuckling, Sheldon replied, "No. Our inspection procedure requires us to look for loose pieces of masonry and cracks. We also have rubber mallets that we use to tap each stone and listen to the responding sounds. Those sounds also tell us if there are any issues. We're also required to record everything we inspect. To do that, we have digital cameras and recorders. I just e-mailed one of the digital recordings to my iPhone so I could show you tonight. Here, let me show you."

Sheldon pulled out his iPhone from his pocket and scrolled to his photos. In a matter of seconds, he presented the phone to Moore. "Here's the picture I was talking about."

Moore looked at the photo. Without a doubt the Laus Deo was more deeply cut into the stone. Below that was a dash followed by the name of the stone carver, Sandustee. It was not as deeply cut as the Laus Deo inscription.

Moore looked up from the iPhone to Sheldon, "You ever hear of this stone carver?"

Sheldon shook his head negatively. "Nope. I don't know beans about stone carvers."

"Any chance you could e-mail this photo to me?"

"Sure," Sheldon said as he took back the phone and began to change screens. "It's not classified or anything. What's your e-mail address?"

Moore provided it and picked up his phone. Within ten seconds, his cell phone buzzed and he confirmed that the picture had come through. "Looks like I have it. Thanks, I appreciate it." Slipping his phone into his pocket, Moore asked Sheldon a number of questions regarding the dangers of his career throughout their dinner.

Nicholas' Office
The Next Day

The door buzzed open and Moore entered Nicholas' townhouse.

"Thanks for sending me the e-mail last night," Nicholas said with a raspy voice. "It does sound like you had a productive meeting last night."

"I did. You coming down with something?" Moore asked with concern. "Your voice sounds raw."

"I've got a raspy throat. There were a couple of youngsters at the event last night. I ended up chatting with them for a while. Little germ factories, I call them. More like Petrie dishes on legs. I may have picked up a virus."

"Take two aspirins and call the doctor in the morning," Moore suggested.

Nicholas nodded his head. "I'm ahead of you. I went into Jody's office and found her bottle of Tylenol. I took two. About an hour ago, my head began to swell up. Then, I remembered Jody kept her birth control pills in a Tylenol bottle."

Moore couldn't help but laugh. "Okay, forget about calling the doctor in the morning. Go see an OBGYN."

"Not funny, Emerson," Nicholas said as he sipped his hot tea. "I read your e-mail last night, but all you said was that you had breaking news."

"I do. Below the Laus Deo quote is the name of the stone carver. It's Sandustee, and I bet he's a Mason."

"Good." Nicholas began to key in an information request on his keyboard.

"I Googled the name last night. Didn't have a hit on Sandustee, but my search listed a number of items under Sandusky from that Penn State football coach to two cities with the name. One is in Michigan, north of Detroit, and the other is on Ohio's north coast, close to Put-in-Bay. It's also the home of Cedar Point, a great amusement park filled with roller coasters." Moore remembered one other search result. "I did see a linkage to stone masons in the U.K. What do you think?"

"Let's see what my search turns up. I can bet you that my search engine has far greater capabilities than yours." Nicholas stood and walked over to a Keurig coffeemaker on a stand in a corner of his office. "Would you like a coffee?"

"Sure. Breakfast blend if you have it." Moore joined Nicholas at the coffeemaker. "Here, better let me do it. I don't want your germs infecting me." Moore winced after he said it.

"Something wrong?"

"Not really. From time to time, I still get a pain in my lower jaw. I may have a cracked tooth from when Gorenchenko hit my jaw a couple of weeks ago. The pain comes and goes."

"You need to have that checked," Nicholas said as he returned to his desk and looked at the monitor.

Moore finished making his coffee and joined Nicholas. "Anything?"

Nicholas' fingers were keying in instructions as he deepened the search. "I'm building a tree of data. Nothing on Sandustee yet. But here's something of interest. I've got a link of data on statue casting and Masons and the German Teutonic Knights." Nicholas keyed in additional instructions and sat back.

"Hmmm. Look at this. There's an old practice of hiding a message inside the heads of statues, sort of like a time capsule. What if a clue could be there?"

Moore had an incredulous look on his face. "Steve, how many statues are there in the world? I don't think so."

"Patience, my boy. Patience. We aren't looking across the whole world. Only the United States and more particularly D.C. Let me try something here." He made a few more entries into his computer.

Less than a minute passed. "Look what we have here. The statue of Andrew Jackson on his horse in Lafayette Park across from The White House. Each of the three key words, Andrew Jackson, Lafayette Park and The White House has thirteen characters."

Moore's eyebrows rose at the revelation. "But, how does Sandustee tie into this?"

"Don't know. What if he was a stone carver and cast statues? Or had a friend who did?"

"When was the statue dedicated?" Moore asked.

"January 8, 1853. The bronze statue was made on site by an American named Clark Mills. The horse was cast in four pieces and Jackson was cast in six pieces."

"You really think there's something hidden in the statue's head?" Moore asked skeptically.

Shrugging his shoulders, Nicholas said, "One never knows. May be worth a check."

"And how do we do that?"

"It'd require an approval from the Park Service."

"That would take ten years to get," Moore fumed.

"Not with my contacts," Nicholas reminded him.

Glancing at his watch, Nicholas said, "It's almost time for our call to Andreas and Kat."

Moore sat in his chair and inched it closer to the speaker phone on Nicholas' desk. At the same time, Nicholas keyed in the number. The call was answered on the second ring.

"Good morning, Steve. I trust Emerson is with you," Andreas greeted Nicholas.

"Yes, we're both here."

"Good morning, Emerson," Bieber warmly greeted Moore.

"Hi, Kat. When are you going to come here for a visit?" Moore asked eagerly. He tried to sound cool but failed miserably.

"Soon, I hope," she responded.

"And what have you two found since our last call?" Kalker asked, anxious to get to the point of the call.

"I understand that Emerson told you about his escapade at Ft. Jefferson," Nicholas said.

"Yes, he did. He's very fortunate to be alive," Kalker observed. "These Russians are a bad bunch. We have been able to determine that Karapashev is directing Yarian in the search for the Nazarene's Code."

"Any luck on tracking down Karapashev's location?" Nicholas asked.

"Yes. We have one lead of particular interest."

"How's that?" Nicholas asked.

"He appears to now be in the United States."

"I wouldn't be surprised the way things have been heating up for Emerson. Karapashev must be on the ground here and directing surveillance on Emerson." Nicholas looked at Moore. "And you, my young friend, had better be more careful and watch your back better."

Nicholas then gave them a briefing about their investigation over the last few days.

"You two have been busy," Kalker offered.

"That would be an understatement," Moore responded.

"There's one more thing that we're running down," Nicholas said.

"Oh?" Kalker asked.

"We have a theory that there may be something hidden in the Andrew Jackson statue across from the White House."

"In a statue?" Kalker asked incredulously.

"Yeah. There's an old practice that messages or notes were hidden in the head of statues. It's like a time capsule," Nicholas explained.

"What's your next step?" Kalker asked.

"We'll talk to the Park Service. They may or may not cooperate with us."

"Think they could run a scan of some sort? Take x-rays?" Moore asked.

"Don't know." Nicholas began to wrap up the call. "We had better go now."

"We'll be in touch," Bieber said as they concluded the call.

Moore stood. "I guess I'm heading over for a visit to the Andrew Jackson statue."

"You and your x-ray vision eyes?" Nicholas grinned.

"Don't I wish!" Moore said as he began to walk out of the office. "I'll let you know if I can determine anything."

"I'm counting on that," Nicholas said as his friend walked down the long hallway to the front door and exited.

Lafayette Park
Across from The White House

Across from The White House was the seven-acre park named in honor of General Lafayette of France. The park was originally a part of The White House grounds until 1804 when President Jefferson had Pennsylvania Avenue cut through the park.

The park's four corners were anchored by statues of Revolutionary War heroes: France's General Marquis Gilbert de Lafayette and Major General Comte Jean de Rochambeau, Poland's General Thaddeus Kosciuszko, and Prussia's Major General Baron Friedrich Wilhelm von Steuben. In the center of the tree-shaded park was the equestrian statue of President Andrew Jackson.

Walking around the statue, which was enclosed by a black wrought iron fence, was Emerson Moore. He looked up at the statue, which was set on top of a white marble base. Jackson's horse reared back on its two hind legs. Jackson held his hat high in the air as he looked toward The White House.

Moore sat on one of the nearby park benches and stared at the back of Jackson's head as he thought about the possibilities. It would take an act of Congress to obtain permission to open up the back of the statue's head, he thought. After a few minutes, Moore stood and returned to his car, which was squeezed into a small parking space.

Moore didn't notice that a man wearing dark sunglasses and a straw hat had been watching him. The man pulled his cell phone from his pocket and speed dialed a number.

When the phone was answered, the man spoke first. "It can be done. It will be dangerous with so much security around here, but it can be done."

"Then, do it," the callee said before he disconnected the call.

The man speed dialed another number in his phone. When the phone was answered the man spoke, "This is Yarian. Find us a van. We have a project."

Moore's Houseboat
Alexandria, Virginia

The ringing cell phone awoke Moore from a deep sleep. He rolled over and tried to focus his eyes on the caller's name. He saw that it was Nicholas.

"Hello, Steve. What's so urgent that you're calling this early?" Moore asked as he saw the time on his alarm clock read 6:17 AM.

"You probably haven't seen the online news this morning?"

"Nope. The only thing I've seen was this beautiful redhead I was dreaming about. Now, I won't know what happened!" Moore responded, mildly irritated at his dream being interrupted.

"You need to review the local news. Right in front of the White House, two men parked a van on the far side of Lafayette Park. They were wearing uniforms and carrying a ladder, cleaning brushes and buckets. You wouldn't think twice that they were up to something."

"Go ahead," Moore urged.

"They approached the Jackson statue and set up the ladder. One of them apparently affixed a small explosive to the back of Jackson's head and detonated it. They had flashlights and quickly looked inside the statue's head and left. They left the ladder, cleaning supplies and van. They rode away quickly on a motorbike from the back of the van."

"How did the news know all of this?"

"The story indicated that there were surveillance cameras in the park and they captured all of it."

"Did it say if they pulled anything out of Jackson's head?"

"No, they're still investigating. I'm going to call my friends at the Park Service and see what they can tell me. The story did say that they were able to capture the motorbike's license plates and they are running them."

"Probably a stolen motorbike – and van," Moore surmised.

"Think it was Karapashev and Yarian?"

"Probably. And that's why I'm going to ask you not to use your cell phone again. We thought Kalker's line was bugged, but it could be yours or mine. I'm having my land line checked within the hour."

"I can't believe this. I may as well cc Yarian on everything I say and do."

"I'll plan on giving you a call from my new number two hours from now at your favorite waterfront restaurant in Alexandria."

"Got it," Moore acknowledged.

Two hours later, Moore was sitting on the deck at Indigo Landing. A waitress approached him with a phone.

"Emerson Moore?"

"Yes?"

"There's a gentleman on the phone asking for you," she said as she smiled at the nice-looking reporter.

"Thanks, I appreciate it." Moore held the receiver to his ear. "This is Emerson."

"Emerson, I had a team of specialists sweep my place and check all the phone lines. I'm clean."

"That's good news."

"For me, yes. For you, no. Your cell phone must be compromised. I'd suggest tossing it and getting a new one today."

"I can do that."

"One more thing. There's a statue of Andrew Jackson in New Orleans."

"That's right. I forgot about that one. I know right where it is. It's across from the River's Edge Restaurant in the French Quarters Jackson Square. Friends of mine own the restaurant."

"Thirteen again," Nicholas said.

"What?"

"Jackson Square and French Quarter. Each has thirteen letters."

Moore quickly counted the letters. "They do," he agreed. "So do, Bourbon Street and Decatur Street."

Nicholas counted the letters and nodded his head in agreement. Then, he gave Moore his instructions.

"First, I want you to get a new cell phone and call me with the number. Then, I want you to book a flight from Reagan to New Orleans. There's no reason why you can't be there by late this afternoon."

"And then what am I supposed to do? Walk into Jackson Square and blow off the back of the statue's head?" Moore asked with a tone of skepticism.

"No, I'm working on that. The New Orleans' statue is a duplicate of the one here and was built by the same sculptor, Clark Mills. Just do as I ask. This may be a long shot, but you never know."

"Okay, Steve. I'll do as you ask," Moore said as he thought about seeing some of his friends in the French Quarter.

River's Edge Restaurant
New Orleans, Louisiana

Downing the last of his rum and coke, Moore thanked the affable restaurant owner, Chellie Smith, for the complimentary beverage. The two had established a friendship a few years earlier when Moore was investigating serial murders in the French Quarter that were linked to serial murders in Put-in-Bay.

The open-air, sunlit restaurant at the corner of Decatur Street and St. Ann Street was located across from Café du Monde and next to Jackson Square in the historic Pontalba Building.

Moore stepped out of the restaurant and walked through the sidewalk crowded with tourists looking at the art for sale along the fence in front of Jackson Square. He saw the long line of horse-drawn carriages awaiting their next passengers for a slow tour of the French Quarter.

Moore's flight had been uneventful. He had caught a cab from the airport to the Place d'Armes Hotel, the historic hotel on St. Ann Street, a few blocks from River's Edge Restaurant. He had checked into a room in the brick hotel that had a lush tropical courtyard surrounding an inviting pool.

Moore stopped in front of a carriage and turned suddenly to look behind him. He watched the faces of people approaching him to see if he recognized anyone. He wanted to be sure that he wasn't being followed. After a minute, Moore walked through the main entranceway into the one block square park named Jackson Square and headed toward the centerpiece. He gazed at the statue dedicated to Andrew Jackson for saving New Orleans during the Battle of New Orleans in 1815. Jackson had laid the cornerstone for the statue, but he died before the statue was unveiled in February of 1856.

As he walked around the statue, Moore saw that Nicholas was right. It looked exactly like the statue in D.C.'s Lafayette Park. Moore found a nearby park bench and sat down. Reaching into his pocket, he pulled out his new cell phone and called Nicholas.

"Steve, I'm here," Moore greeted his wise mentor.

"Good. I'm still running down approvals for a minor biopsy. Tell me, have you been followed?"

Moore looked around Jackson Square once again. "No, not that I can tell," he responded.

"Good. It must have been your cell phone for sure."

"I guess so. What do you want me to do now?" Moore asked.

"You can sightsee as far as I'm concerned. I hope to have the approvals no later than tomorrow morning. Then, we can see what's in Jackson's head – if anything."

"All right, then. Call me when you have something."

"I'm close," Nicholas said as they ended their call.

Moore decided he'd walk the two blocks to Royal Street and visit his friends at Cohen's.

Moore stood and walked to his left, through the Square and toward its north side. Three buildings dominated the north side. The centerpiece was St. Louis Cathedral flanked to the left by the Cabildo, where the Louisiana Purchase was signed. On the right, it was flanked by the Presbytere, the original housing for the Catholic priests. Both buildings were museums while the cathedral was still the site of daily worship services.

Walking down an alley on the west side of the church, Moore

turned left and walked the short distance to 437 Royal Street, the home of James H. Cohen and Sons' Antique Weapons and Old Coins. The Cohen family warmly greeted Moore as he entered the shop. Moore spent an hour visiting with Mr. Jimmy, Jerry, Steve, and Barry while admiring their collection of Kentucky long rifles, dueling pistols, and handguns from the Civil War as well as their swords and sabers. Moore always enjoyed his visits with the Cohen family.

Leaving the store, Moore continued walking west on Royal to Orleans Avenue. He turned right and walked the short distance to the Orleans Grapevine Wine Bar & Bistro owned by his friends, Pam Fortner and Earl Bernhardt. Moore had met them years ago when they attended the Jimmy Buffet Parrothead celebration at Mr. Ed's Bar in Put-in-Bay. The two hosted the New Orleans' Parrothead event at one of their other bars on Bourbon Street, The Tropical Isle. The Tropical Isle also hosted Put-in-Bay singer and guitarist, Ray Fogg, during the month of March.

Entering the doorway of the two-story structure, built in 1809, Moore paused to breathe in the ambiance of the restaurant's warm, dark stained wood trim, which accented the red brick interior and the tin ceiling. Moore loved the atmosphere that was heightened by a pianist, playing a variety of tunes.

"Emerson!" greeted a man seated at the bar. He was stocky, had a goatee and wore his gray-streaked hair combed back. He was wearing a black shirt with a piano keyboard printed vertically down one side.

"Mr. Earl," Moore returned the greeting. From the day they first met, Moore had called the two owners Mr. Earl and Miss Pam. It just felt right. It was a "Southern" tradition.

"What brings you to town?" Bernhardt asked with his Southern drawl. Before Moore could respond, Bernhardt asked, "Anything to do with that female detective you met here?" Bernhardt was referring to Melaudra Drenchau, a romantic interest of Moore's who vaguely looked like Halle Berry.

"He wishes!" a feminine voice said behind Moore.

Moore turned and greeted the perky, blonde co-owner. "Miss Pam, it is so nice to see you." Moore gave her a big hug.

"You didn't answer my question, Emerson. What about that Drenchau woman?"

"Miss Pam's right. I wish I were here to see her. I don't know what I did, but that relationship went cold really fast, even before it started."

"Are you going to give her a call while you're in town?" Fortner asked.

"It's too short of a trip. I'm in this afternoon and out tomorrow afternoon," Moore explained with a tone of exasperation.

"Business?" Fortner asked.

"Yes, but let's talk about you folks and what's been happening."

"I suggest we do it over dinner. Have you had dinner yet?" Bernhardt asked.

"No, but I'd love to dine here."

"Can I order for you?" Bernhardt inquired.

"Sure."

"We can eat here at the bar." Bernhardt motioned to the bartender to take the order. "Let's try the Evangeline chicken and the C'est la Vie."

The bartender nodded.

"And what exactly is that?" Moore asked eagerly.

Fortner responded. "You'll like it. It's a tender and moist chicken breast wrapped in Neuskes bacon and fresh sage. It's served with a Southern Comfort glaze, peppered sweet potatoes and baby vegetables."

"And the C'est la Vie is a Chardonnay-Sauvignon blend. If my memory serves me, you liked it when you tried it here last time," Bernhardt mentioned.

"Good memory," Moore said as the bartender returned with the wine.

The three spent the next hour catching up on happenings in Put-in-Bay and the French Quarter. After finishing off a dessert of fromage au chocolate – Wisconsin fudge with fresh fruit – Moore agreed to accompany Fortner to the Tropical Isle on Bourbon Street for an after dinner drink since she needed to be the on site manager for the evening.

The Tropical Isle's atmosphere was the opposite of the Wine Bar's laid-back atmosphere. It hosted a wilder crowd and loud, raucous music. It was also the home of the famous Hand Grenade drink, which had a federally registered trademark. The melon flavored drink had a high alcohol content and was served in a green, plastic yard glass with a base shaped like a hand grenade. It was often referred to as "New Orleans Most Powerful Drink!"

Moore bid Bernhardt farewell and walked out of the Wine Bar with Fortner for the Tropical Isle where Moore would listen to music and drink a third of a Hand Grenade before returning to his hotel room.

Had Moore not been so engrossed in his conversation with Fortner, he may have noticed that a man had stepped from the shadowy doorway of a building and began to follow him.

As he followed them at a discreet distance, Yarian smiled to himself. Moore may have replaced his cell phone, but Yarian had a back-up plan. It was working just as well, if not better.

The Next Morning
Jackson Square

The morning sun cast shadows across the well-kept grounds filled with a variety of flowers and trees. Two vans were parked in the center of the square. A team of four workers unloaded ladders and equipment from the rear of the vans. They were supervised by a middle-aged, black woman with graying hair.

"I want you to know that this is highly irregular," she said in her Southern drawl to Moore, who was standing next to her.

"Miss Larose, I do appreciate all of your help in this matter," Moore replied.

Moore had been awakened by an early morning call from Nicholas. He had told Moore that he had been able to set up this operation by calling in a favor from one of Louisiana's senators. Nicholas had instructed Moore to meet Larose in the Square at 6:30 AM before the tourists began to fill the area.

"This type of thing has never been done before," Larose fretted.

"I'm sure that it hasn't."

"This is most unusual," she continued as she watched the workers finish setting up scaffolding and ladders, then hoist their cutting tools to the top level. "I suppose you will want to join them?"

Nodding his head, Moore began to walk to the ladder. "Yes, I'll need to be with them."

Moore quickly climbed the ladder and joined the two men on top of the scaffolding. They were beginning to make an incision in the rear of Jackson's head. Sparks flew from their cutting tool as they carefully cut open a six-inch by six-inch opening. Cautiously, they removed the cut section.

One of the men turned to Moore as he stepped away and said, "He's all yours."

Pulling a flashlight from his pocket, Moore stepped up and shined the light inside the back of the skull. Not seeing anything, Moore pocketed the small flashlight and reached his hand inside the skull. Feeling around, he found a wide ledge near the base of the skull. On the ledge, his fingers encountered an oilskin-wrapped packet.

Carefully, his fingers closed around the packet and he withdrew it from the skull.

"What do you have there?" the worker asked as the packet emerged.

"Don't know," Moore responded.

"Don't ask him any questions," Larose's voice shouted from below. "Orders from headquarters. We don't get to know what he does and are not to interfere," she huffed with obvious irritation.

Moore reached into his pants pocket and withdrew a folded plastic bag into which he inserted the packet and zipped it shut. "And I won't know what we have here until I return to Washington," Moore said as he descended the ladder.

"Thank you, Miss Larose, for your help today."

"You are welcome," she said in a cold tone. She was put off by the whole operation.

Moore turned and bumped into two police officers. "Excuse me," Moore said, embarrassed.

"No need for that. We're your escorts to your hotel and the airport," one officer said.

"Now, that's a pleasant surprise," Moore said as he began walking with them to his hotel a block away.

As they walked, Moore called Nicholas on his new cell. "Got it," he said when Nicholas answered. "You were right."

"Good. Did you open it?"

"No, it's wrapped in oilskin. I didn't want to risk opening it in the sunlight. I'll wait until I get to your office this afternoon. I'm on the way back to my hotel and then to the airport."

"Excellent. I'll look forward to seeing you and your prize," Nicholas said as he ended the call.

Moore paused and then asked, "By chance, did you arrange for a police escort for me?"

"Yes, I did. At this point in the game, we don't want to take any chances."

"Good. Just wanted to make sure they're legit."

From a corner of the Square, a tourist ground his cigarette into the concrete. It was Yarian. He fumed at missing the Jackson Statue in Jackson Square, but then he didn't know American history. His mind worked as he watched Moore leave the Square. He plotted how to examine the contents of Moore's bag.

Yarian followed Moore and the two police officers to Place D'Armes, but he wouldn't have an opportunity to examine the contents. Moore was too well protected this time.

Moore disappeared into his room where he quickly packed his suitcase. He returned to the lobby and checked out, then rode in a police car to the airport.

Nicholas' Office
Washington, D.C.

"You're sure it was Yarian?" Nicholas asked, incredulously.

"Positive. I saw him following me from the Square. I saw his reflection in the windows of a store on St. Anne when I was returning to my hotel. I checked twice," Moore replied.

"And he didn't accost you?"

"Not this time, especially with the two police officers accompanying me," Moore said. "I'm not quite sure what his game is." Moore then added, "I'm not even quite sure how he found me."

"You replaced your cell phone?"

"Yes."

"And you didn't tell anyone that you were going there?"

"No."

"What about Kalker or Kat?"

"I didn't tell a soul."

Nicholas rubbed his chin as he thought and looked Moore up and down. "I don't understand how they knew you were there."

"Join the club."

Nicholas was obviously agitated. "Well, we'll figure this out. Let me see what you have there."

Moore slid the plastic bag across the desk toward Nicholas. He then sat back in his chair.

"We'll want this opened by some of my friends at the National Archives. I don't know what we have here, but I don't want it damaged. If it's been in that statue, we don't know its condition."

"How soon can you get it to them?" Moore asked as he rubbed his right jaw.

Nicholas glanced at the nautical clock on his desk. "Today. I still have time." He looked closely at Moore. "Your jaw still bothering you?"

"No. More like a tooth."

"You rub your jaw quite often. When did all of this start?"

"Oh, it's nothing. Just a toothache."

"When did it start?"

"It must be cracked. I'll get it checked when I have a chance."

"How did it crack?"

"It was in Turkey. Gorenchenko hit me in the jaw, among other places. It's been hurting ever since I regained consciousness."

Nicholas reached for his phone and punched in a number.

"What are you doing?" Moore asked.

Nicholas held up his finger for Moore to wait. "Yes, is he in?" Pause. "Good. This is Steve Nicholas. Could you let him know that I have an emergency and am sending Emerson Moore over for an examination?" Pause. "Thank you very much."

Nicholas ended the call and wrote an address on a notepad. Tearing off the note, he handed it to Moore. "I want you to see my dentist. His name is Alan Keifer, one of the best dentists here on the Hill. A cracked tooth is nothing to fool around with."

Moore protested, "But I have my own dentist."

Nicholas stared into Moore eyes as he spoke in a no nonsense tone. "Emerson, I need you to do as I say on this one. Trust me. My instincts are at work on this one."

Moore reluctantly took the paper from Nicholas. "I don't get it, but I'll do this for you."

"Good. Now off with you. I've got to get this packet to my analyst friends."

Moore did as he was told and left Nicholas' office for the dentist's office. It was five blocks away. He hated to interrupt his work with something like this.

An hour later and after the dental assistant had taken x-rays, Dr. Kiefer walked into the examination room where Moore was seated in the dentist's chair. Kiefer was a kind man with white hair and a gentle manner.

"Another referral from my friend, Mr. Nicholas?" Kiefer greeted Moore.

"Yes. Steve was adamant that I come right over."

"Yes, he can be that way. I've helped him from time to time with some of his friends, if you know what I mean," Kiefer said with a raised eyebrow. "Tell me what the problem seems to be."

"I've had a nagging pain in my right lower jaw for the last few weeks." Unconsciously, Moore raised his right hand and rubbed the area. "I was, um, in a fight and think I may have a cracked tooth."

He then turned to his display. "Let's see what we have here on your x-ray."

Moore turned so that he could see the display on the monitor. "What's that?"

"I was wondering the same thing," Kiefer mused. "Have you had dental surgery, recently?"

"No."

"Let me ask you a delicate question, one which I'd primarily ask only of Steve's friends. Have you been unconscious at any time in the last few weeks?"

"Yes," Moore responded. "It's a long story…"

Kiefer cut him off. "I don't want to know. I don't need the details."

Moore nodded. "What is it?"

"My guess is that somebody implanted a tracking device in your tooth cavity." Kiefer swung around on his stool and began to lean forward. "Open up and I'll take a look." Kiefer probed a bit and leaned back on his stool. "I'm going to numb you up a bit so that we extract it and fill in the cavity."

"Numb away," Moore grinned as he tried to relax in the chair.

Twenty minutes later, Kiefer had extracted the device and filled in the open tooth cavity. He sat Moore up in his chair and said, "I'm going to give this to you so you can do whatever you and Steve think you need to do with it."

Moore was dumbfounded. He was skeptical that his cell phone had been bugged, but couldn't think of any other way the Russians could have tracked him. He knew now.

"You don't want to keep it here?" Moore asked as Kiefer placed the device in Moore's open palm.

"I don't think so. I don't need whoever is tracking you to pay a visit here."

Moore rose from his chair. "Of course not. Thank you, Dr. Kiefer. Do I pay on my way out?"

"That won't be necessary. I have an arrangement with Steve and I'll bill him direct."

"Thanks again." Moore walked down the hall and outside the building where he stopped and looked at the device in his hand. He was relieved to finally know exactly how Yarian and Karapashev were able to track him. He had started to suspect Bieber and Kalker, and was ashamed to think that he may have soon accused them of treachery.

Moore retrieved his cell from his pocket and called Nicholas to report the results of the dental visit. During the call, Nicholas instructed Moore to destroy the tracking device by smashing it against the concrete.

After they finished their discussion, Moore found a large stone, placed the tracking device on the concrete sidewalk and smashed the stone on top of the tracking device. He then tossed the stone and the shattered device in the nearby shrubbery.

Nicholas' Office
Washington, D.C.

In response to Nicholas' late evening call, Moore arrived early the next morning at Nicholas' office. He was anxious to see what Nicholas' analysts had discovered in the packet.

"Good morning," Moore said as he entered the cluttered office.

"Sleep well?" Nicholas asked.

"No. I tossed and turned all night. Between thoughts of that tracking device and this packet, I'd be surprised if I had three hours of sleep last night."

Nicholas smiled as he motioned for Moore to sit. "Let me put one of those issues to rest. The packet."

"Yes?"

Nicholas began to open it, but then stopped. He wanted to tease his friend for a few more minutes. "The contents are very interesting."

"And they are?" Moore fidgeted.

Nicholas opened the oilskin to reveal what had originally been a white parchment. It was stained and aged yellow. The black ink was blurred in places and faded.

"I'm not sure that I can make out what this is saying to us," Moore said as he squinted.

"My analyst friend explained it to me when he dropped it off last night. It says that the final clue rests with the boy with the boot."

"The boy with the boot? What boy with the boot?" Moore asked perplexed. "How are we going to find some boy with the boot in the 1850's?"

Nicholas ignored the questions as he continued. "It goes on to say that the boy will give you directions to the answer you seek. It's at the base of the thirteenth obelisk."

"Great. Once we locate this boy's grave, we're going to have to have a séance so we can ask him directions," a frustrated Moore growled as he shifted positions in his chair. "This is going no-where."

"I know you're growing frustrated. You've been through a lot. But relax," Nicholas urged Moore. "And think what you haven't asked me."

Moore's head felt like it was going to explode. He recognized the onset of a migraine. "I don't know. What do you want me to ask you? Stop playing games."

"Think about what we've been discussing," Nicholas coached. He wanted his friend to engage his logical thinking process.

Moore sat back and tried to clear his mind. If only he had had a better night's sleep, he might be thinking more clearly, he thought to himself. He took several deep cleansing breaths and looked at Nicholas. "Is there a signature?"

"Yes."

"And who signed it?"

"Sandustee."

Moore let out a deep breath. "The name on the Washington Monument. So it is all connected, after all."

"So it seems."

Moore looked at Nicholas and smiled. "Okay, you're playing with me. You've had this information since last night. You've probably been up all night doing your own analysis."

Nicholas nodded. "We need to find the boy and the boot and then the obelisk he's pointing us toward."

"But what boy, what boot, and what obelisk?" Moore's frustration returned.

"I did some research last night."

"What a surprise!" Moore said in a sarcastic tone. Lack of sleep had a tendency to make Moore cranky.

"There are twelve major obelisks in the world today. There were thirteen obelisks at one time. They surrounded the city of ancient Rome."

"Looks like I'm heading to Rome," Moore groaned.

"Not so fast. You need to find the boy and the boot first. Remember that he points toward the thirteenth obelisk. The twelve obelisks today are the Washington Monument and the ones located in St. Peter's Square in Rome and in New York City's Central Park." Nicholas continued naming the remaining locations, which were scattered around the world.

Moore finally put up his hands as if surrendering. "I'm in information overload. I feel like I'm drinking from a fire hose the way the pieces of the puzzle are being thrown at me. You've got the Legend of 13 weaving like thread through this entire escapade.

You've got the thirteen obelisks. You've got some boy and his boot. You've got the Nazarene's Code. You have the Andrew Jackson statute. How in the world does this all tie together?"

"You've got me," Nicholas said with a wide grin on his face. "I'm just a code breaker. You're the investigative reporter. Work your story."

Hearing a car door slam, Moore strode to the window and peered through the shutters onto the street. He saw a man walking away from the car, parked in the previously empty space behind Moore's car.

"You're edgy," Nicholas observed. "Not the typical Emerson Moore I'm used to seeing. You've always been calm and collected."

Whirling around to face Nicholas, Moore reacted. "This is just getting to me! Well, let's see. I've been tortured, beaten, followed, chased, threatened, and almost murdered more than once. This investigation has caused the death of innocent people. I'm overwhelmed!"

"Whoa there. That's a first!"

"What?"

"I don't think I've heard Mr. Emerson Moore ever say he's overwhelmed," Nicholas responded with a more serious look.

"Well, I am."

"We should call Kalker and your friend, Kat. We can get them more involved."

"Yes, maybe they can assist more."

Nicholas looked at the clock on his desk as he reached for his phone and dialed Kalker's number. The phone was answered on the third ring.

"Yes?" Kalker answered.

"Andreas, it's Nicholas and I have Emerson with me."

"Steve! It's good to hear from you. And you too, Emerson. I'll put you on speaker. Katrina is here and I'm sure she'd like to be a part of this conversation."

"Hello, Steve," she said. Then in a warmer tone, she said, "Hi, Emerson."

They exchanged greetings and Nicholas and Moore updated them on what had transpired, including the event with the Andrew Jackson statues and the tracking device.

"They must have implanted it when we were in Turkey," Bieber said.

"Exactly," Moore responded. "That's how they could track us wherever we went."

"It's behind you now," Kalker observed. "What are you going to do next?"

Moore looked at Nicholas, who just smiled. Moore then continued, "I guess we need to find this boy and the boot and wherever this thirteenth obelisk is."

"It sounds like you're getting close," Kalker said.

"It does, Andreas," Nicholas answered. "At this point, I'm thinking that the Nazarene's Code is somewhere in the United States. And we need to step up our efforts to make sure we find it before Karapashev and Yarian find it."

"I agree," Kalker responded. "It's too powerful to fall into the wrong hands."

"Exactly," Nicholas agreed.

"The time for talking and trying is over, Andreas," Moore said firmly as he looked at Nicholas. "You and Steve need to find who is putting me and my friends in danger and stop them now. With your connections, this shouldn't be taking so long. If you can't stop them, I'll consider dropping out of this search."

Nicholas looked at Moore in undisguised surprise. He didn't expect Moore to be so harsh or demanding.

Kalker and Bieber were silent on the other end of the phone. They were probably just as startled, Nicholas thought.

Nicholas broke the silence. "Emerson didn't get much sleep, so –"

"Sleep or no sleep, I'm getting to my wits end. Seriously, I respect you both, but you need to produce results," Moore stormed.

Nicholas was speechless for a change.

"I understand your frustration," Kalker said carefully.

"Of course," Bieber agreed. "I haven't said much because I'm not having much luck, but I am researching what I can from here. I'm sorry I haven't contributed much lately. I promise I'll –"

"Just do what I ask," Moore interrupted as he stood to leave. "I'm heading back to the marina to research the boy and the boot."

"That's fine," Nicholas said.

"I'll let you know if I find anything," Moore said as he began to walk down the hallway.

"Oh, Emerson," Nicholas said.

"Yes?"

"One more thing."

"What's that?"

"Boy and the boot."

"Yes?"

"It has thirteen letters."

Moore didn't respond. He walked briskly to the front door and left the townhouse, slamming the door as he exited.

Nicholas turned back to the phone. "Emerson is very edgy," he offered as an explanation. "He's usually unflappable."

"Steve, it's obvious that the stress is building on him. We'll see what we can do from this end."

"And I think we should make a trip there," Bieber added. "I'm concerned about Emerson's emotional state."

"I think we all are beginning to become concerned," Nicholas said.

After a few more comments, they ended the call.

Tunnicliff's Tavern
Washington, D.C.

Driving past the Capitol, Moore continued toward the Eastern

Market, the yuppie-filled housing area off of Pennsylvania Avenue on the Hill. Moore's luck was with him as he spied a car pulling out of a parking space on Independence Avenue and quickly pulled into it. Finding a parking spot near the Market was always difficult.

Moore locked his car and began to walk toward the Market where he was to meet Nicholas for a mid-afternoon lunch to continue their conversation from the previous day. He knew he owed everyone an apology. He wasn't himself yesterday. The lack of sleep and weight of everything that happened to him had crushed his etiquette to shreds.

He had been in dangerous situations before, but hadn't let it get to him. He'd also need to let Nicholas know that his frustration got the better of him and he didn't do any research on the boy and the boot. As he walked, he allowed the change in scenery to attract his attention.

The carnival-like atmosphere of the open-air market was filled with a blend of artisans, craftsmen, weavers, and seamstresses. Canopies covered each of the vendor's stalls, some of which were filled with exotic fragrances and the scents of ethnic food being cooked over nearby grills.

The wide variety of food and merchandise attracted a mixture of visitors. Moore relished the diversity in the marketplace as he made his way through the crowded venue and onto an equally crowded 7th Street. He walked past a number of establishments until he saw Tunnicliff's Tavern, a local watering hole filled with Irish tradition.

As he approached, he saw Nicholas seated at one of the tables in the fenced patio, which was covered by a dark green awning with the tavern's name printed boldly in white letters. Nicholas waved his hand at Moore. Moore nodded his head and joined Nicholas.

"Sitting outside today?"

"Emerson, it was just too nice of a day to sit inside," Nicholas responded. "Besides, the scenery out here is much more enjoyable," Nicholas added with a twinkle in his eyes as two attractive females walked by.

Feigning misunderstanding, Moore commented as he looked at two five-year-olds carrying balloons, "It's always fun to see kids enjoying themselves."

"Now, Emerson. You know exactly what I meant," Nicholas chuckled.

"Got to have a little fun with you. You're always so serious."

"Me? It seems you're the one so serious lately."

The waiter appeared and took their order. Moore chose a Guinness and Greek salad and Nicholas ordered jumbo lump crab cakes, sesame tuna salad and a Guinness.

Nicholas looked closely at his friend. "I don't know if I should bring this up."

"It's about my conduct yesterday, isn't it?" Before Nicholas could respond, Moore continued, "I was out of line yesterday. I'm sorry. I'll call Kalker and Bieber to apologize later today. I'm caught up on my sleep and –"

Nicholas waved his hand dismissively. "No apology needed. Everything you said was right, and necessary to shake Kalker and Bieber to help more. But that's not what I was going to bring up."

"Oh," said Moore, confused. "Then what are you not sure about bringing up?"

"Eastern Market has thirteen letters," Nicholas said as he settled back in his chair.

"Why doesn't that surprise me?" Moore looked around and then back at Nicholas. "Steve, you need to excuse me for a second. Got to pay a visit to the loo."

"Go ahead. Take your time."

Moore stood and walked into the tavern with its dark stain wood trim and inviting interior. Some of the walls were painted dark green or tan while one wall was covered by red and white vertically striped wallpaper.

Moore visited the restroom and was returning to the front door when he saw a bearded man wearing dark sunglasses and a fedora. He was seated in the front of the tavern at one of the highboy tables and looked through the open window. Moore thought that he was staring at Nicholas.

When Moore rejoined Nicholas, he saw that their drinks and food had arrived. As he picked up his Guinness, he toasted Nicholas, "May your life be filled with fair winds."

Nicholas returned the toast and asked, "Still sailing?"

"When I get a chance." Moore set his glass on the table. "Steve?"

"Yes?"

"If you look over my left shoulder, you'll see a man with a beard and dark sunglasses. He's wearing a fedora."

Nicholas looked over the edge of his glass, took a sip and then looked at Moore. "Yes, I see him."

"Do you know him?"

"I can't tell. Why?"

Moore had cut his Greek salad and was in the process of placing a small portion on his fork. "I thought he was staring at you when I walked back."

"Hmmm. Interesting. Let's see what he's up to." Nicholas glanced in the man's direction again. As he did, the man in the window looked away.

Nicholas and Moore were so distracted by the man in the fedora that they didn't notice a thin man with dark hair walk brusquely by the hostess and toward their table. As the man neared the table, he stopped and pulled a Beretta Px4 subcompact handgun from his pocket. He fired two shots at Nicholas' chest and blood erupted.

Nicholas slumped over as blood trickled from his mouth onto his tuna salad.

The outdoor patio was filled with screams from patrons as the gunner brandished his weapon and ran out of the covered patio.

Moore, in utter shock at what had just transpired, jumped from his chair and went to his friend's side to try to keep Nicholas' from slumping to the concrete. "Steve, Steve?" he shouted. "Stay with me."

Nicholas moaned as his skin color paled in front of Moore.

Looking at the hostess, Moore yelled, "Someone call 9-1-1. We need an ambulance."

A woman, who was seated two tables away, rushed to Nicholas. "I'm a nurse. Let me help."

Moore assisted her in lowering Nicholas to the floor and she began checking his vitals.

Moore stood and saw several policemen, who were usually on hand for events at the Eastern Market, approaching. He said to the nurse, "Tell the cops I'm going after the shooter."

The nurse nodded as she bent over Nicholas and Moore ran out of the covered patio, through the chaos and in the direction the assailant had run. He was mentally kicking himself for his slow reactions, but wanted to make an attempt. He ran two blocks down the street, but to no avail. The assailant had disappeared.

Moore returned in a daze to the tavern where he saw Nicholas being wheeled into the rear of an ambulance, which had been parked nearby for any emergencies at the Market. Moore saw the nurse as the ambulance's rear doors closed and it pulled away with its sirens screaming.

"Excuse me, miss. I appreciate your help. How's my friend?"

When the nurse turned around and Moore saw the look on her face, he feared her response.

"He didn't make it. The wounds were fatal. I'm sorry. There wasn't anything I could do," she said as her face strained with emotion.

Moore's eyes welled up with tears and he fought to compose himself. He looked at the woman. "Thanks for trying." Moore turned and began to walk away. He was oblivious to his surroundings; otherwise, he would have noticed that the man with the fedora had been standing near him and had overheard the exchange between the nurse and Moore. Moore might have also noticed the small smile on the bearded man's face.

"Excuse me, we need to talk with you," a voice called from behind Moore.

Moore turned and saw two police officers approaching him.

"Yes?"

"We understand the gentleman, who was shot, was dining with you. You were a witness to the shooting?"

"That's correct."

"Could you come with us to our car? The detectives will want to talk with you as soon as they get here."

Nicholas' House
Capitol Hill

An hour had barely passed since the shooting at the Eastern Market. The man in the fedora walked up the sidewalk to Nicholas' front door. He looked over his shoulder to make sure that no one was watching as he pulled a device from his pocket. He inserted it in the keyhole and the door unlocked.

Once again, the man looked over his shoulder as he walked into the townhouse and then carefully closed the door behind him. He began walking down the hallway and past the open door to Jody's office. When he reached the closed door to Nicholas' office, he tested the doorknob. The door was locked. Once again, he pulled the device from his pocket and inserted it in the keyhole. It quickly unlocked the office door.

The man returned the device to his pocket and swung open the door, revealing Nicholas' office. A smile crossed the man's face as he imagined the access to highly secret data that this office held. And he was going to enjoy hacking into it.

The man walked toward Nicholas' large desk. A noise caused him to stop suddenly.

Nicholas' chair swung around. The man sitting in it was holding a Glock pistol. It was pointed squarely at the bearded man's chest. "I've been waiting for you."

The intruder's face was filled with shock. His body jerked in reaction to seeing the man seated in front of him.

"So have we," a voice spoke from behind the intruder. "We have a number of questions to ask you."

The bearded man turned around and was greeted by two U.S. government agents. Their pistols were pointed at the bearded man.

"Then, you won't mind if I end this charade since you know who I am." The bearded man placed his hat on Nicholas' desk. Then he quickly removed the sunglasses and peeled the fake beard from his face. "So, after all of these years, I was finally lured to the lion's lair."

"Andreas, we knew that this one was too big for you not to get involved."

Kalker nodded his head. "The Nazarene's Code is irresistible. Finding it became my addiction – and my downfall."

"Where's Katrina Bieber?" one of the agents in the hall asked.

"She's my niece. She doesn't know anything about the things I'm involved in," Kalker explained as he sought to defend her innocence.

"But, because of her background in antiquities and archeology, you allowed an innocent girl to be involved and almost be murdered?" the agent in the hall asked.

"Of course, I didn't mean for some of that to happen," Kalker replied with a tone of indignation.

"You need to come with us," the agent said.

"That's not going to happen," Kalker said aggressively as he pulled the device from his pocket and began to aim it at the agents. Before he could fire, the agents' guns fired, killing Kalker as he dropped to the floor.

One of the agents rushed to Kalker's side and picked up the weapon. "It's an electronic lock picking device," he exclaimed.

The man in the chair spoke. "Kalker knew what he was doing. He wasn't going to allow you to take him alive. That's two murders today."

Moore's Houseboat
Alexandria, VA

Moore was seated on the rear deck of the houseboat as the late afternoon sun cast long shadows across the marina. He was unconsciously shaking the ice cubes in his empty glass as he mindlessly watched a variety of craft entering and exiting the harbor.

Five hours had passed since he had talked with the detectives, left the tavern and returned to the marina. It was as if Nicholas' death had catapulted him into another dimension; one where he could escape from the realities of his dear friend's passing.

"Emerson," a soft voice called from the dock.

Moore's mind returned to reality and he stood to look around the edge of the craft's cabin.

"Kat!" he said. "What a surprise! What are you doing here?" His entire countenance changed when he saw her.

"I thought you might need some company. I heard about Steve Nicholas. I am so sorry," she said softly as she stepped aboard the stern and placed her hand lightly on Moore's arm.

Looking into Bieber's blue eyes, Moore said, "Thanks. I'm going to miss him. He was always my answer man. He knew everything, or," Moore reminisced, "acted like he did. His network of contacts was just amazing. And – he was a good man. A friend. "

Bieber nodded her head in agreement.

Moore continued, "And on top of that, he helped people like me grow. He helped me develop a questioning style. A lot of the time, he knew more than he'd tell you so that you'd go out and find the facts for yourself."

"Men like that are scarce," she said as her fingers began rubbing Moore's arm.

"When I think about it, I realize that the scars on my body will fade away. Steve's death leaves a scar on my soul that will never fade away."

"Need a hug?"

Moore smiled for the first time that late afternoon.

"That would be nice."

Bieber's arms encircled Moore, who reacted in kind. Bieber molded her firm body against Moore as if she could transfer emotional strength between the two. They stood that way for a few minutes, and then Moore pulled away.

"Listen, I'm sorry I sounded off on you and your uncle. I didn't mean it. I know you're doing all you can."

"Don't worry about it."

"I was such a jerk," Moore lamented. "I overreacted to the pressure of these last few weeks."

"I understand," she said as she ran her hand along the side of Moore's face.

"Thanks for being so understanding." Moore was glad that she had made the surprise visit. He smiled and asked, "Would you like a drink?"

"Yes. A cosmopolitan."

"Not sure I can do that for you. I just have rum and whiskey."

"Then, I'll take a rum and Coke."

She accompanied Moore to the small galley where Moore opened one of the cupboards and pulled out a bottle of Captain Morgan. He quickly made her a rum and coke and one for himself. He put two shots of rum in his glass.

With drinks in hand, Moore guided her to the seats in the salon. "Where's your uncle by the way? Did he come with you?"

She nodded. "He said he had some meetings with your government people."

"I see," Moore said as he sipped his drink and unconsciously began to withdraw.

Bieber sensed his continued sorrow and made a suggestion as she scooted closer to him and draped her arm around his shoulder. "You need a change of scenery."

"I certainly need something," Moore offered. "I've been so embroiled in this Nazarene's Code stuff that my head is spinning. I just can't think straight. I don't even know where to go from here now that Nicholas is gone."

"Why don't we go visit your island home?" she asked as she stroked his thick hair.

The spark returned to Moore's eyes. "I could use that. I could show you around. One of my friends in Huron has a new sailboat that he wants me to try. I could take you sailing."

"I'd like that."

"Sure, and you can stay at my aunt's house."

"When do we go?"

"Right after Nicholas' funeral."

"Splendid," she said as she began to nuzzle Moore's neck.

Moore felt his body react to her comforting and affectionate advances. The rum also was contributing to his relaxed inhibitions. His arm reached behind them and flicked off the lights in the salon. Only the light from outside the marina was able to slightly penetrate the cabin's warm interior, which was heating up by the minute. Their lips met in a tender kiss. A moan escaped from Moore as his arms encircled Bieber.

The Next Morning
Moore's Houseboat

The savory fragrance of bacon cooking filled the houseboat. Moore expertly flipped the pancakes he was making on one of the burners while keeping an eye on the bacon.

Hearing the shower water turn off, Moore yelled toward the stern cabin. "Breakfast will be ready in a few minutes."

"Good. I'll have time to blow dry my hair," Bieber yelled back.

Moore could hear the blow dryer and turned his attention back to cooking. He was distracted when his cell phone rang.

"This is Emerson," he answered.

"Emerson Moore?"

"Yes."

"This is Jody from Steve Nicholas' office."

"Jody, we finally get to talk. I want you to know how sorry I am about Steve's death. I wish I could've stopped it."

"Thank you. We all are going to miss him. He was a very special person."

"Indeed he was. And very unique," Moore said. "When can I pay my respects?" Moore asked.

"That's why I'm calling. Steve had instructed us that he didn't want a funeral or calling hours. In fact, he's being cremated this morning. He just wanted to quietly fade away."

"I see. I guess I shouldn't be surprised. That sounds like him."

"Well, I just wanted to let you know."

"Thanks. Maybe on one of my trips into D.C. I can have lunch with you."

"That would be wonderful. You can reach me at Steve's office number for the next sixty days."

"Good. Thanks again, Jody," Moore said as he ended the call and slid the pancakes onto a serving plate.

"Smells yummy," a voice from behind Moore called.

"I hope it is," Moore said as he turned to see Bieber walking toward him.

She was wearing one of his gray tee shirts, which hung mid thigh. She looked fresh and naturally stunning. Bieber walked up to Moore, threw her arms around him, and gave him a long kiss.

When they broke the kiss, Moore grinned and teased her. "Maybe I should just cover the bacon and pancakes for a while."

Playfully, Bieber pushed Moore away and walked to the galley table. "Ah, but you made me hungry for breakfast." Her blue eyes looked seductively over the rim of her juice glass at Moore as she tasted the orange juice. "Ummm. *Das ist gut.*"

"Freshly squeezed," Moore responded.

"And that's not all that's freshly squeezed," she teased back.

"I had a phone call from Nicholas' office," Moore said as he set the bacon and pancakes on the table and took a seat.

"Oh?"

"They're cremating Steve today and there won't be any calling hours or memorial service. That's what Steve wanted. So, we can leave for the islands this afternoon if you're available." He was sad about the lack of closure with Nicholas, but glad she was here to help him move on. She gave him hope and boosted his spirits.

"I'm sure that I can, but I'll need to check with my uncle to be sure that he doesn't need me," she said as she tasted her first bite of the pancakes. "Delicious."

"I'm still learning. I used to make athletic pancakes."

"Athletic pancakes? What are they?"

"They run in the middle," Moore grinned at his explanation.

"These are definitely not athletic pancakes," she chuckled as she continued eating.

He laughed with her. It felt good.

Aunt Anne's House
Put-in-Bay

As Moore's car neared the Perry Monument, Bieber looked out the driver's window of the Mustang convertible at Put-in-Bay's picturesque harbor. "This is beautiful," she exclaimed.

Smiling, Moore commented, "I thought you'd enjoy this. My aunt's house is straight ahead, where the road curves. If you don't make the curve, you'd drive straight into it."

He followed the curve and turned left onto the side street and left into the vacant parking space, next to the single car garage. He had been pleased that they had been able to catch an afternoon flight to Cleveland where they picked up his car. An hour later, they took Miller's Ferry from Catawba to South Bass Island.

Exiting the car, they grabbed their bags and started for the house.

"Oh, my! I love this truck. Is it your aunt's?" Bieber asked as they passed the open garage door and saw the 1929 Ford Model A truck.

"Yes. It was my uncle's pride and joy until he passed away." Moore continued, "After we get settled, I'll take you for a tour of the island in it."

"I'd like that," she said as they rounded the corner of the house and walked into the back door.

"Aunt Anne, we're home," Moore called as they walked into the kitchen at the rear of the house.

Seconds later, the highly energetic Aunt Anne rushed into the room to greet them. She hugged Moore first and then Bieber.

"It's about time you came back here." Looking at Bieber, she exclaimed, "And look how pretty you are. Much prettier that Emerson described on the phone."

"Aunt Anne…" Moore began.

"Don't you Aunt Anne me," she warned with a twinkle in her eye. "Come along, honey," she said as she placed an arm around Bieber, "I'll show you where you can put your things. You must be pretty special for him to bring you here."

They walked from the kitchen into the front of the house where Moore commented with surprise. "What happened here?"

"You like it?" Aunt Anne asked.

"Yes, but what happened to all of the antiques?"

"I gave them to the resale shop over at the museum. I thought it was time for a change."

"Looks really nice. Feels beachy."

"That's the look I wanted," Aunt Anne said in response. "I was hoping you'd be surprised."

"I like it, too," Bieber said as she looked around the large living room that contained comfortable white wicker furniture and cottage style accessories. The old pictures on the wall had been replaced with beach scenes and the walls had been painted a light sea foam green.

"Let's get you upstairs to your room," Aunt Anne said as she began to climb the stairs.

Thirty minutes later, Moore and his aunt were standing in the screened porch overlooking the bay. They could see Bieber on the dock using her cell phone.

"She sure is a pretty girl, Emerson," his aunt commented.

"Hmmm," Moore replied.

"How serious is this?"

Moore smiled in response.

"Going quiet on me, eh?" she asked,

"As I said on the phone, we've spent a lot of time together, working on this story. I'm still evaluating her."

"Oh, and is that what they call it now? Evaluating? Never heard of such a thing. You either like the girl or you don't. You're ready to get back in the saddle or you're not. The fact that she's here tells me a lot," his aunt teased as she went into the house and to her kitchen, her inner sanctum.

Moore smiled again and opened the screen door. He paused for a moment as he thought about telling his aunt about Bieber's health condition. Deciding to delay the news, he walked down the steps and out to the dock to join Bieber.

"Any luck in getting in touch with your uncle?"

With a look of concern on her face, she looked up at Moore.

"No. My calls are rolling into his voicemail. I don't know where he is, but then again, he knows so many people in Washington. He may be off visiting with his friends. It's not like him to not answer the phone when I call. I'm all he has."

Trying to reduce her concern, Moore said, "I'm sure he's fine and that he'll return your call when he's available."

Bieber nodded her head. "Maybe later today, I'll catch up." She turned to look at the bay and Gibraltar Island on the horizon. The Jet Express, filled with island visitors, was passing through the harbor entrance on its way to its dock.

"Emerson, this is so relaxing. I now know why you prefer to call this home rather than Washington."

"This is a touch of paradise." Moore pointed to a marina complex that had several brightly colored buildings.

"That's the newest bar and restaurant complex. It's called the Keys. I thought we could have drinks there tonight after the island tour. Either Alex Bevan or Westside Steve will be singing there tonight. After that, we'll head to T&J's Steakhouse about a block away and you can ride the mechanical bull."

"Mechanical bull?" she asked.

"Yeah, it's a lot of fun. And when you get thrown, because you will be thrown, you'll land in a sea of foam."

"Sounds fun," she said as she looked warmly at Moore. "What's on the agenda for tomorrow?"

"We're going sailing out of Huron. My friends at Harbor North are going to let us take out one of their new boats. It's a 28-foot Hunter with a couple of special features."

"I'd like that."

Bieber's cell phone began to ring.

"Is that your uncle?" Moore asked as Bieber glanced down at it.

"No. Looks like it's one of my girlfriends in Germany calling me."

"You two go ahead and talk. I'll be in the garage, cleaning up the truck for our tour. You can meet me there when you're done."

Bieber nodded her head as she answered her phone, "Hello Dagmar."

Moore walked down the dock and to the garage at the rear of the house. He found a couple of clean rags and began wiping down the truck.

Fifteen minutes later, Bieber appeared at the garage door.

"I'm ready to go if you are."

"Hop in," Moore said as he took a seat behind the old Ford truck's steering wheel.

"My friend, Dagmar, is going to call some of my uncle's friends in Washington to see if they can help locate him."

"That's good that she can help."

"It would make me feel better once I know where he is." Bieber sat in the passenger seat as Moore started the truck. "This is going to be fun!" she said. A night in Put-in-Bay would also help take Moore's mind off Nicholas's death, she thought to herself as the Ford backed out of the garage.

Throwing the truck into first gear, Moore eased the truck up to the nearby stop sign. Seeing no traffic approaching, he turned right and shifted through the gears as the truck drove along the road overlooking the harbor and past the Perry Monument.

"What a beautiful view!" Bieber exclaimed as she looked at the variety of power and sailboats at dock and moving through the harbor.

Moore drove along Bay View Avenue that separated the public marina from DeRivera Park. He pointed out the Boardwalk Restaurant complex, the private club at the Crew's Nest and its marina, and the Miller Marina. He parked the truck in a space on Oak Point where the two stepped out of the vehicle.

"Oh, this is a wonderful setting," Bieber said as she looked across at Gibraltar Island and then to the harbor.

"It's one of my favorite spots on the island. It's not as hectic here," he said as they sat on a picnic table.

"Very peaceful."

"It is."

"And romantic," she said as she leaned into Moore. Her lips found Moore's and they engaged in a long kiss. Their quiet moment was interrupted by a shout from the harbor.

"Way to go, Emerson. Give her one from me!"

Their heads separated and turned toward the source of their distraction. There, in the harbor and aboard an idling jet ski, was Mad Dog Adams.

Feigning innocence, the rugged Adams yelled, "Oh my, did I interrupt anything? Gee, I'm sorry, Emerson. You know I wouldn't want to do anything like that!"

"I don't believe that for one second," Moore replied to his friend.

"Are you going to introduce me to the new beer babe or what?"

"New beer babe?" Bieber asked as she turned and looked at Moore.

"He's always joking. Mike sings at the Round House Bar. He's been there for over thirty-two years," Moore said. "Mike, this is Katrina Bieber. You can call her Kat."

"Kat, nice to meet you." With a mischievous look in his eyes, Adams looked directly at Moore. "Good thing I showed up when I did to rescue you."

"Rescue me?"

"Looked to me like the Kat got your tongue!" Mad Dog Adams guffawed.

"That's funny! The Dog saying the Kat got your tongue," Moore grinned.

"Bring her over to the Round House tomorrow. I'll have her come on stage for the conch segment of my act," Adams said as he gunned his jet ski.

"Can't. We'll be sailing tomorrow. Maybe the next day."

"Whatever," Adams said as he began to pick up speed on the jet ski. "Hope to see you two lovebirds later. I can tell that you're going to need some close adult supervision," he chortled.

As they watched Adams accelerate and dodge watercraft in the harbor, Bieber asked, "What happens during the conch segment of his show?"

Laughing, Moore explained. "He has women from the audience join him on stage and gives them his conch shell to blow. While they try to blow it, he makes all kinds of sexual innuendos to the delight of the crowd and embarrassment of the poor women."

"I'll make sure that I don't get called on stage," she laughed playfully.

"Since the mood has been broken, for now, let's continue our tour."

"Oh, if we must," she responded light-heartedly.

The two returned to the Ford and drove back to the Boardwalk where they turned right on Catawba. Making a quick left on Delaware Avenue, they drove past the bars, restaurants, hotels and gift shops along Delaware Avenue. At the stop sign, they turned left onto Toledo Avenue and pulled into a vacant parking space at Blu Luna Ristorante Italiano in Harbor Square.

The restaurant had an open-air bar at the corner of Toledo and Delaware. An outdoor dining area flanked by a rock wall and filled with lush plants faced Toledo Avenue and led to the indoor restaurant.

"Let's sit outside," Moore said as the two emerged from the truck.

They walked to the outdoor dining area and took a table next to the rock wall.

As Bieber sat, she looked across the street at the National Park Service's Visitor Center and the Perry Monument, which towered over the building. "You certainly can see that monument just about wherever you go on this island."

Before Moore could comment, the restaurant's high-energy general manager, Milos Ljubenovic, walked to their table and greeted Moore. "Emerson, it's good to see you again, my friend."

Moore smiled at the gregarious manager. "Hello, Milos. This is my friend, Katrina. She's from Germany and it's her first trip to Put-in-Bay."

"Hello, Milos," Bieber said as she greeted him.

"Welcome to Put-in-Bay and the finest Italian restaurant on the island."

"I'm looking forward to our dinner tonight," Bieber said.

"And, if you allow me, I will make your meal selections."

"Sounds fine. What would you pick for me?" Bieber asked in eager anticipation.

"Since you're from Germany, I'm going to serve you a sampling of our wienerschnitz. Then, I'll bring out samplings of our stuffed peppers, chicken paprikash, and Hungarian goulash. We'll top off the meal with a serving of German apple strudel."

"That sounds wonderful," she smiled.

"Good. I'll have a bottle of red wine sent to the table," he added as he began to walk away.

"That guy never sits still," said Moore. "I've been here when he's tried to sit down for a meal and I don't know that he gets to finish it. He always has his eyes on his customers and is constantly jumping up from his table to take care of them."

"He seems so nice," Bieber said as she relaxed. "What nationality is he?"

"He's Serbian. The local island mystery adventure author is also Serbian and introduced us to each other. He knew that I'd enjoy meeting Milos."

"Why's that?"

"When I was a cub reporter, one of my first assignments was covering the war between Croatia and Serbia in 1991. The atrocities were devastating! Milos and I had similar experiences although his experiences involved his family."

"Tell me more."

"I'd rather not. That's a story for another day," Moore stated as Milos appeared with the wine.

After a delightful dinner, the two drove the Ford truck down Toledo and turned left on Bay View, followed by a quick right into the parking lot of The Keys complex.

Emerging from the truck, they entered the complex of buildings, brightly painted in Caribbean hues. The grounds were a mixture of lush tropical plants, colorful umbrellas over outdoor tables, and misters, which provided patrons with a cooling relief from the hot sun.

The first building they passed was Local Color, a tee shirt shop that also housed the dockmaster's office. On their right was The Crazy Chicken, a patio grill offering jerked chicken, smoked brisket and St. Louis ribs.

They stepped up to the top level and walked past the Tortugas Rum Nation, a restaurant with open windows overlooking the harbor. Its upstairs housed Hemingway's, a sushi bar.

"We're going to Lola's Key," Moore said as they walked into the small waterfront bar. "This is one of my favorite spots on the island. You can sit here, enjoy a drink and watch the boat traffic."

"I like it," Bieber said as she sat on one of the bar stools.

They placed their drink orders and swiveled around on their stools to enjoy the captivating view in front of them. As they sat, Moore returned a wave from island singer, Westside Steve. They listened to the entertainment from Westside Steve, chatted about island life and sipped their beverages.

After enjoying the waterfront ambiance for about an hour, Moore turned to Bieber. "How about a change of venue?"

"Oh, but this is so beautiful," she said as she looked back at the moonlight shimmering on top of the gentle waves in the harbor.

"It is, but I promised you a ride on the mechanical bull. Let's head over to T&J's Steakhouse," Moore said as the two stood. "We'll walk across the park. It's not far."

Minutes later, they walked into the complex, which had previously housed the Crescent Tavern. The country-themed complex was managed and owned by brothers, Tim and Josh Niese. Their father, Tim, was a close friend of Moore's.

"We'll stop here tomorrow night for some of their smoking hot ribs," Moore said as they approached Josh Niese, who was collecting five dollars for each ride.

"I'm sure it will be a wild ride," Bieber said as she entered the foam-lined enclosure around the mechanical bull. She put both hands on its hindquarters and boosted herself aboard on her first try. Her skilled mount was greeted by a round of applause and shouts from the people who stood around the enclosure.

"That wasn't too bad," she said as she gripped the rein. "Let her rip!" she yelled with an assured smile.

Niese said softly to Moore, "I'll start her out easy and build her confidence. Then, we'll turn it up."

"Exactly what I was hoping for," Moore grinned as he focused on Bieber's undulating body on the mechanical bull.

Bieber's strong thighs were gripping the sides of the bull. Her upper body was relaxed and flexible like a tree in the wind. One arm was in the air as she tried to maintain her balance much like a tightrope walker does.

For the first two minutes, she rode well through initial spins and bucks of the bull, then Niese turned up the heat and the bull threw her. She landed in the foam and, laughing, stood up.

"This is fun. Come on, Emerson. Mount up behind me! We'll ride it together!"

Feeling his face redden like an embarrassed schoolgirl, Moore replied, "I'll pass. I'm enjoying watching you ride. So is everyone else."

A few minutes later, Bieber found herself thrown into the foam again. She returned to Moore's side. "It would have been more fun if you had joined me for the last ride."

As they started to cross Delaware Avenue and return to the truck, Moore said, "No, really, I would've ruined the view for everyone."

"Bad boy!" she teased.

Laughing, they walked through the park to the truck and returned to Aunt Anne's house. They parked the truck in the garage and walked around the house to the dock that stretched into the harbor toward Gibraltar Island. Sitting on the edge of the dock, they linked arms around each other and gazed at the darkening sky and the first hint of twinkling stars.

The Next Morning
Aunt Anne's House

Moore walked into the kitchen and greeted his aunt as he sat down at the kitchen table. "Morning, Aunt Anne."

His aunt gave him a peck on the cheek and poured fresh orange juice in a glass for him. "Morning, Emerson. And where's your sweetness this morning?"

"I knocked on her door and she said she'd be down in five minutes."

"Good. I'll start cooking the eggs." She slid a copy of the day's *Sandusky Register* across the table. "Interesting story in there. Somebody's on a weird vendetta."

"How's that?"

"They're going around the country, decapitating the boy with the boot water fountain statues."

Moore immediately sat straight up in his chair and reached for the paper. "You've got to be kidding!"

"No, it's all there."

Moore began reading the article.

In Fresno, California, the Boy and the Boot statue, which had been erected in 1895 at the Fresno Courthouse Park on Tulare Street, was discovered two days ago to be missing its head. It also happened to the statues in Penrose, Colorado; El Paso, Texas; Steven's Point, Wisconsin, and New Orleans.

"They better put an armed guard around our statue in Sandusky," Aunt Anne murmured as she set a pot of fresh coffee on the table.

"There's a Boy and the Boot statue in Sandusky?" Moore reacted in surprise.

Before she could answer, a cheery voice called, "What's all this talk about a Boy and the Boot statue?" Bieber swooped into the small kitchen and walked behind the chair in which Moore was seated. She threw her arms around him and gave him a kiss on the cheek.

"Morning, sleepyhead," Moore teased as he stroked her arm.

"Somebody has been decapitating the heads off the Boy and the Boot statues all around the country," Aunt Anne responded. "It's right there in the newspaper."

Bieber's eyes widened as she looked at Moore. "And, there's one in Sandusky?"

"Yes. I wasn't aware of that. Look, Kat. There's a photo of it on Washington Row and a photo of the decapitated one in New Orleans. We'll stop and check it out after our sail this morning."

"Okay," she said as she sat and began to pour a cup of coffee.

"Did you hear anything back from your uncle?" Moore asked.

A look of concern crossed Bieber's face. "No, I've left several voice messages."

"Should we contact the police?"

"Oh, no," she responded quickly. "I'm sure that he'll turn up. I've known him to misplace his cell phone or not check voicemail. Let's wait another day," she said. "Then, I'll feel free to panic."

She picked up her fork and began to eat her eggs and toast. "This is very good, Aunt Anne."

"I'm glad you're enjoying it," Moore's aunt beamed.

They finished their breakfast and Bieber excused herself to step outside to try to contact her uncle once again. When she returned, she joined Moore in his Mustang convertible and they drove to the Miller Ferry dock for their short trip to Huron, which was located east of Sandusky.

Harbor North
Huron

Moore's car made its way to 400 Huron Street where it pulled into the Harbor North parking lot. The sales and marina office was set on a hill overlooking the marina on the Huron River.

"You're going to love these guys," Moore said as he and Bieber exited the car and started walking toward the office to check in.

"How do you know them?" Bieber asked.

"Harbor North is the home of the oldest sailing school on the Great Lakes. I took my sailing lessons here." Moore pointed to a Hunter at its berth. "That one belongs to T.J. He lives aboard it year round."

"In the winter, too?"

"Yes. He truly has the love of sailing running through his veins," Moore said as they walked into the marina's office.

Two men were huddled over a nautical chart. The tall one with the reddish blonde hair was friendly owner Bruce Roberts. Standing next to him with a beard and hair pulled back in a ponytail was T.J. Wright, a free-spirited pirate and sailing instructor.

The group exchanged greetings and introductions.

"So, where's this new Hunter you've told me about?" Moore asked.

"You're going to like this one. She's a 27-footer and carries 333 square feet of sail," Roberts explained.

"But, the real surprise is her outboard," Wright grinned.

"How's that? Bigger than a ten horsepower?"

Roberts and Wright looked at each other and chuckled.

"Would you believe a 75 horsepower?" Wright asked.

"No way, T.J.," Moore responded.

"He's right, Emerson. You could water ski behind it," Roberts added.

Moore turned and looked at Bieber. "I have to see this."

"Let's go," Wright said as he walked toward the door, followed closely by Bieber and Moore.

"Have a good sail," Roberts called as he looked back at his chart. "And treat her carefully. I have a serious buyer coming to look at her tomorrow."

"I'll take care of her. Thanks, Bruce," Moore said as he closed the door behind him.

They walked down to the Hunter's berth where she rocked gently in the water.

"I checked out your inventory online last night. Looks like you folks have been moving a lot of boats."

Wright nodded his head. "It's been a good season for us. Hunter sales have been especially strong."

Moore walked to the end of the dock and looked at the large outboard at the boat's stern. "Would you look at that? It's a 75 horse Mercury!" Moore said in amazement.

"This baby can get up and go," Wright explained. "Ready to take her out?"

"Sure," Moore said as he helped Bieber board.

As the two boarded and prepared to pull away from the dock, Wright untied the lines and threw them onto the craft. "One more thing, this craft is beachable. All you have to do is pull up the centerboard and you can run her up on the beach."

"Cool," Moore said as he started the outboard and began backing away from the dock and into the river. "We'll see you in a few hours."

"Enjoy yourselves," Wright called as Moore straightened the boat in the river and began to head north for a quarter of a mile to enter Lake Erie. The two waved to Wright.

"Nice breeze," Bieber commented from her seat near Moore who was at the wheel.

"Yes, it is. I'd say about twelve knots and from the northeast," he said as he looked aloft at the burgee. He brought the boat about into the wind, the no go zone, and turned to Bieber. "Kat, I'm going to need your help."

"Sure. What can I do?"

"Take the wheel and hold it steady into the wind." Moore pointed to the windex on top of the mast. "I'm going to run up the main sail and jib."

"I've never done this before," Bieber said nervously as she took control of the helm.

"You'll do fine. Just keep the nose into the wind." Moore moved forward and unfastened the sail bags for the main sail and jib. He then began hoisting the main sail. He quickly returned to the helm and took the wheel from Bieber. "Now, for some fun."

As they fell off the wind, he unfurled the furling jib. The boat accelerated under sail and they began their reach.

"Where to?" Bieber asked.

"We're going to that strip of land. That's Cedar Point. It's one of the world's largest amusement parks and the Roller Coaster Capitol of the world!"

"How fun!" she said as she looked toward the horizon that was dotted with a number of amusement park rides and coaster tracks twisting in every direction. "I can see them. It looks like they have a lot of them."

"They do. As we get closer, you'll hear the riders' screams," Moore grinned as he looked at the 364-acre park that had been founded in 1870 and was the second oldest amusement park in the United States. "Then, we'll sail around the tip of the peninsula and into Sandusky Bay."

The boat flew through the water as waves sent a soft spray over the bow. There were several other sailboats out, enjoying the stiff breeze. There was also a powerful cigarette boat. It was heading at a high rate of speed toward Moore's boat.

There were two men aboard. One was at the controls while the other was holding a pair of powerful binoculars to his eyes. They had been scanning the occupants of sailboats for the last fifteen minutes. But, they hadn't identified their target.

Their luck changed when Yarian spied Moore at the helm. "That's the one," he yelled to his companion. Yarian placed the binoculars in a storage compartment and raised a semi-automatic rifle to his shoulder. As they neared Moore's boat, Yarian fired several rounds over Moore's head.

"What in the world?" a stunned Moore exclaimed when he heard the bullets whizzing by. He looked at the approaching boat and recognized Yarian. "We've got trouble."

"What do you mean?" Bieber asked as she swung around to face the other boat. "Oh no, it's Yarian."

The powerboat cut back on its engines as it closed the distance between the two boats.

Pointing the gun in a menacing fashion at Moore, Yarian yelled, "Drop your sails."

"What are we going to do?" Bieber asked.

"Exactly as he says," Moore said. "For now." Moore looked cautiously at Yarian as he formed a plan in his mind. He brought the boat about and turned to Bieber. "Take the helm again and keep us pointed in this direction," he said as he stood and Bieber quickly replaced him.

Moore began furling the jib and then lowered the main sail. As he did, he looked toward Cedar Point's beach, calculating the distance. He then returned to the wheel and Bieber took her seat.

The powerboat moved next to the sailboat, which had begun to drift in the wind.

"We meet again," Yarian said with an evil look of glee.

"What do you want, Yarian?" Moore shouted.

"Oh, just a word with you."

"I've got a word for you."

Yarian snickered. "And what would that word be?"

"Good-bye!" Moore, who had started the outboard, now threw the outboard to full speed. The sailboat leapt out of the water, catching the powerboat's occupants off guard.

"Can we outrun them?" Bieber asked as she hung on tightly.

"No way, but we just got a head start on them. They'll catch up and probably overshoot us," Moore said confidently as he looked over his shoulder.

Yarian swore at the unexpected action and screamed at his helmsman to catch up to Moore. As they neared Moore's boat, Yarian leveled his semi-automatic rifle at the craft and unleashed a stream of bullets. The bullets stitched a line along the craft's hull as the powerboat went flying by as Moore had predicted.

"Bruce is not going to be happy with the damage to his boat," Moore said as he recalled Roberts' warning to take care of the

Hunter.

The powerboat was executing a wide turn and preparing to run by Moore's boat for a second deadly pass.

Moore had his eye on the beach ahead. "Kat, I need you to pull up the centerboard."

"Why?" she asked with eyes filled with fear.

"We're going to run this up on the beach. Too many people around for them to follow us."

"What's a centerboard?"

"It's a piece of the boat which goes down about five feet instead of a fixed keel. It should be that line on the starboard side of the cabin top."

"Line? Starboard?" she asked with a puzzled look.

"Right side," he said as he pointed to the line. "And that line."

Bieber didn't have to be told a second time. She quickly found the centerboard pennant and pulled it up as bullets imbedded themselves in the fiberglass hull.

When she finished pulling up the centerboard, Moore yelled. "Better brace yourself!"

Bieber did as she was told as she looked at the rapidly approaching beach.

Within moments they ran up on the beach and Moore cut the engine. They jumped off the craft as onlookers watched the action in front of them.

The powerboat surprised Moore with its next move. It slowed its engines and prepared to run up on the beach in pursuit of Moore and Bieber.

"We can't jeopardize the safety of these beachgoers," Moore said as his attention turned to the parasailing boat, moored nearby. "Come with me," he said as the powerboat struck the beach and Moore and Bieber ran toward the parasailing craft. It was a 29-foot premium parasail boat powered by a 240 horsepower Volvo diesel engine.

Moore approached one of the operators and quickly explained their dilemma.

"Yeah, I thought something was wrong when I heard the gunshots and saw you two on the water. Looked like you were trying to get away."

Moore quickly suggested how they could help and how the expenses would be covered.

"Yeah, we can do that. Let's go," the operator said as they boarded the boat and started its engine.

In seconds, they were pulling away from the beach to a point outside of gunshot range. As the boat's operator stood at the controls and radioed the police about the shooting offshore, a crewman helped Moore and Bieber into the rigging and harness. Soon, the boat began picking up speed and the parachute began to fill with air. The crewman stood at the winch and slowly began unwinding the towline. As he did, Moore and Bieber felt themselves being lifted into the air.

"Aren't we easy targets up here?" Bieber asked nervously as they began to soar.

"Bear with me," Moore said as they attained their maximum

height of 300 feet. He signaled to the crewman below and then pulled the safety pin to release them from the towline.

As the line fell away, a wide-eyed Bieber asked, "What are you doing?"

"We're going to paraglide to Sandusky," he smiled confidently.

"What?"

Moore repeated himself. "We're going to paraglide to Sandusky. You just steer the parasail by pulling down on these risers."

"You've done this before?"

"No, but I'm a quick learner."

"I hope so."

They quietly glided over the beach where they could see Yarian and his crony oblivious to them overhead. The two men were focused on pushing their beached boat off the beach before the police or Cedar Point security arrived.

They floated above the Wicked Twister and the Giant Wheel, a Ferris wheel that towered 145 feet over the amusement park. Looking down on the lushly landscaped park, they sailed over the sky ride, Raptor, Carousel and Blue Streak roller coaster as park guests pointed skyward and waved at them. Next, they flew over the Cedar Point Marina, which was filled with boats of all sizes and, then, Sandusky Bay.

"Good thing we have this strong wind from the northeast, otherwise we'd end up swimming to Sandusky," Moore observed as they began approaching Sandusky's Battery Park Marina on the east side of downtown. "There's a park behind the sailing club where we'll land."

"This is an unexpected respite," Bieber said as they glided through the air.

"Nice and quiet. When we started our sailing adventure this morning, I didn't expect us to end up sailing through the air," Moore grinned as he tugged on the risers to position their approach to Battery Park. He pulled on a line to start their gradual descent.

Soon, they were skirting the masts of several sailboats in the sailing club.

"Get ready, Kat," he cautioned as they dropped closer to the ground and then impacted. They both tumbled to the ground and rolled a few feet before coming to a stop.

"I don't think that was the proper way to land," Bieber commented.

"Right. But I'd think that anytime you can land and walk away with nothing broken could be considered a good landing," Moore teased her. Spontaneously, he reached over and kissed her on the lips.

After returning the kiss, Bieber looked at Moore, "What was that for?"

"For being such a good sport today."

"What else could I do?" she asked as she leaned into him and kissed him again.

"Maybe, you two should get a room!" a voice called from behind them.

They turned around and saw a Sandusky police officer calling to them from the open window of his police car. "You the two, who were being shot at?" he asked as he looked at the parachute and rigging on the ground, then back to them.

"Yes," Moore responded as he and Bieber stood to their feet and the officer exited the vehicle. "Did you catch the two shooters?" Moore asked as he read the officer's name on his name badge. It read Cozart.

"Just missed them. Cedar Point Security arrived quickly, but those two were able to push their boat off the beach and take off. The Coast Guard and one of our police boats are looking for them." Cozart leaned against his car as he prepared to write out the incident report on his clipboard. "Any idea who it was?"

"The one guy's name is Yarian. I don't know who the other guy is," Moore said.

For the next thirty minutes, Moore and Cozart worked together in completing the incident report. Moore was careful and decided to withhold detailed information regarding their previous encounters with Yarian.

Once they completed filing the report, the officer returned to his car and drove away.

"What next?" Bieber asked.

"The Maritime Museum of Sandusky."

"What?"

Moore pointed across the street. "I know the museum's executive director and I want to see if she'll loan us her car to visit the boy and the boot statue. Besides, we may want to clean up a bit."

"Sounds good to me," Bieber responded as they crossed Meigs Street and entered the museum.

To their left, Moore spotted the museum's executive director, Annette Wells. "Hi, Annette."

"Hi, Emerson," she responded. "Bringing a visitor to take a tour today?"

"A quick one if that's okay with you," Moore said. "Meet my friend, Kat Bieber."

"Hello, Kat. I hope you enjoy our museum," Wells responded.

"I'm looking forward to it," she replied.

After a brief visit to the restrooms, the two quickly toured the museum, which was filled with exhibits and information. The displays included area shipwrecks, the Australian convict ship, *Success*, Sandusky area boat building, ship models, passenger ferries and ice harvesting in the winter.

When they returned to the entranceway, Moore asked, "Annette, would you loan me your car for about an hour? We'd like to visit the Boy and the Boot fountain."

"Sure, go ahead and take it," she answered as she reached for her keys. "It's parked in the third space."

Moore took the keys and, accompanied by Bieber, walked to the car and drove to the fountain a short distance away. As he entered Washington Row, which fronted the park, he found a vacant space across from the Sandusky Chamber of Commerce office and parked the car.

"The fountain should be across the street. That's where my aunt said to look for it," he said as they emerged from the vehicle and walked through Washington Park.

The park was filled with tall shade trees, flowering shrubs and numerous floral beds and mounds. One mound contained a large floral clock. Another mound had the city name spelled out by using flowers. An antique red popcorn wagon stood at the corner of Washington Row and Columbus Avenue. There were several memorials throughout the park, including one dedicated to fallen police officers.

"If we have time, my aunt said we should check out the Merry-Go-Round Museum," Moore said as he pointed to the former Post Office building with a large rotunda across from the park.

"That would be fun," she grinned.

"There it is," Moore remarked as he pointed to the Boy and the Boot statue mounted on a pedestal of tufa rock in the middle of the fountain, which was also made of tufa rock. Water sprayed up and encircled the statue like a wall of mist. Water also streamed out of the leaky boot, which the boy was holding in one hand.

"Too late," Bieber observed as they neared the statue and saw that the boy's head was missing.

"Oh, no," Moore echoed with disdain. "They got him, too."

"Interesting that it wasn't in the newspaper," Bieber said.

Moore didn't respond. He just shook his head from side to side.

"Emerson!" a deep baritone voice called.

Moore looked around and saw Barry Vermeeren, a prominent Sandusky attorney and one of Moore's friends, walking toward them. "Hi, Barry. Meet my friend, Kat. She's in town visiting me."

"Hello, Kat."

"Hello," she responded to the affable attorney with movie star good looks.

"What brings you to beautiful downtown Sandusky?" Vermeeren

asked.

"The Boy and the Boot statue," Moore replied. "Looks like it's been damaged."

"Yes, that's what I heard this morning when I was leaving the courthouse. Apparently vandals did it sometime between sunset and dawn. But, you can still enjoy the rest of him," Vermeeren suggested.

Bieber nodded her head as she looked at the statue.

"Did you see today's *Sandusky Register*?" Moore asked.

"If you're referring to the story on the statues and vandalism, I did," Vermeeren responded.

"We're involved."

"What?"

Moore gave Vermeeren a synopsis of what had happened over the last few weeks, including the disappearance of the city survey-or, who had assisted L'Enfant in planning Washington, D.C. and headed to Portland. "Sometimes, I think I should go to Portland, Oregon to see if I can pick up his trail. But then again, there's no Boy and the Boot statue there and that seems to play a key in un-locking this puzzle."

"How do you know it's Portland, Oregon? Could it be Portland, Maine? Or could it be Portland, Ohio?" the good-natured attorney probed.

"Portland, Ohio? There's no Portland, Ohio."

A smile crossed Vermeeren's face. "There used to be."

Moore was stunned. "Where?"

"Here."

"Where's here?"

"Sandusky," Vermeeren grinned.

"How's that?" Moore asked with a puzzled look on his face.

"It's right over here. I'll show you." Vermeeren led the two to a historical marker. "Read this."

Moore was stunned after he finished reading. "So, the original name of Sandusky was San Dus Tee. And it was named by the first settlers, the Ogontz Indians."

"Right," Vermeeren affirmed. "But, when the town was platted in 1816, it was platted as Portland. We can check at city hall to see who platted it. It may have been your guy or one of his descendants. The name changed to Sandusky in 1818."

"How ironic that this comes together in your backyard," Bieber observed.

"It is," Moore said.

"Must be your day, Emerson. The stars are all aligned," Vermeeren smiled.

"Not quite. We don't have the Boy with the Boot's head," Moore said, frustrated with the near miss in finding the right statue first.

"But, we do have it," Vermeeren grinned.

"Huh?"

"This statue was a four-foot high, hollow bronze cast of the original zinc statue. After the original statue was vandalized a few years ago, it was relocated to the atrium of City Hall. I'd venture to say that it's untouched, especially since the police department is located next to it."

"What are we waiting for? Let's go! Can you join us?" Moore asked.

Vermeeren looked at his watch. "Yes, I should be okay for the rest of the day."

The three walked over to Moore's borrowed car and drove to City Hall.

"Barry, do you know how the Boy and the Boot statue ended up in Sandusky?" Moore asked as they drove.

"As a matter of fact, I do. Two prominent Sanduskians, Voltaire Scott and his wife, had it shipped here in the 1870's. There's some controversy as to where the statue was manufactured. Some say New York City; others say Germany."

"Any idea why there are so many versions of this statue around the United States?" Moore asked.

"No, but it's interesting that they've popped up in those locations," he replied.

They parked the car in the City Hall parking lot off Meigs Street and walked to the building. Upon entering the atrium, they saw the original Boy and the Boot statue. It was inside a glass display case.

"There it is," Vermeeren said with a twinkle in his eye.

"The big question is how do we get permission to open the back of his head?" Moore asked.

"I'm sure that won't be easy," Bieber suggested.

"You two stay here. I'm going to see if the city manager is available," Vermeeren said as he began to walk away. "We grew up together," he added with a mischievous wink.

Ten minutes later, Vermeeren returned with the city manager in tow. They were soon joined by two maintenance men with cutting tools and a ladder. Several other high-ranking city employees also appeared to watch the operation.

It didn't take long for one of the men to remove the back of the glass case and to cut a four by four inch square from the back of the boy's skull. He flashed a light inside and then reached inside. When he withdrew his hand, he was holding an oilskin wrapped packet. "Is this what you were looking for?" he asked as he handed the packet to Moore.

"Yes, it is," Moore responded excitedly as he carefully held the oilskin. "Thank you very much."

"Why don't we all return to my office so you can open your treasure," the city manager said as she began to walk back to her office. Moore, Bieber and Vermeeren followed closely on her heels.

In her office, Vermeeren asked, "Do you know who plotted Sandusky?"

"Let me think a minute," she said. After a moment, she responded, "Yes, he helped plot Washington, D.C. His name was Williames. John Williames."

"That's him," Moore said exuberantly.

"We've been trying to track Williames," Bieber added as she watched Moore, whose hands started to shake with excitement as he began to open the oilskin on the desk.

Inside the oilskin was a parchment. It read: San Dus Tee points to the 13th obelisk.

"Now, that's confusing. How can a city point to an obelisk?" Moore asked.

Vermeeren turned to the city manager. "Do you have a street map, showing the surrounding area?"

"Yes," she said as she turned and asked her assistant to bring one into her office.

Within a minute, the assistant was spreading a large map on the city manager's desk.

After studying the map, Vermeeren was the first to speak. "If you look at the street patterns, what do you see?"

"Streets running horizontally and vertically. There are a few streets running diagonally." Moore looked more closely at the map. "It's almost a diamond-like pattern."

"Right. So, if we remember that our city designer was a free Mason, what else do you see on this street grid?"

Moore's eyes widened with amazement. "The square and compass."

Before Vermeeren could ask any more questions, Moore saw the next answer. "And a compass can point the way." He looked closely at the area where Central and Columbus Avenue came to a point at the intersection with Market Street. It would be the apex of the compass.

Moore saw a ruler and picked it up, then placed it carefully on the compass. "It points to the Marblehead Peninsula," Moore said as he moved the ruler on a direct line to where the compass and street grids led him. "But, there's no obelisk there unless we consider the Marblehead Lighthouse."

"Bear with me a moment," Vermeeren said as he reached over and moved the ruler in the same vertical direction. "Now, where does it lead you?" he asked with a wide grin.

"It's the Perry Monument! Of course, it would be the thirteenth obelisk."

"I'd venture to say that what you have here is a symbiotic relationship," Vermeeren said.

"How's that?" Moore asked as he wrinkled his brow.

"It's a relationship which is interdependent. It's like the bumblebee and the flower. They both need each other. In your case, there's the relationship between the Boy and the Boot statue, the square and the compass, and the Perry Monument. They are interdependent on each other."

Moore nodded his head. "And when you count the letters in the two words – square and compass, they add up to thirteen letters. There's also thirteen letters in the Perry Monument."

"Anything else I can do for you today?" Vermeeren chuckled.

"Barry, how can I ever thank you?"

"You bring the salmon for the next cookout at my house," he teased, knowing that Moore had attended a cookout at his waterfront home on the Cedar Point Chaussee and had eaten half of his salmon even though salmon was not on Moore's list of edible foods.

"That's a deal. Although, I'll also bring one rib eye steak for me," Moore responded.

They thanked the city manager for her assistance and left the building. They headed for Moore's borrowed car where Vermeeren offered to drive Moore to Huron to retrieve his car. They picked up Vermeeren's car and returned the borrowed vehicle to the museum, then headed for Harbor North.

They chatted about a number of items as they drove eastward on Cleveland Road from Sandusky to nearby Huron. A few minutes into their drive, Vermeeren looked over his shoulder at Bieber and then pointed to his left. "There's Sawmill Creek Resort. A great place to stay."

"Looks very nice," Bieber said from the back seat.

"This barn in front houses the Sawmill Creek Shops, a very nice boutique of clothes and quality gift items."

"Can we stop?" Bieber asked.

"They're closed now. But you can come back for a visit. I'm sure a nice guy like Emerson would bring you back here," Vermeeren said.

Grinning, Moore turned in the passenger seat to look at Bieber. "What he didn't tell you is that his wife, Dixie, and her business partner, Holly McGory, own the shop. Dixie is from New Orleans and epitomizes southern charm and beauty. Holly looks like actress Gwyneth Paltrow."

"I'd love to come back here for a visit. Emerson, can we?" she asked with pouted lips.

"Sure, Kat. I'll bring you back after we solve this puzzle."

Within minutes, Vermeeren delivered his passengers to Harbor North.

Moore and Bieber expressed their appreciation and turned to find themselves face to face with Bruce Roberts and T.J. Wright.

"And where is our Hunter?" Roberts asked although he already knew the answer. The Coast Guard had alerted him and he had retrieved the boat. It was safely back in its dockage.

Moore explained the encounter with the gunmen and their escape to Sandusky, but left out the issues surrounding the Boy and the Boot statue.

"I may have second thoughts about crewing with you next time if that's the kind of friends you have," Wright teased.

"I'll crew with him anytime," Bieber said as she defended Moore.

"I bet you would," Wright joked.

"She's back in her slip," Roberts said. "And we've looked over the damage to her. Bullet holes above and below the waterline. Our insurance agent will be out tomorrow." He added, "It's Christine Crawford."

"I remember Christine. She was one of the pirates during Put-in-Bay's Pyrate Fest," Moore recalled. "She wanted to hang me from the yardarm."

"We might just help her," Wright kidded Moore.

"Yes, she was there. I'm sure that she'll do her best to handle our claim," Roberts said.

Looking toward the parking lot and an escape from the ribbing he was receiving, Moore said, "We should be hitting the road. We've done enough damage around here."

"That you have," Wright quipped.

Moore and Bieber bid their farewells and headed for the car and the short trip back to Put-in-Bay. While on the Miller Ferry, Bieber excused herself to call her uncle again.

When she returned, Moore asked, "Any luck?"

"No, I'm really getting nervous about him. He's never been out of touch for this long. Dagmar is still trying to find him."

"Do you think he may have taken a turn for the worse?"

"I just don't know," she said with a worried look.

Moore placed his arm around her and they looked over the rail as the ferry closed the distance to the island.

The Next Morning
Aunt Anne's House

Carrying her morning coffee, Bieber joined Moore on the enclosed front porch where Moore was using his iPad.

"Anything interesting?" she asked as she pulled a chair closer to Moore and sat down next to him.

"Yes. I was reviewing the Sandusky Mason's website," he said as he turned to look at her. "It says that Sandusky and Washington, D.C. are the only two cities in the world, which are laid out on the Masonic square and compass."

Moore turned back to his iPad. "And the original plat of the city represents an open Bible. If Columbus Avenue is treated as the center of the book, the blocks and squares are equal in number and dimension."

"That is interesting," she commented as she looked at the map on his iPad.

"Here's something else I found. Sandusky has a chapter of the Knights of St. John. The Knights date back to the eleventh century and worked with the Knights Templar in the Holy Land during the crusades."

"I'm stunned how everything points to this area," Bieber said. "What about this Perry Monument?"

"I've already made a phone call to the Superintendent, Blanca Stransky, and she's arranging for us to take a tour of the monument. We'll also get a chance to check out the monument's basement."

Moore paused and looked at Bieber. "Do you know how they protect the monument from the winter snow and ice?"

"Wrap it in plastic?" she guessed.

"No. This was a major engineering feat. Each November, before the first snow hits, the monument is retracted into the ground and then emerges each spring like a groundhog," Moore said with a straight face.

Bieber looked at him in disbelief. "You really don't expect me to believe that, do you?"

Chuckling, Moore responded, "It's an old island joke we play on tourists."

"This tourist didn't buy it." She grinned at him and then leaned toward him to kiss him on the cheek.

"Hey, you caught me off guard. Try it again."

This time, he turned his head and caught her kiss full on his lips.

"What are you two doing out here? Smooching away like two high schoolers?" Aunt Anne asked as she unexpectedly entered the room.

Pulling away from Bieber, a red-faced Moore responded, "Caught us red-handed."

"More like red-faced," Bieber snickered.

"Don't you two have an appointment at the monument?"

Moore looked at his watch. "Oops, the time got away from me. We had better go."

Moore and Bieber went to the rear of the house and out the kitchen door. They walked around the corner of the house and to the garage.

"We'll take the golf cart," he said as he began to swing into the seat.

They drove out of the garage and the short distance to the monument, parking in front of it. Climbing the stairs, they walked toward the entrance where one of the park rangers was waiting for them.

"Good morning, Emerson," tall and bespectacled ranger, Ted Klimczak, greeted the two.

"Hi, Ted. You giving us a tour today?"

"Yes. Is this for your friend?" he asked as he looked at Bieber.

"Somewhat - and a refresher for me. It's been awhile since I've toured it. This is Kat Bieber."

"Hello, Kat."

"Hi," she responded as she looked upward at the towering structure.

"Pretty tall, isn't it?" Klimczak asked as he noticed her eyeing the monument.

"How tall is it?" she asked as they moved toward the inside of the monument to ascend to the top in the elevator.

"It's 352 feet high, but we're going to the observation deck. It's at 317 feet. There's a magnificent view of South Bass Island and the surrounding islands from the top," he said as they entered the elevator and began their ascent.

Klimczak continued, "The Perry Monument is the third tallest monument in the United States and commemorates Oliver Hazard Perry's American victory in the Battle of Lake Erie during the War of 1812. Beneath the rotunda floor are interred the remains of three American and three British officers, who were killed during the battle.

"The construction was completed in June, 1915, and cost $480,000. It's comprised of seventy-eight courses of pink granite from Milford, Massachusetts and topped with an 11-ton bronze urn. You'll be able to see it when you look at the top of the monument."

As the elevator came to a stop, Klimczak opened its doors and allowed the two to step out onto the open-air observation platform.

"Here we are. You let me know if you have any questions," he said as he leaned against the wall.

"This is breathtaking," Bieber said, scanning the harbor below.

"It is," Moore said as he swept his eyes above at the urn and the sides of the column. "Not as breathtaking as you, though."

She nudged him playfully. "What are you looking for?" she asked, when she turned to look at him.

"I'm not quite sure. I'm looking for a clue. I really don't know what it would be," Moore said as the two walked around the platform. "The Washington Monument has the Mason's compass and square etched on its base. I haven't seen one here yet."

"It's hard to know what you're looking for when you really don't know what it is," she observed.

Moore nodded. "The life of a journalist."

After twenty minutes, they returned to the elevator and began the descent to the main floor. "We'd like to walk around the base of the monument and then take a look underneath if that's okay." Moore said to Klimczak as they stood in the elevator.

"No problem. Blanca asked me to do whatever you two needed done."

"Good."

When they arrived on the main level, Moore and Bieber, followed closely by Klimczak, exited the monument and began examining its walls as they walked around it.

"Anything in particular you're looking for?" Klimczak asked as he noticed their examination of the walls.

"No, but we'll know it when we see it," Moore responded.

When they finished, the three of them descended the steps and walked to the side where they approached a locked construction gate and fenced area.

Klimczak produced a key and unlocked the gate. "We still have some construction work going on as we ready the monument for the September 2013 anniversary celebration of Perry's victory over the British." Klimczak glanced at Bieber. "The naval battle took place just northwest of here."

"I see," she said as they walked through the gate, which they left open, and headed toward the entrance to the monument's basement.

Arriving at the doorway, Klimczak produced another key and unlocked the door to the basement level. "It's like a cave in here," he said as they entered. He flicked on a light switch and the basement's interior was illuminated.

"If you look above, you'll see several stalactites hanging from the ceiling. They're like icicles that form as water works its way through the granite," he explained.

"Never seen stalactites in a basement before," Moore commented as his eyes began to sweep around the area in front of them.

"Careful where you walk," Klimczak said. "The floor is only concreted in areas. The rest of the area is gravel." As they walked around, Klimczak stopped and pointed to a spot. "That's where the remains of the six officers are interred."

Moore nodded. "The monument construction was finished in 1915?"

"Yes."

Moore looked at Bieber, who had also been carefully scrutinizing the area. "I'm not sure that we're going to find anything here," he said quietly.

"Why?"

"It just seems like everything we've been following up on leads us to the 1880's," Moore said.

"I'm not sure I'd be so quick to jump to conclusions," Bieber cautioned.

"It's my gut talking to me. It's been pretty spot on in the past."

"Sure that it's not just hunger pangs you're hearing?" she teased.

Moore smiled. "What's in the rooms along the side?"

"Storage. You can look into them if you like. I'll unlock these two." Klimczak unlocked the two rooms to show a room with artifacts.

Moore and Bieber entered the room and spent some time examining the items for any clues to the Nazarene's Code. Finding nothing, they left it and entered the other room.

"We store the costumes for the re-enactors here," Klimczak said as he pointed to a variety of costumes and soldiers' uniforms. "Over here we have the rifles."

"These look interesting," Bieber said as she looked at one of the rifles. "Certainly not a semi-automatic," she teased.

"Nothing automatic about those," Klimczak commented. He went on to explain, "With these, you have to open the pan, then draw a cartridge from the pouch." He pulled a cartridge out of a nearby pouch. "Then, you'd bring the cartridge to your mouth and twist the end off with your teeth. You prime the pan with a touch of powder from the cartridge, then, you stand the rifle up and drop the cartridge down the barrel, ramming it home with this ramrod. Now, you'd be about ready to fire," he said as he replaced the rifle in its rack.

"Do you mind if we wander around a bit?" Moore asked.

"No, go right ahead. I need to spend some time in tidying up this room," Klimczak said.

Moore and Bieber walked out of the room and separated as they continued their examination. Moore made his way toward the weapons room.

Only a few minutes had passed, when a deep voice spoke from the basement doorway. "Well, well, Mr. Emerson Moore!"

Moore swung around and saw Yarian and the man, who had piloted his boat, enter the basement. They were holding weapons. Yarian's was pointed at Moore.

"You've been slippery to catch lately," Yarian stormed. "This time, you're not getting away."

"Maybe this is the time you don't get away, Yarian," Moore said in a challenging tone.

With a look of disdain, Yarian ignored the comment. "Where's your girlfriend?"

Out of the corner of his eye, Moore saw Bieber behind a piece of tall machinery and near a pile of tools. "She's not here!"

Yarian's partner began to walk around the basement and neared the spot where she was hiding. "You're lying, Mr. Moore. We'll find her," Yarian growled.

"I'd say that you are such a sorry piece of humanity, but that would imply that you were actually human," Moore responded boldly as he tried to stall them in starting their search for Bieber.

"Enough!" Yarian screamed as anger boiled inside of him. Yarian's eyes narrowed with hatred as he stared at Moore. As his finger began to increase the pressure on the trigger, he was distracted by a noise to his right.

From her hiding place, Bieber stepped into the open. She held an axe in her hand. She threw the axe toward Yarian's surprised partner and ducked behind the machinery as Yarian fired twice in her direction. The bullets missed her, but the axe struck home.

Yarian's partner screamed for a brief moment as the axe landed squarely in his chest. His body crumpled to the floor from the fatal throw.

From the storage room, Klimczak had watched the scene begin to unfold in front of him. He had quickly loaded a rifle and softly called to Moore, "Catch. It's loaded. Cock and fire."

With Yarian's attention distracted momentarily to his partner on the floor, Klimczak tossed the rifle to Moore. Moore caught it and, in a fluid motion, brought it to aim at Yarian as he cocked it.

Yarian turned to face Moore. A look of disbelief crossed Yarian's face. "Put down the toy gun," he said as he cast his eyes from Moore to where Bieber was hidden. He wasn't sure what might be flying through the air next.

"Drop it, Yarian," Moore commanded.

"This is so silly," Yarian said in response as he began to raise his gun and point it at Moore. "You're gone," he sneered.

Before Yarian could pull the trigger, a flash of light and an explosion rocked the confines of the basement as Moore fired. When the smoke cleared, Yarian's body was on the floor. The musket ball from Moore's rifle had flown straight and true across the basement, impacting below Yarian's left eye and killing him instantly.

Moore, with Klimczak on his heels, rushed over to first check Yarian and then his companion to be sure that they were dead.

"Ted, thanks for thinking fast and tossing me the rifle," Moore said appreciatively as he looked at the two bodies.

"Great shot," Klimczak said as he held a re-enactor's sword in his right hand.

"Not really. I was aiming at his shoulder. The sight must be off." He then turned to face Bieber, who was trembling. He walked to her and held her close. "Are you okay?"

"Yes. I, I can't believe I did that," she stammered as she shook.

"Neither can I," Moore said as he soothed her. "Nice throw."

"Who were these guys? It was apparent they were up to no good," Klimczak said.

Before Moore could respond, a number of policemen and park rangers entered the monument's basement. They had their guns drawn, but holstered them when they saw the two men on the ground.

"Emerson," the Put-in-Bay police chief said as he greeted his old friend. "I should have known you'd be involved with this mess."

"I guess I have some explaining to do."

"I'd say you guessed right."

Two hours later Moore and Bieber were sitting on the dock in front of Aunt Anne's house. They were recounting the events of the last two days and trying to determine how the Perry Monument was tied into the final clue for the Nazarene's Code.

"Hey, Emerson," a voice called.

Moore and Bieber turned to see Mad Dog Adams riding his bicycle across the yard and toward them.

"Hi Mike," Moore greeted his friend.

"And how's our friendly beer babe doing today?" Adams asked as he leered at Bieber.

"Purrfect," Bieber teased.

"Kat, you can make me purr anytime," Adams joked. "I hear that cats like to have their bellies rubbed. Want me to rub yours?"

Bieber had identified Adams for the rapscallion he was. "No, I don't need my belly rubbed."

"Want to rub mine?" Adams asked, although he already knew how she'd respond.

Bieber just laughed.

"What brings you here this afternoon? Don't you have a show at the Round House?" Moore asked.

"In about an hour. I was just riding my bike and a guy asked me if I knew you. I told him for a long time. He handed this envelope to me and asked me to deliver it to you. So, here I am," Adams said as he handed the envelope to Moore.

Taking the envelope, Moore asked, "What did the guy look like?"

"White ball cap, blue shirt and khaki pants. Gray hair and dark sunglasses. Nobody that I can recall seeing on the island."

"Thanks, Mike," Moore said as a puzzled look crossed his face.

"I've got to go. Bring the Kat over to the show. I'll have her come up on stage and show her my conch shell," Adams chuckled with a mischievous twinkle in his eyes.

"Be careful what you ask for, Mike. You may find that you've met your match."

"Haven't yet," he called as he pedaled away. "She'd just be purrfect on stage with me," he yelled.

"He is a scoundrel, but a nice one," Bieber observed.

"Let's see what we have here," Moore said as he opened the envelope and read the contents. His eyes widened in amazement.

"What is it?" Bieber asked as she watched Moore's reaction.

"The answer has been staring us in the face."

"How's that?"

"Jay Cooke, who grew up in Sandusky and helped finance the Civil War, owned Gibraltar Island." Moore paused and pointed at the small island that guarded the entrance to Put-in-Bay's harbor. "According to this note, he wanted the Perry Monument constructed on his island!"

"But it wasn't. It was built here."

"Right, but the original location was going to be on Gibraltar Island. There's a small monument there. Want to bet as to whether or not it has the square and compass on it?"

"No, let's go and check it out," Bieber urged.

"We'll take the Zodiac," Moore said as he began to walk toward the dinghy tied to his aunt's dock.

"Who sent you the note?"

"It's not signed. I don't know, but I'll take the clue nonetheless," Moore said as he assisted her in boarding the Zodiac. He took a seat at the stern and started the small outboard. In seconds, the small craft was cutting across the harbor, aimed at the small island's dock in front of Stone Lab.

Five minutes later, the nose of the Zodiac bumped against the dock where the island's two large workboats were tied up. Moore grabbed a line and stepped up onto the dock and secured the craft. He then extended his hand and assisted Bieber in joining him on the dock.

"Not very crowded," Bieber observed as she looked around.

"Classes are in session," he said as he looked around and then pointed toward an area on the far side of the Stone Lab. "That patio area is covered by solar panels and sometimes they hold classes there."

"Is that where the original monument was going to be built?"

"No, it's up the hill on our right and in front of Cooke's Castle," he said as they started walking along the sidewalk.

"We can see the top of the Castle's turret from your aunt's house, correct?"

"Yes. Cooke built the place as his summer retreat. He'd invite all kinds of important people here, including presidents and former Civil War generals."

"The castle is stunning," she said as they approached the side of the building where they could see the steps leading to the main doorway.

They rounded the front of the building and saw the monument in front of them. The ten-foot tall structure was made out of white limestone and topped with a large round bluish urn. There was a plaque on one side and symbols on each of the others.

"Look," Moore said. "The Masonic square and compass. The final clue must be here."

"How will we get permission to dig?"

"That won't be necessary," a familiar voice called from behind them.

As they turned to identify the speaker, a number of government agents, wearing camouflage, stepped out from the nearby shrubbery and trees. They were holding weapons, which were pointed at the two of them.

"Steve!" Moore exclaimed as he recognized his dear friend. "I thought you were dead!"

Nicholas was standing at the corner of the Castle. Next to him were two more armed government agents. "Not really. Bullets bounce off my chest like Superman," he kidded.

"But, I saw you go down. The blood, and then they told me you died."

"I'm sorry for having to trick you, Emerson, but my friends from the agency assisted me in pulling off that stunt."

"But, why? And why are your guns pointed at us?"

"It's a long story. It's taken a long time to put this in place and, I'm sorry to say, you've been nothing more than a pawn in this adventure. But, a pawn that was well played."

"I don't get it," Moore said, with a puzzled look on his face as Nicholas walked closer to the two.

"The Nazarene's Code."

"What about it?"

"It's not here," Nicholas said.

"What? But all the clues led here," a wild-eyed Bieber stormed.

"That's right," Moore added.

"All a part of our master plan. It was an elaborate ruse, which took some time to put together. It didn't all work according to our plans, but you kept your wits about you and were able to survive."

"A ruse! I was your patsy! You used me! To what end? People have died, Nicholas! I almost died!" Moore glared at his friend. "Why? Just tell me why!" a deeply frustrated Moore demanded.

Nicholas held up his hand with his palm outward toward Moore. "Yes, I used you," Nicholas confessed. "I knew we'd have our day of reckoning, but trusted that once I explained, you would understand and accept the role you unwittingly played in making our nation safer."

"How's that?" Moore asked. His emotions were on edge at this unexpected revelation.

"Let me start somewhat from the beginning, but I'll caution you this is not for print and you're going to have to sign a secrecy act agreement before I can let you off this island."

"Great. All this and no story to show for it. But go ahead," Moore urged anxiously.

"It started some time ago when East Germany and their Stasi intelligence operation existed. A number of our agents were murdered in East Germany and worldwide. After the reunification of Germany, the two German intelligence agencies combined.

"There was a rogue unit. It was like our Mafia's Murder, Inc. They continued to identify and murder our overseas agents. Then, they moved into drug trafficking and linked up with opium growers in Turkey and Afghanistan. A few years ago, they began to quietly provide funding to terrorist organizations."

Nicholas paused as he glanced at a passing boat, which was entering the harbor.

He continued. "And do you know who headed this organization?"

"No," Moore replied. "Who?"

"Kalker. We developed a ruse to lure him into visiting the United States so that we could easily take him into custody. Something as powerful as the Nazarene's Code provided the bait to attract him to our soil."

"What? But he was our partner – and he was dying," Moore stammered. He looked at Bieber, who had turned pale.

"Also, a ruse. He took pills that made him sweat and faked the cough when you were around. He was very sharp. In fact, he was in disguise at the site of my purported murder."

"He was at Tunnicliff's Tavern?" Moore asked, stunned.

"Yes. He was the guy inside with the beard and Fedora. You were suspicious of him."

"Where is he?" Bieber asked.

"After my so-called death, he broke into my office and was shocked when he found me sitting there, waiting for him. Then, things took an unexpected twist. When we tried to take him into custody, he resisted. One of our agents thought he produced a weapon and killed him instead of wounding him."

Bieber's eyes narrowed as she stared with deadly hatred at Nicholas. Moore touched her arm to comfort her, but she pulled away.

The look was not lost on Nicholas, who swung his head toward Bieber. "Today, your efforts at the Perry Monument resulted in the elimination of two more of the top players in Kalker's network. Our entire plan culminates with luring the top six members of his organization to the United States so that we can put them in custody and don't have to worry about any extradition laws or international political issues. We got Kalker. You two took care of Yarian and Yarian's sidekick, Monchelov, today as well as Gorenchenko in London."

"Who are the missing two?" Moore asked.

"We've had Karapashev in custody the entire time. We knew that Kalker was giving us false information about him. But, we played along as if we didn't know his whereabouts."

"Who's left?" Moore asked, with a sinking feeling in his gut. He feared where this may be heading.

"Their top assassin. She's skilled at murder and in being a honey trap, reeling in unsuspecting men by pretending to fall in love with them. She's a widow maker of the worst kind."

Moore knew the answer before he asked. He looked at Bieber. "Kat? No."

"Katrina Bieber is the name she's using today, but her real name is Erika Fleischer. Fleisher is German for the word butcher. Very appropriate," Nicholas answered.

"Is that true, Kat? Say it's not true." Moore knew it was true even as he said it, but wanted to be wrong because he had fallen in love with her. His gut wrenched as he realized she betrayed him and played him for a fool.

Bieber didn't respond. Her face had tightened. She stood defiantly as she clenched and unclenched her hands.

"And your story about the tumor and dying, was it a lie, too?" Moore asked.

"All lies, Emerson," Nicholas answered for Bieber.

"You played me like Steve played me," Moore said as his frustration grew. "What about in Turkey? When I thought they killed you?"

Bieber's body relaxed as she resigned herself to her fate and allowed all pretenses to disappear. "Emerson, you were such an easy mark in this whole thing. You were putty in my hands. They dragged in another man and shot him. They dripped his blood on you while I watched. I laughed to myself when I thought how it'd make you feel," Bieber responded in a hard tone.

"But, I saw you kill Gorenchenko and that guy today. They were your partners!" Moore said.

"They were expendable, especially that ass, Gorenchenko! I enjoyed taking him out," she said quietly as she reached into her pocket and pulled out a tube of lipstick. "I never did like him. As for the others – we were so close to finding what I wanted, and I couldn't let them ruin it. I didn't need them."

"I should have seen the funnel clouds on the horizon," Moore said sadly as he looked at Bieber.

"It's difficult to have clarity when she pulled you into her love nest," Nicholas said.

"And my supposed calls to my uncle the last few days were actually calls to Yarian so that he'd know where to find us." She took the cap off the lipstick tube and began to point the tube at Nicholas.

Moore leapt at her, yelling, "It's a gun!"

Tangled together, the two rolled down the slight incline as they fought over the loaded lipstick tube. Before they came to a rest at the bottom of the hill, the weapon fired. The two entangled bodies lay at rest until one moved.

Moore rolled off of Bieber and sat up. When he looked at her, he saw that the bullet had entered her head under her chin. She was killed instantly. Blood flowed from the entrance and exit wounds onto the ground next to her body.

As several agents surrounded him, one helped Moore to his feet. Moore looked back up the hill and saw Nicholas beckoning to him. Moore walked up the hill to Nicholas.

"I'm sorry about all of this, Emerson. I hope you'll forgive me," Nicholas said as they walked toward the edge of the cliff and down an iron stairwell to a rocky edge above the graveled swimming beach. "Sit down. I have some explaining to do."

Moore just nodded his head. He was still in disbelief, shock, and grief over what had transpired during the last fifteen minutes.

The two men stared at the water. They watched as a fish caught a bug floating on the surface.

Nicholas began his explanation. "In order for us to catch these big fish we had to have the right lure. That's why we concocted this entire scheme about finding the Nazarene's Code with its power-filled attributes. We knew that the more believable we made this look, the better our chance at luring them to the U.S."

Moore turned his head to look at Nicholas. "Does the Nazarene's Code exist?"

"Rumors about its existence have circulated for centuries, but no one knows for sure. We just used that as the basis for our ruse and then allowed the coincidence of the Legend of 13 to act as the thread to help pull it together."

Moore looked from the water to Nicholas. "You sure made this intricate."

Nicholas interrupted. "It took a lot of planning. And we had to get special permission to cut open the statutes' heads so we could insert the clues. We did it under the auspices of cleaning teams. Then, we had to make it look like they'd never been touched so that you and they would go along with it."

"You did this with the Boy and the Boot statue, too?"

"Yes. One of our teams placed the packet a few weeks ago. We used the coincidence of Sandusky and D.C. being laid out like the compass and square. And it coincidently pointed to the Perry Monument. Then, we learned about the site of the original monument being here on this secluded island. It was just a matter of how coincidence worked into our planning."

"But, how did you know that I'd pull all of this together?" Moore asked, somewhat bewildered. "And why didn't you just let me in on it from the beginning?"

"You're my intrepid reporter. You use logic and we were counting on your logic. And, I was playing the role of Grand Chess Master. I was watching most of your moves and gently pointing you in the right direction when necessary. You couldn't know about the plan because you're a reporter, not an actor."

"Kat was the real actress here. She played her role to the hilt," Moore said sadly.

"She did. I couldn't tell you. You had to be believable. I just – didn't know it would get so dangerous for you. I'm sorry for that."

"What about the San Dus Tee etchings on the top of the Washington Monument?"

"There are none. We retained the engineer, Nick Sheldon, to mislead you."

"But he showed me a picture of the etching," Moore said.

"Photoshopped."

"And the clue in Mudd's cell?" Moore asked.

"Planted by us. There really was a letter from the German ambassador, but it's in the National Archives. We created our own version."

Moore shook his head from side to side as he realized the intricacies of their plan. "What about Levy's notebook that I found in his desk?"

"Planted."

"And the deaths of Levy, Lawsons in London and the Turkish police officer, were they planned?" Moore asked with clenched teeth.

"No. They were unfortunate. So was your captivity and torture."

"I hope this was worth their deaths, and my pain. You sure went to a lot of trouble to set this all up."

"Well, it was for national security, so I hope it was worth it. I just wish that we had taken Bieber and Kalker alive," Nicholas lamented. "We hoped you could skate through this entire plan with minimal damages."

"Oh, I skated through it all right. It was like a roller derby with dead bodies strewn around the world's rink," Moore responded cynically. "And, really? A tracking device in my tooth?"

Nicholas shook his head. "We had nothing to do with that, I promise. And we didn't expect you to become emotionally attached to Bieber. You're known to be aloof and emotionally detached with women – even the most beautiful ones."

"That's true. This one was different. I was such a fool," Moore commented.

"All men can be at times," Nicholas agreed.

Moore watched the Jet Express, carrying a boatload of island visitors, round Gibraltar Island and enter Put-in-Bay's harbor. He allowed a deep sigh to escape from his lungs. It was one thing to be played by Nicholas, but it was another to be played by Bieber. It would take time for the emotional scars from both of them to heal, Moore thought to himself.

"You've put me through hell," Moore said quietly as he looked at Nicholas.

"I'm not sure about that. Maybe just on the edge of it," he said.

"Close enough that I smelled the smoke, felt the heat and got singed by the flames," Moore said. "And I got burned romantically, too."

"I'm sorry about the way things had to turn out with Kat," Nicholas said, with a tone of remorse.

"Yeah, me too." Moore looked down at his feet. "The person she played was one I could've spent a lifetime with. I just didn't realize how one-sided it was. It was a hoax. But at least I know I can love again. It just has to be the right one the next time."

The two stared out over Lake Erie where dark clouds on the western horizon signaled an approaching storm. Lost in their respective thoughts, neither one of them spoke for five minutes.

"Geez, Steve, what will I tell my editor?"

Nicholas chuckled. "I'll handle it."

Then, Moore realized how he might have a touch of revenge on Nicholas. He looked at his watch and turned to Nicholas. "I need a drink. Want to join me?"

"Yes, I would. This has been a difficult hour of reckoning. I need to atone for my guilt. As far as a first step, I'll buy the first round."

"It's going to take a lot more than buying me a drink for me to grant you redemption. Forgiveness will come, but it will be a while in coming," Moore said seriously.

"That's what my wife used to say to me. And boy, did she ever make me pay," Nicholas said as he recalled his wife who had passed away five years earlier. "She made my life difficult until she would finally forgive me."

"Sometimes, you do reap what you sow, Steve."

"I am sorry that I used you, Emerson. I hope you understand," Nicholas said somberly.

"I know you're sorry, but it's going to take time for me to process all this. You'll need to wear sackcloth for a long time and crawl through a mile of broken glass as you repent. Then, I can probably think about forgiving you for betraying me."

"I'd expect that it's going to be awhile before I'm back in your good graces."

Two minutes passed before either commented. They were lost in their thoughts.

Changing gears, Moore said, "Let's go across the harbor and grab a drink at the Round House Bar. Mad Dog Adams' show will be starting shortly. I'll talk him into having you go onstage for the conch shell portion of his show."

Moore chuckled silently to himself as he stood and imagined Nicholas on stage with the ornery Adams. It would be the first step in payback – and payback would continue for some time, Moore thought to himself. His revenge against his friend would be ever so deserving.

"That sounds like a needed break from what we've been dealing with," Nicholas said unknowingly as he followed Moore up the staircase.

There was one more place in Put-in-Bay that had thirteen letters and Moore wasn't going to tell Nicholas. He'd let Nicholas find out for himself when he was on stage with Mad Dog at the Round House Bar.

Coming Soon
The Next *Emerson Moore* Adventure

Zenobia

PostScript

When I began researching this novel, my wife, Cathy, and I had dinner at Kelley's in Key West with treasure hunter Kim Fisher and his wife, Lee. They told us about the Legend of 13. Later, I was amazed as I sat with a pad of paper and began to look at words with thirteen letters and how thirteen was significant. It was very useful as a thread to run through the novel. I was also surprised to see that the names of two characters I had already developed coincidently had thirteen letters – Katrina Bieber and Steve Nicholas.

Following are a few more notes about the Legend of 13:

- The Thomas Jefferson Memorial was dedicated April 13, 1943.
- The Supreme Court Building cornerstone was laid on October 13, 1932.
- The Cuban Missile Crisis lasted 13 days.
- Princess Diana and Dodi Fayed died when their Mercedes struck the 13th pillar in the Alma tunnel in Paris on August 31 1997.
- The Apollo 13 spacecraft exploded at 1:13 in the afternoon (1313 military time) on April 13, 1970.
- Michael Jordan retired from the NBA after 13 seasons on January 13, 1999.
- Companies file for Chapter 13 bankruptcy.
- There are 12 jurors and one judge in our court system.
- Our barcode system is made up of 13 characters.
- There were typically 13 steps leading to the gallows.
- The hangman's noose has 13 turns of the rope.
- The moon moves 13 degrees around the earth.
- The 13th amendment passed during Abraham Lincoln's term as U.S. President outlawed slavery.
- *Sandustee* was published in 2013.

The town of Sandusky, Ohio, was laid out by a surveyor named Hector Kilbourne who was a Mason. There's an interesting YouTube video on the Masons and the City of Sandusky layout at **http://www.perseverance329.com/history_1.html.**